SUCH THY
MERCIES

SUCH THY MERCIES

WALKER BUCKALEW

Providence House Publishers
FRANKLIN, TENNESSEE

Printed in the United States of America

1 2   1 1   1 0   0 9   0 8   0 7   1   2   3   4   5   6

Library of Congress Control Number: 2007924732

ISBN: 978-1-57736-394-1

Cover illustration by Jeff Whitlock, Whitlock Graphics
Cover design by Joey McNair

Scripture quotations marked KJV are taken from the Holy Bible, King James Version, Cambridge, 1796.

Scripture on page 152 taken from the HOLY BIBLE, NEW INTERNATIONAL VERSION®. NIV®. Copyright© 1973, 1978, 1984 by International Bible Society. Used by permission of Zondervan. All rights reserved.

This is a work of fiction. Names, characters, places, and incidents are products of the author's imagination or are used fictitiously.

PROVIDENCE HOUSE PUBLISHERS
238 Seaboard Lane • Franklin, Tennessee 37067
www.providence-publishing.com
800-321-5692

In gratitude:

Frances S. Buckalew (1911–)

PREFACE

This story can be read by itself, but it is also a sequel to *The Face of the Enemy* and *By Many or By Few*. In this episode, approximately one year has passed since the conclusion of the second book in The Rebecca Series.

Readers are reminded that these stories are set in the 1970s, and that being the case:

- telephones will have rotary dials,
- long-distance calls will involve conversations with long-distance operators,
- there will be no cell phones,
- there will be no Internet, and
- there will be no automobile/train link between England and the European continent.

For we wrestle not against flesh and blood, but against principalities, against powers, against the rulers of the darkness of this world, against spiritual wickedness in high places.

Wherefore take unto you the whole armour of God . . . the breastplate of righteousness . . . the shield of faith . . . the helmet of salvation . . . the sword of the Spirit, which is the word of God.

—Ephesians 6:12

PROLOGUE

Special to: *San Francisco Times*
Filed from: New York City
Filed by: Joe Robinson, *San Francisco Times* feature writer
Date: January —, 19—

Congressus Evangelicus III, the third in a series of international conferences dealing with themes and issues common throughout Christendom, will be held in the Bay area in early summer. Dr. Eleanor Mason Chapel, senior professor and chair of the Old Testament Department at Union Theological Seminary in New York City, will co-chair (with Dr. Niccolo Giacomo of Rome) the powerful Congressus steering committee during her impending one-semester sabbatical in Berkeley. While packing her Manhattan office for the move, Dr. Chapel granted this interview to Times *feature writer Joe Robinson, who is on special assignment this year to cover Congressus events worldwide as they build to their climax in San Francisco.*

THE REPORTER TOOK HIS CHAIR SOMEWHAT UNCOMFORTably, conscious of the fact that Dr. Eleanor Mason Chapel did not suffer fools—or reporters—gladly. She eyed the visitor, and especially, his already-in-motion tape recorder, warily. He stirred nervously under her gaze. The blue-green eyes did not seem hostile, exactly. They seemed impatient to move on to something truly important, like packing for the six-month sojourn in California.

Interviews with major newspapers clearly did not make it to the "important" category in her estimation.

She sat perched behind her desk in an oversized swivel chair that made her seem even smaller than the four feet ten inches and eighty pounds she claimed for her own. She had risen quickly to greet Robinson, an interloper in her cluttered sanctuary, swiftly circling her desk to shake hands, then just as swiftly circling back to her throne.

She was dressed now, as she reportedly was dressed always, in a gray two-piece suit; a white blouse; a red silk scarf; and faded, scuffed, once-white tennis shoes. The hem of her drab skirt was mid-calf in quiet defiance of the fashion of the day. Her gray hair, presumably of considerable length, was bound tightly behind her head in a bun that accentuated a certain pixie-like quality in her face.

But readers must not misunderstand.

In Eleanor Chapel's case, near-opposite physical descriptors—such as pixie-like and austere, pretty and harsh, cute and intimidating—somehow fit together into a non-contradictory whole. And adding to the riot of images that emanated from her person was the gray-whiteness of background—clothing and hair—set against the nearly iridescent redness of the scarf and the startling blue-greenness of the eyes.

All in all, a picture as arresting as it was discomfiting.

And Robinson found he had hesitated too long in his strange confusion of mind. For he was suddenly assailed by a flurry of questions from his interviewee: "How did you come to be called to a journalistic vocation? What do you know about the Old Testament? How large is your family? Where is your family? How in heaven's name could your editors consider me newsworthy?"

And so, after having admitted that he never really thought about the subject of vocation, that he knew almost nothing about the Old Testament, and that he had no family at all, the reporter leaped desperately in the direction of his diminutive inquisitor's final question. "Well, ma'am," he blurted as fast as he could speak (it was all in the little tape recorder she had irritably agreed to admit), "the fact is that *Congressus Evangelicus III* is already big news in the San Francisco Bay area, and will get bigger over the next few months as the actual event gets closer, and with the announcement that you'll be coming to Berkeley for a one-semester sabbatical and that you've agreed to co-chair the conference's steering committee . . ."

"Oh please," she interrupted, her high, joyous, tinkling laugh suddenly letting the air out of Robinson's tension-filled balloon and leading him to realize in a flash that this was a happy—if brusque—woman with a finely honed sense of the absurd. "These colossal international *Congressus* assemblies most certainly are newsworthy; on the other hand, and in utter contrast, my going to the San Francisco area for a few months and co-chairing a steering committee mean absolutely nothing from a news standpoint except that I'm a novelty, sir."

"A . . . a novelty?" he managed to stammer.

"Yes, a novelty. Of course. Just think about it. I'm a Southern Baptist. I'm an Old Testament scholar. I'm a Caucasian member of an African American church in Harlem. I'm a woman. I'm an old person: in my sixties, you know. I was a widow most of my adult life, but now am newly married to a retired New York City detective who happens to be Roman Catholic. If all of that doesn't make me a novelty, I can't imagine what would."

And immediately he saw that she was right. The real news was indeed the conferences themselves. The first two *Congressus Evangelicus* conventions established this once-per-decade extravaganza as Christendom's largest recurring ecumenical event. Held first in Rome and then in Rio de Janeiro, each of the first two assemblies produced memorable position statements endorsed by acclamation of the conferees. The Rome statement, now almost twenty years old, was still widely considered the best short argument for ecumenism ever written, and continued to be quoted in pulpits around the world.

Knowing she agreed to a *brief* session, he decided to plunge in.

"All right, ma'am," he said deferentially, "let's say the conferences—not you—comprise the real news here. Give me your thoughts about the Rome position statement. It seems to have had tremendous impact over the last two decades."

"Yes," she said quickly, "it has."

She popped up from her chair, took three short steps to her window overlooking Broadway, looked out at the pedestrian profusion of January humanity tightly bundled against wind and cold, and offered this:

"I don't think very highly of ecumenical efforts myself, Mr. Robinson. It's not that I think of myself as an actual opponent of them, you understand. I just don't view the ecumenical movement as worth much time and effort."

"How do you mean?" he ventured.

Still looking out her window, she sighed, shrugging her small shoulders, and continued. "I'm a simple soul, Mr. Robinson. And to me, Christ's charge seems straightforward. I'd be happiest if every Christian group and every Christian person on the globe just poured 100 percent effort into their own every-single-day devotional lives, their own families, their own jobs, their own Christ-based ministries to the poor and disenfranchised, their own sacred traditions. And I may be wrong, sir, but that's how I've felt all my life. And that's quite a long time, you'll agree."

The journalist paused to consider her response. Then he asked: "Does that not make you an odd choice to co-chair the steering committee for *Congressus III*, or am I missing something?"

She wheeled around to answer, her back now to the window. "I am indeed an odd choice, sir, but less for that reason than for this one: I stand in complete opposition to the old-line steering committee leaders' draft position statement for *Congressus Evangelicus III*, and I'd think that would bother them a great deal more than my lack of enthusiasm for their previous statements or for ecumenism in general.

"As you know, the theme for *Congressus III* has to do with leadership, power, and organizational structures. The draft position statement, if adopted by the conferees, will have profound implications for the shape of seminary education, for the character of those seminarians' ministries after they have graduated, for theology and practice in all the churches ultimately served by them, and finally for the basic nature and structure of the church universal. And I don't like it one bit."

"You mean you're actually opposed to the tentative position statement, Dr. Chapel? Do they—the old-line steering committee leaders, I think you called them—know that?"

"Of course. It's the first thing I talked about when they telephoned me."

"And they asked you to serve anyway?"

"Clearly."

"Why?"

"That's what I asked them. They replied that I would help them, well, promote their diversity efforts by co-chairing. You know. A woman. A Southern Baptist married to a Roman Catholic. A Caucasian in an African American congregation. An old person. All that stuff.

"I'm a novelty, that's all."

"But aren't they worried," Robinson persisted, "that you'll influence people in a direction they don't want? In a direction opposite the position statement they'll be promoting?"

In response to this, he was bathed once more in the tinkling laughter, the kind that makes you laugh, also. The kind that somehow makes you

happy. Makes you want to do something in hopes of getting the person to laugh again and again.

"I think you mean to ask, don't you," she finally said, recovering, "whether or not they're *afraid* of me?"

"Yes," her questioner acknowledged after a moment.

"Well, no, they're most decidedly not afraid of me, sir."

"But if you're the co-chair . . ."

"I am the co-chair. But I'm also their pet, you see. They're quite sure I'll be a good little kitty."

"And will you?"

And then Dr. Eleanor Mason Chapel, senior professor and department chair of Old Testament at Union Theological Seminary, author of dozens of scholarly books and hundreds of scholarly articles, laughed and laughed and laughed, head thrown back, hands covering her mouth, tiny shoulders shaking.

When the laughter abated, Robinson ventured one more question, and he saw that she tried hard to listen, now holding her abdomen with both hands, her sides obviously aching from the prolonged outburst.

"Dr. Chapel," he asked, apprehension on her behalf creeping into the timbre of his voice, "if you're not going to be a good little kitty, won't someone be upset? After all, there is a lot of marketing money being poured into this. There will be global organizational consequences of considerable magnitude. These are powerful people standing within— or atop—powerful organizations. Couldn't the steering committee's process and the eventual outcome of all of this be, well, threatening in some fashion?"

He watched while Eleanor Chapel, now almost expressionless, turned slowly and again looked out her window. After several moments, she replied quietly, evenly.

"When Almighty God throws messages at my brain, sir, I'm not allowed to consider the consequences to myself. And since I believe that He wants me to do this, the truth is that I'm not *allowed* to think about anything except that charge—that charge from Him to me.

"I have been given a very explicit direction to take. I will take that precise direction. That's all."

The reporter watched for some time while Eleanor Chapel continued to look out her window, seemingly lost in thought. Finally, he thanked her,

took several moments to shut down the tape recorder and pack up his things, rose from his chair, and moved to the door.

When he looked back, he saw that she remained at her window, absolutely motionless and silent.

And just at that instant, as the journalist turned again to go, he heard something. It took a moment to identify the sound. It was the low octave, continuously exploding rumble of distant thunder, immediately filling the auditory horizon and advancing on its prey, inexorable.

His hand now on the doorknob, he once more glanced back at Eleanor Chapel.

And still she stood facing the approaching storm, unflinching, small as a child and yet . . . mysteriously . . . as formidable as the lightning itself.

CHAPTER ONE

TIME PASSES ONLY IN THE MIRROR.

The thought came to the senior professor of Old Testament unexpectedly, striking her as the voice of common vanity, and so, somewhat embarrassed, she moved quickly on. Then, following an impulse of uncertain origin, Dr. Eleanor Mason Chapel cautiously returned to the unsettling thought and began gingerly to turn it over in her mind, looking around and behind it for something.

We think memory holds that truth, she mused, the truth of time's passage. And that's dead wrong, she replied to herself with some emphasis. A husband thirty-five years gone is still right there, in memory. And will be in twenty more. A sister two years gone is still right there, in memory, and not more so or less so than the long-passed husband, but equally so. In each case, *it seems like yesterday*, we say to ourselves. And of course it does.

Time's passage might, in fact, pose as complete chimera, she thought, except for the physical self's testimony to the contrary. And her mirror was at that very moment supplying that testimony unflinchingly. She sighed audibly.

It all made sense, though, she told herself. Christianity values the body in ways that nothing else ever has. Christians believe in the resurrection *of the body*. Reasonably, in such a case, God's way would be to remind a person more or less continually that the body is at all moments on its way to becoming something else, something for the long run, so to speak. Without that daily reminder, why, we would all be perfectly free to imagine time's passage as of no more consequence than the addition of another snapshot of memory to our bulging mental scrapbooks.

Yes, she continued in her reverie, but with the mirror's unrelenting message to the contrary, we are forced to consider the obvious: *time passes*

and this life will end. And then what? For Christians, she thought, the answer shimmers like an Alpine peak: distant, fearsome, thrilling, magnificent. . . .

And, at times, not so *very* distant.

Therefore, she concluded with satisfaction, it is not enough merely to say that time passes only in the mirror. It is much more than that. The simple fact turns out to be this: *Time passes in the mirror . . . and the face of eternity looks back from the glass.*

Peering over the half-glasses perched on the end of her small nose, Eleanor Chapel tried to penetrate the shadowy reflection of her own elfin face, illumined weakly by the overhead bulb in the high-ceilinged bathroom of her temporary quarters on Scenic Avenue, high above the University of California campus at Berkeley. Squinting and frowning now, the blue-green eyes traced her own symmetrical features critically.

Suddenly she laughed aloud, a girl's tinkling laughter. Sixty-three years old, she thought to herself, and looking every day of it. Thank God, she added, for those wrinkles and creases and saggings and grayings. Every one of them told her that her life was a preparation, and in partial consequence, a great joy.

Still smiling, her own laughter lifting her spirits, she reached behind her head and wound her still-thick, gray hair into the tight bun that for decades she had preferred. Then she donned her trademark red silk scarf to stir a dash of color into the equally trademark drabness of her white, long-sleeved blouse and gray skirt. Next, she turned from the mirror, left the bathroom, and stepped into the modest bedroom containing the plain, double bed in which she slept alone. Sitting on the side of the bed, she demurely pulled up first one foot and then the other, lacing on her faded and fabled white tennis shoes. Standing, she finally drew on her gray suit jacket.

She snugged the jacket around her neck, tugged the garment down, and then reached to the left lapel, turning it upward toward her face. Her right thumb and forefinger briefly caressed the delicate pin that graced the lapel. The tiny, intricately crafted replica of a fountain pen nestled against the gray fabric, the pin's own metallic grayness taking on a lustrous, silver cast and standing out in its stark elegance as her only accessory, other than her wedding and engagement bands. It was her husband's wedding gift to her, and she knew, had been selected with all the care, and indeed, anguish that a near-fifty bachelor could bring to the joyous and terrifying task of selecting his first adornment for his first love.

She raised the pin to her lips, then pressed the lapel back into place. She was ready.

A hundred yards away from her apartment lay the compact campus of the multi-denominational Pacific School of Religion, known to its faculty and student body as PSR, occupying a commanding position above the northern reaches of San Francisco Bay. In just minutes, the PSR faculty would assemble for the first of several year-end meetings, a series held early each June to review the academic year just ended, and to plan for the next.

Dr. Eleanor Chapel, widely considered the world's preeminent Old Testament scholar, could, in fairness, contribute little to these meetings. She was but a guest, completing her one-semester research and teaching sabbatical before returning in three more weeks to her academic home in New York City, at the famed Union Theological Seminary, just across Broadway from Columbia University.

As chair of the Old Testament department at Union, she would spend the month of July in an administrative fury, preparing for the upcoming academic year. Then, in a two-week vacation that she had taken annually on the first of August for years, she would head for Rome, home to her dear niece and to her greatest of treasures, grandniece Maria and grand-nephew Paulo.

As a Southern Baptist and as a woman, Eleanor Chapel was very much in the minority in her home faculty at Union Seminary, but she loved her school and her work. Although her sabbatical in Berkeley had provided the rejuvenation she had sought, she yearned not just for the August vacation in Italy, but in a way even more, for what would come before: her July return to New York City. And she longed for the city for more reasons than the strictly academic and professional ones.

There was a personal treasure there, too.

Now, she would dutifully attend PSR's end-of-year faculty meetings, despite her incipient departure. It was not just the rigor of her commit-ment to this, her temporary institutional home, that made her attendance obligatory in her mind. Rising above and beyond that, the eminence known as *Congressus Evangelicus III* loomed high over them all. The third international gathering to bear the encompassing Latin name, this year's specific conference theme was as imposing in prospect as the over-arching Latin title was mysterious: *Christianity, Leadership, and Power—Organizational Structures for the New Decade and Beyond.*

PSR would serve as one of the host organizations for the conference, and its own curriculum and external relationships were in readiness to move in the directions implied by the theme. And Eleanor Chapel was not only to be a featured presenter, panelist, and television interviewee during the conference, but she had been named a co-chair of the conference steering committee even before she had arrived in Berkeley that winter. All of that being the case, her absence, if she dared consider such, from these end-of-year faculty meetings would, she knew, worsen the image some of her colleagues already held of her as "East Coast royalty." Tensions—and, truth be told, jealousies—were riding high enough already; any truancy whatsoever on her part would salt the wounds.

She glanced at her black plastic, ridiculously inexpensive, digital watch. The display read 7:53. There was just time to begin the five-minute walk from her apartment to the meeting. She lifted her battered, tan leather briefcase which she had carefully packed the previous evening, and closing and locking the apartment door, scurried down the interior stairway and out the front of the twelve-unit, three-story, white stucco apartment building. She looked up at a bright blue sky, then down at the neatly trimmed, emerald squares of grass that framed each side of the short walkway from front steps to sidewalk. She smiled at the sheer freshness of it all.

Her wide blue-green eyes, thus transported, did not fall upon the mountainous figure of a man standing motionless on the other side of the quiet intersection just to her left. Nor would she have taken notice in any case, since the figure stood almost with his back to her, perhaps waiting for the next cross-town bus.

She turned right in the direction of the PSR campus, and trotted along the sidewalk, delighting in the invigorating early summer breezes that rose from San Francisco Bay into the Berkeley hills, across and through the small, open campus, and down the length of Scenic Avenue. The northern California climate had proven to be everything she had been promised when these arrangements had been made the previous summer: cool, windy, bracing, uncertain.

Hurrying toward the campus, her mind equally on the glory of the day and the significance of the agenda before the faculty, she did not realize a man was following forty yards behind her along the opposite side of Scenic Avenue. Had she noticed, she might have marked the huge man's grace of movement, incongruous in view of his enormous girth and the sense of ponderous heaviness that somehow marked his entire frame.

In any case, her fleeting thought of the previous summer had already led her mind on a swift detour that, had she allowed it, might have consumed her entirely, something she from time to time deliberately invited. In the seconds that passed before she forced her mind back to business, the mostly unwelcome recollections flooded her consciousness in a swift succession of images. First, she recalled the fantastic and very nearly successful plot to install new reading textbooks in all public elementary schools in all fifty states, for grades first through third.

This was followed by an initially civil debate on the New York City campuses of Columbia and Union regarding the plus factor offered by the texts: the enhancement of self-esteem for all youngsters using the books by means of a powerful dose of moral relativism, labeled by the publisher, its advertising firm, and its lobbyists as "universal morality." All ideas were to be seen as equally good, equally valid, equally true. In insidious consequence, a child's self-esteem was to be built upon the "fact" of the infinite worthiness of *every* idea, *every* thought, *every* action.

Then had come the rapid deterioration of the superficially courteous debate into outright violence and crime: financial and physical threats against legislators, educators, and administrators and their families throughout the United States; bribery and extortion; kidnapping and torture; a gruesome murder; and even a brazen assassination attempt directed at the First Lady of the United States, who along with Eleanor Chapel had become an outspoken opponent of the so-called reading and self-esteem project.

Now approaching the crosswalk to the PSR campus, the Old Testament professor's hand rose to her mouth and she fought back a shallow wave of nausea. Tears welled behind the half-glasses.

And finally, she recalled for perhaps the hundredth time, the incomprehensible. Her esteemed colleague was arrested, convicted, and imprisoned. Although regarded by most as the chief engineer of the plot, a jury, deliberating for two long January weeks, had been unwilling to convict him of the most serious charges: his part in planning and commissioning, first, a reporter's murder, and, second, the assassination attempt.

It had all seemed so . . . well . . . so *medieval*, she reminded herself. And yet, there they were, in a perfectly civilized society, caught in the throes of evil and intrigue and subversion and corruption beyond anything she could ever have imagined. And it had all ended so suddenly, so dramatically, and with such finality.

Or had it?

She allowed the question entrée, but denied it lodging. She passed mentally, in a heartbeat, through the lingering shadow of the past and into the breathless sunlight of the present. Coming to a halt at the edge of the small campus, she stooped and placed the tan briefcase on the sidewalk. Then she raised both hands to her face, pushed the tears from the corners of her eyes with the tips of her index fingers, and took one long, deep breath. Then, lifting the briefcase again, head high, she resumed her scurrying gait.

Perfectly civilized society indeed, she thought, acknowledging her earlier choice of words. *Downright barbaric and dangerous*, she corrected herself, if you dared to see everything that was actually there.

Turning now toward the near doorway of the administration building, she broke into an efficient little trot, her tennis shoes a blur against the dull gray of the campus walkways. As she reached for the wrought iron handle on the heavy wooden main door, she considered the irony. She was about to participate in a faculty meeting in which those very things—contemporary society's civility, barbarism, and danger—would be confronted. *Congressus Evangelicus III—Christianity, Leadership, and Power: Organizational Structures for the New Decade and Beyond*, she murmured the words aloud to herself.

Who in the world had thought of that awful title for this monumental international conference in which she was to be a reluctant centerpiece? Something about the whole affair called to mind the words her late grandmother from Alabama had habitually offered, usually with much emphasis, when that esteemed octogenarian had been faced with some onerous but unavoidable obligation: "Instead of that," Grandmother Mason had liked to declare with finality, *"I'd rather be turned inside out and hung out to dry in an ice storm!"*

Now inside the administration building, Eleanor Mason Chapel headed for the faculty meeting, thinking of her dear grandmother. As she trotted toward the meeting room, her infectious laugh echoed down the empty hallways like the sound of a children's bell choir at Christmas.

Behind her, unobserved, the heavy wooden door closed slowly until, inches before it reached the frame, its movement was arrested by a thick, muscled hand the size of a bear's paw.

The athletically built young woman, twenty-eight years of age and clad in a light blue summer nightgown, sat up in bed, bolt upright, immediately awake. She stared hard into the early morning darkness of the compact London bedroom. Sinews tensed throughout her lean body, the captivating gray eyes wide.

Nearly a year had passed since she had last been recipient of the eyes-open visions that had come to her repeatedly during those early June days in New York City. Mentally acknowledging this in the first instant of recognition, she reached tentatively with her left hand for her husband's sleeping form, making gentle contact in the darkness with his muscular right shoulder to reassure herself of his presence in the room.

Her eyes still boring into the blackness of their small, minimalist bedroom, she tried to breathe normally, alerting her brain to prepare to commit to detailed memory every feature, every subtlety, of what she knew would be coming. And in just seconds, there it was again, appearing in the form she had long before learned to recognize: sharp outlines and bright contrasts against a circumscribed field of view, and within that field, a picture, materializing rapidly . . . and now. . . .

She saw as through the eyes of someone else, someone looking out through a tightly shut window located well above ground level, perhaps on a third or fourth floor, and across an expanse of open courtyard. On the opposite side of the courtyard she observed at first only steps, an astonishing, impossibly long flight of stone steps leading to a structure that she could not see clearly. But then that image, too, sharpened itself as the seconds ticked by. She could now make out the distant detail of immense, ornate double doors, massive in form.

Above the doors she now began to perceive a semicircle, perhaps of stained glass. The glasswork portrayed an image that remained indistinct, a dark form against a still darker background. Somehow this unrecognizable, dark image initially brought to her an unexpected sense of comfort and reassurance. And then it suddenly brought something else. Something both fearsome and arresting. Something that seemed to require—no, beyond that, to demand—a response from her.

But what response?

She did not know.

The vision held itself steadily before her eyes for some time, and then, as in the past, it began gradually to fade from her view. As it did, she found herself, the self in the vision through whose eyes she saw, looking down. The eyes of the envisioned person looked down and saw her own hands—youthful, feminine hands with fingers that seemed short and pudgy in contrast to Rebecca's own—hands that rested on the windowsill against which the person stood. And, through this person's eyes, Rebecca saw on one hand both an engagement ring and a wedding band, and on the other, a single ring, also worn on the third finger, but of indeterminate character and symbolism.

And these hands—these hands that were the dreamer's hands and yet not her hands—changed as she watched them, turning slowly into angry fists, fists that began to pound on the wooden sill in fury or frustration or terror. As the vision continued to fade, its edges contracting and tightening, its center weakening in detail, the pounding ceased, and the hands slowly spread themselves into feminine claws on the sill, a woman's fingernails digging into the polished wood. And in this attitude, perhaps for a full five seconds before the vision disappeared entirely, the lone ring's details crystallized in the visual mind of the seer. And she saw that it was a cameo, a bright white figure standing out strongly against the pale green of the background surface.

And then it was gone.

As the vision disappeared completely, the dreamer experienced the familiar sense of being emptied of all strength, of all muscular capacity, and she sank slowly back to her pillow. Breathless and gasping, indistinct murmurs escaping her throat, her whole body quickly became very, very cold. Weakly, she reached for the lightweight bed sheet and pulled it up to her chin.

After a moment, reluctantly, in response to an impulse that she knew was to be obeyed immediately and that, though subtle, was to her mind just as clearly from the Source beyond herself as was the vision, she reached timidly to her husband and once again touched his right shoulder.

Something in that touch caused him to awaken instantly, and he rolled over quickly from his left side onto his right. Now facing her, his brown eyes were wide and alert.

"The dreams, dear," she whispered softly. "The visions again."

Immediately, he slid his right hand and arm under her neck and moved himself against her, pushing her head gently onto his chest with that same hand and arm. Sensing her weakness, he used the fingers of his right hand to move her long, thick, black tresses from the confused tangle into which they had fallen, pulling them back from her face and realizing as he did that her hair was as wet as if she had just stepped from a river. She was saturated in perspiration.

He understood.

"Wait," he whispered in her ear, as he moved his chest quickly from under her head, then stood, crossed the bedroom floor, and retrieved two blankets from the closet shelf. Leaning over the bed from behind her, he covered his wife. He then circled the bed again and resumed his previous position, her head once more on his chest. He knew she would speak when she could.

Idly, he again caressed her sweat-soaked hair with his right hand. And thoughtfully, he traced the elegant lines of her face and, smiling down at her, stroked with his fingertips the ragged, shallow V of the scar that ran across her right cheek. The scar tissue rose dramatically from a point near the corner of her mouth and extended itself in a thick, tapering line that ended near her right ear. To him, everything about her was beautiful, the arrow of scar tissue no less than the magnificence of her eyes and the glory of her hair.

But, he thought to himself, his wife had just experienced another of "the visions." And he knew what that meant. He knew what that had always meant.

And so he closed his eyes, feeling her shallow breath on his chest, and he began to pray the only prayer he could, speaking the words softly aloud, as she had taught him to do: "Father, please help us to be equal to the tasks that You now set before us. May we act in obedience. May we *always* act in obedience. And may we be granted through Thy Holy Spirit the wisdom, the strength, and the courage to enact Thy will for us. We pray in the Holy Name of Thy Son, our Savior, Jesus Christ.

"Amen."

Nearly two hours later, as first light cautiously made itself known outside the bedroom's only window, the long-limbed, long-muscled young man, almost a full year older than his bride of ten months, kissed her still-damp hair until she stirred. Feeling her head move slightly on his chest, he whispered, "Sweetheart, let me telephone the headmistress and tell her you'll come in at midday. I'd like you to get several more hours of sleep after what's happened."

She shook her head weakly against him. "No," she murmured, "I can't do that on the last day of school, darling. The girls would be devastated if I were not there on the final morning. They'd be crushed, and they're too young to understand anything other than 'She wasn't here on our last morning.'"

Knowing she was right, he kissed her hair once more and slipped from under her, rolling to the edge of the bed and rising quickly. "I'll start your tea, dear. Don't try to get up yet."

As his footsteps retreated down the hallway of the small flat, the young woman turned her mind once more to the night vision, pulling the details again to the forefront of her mind's eye, as she had set herself to do just before the vision's onset. Twice she took herself in memory through the vision from start to finish, driving the images before her internal view with practiced discipline. Finally satisfied, she pulled her husband's pillow on top of her own, fluffed their soft shapes into a billowing mound against the head of the bed, and sat up against them. And now, for the first time, she brought her mind to bear on the vision's meaning and message—if indeed, a trace of either could be extracted.

She found nothing. The vision comprised a series of images without either meaning or message, insofar as she could tell on first analysis. The mysterious, unrecognizable stained glass image had seemed to demand a response from her, but she could no more ascertain the nature of the demand now, upon studied reflection, than during the dreamed sequence itself.

She drew her hands to her face, closed her eyes, and concentrated. Always before—no, not *always* before, but nearly so—a firm, clear command had accompanied any such series of images. This time there seemed to be little beyond the images themselves, which continued to suggest nothing to her that she could meaningfully translate.

She heard her husband returning, and looked up to see him entering the bedroom with her tea. He placed the cup and saucer on her nightstand and sat on the side of the bed, taking her right hand in his. He searched her eyes.

She smiled and shook her head. "Nothing. I simply have a series of images. And I'm fairly certain I'm recalling everything."

He returned her smile. "Then more images will be sent."

She nodded and then described for him the scene that had presented itself to her, and the actions of the person—apparently a young woman—through whose eyes she had been invited to observe.

As she had learned to expect, his detailed questions drew from her memory more than she had realized she had seen. She found, for example, that she knew that the stone steps rising to the edifice across the courtyard numbered more than fifty, that there were perhaps three or four dozen people standing in the courtyard far below the closed window through which she observed, that this small crowd seemed to be watching the steps or the edifice with apparent expectancy and even excitement, that "her" hands—not just her fingers—were soft, small, and plump, and that the cameo's white relief figure actually comprised two figures: that of Madonna and Child.

They sat silently in thought, his hand resting on her drawn-up knees as she sipped her tea gratefully. Then she sighed, glanced at the clock on her nightstand, and said, "Thank you, Matt." She leaned toward him to kiss his lips softly. She then placed her cup and saucer on the nightstand and swung her legs past him to the floor, rising carefully to her full height. "I feel strong enough now, I think. I've got to hurry. I want to be early to school."

With practiced dispatch, the two of them moved rapidly through the weekday morning ritual: washing up, devotions, a quick bite of something from the pantry. And finally, as if the thing had been fully choreographed, they found themselves approaching the front door from opposite directions, depositing their briefcases there at almost the same moment. They laughed, kissed again, and joined hands, his right hand cradling both of hers, a silent prayer on the lips of each.

Then, without apparent signal, they wordlessly enacted the final steps in their every-morning dance. They circled in opposite directions through the apartment, looking systematically out every window in the flat and yet staying well away from each window, as though taking pains to ensure that they could not be seen by anyone from the street in front, nor from the alleyway behind.

As the young husband approached the front door once more, he saw his wife standing absolutely still, eyes fastened on something in the medium

distance. He moved to her side and followed her gaze. Across the street he
saw a small, nondescript sedan, possibly a rental. Behind the wheel sat a
young woman. She held a newspaper near her face, but her eyes swept
incessantly across the front of their apartment.

And thus, both husband and wife understood in a flash of recognition.
They were—yet again—under surveillance by an enemy.

The haggard observer, a woman of perhaps thirty difficult years, sat in
the oft-dented rental automobile on this tree-lined street in what she
regarded as one of London's more questionable neighborhoods. She sipped
stone-cold coffee and pretended to read the morning newspaper that she
had finished two hours earlier. She was slight of figure, no more than two
inches over five feet in height, with somber Mediterranean features, and
she had allowed her short, imperfectly dyed, now sandy blonde hair to lie
in the same dishevelment that it had chosen for itself during her brief sleep.
She wore a pair of lightweight beige slacks, and a dark blue medium-weight
jacket that seemed much too large for her small frame.

Her eyes burned with fatigue. She fought against her need to close
them. Periodically she raised her eyes and discreetly, she thought, studied
the door and the three front-facing windows in the deteriorating flat immediately across the street.

Each time she glanced at the apartment, a word emerged instantly from
somewhere (the psychiatrists will say they can tell you from where) and into
her consciousness. The word, she felt embarrassed to acknowledge, was
"menacing." The look of the small flat with its hollow-eyed windows was
somehow menacing at the same time that it was thoroughly unprepos-
sessing. *How was that possible?* she wondered to herself, now for the first
time actually forming the question in her mind, stringing the words
together into an unspoken sentence.

How, indeed?

And as soon as she went so far as to speak the question to herself, she
knew. It was the apartment's occupants—no, her *image* of the apartment's
occupants, especially one of them—that menaced her. The apartment

itself was nothing: small, undistinguished, easily ignored. But the people it housed were not. They were not small, they were not undistinguished, and they were—to say the least—not easily ignored by anyone on the globe who had even the faintest idea what these people had done in the last two years.

Their reputations threatened at times to overwhelm the faux blonde as she sat alone in her car, forcing herself to believe she was competent to execute what the Americans liked to call a stakeout. *What could they possibly mean by that?* she wondered. As far as she could tell, "stakeout" meant exposure and risk and . . . and even capture . . . physical capture, perhaps, or more likely, another sort of capture. The threat posed by these individuals was real.

And so the observer's mood alternated between the excitement that stirred in her in this utterly new, danger-laden assignment, and a terror that is borne of raw, bleeding fear. Which, in her case, included a mixture of what her psychiatrists called her fear of failure and something beyond the genuine, profound, and to an extent, understandable physical and emotional fear of one of this apartment's two occupants.

These ingredients had begun, weeks before, to form themselves into a pulsating, virulent mixture in her soul, a mixture that she fought into submission again and again. It was exhausting. And this last, crippling infusion of self-doubt was now present in force, she knew, simply because failure in this assignment could not be contemplated, not even for a moment.

And so, in that frame of mind, she summoned something that she told herself was self-assurance. (The experts had told her she could do that for herself.) So she worked to inject an emergency measure of this self-induced confidence into the roiling emotional cauldron within. And she embraced this force-fed assurance with the desperation of one who knows that "life-or-death" is more than a phrase for the novelists and the playwrights.

Her life could end right now, right here.

And she did not want that, though she would have been pressed to provide a reasoned explanation for the strength of her desire to live beyond the next few minutes. And in that lack of certainty, too, she knew the psychiatrists would be disappointed in her.

But she did know one thing. She knew that she was very, very tired. Had anyone watched the quiet street overnight, such a sentry would have seen

the woman arrive, automobile headlamps extinguished, a full hour before daybreak. Nearly three hours had now passed without her so much as adjusting her position behind the wheel except to turn the pages of the newspaper and occasionally to nurse the large cup of strong coffee she had brought with her from her small hotel room nearby. She sipped again at the dregs, then threw her head back and drained the cup, her eyes closing as she did.

Swallowing the remains of the bitter substance, she kept her eyes blessedly closed for moments, then gradually allowed her head to drop forward toward her chest. And almost instantly she slept. The empty cup slipped from her hand. Her breathing slowed and her jaw muscles relaxed. Her lips parted slightly.

Suddenly a door slammed and her eyes flew open. Heart racing, she jumped in her seat, hitting both knees hard on the steering wheel.

Recovering, she pulled the newspaper up to her face, swung her eyes toward the flat, and saw that a young couple had emerged from the apartment, the woman waiting while her companion turned to lock the door. And there they stood, both of them, not more than thirty yards away.

She felt herself unable to breathe. She opened her mouth and gasped for air, now averting her eyes. Steeling herself with the words, *You can do this, Andrea,* and then, *You must do this, Andrea,* she positioned the newspaper more carefully. Looking just over the top of the page, she examined her quarry.

The woman appeared to be six feet in height, with thick, straight, lustrous black hair that she had caught up in a bright yellow bow, the resulting ponytail trailing more than halfway down her back. She wore a light blue, sleeveless blouse with a long, cream-colored skirt. She seemed strikingly muscular, though not at all in a bulging, masculine way. Rather, there seemed something feline in her sleek musculature, something that brought to mind the image of the internationally ranked amateur tennis player this woman had become in her late teens and early twenties. Her physical presence suggested to the observer the possibility that she might be no less fit now, at age twenty-eight, than then.

Even at the thirty-yard distance that separated the blonde observer from the couple, she could distinguish clearly the shallow V-shaped line of the ragged scar that altered the natural elegance of the tall woman's face. She could see that, as she had expected, the scar tissue indeed began at a point near the right side of her mouth and extended almost to her ear.

Odd, thought the observer. The woman surely could not have been more beautiful before receiving the supposedly disfiguring wound than she was at this moment. The line of the scar seemed, if anything, to have created a more interesting countenance, one with its own special mark: an arrow drawing the eye first to the dark magnificence of her hair and then to the exquisite symmetry of her mouth. Neither cosmetics nor jewelry adorned the face; indeed, neither contrivance could have enhanced any aspect of it. Plainly, original elegance of this kind could not be beautified by color, covering, or precious stone, any more than it could be diminished by a superficial interruption of its delicate surface.

The athletic woman's companion turned from the door and smiled at her, taking her left hand in his right. She was tall, but he was taller, probably by four inches or even more. He was handsome in an ordinary fashion, not physically attention-getting in the way the woman no doubt had been all her adult life. And he was physically altered, too, much as she had been, the observer knew, by the battles the two of them had fought together. In his case, his entire left shoulder and arm, though covered by a lightweight, long-sleeved shirt, appeared deformed, even atrophied, to such an extent that he struck the observer as, in a practical sense, missing the left shoulder, arm, and hand entirely. And yet he walked gracefully and athletically, and, above all . . . what?

And she knew. Above all, this man was in love with the woman whose hand he cradled in his own. It showed in some indefinable but unmistakable way, not just in his eyes and on his lips, but in his entire physical being. Indeed, Matthew Clark had loved Rebecca Manguson from the moment his brown eyes had fixed themselves on her stunning gray ones two eventful years earlier.

The observer did not turn her head to watch the couple walk along the sidewalk behind her to the nearest corner. She waited until she could see them in her side-view mirror. She then watched their reflection as they crossed the intersection and turned to walk toward, she knew, the Anglican junior school for girls in which they both taught.

The dyed-blonde woman, her anxiety diminishing slightly as the distance between herself and the apartment's occupants grew with each passing moment, waited behind the wheel for five full minutes. Then, stepping painfully from the car, her muscles protesting after hours of inaction, she timidly traced the couple's route to the corner, turned in the direction opposite that taken by them, and now forcing herself to walk with an affected nonchalance that bespoke her inexperience as a shadow, entered the alleyway behind the apartment.

Moving more quickly, she strode down the alley and stopped at the back door of the couple's flat. She looked up and down the alley, removed a small, odd-shaped implement from her jacket pocket, and then stepped to the door. In Rebecca and Matthew Clark's absence, the observer had work to do.

At almost the same moment on this June morning, across much of a continent, nearly a thousand rugged miles from London toward the south and east, another young woman observed a couple from the window of an automobile. But the two people under observation by Anna Angelini did not ignore the observer, as the Clarks were so studiously doing in London. In fact, they waved happily over their shoulders in their mother's direction. The two children, the older holding her brother's hand, now began to run excitedly toward the long steps that led to the entrance of their Roman Catholic elementary school. Their mother waved at them in return as they climbed the steps, but her mind was at that moment less on her children than on her own mother.

For this June day, the last of the school year, would have been her mother's sixtieth birthday, had she not been taken by cancer almost exactly two years earlier. Margaret Mason's life had been full. She had served in the Second World War as a nurse with the U.S. Army, almost always near the front lines, first in Sicily and then up and down the Italian peninsula.

At war's end, she had married an Italian officer, one Marcus Capo, captured in Sicily by General Patton's forces. Marcus had been a young Florentine whom she had helped restore to robust health. Margaret's postwar marriage to Marcus had not been well received by the Mason family, back in small-town Alabama, with the notable exception of her only sibling, her beloved sister Eleanor.

Many times the young Anna had been told the story of how, despite Margaret Mason's marriage to a former enemy soldier, and despite her subsequent conversion to Catholicism, Eleanor Mason Chapel had embraced her younger sister and her Italian family without reserve, and not just from afar. She had sacrificed financially to travel to Rome for Margaret's wedding, and had continued to cross the Atlantic regularly in the ensuing decades while rising professionally to a position of international prominence as an Old Testament scholar, teacher, and writer.

Her aunt Eleanor's commitment to Margaret and to all of the Capo family members had been viewed as all the more remarkable in view of the tragedy that ended Eleanor's own marriage. She had been widowed when her husband's U.S. Army Air Corps fighter, a hulking, single-engine, P-47 Thunderbolt based at Duxford, England, had been brought down by German ground fire over France.

The war had taken a husband from one sister and provided a husband for the other. The fact that the two husbands had fought for opposing armies had never been of the slightest interest to the widowed Eleanor Chapel. She loved her sister and her sister's husband without reservation.

And there was still another reason beyond that one that led the Old Testament professor's extended Italian family to treasure her. They knew Dr. Eleanor Chapel loved them despite her lifelong membership in the Southern Baptist denomination, a significantly large Christian body (the Capos were given to understand) in the United States. But the denomination was, they were repeatedly told, one that shared little with the Catholic Church beyond the common belief in Jesus Christ as Lord and Savior.

Anna Angelini had often wondered why the thing was said in that way—*"shared little beyond their common belief in Jesus Christ as Lord and Savior"*—as though sharing that belief comprised some small matter, of no more moment than, say, holding Sunday services at the same hour. It had seemed to young Anna that if you shared that belief, you shared the one thing in the universe that mattered most and mattered eternally. The adult Anna felt exactly the same.

In any case, her aunt Eleanor's love and devotion to her only sibling had been one of the brightest and steadiest stars in their lives, from their earliest times together until the hour and minute of death. And now Anna's cherished Aunt Eleanor—the esteemed Dr. Eleanor Chapel, senior professor of Old Testament, Union Theological Seminary, New York City (she had to remind herself from time to time)—would be coming to Rome to see her, the Capo family, and of course, the children: her precious, fragile grandniece Maria, and her irrepressible, rough-and-tumble grandnephew

Paulo. Anna smiled to herself. Her aunt was so like her mother that, when she was with them, it seemed at times as if her mother actually moved among them once more in angelic form. She could hardly bear to wait the seven weeks until August first.

Still smiling, tears rolling slowly down each side of her nose and bringing the salt taste of loss to her tongue, the young mother drove away from her children's school and steered toward the nearby churchyard and cemetery. She would visit her mother's gravesite this morning.

Two blocks from the church, she pulled her car over in front of the neighborhood florist's shop. Her mother had rarely been without fresh flowers in her home. Anna had made a promise to herself that Margaret Mason Capo's earthly place of rest would always be similarly graced.

As she pulled away from the florist's, her mind on things long past, a black Mercedes sedan pulled away from the curb, two cars behind her. Its heavily tinted windows allowed no glimpse of the occupants. When the young mother pulled into the cemetery moments later and slowed to a stop near the Capo family plot, the Mercedes slid quietly to a halt at the main gate.

And there it waited, still and silent as the tree-shadowed gravestones.

Chapter Two

THE OBSERVER ONCE MORE SAT AT THE WHEEL OF HER automobile in urban London, her coiffeur now darker, dirtier, and more confused than at sunrise that same morning. The battered rental car was positioned in very nearly the same spot. Now holding a coffee-stained paperback romance novel, the woman watched irritably from the corners of her eyes as Rebecca and Matthew Clark approached their decaying apartment, their school day and their school year complete, holding hands just as they were when they had departed that morning. Each face inclined toward the other's as they talked quietly and intently, seemingly lost in each other's presence.

"School talk," muttered the observer to herself in English. *"Sciocchezza!"* she then said more loudly than she perhaps intended, and with some vehemence, since, in the observer's experience, schooling had indeed been little but foolishness, and lovers' mindless conversations even worse.

She watched the man stoop to manipulate the key with his good hand, then hold the door for his wife. As they disappeared into the flat and closed the door, she noted the precise time in her logbook, and raised the paperback to her eyes once more.

She had looked down for perhaps fifteen seconds to write in her ledger. Had she not, and had her eyes been able to penetrate the shadowy interior behind the hollow-eyed window to the left of the front door, she would have been stunned to find herself under expert observation from within. A pair of gray eyes examined their prey for the second time that day, studying the observer's face in profile. The gray eyes were joined immediately by a pair of less remarkable brown ones, the latter assisted by a compact and powerful pair of United States military-issue binoculars. Everything about the blonde's appearance and that of her rented automobile underwent professional-calibre scrutiny. Details were swiftly committed to memory, noted systematically, and mentally filed, down to and including the title of the novel she held in her hands.

An odd chill passed through the reader, but she saw nothing now except the pages of her book. She was too weary to be gripped by the debilitating fear that had nearly overcome her that morning. For then, the very breath had been ripped from her by that first glimpse of the flat's occupants—especially one of them. She had then, in fact, been forced to summon every ounce of discipline at her disposal just to remain at her post. But now, nearly nine hours later, no reservoir of energy remained sufficient to reproduce those emotions.

Or so she thought.

Suddenly, just as it had that morning, the concussive slam of the apartment's front door cancelled everything except the fear that had been masked by exhaustion. Her heart thudded dully. Frozen, she stared across the narrow street at the couple, as once more, the man stooped to lock the apartment door while the woman waited motionless at his side.

This time the observer stared, eyes wide, at only one of the two. She found she could not take her eyes from the one human being whose mere presence seemed to change everything. For she knew what this Englishwoman had done. And so the observer, unmoving, holding her breath in incoherent desperation, fixed her gaze on Rebecca Clark and only on Rebecca Clark, and found that it was impossible to look elsewhere.

The observer saw dimly that the ogress was now dressed in tennis clothing: shoes, a short tennis skirt, and a white knit shirt. The long ponytail, its black cascade a shimmering, striking contrast to the bright whiteness of the garments, was no longer secured by the yellow bow, but only by a set of thick, dark-red rubber bands. The woman carried two tennis rackets and a can of tennis balls, holding all three in the long, powerful talons of her left hand, leaving her right hand free. When her husband, also dressed for tennis, turned from the front door, she placed the accoutrements on the walkway and began systematically to stretch the muscles of her back and legs.

To the stricken observer, Rebecca Clark now looked almost superhuman. For not only did the sinews of her exposed upper and lower arms stand out in terrible relief, but more intimidating by far, the rippling musculature of her long-boned thighs revealed a creature whose physical capacities actually seemed commensurate with the lore that surrounded her. Not merely the tennis championships, of course, as impressive as those had been. For any superior athlete could have accomplished as much, given enough training and enough determination. No, it was not those accomplishments that flooded and staggered the false blonde's imagination and led her again to fight for breath itself.

The lore that overawed her had instead to do with other kinds of accomplishments . . . accomplishments and capabilities. . . . And these included not just the speed of foot to outrun would-be assailants or to overtake potential assassins. And not just the strength of leg, torso, and shoulder to carry a six-foot-four-inch, two-hundred-pound man aloft for more than a mile along a treacherous cliff or successfully to fight hand-to-hand with an armed, trained killer. And not just the mechanical acumen and automotive athleticism to drive a temperamental Alfa Romeo two-seater through a phalanx of larger, higher-powered vehicles or to elicit keyless ignition and coordinated movement from a series of darkened engines, all within seconds and while under automatic weapons fire.

No, the sum of those accomplishments and capabilities contributed no more than one part in three to the observer's dysfunction. The other parts were rooted in the observer's knowledge of Rebecca Clark's *other* history. For this Englishwoman had a separate story that ran parallel with, though indissolubly linked to, each of these aspects of her warrior past. Said simply and without embellishment: Rebecca Clark could, under certain conditions, see things before they happened. Could actually *see* them in her mind's eye. And then she could bring her extraordinary physical and analytical capacities to bear on the world around her in ways that could alter these previously envisioned outcomes. And it was *this* capacity that brought the observer to her emotional knees.

It was not said, of course, that the Englishwoman saw visions on a daily basis. She saw them, it would seem, only on rare occasions, but always in the context of some great thing that was about to be done. And the observer knew, if you were to ask Rebecca Clark how or why or by what means these things came to her, she would say she did not know. She would describe herself as an ordinary Christian who tried to be a good church member, a good teacher of the girls whom she shepherded hourly and daily at her school, and now, a good wife to her husband of ten months. If asked, that's all she would say. She would add that she had no idea whether or not she would ever be sent another vision, or whether, instead, she had been sent those images at two particular points in her life, to be sent them no more.

That is precisely the way, if asked, she would talk about her visions: she would say that they had been sent to her. If you asked her by Whom, she would say only that she was a Christian who believed in God's capacity to choose any means whatever to communicate with His creatures. And she might add, at that point, that her life was, with the exception of these rare events, quite ordinary. She might point out that, for example, she arose every morning and said her prayers, worked at her profession throughout the day, and then said her prayers again before bedtime.

The Holy Spirit's communications with her, when they occurred, were of the same order as those of other Christians, she would contend. That is, whether she happened to be engaged in actual prayer or not, there might come an unmistakable sense that some long-deferred obligation could be postponed no longer; or an unmistakable sense that a prudent hesitancy to commit oneself to some good action was becoming plain cowardice; or an equally unmistakable sense that an earlier decision or action had been wrong, and that recompense, penitence, and apology were now required. These, Rebecca Clark would say if asked, were the fruits of ordinary prayer, or just of simple, routine awareness of God's continual presence—of the day-by-day and hour-by-hour urgings and admonitions of the Holy Spirit. And she would insist, these described quite adequately and completely the nature of her own, perfectly ordinary, personal relationship with the Almighty.

Except, of course, she would acknowledge, for those two vision-dominated points in her life. The two points separated by one year, with the most recent occurring twelve months previous almost to the day.

And now, there should be no more reason to expect another series of visions today . . . this week . . . this month . . . she would say, than on either of the other occasions. There had been no suggestion that more such images would be forthcoming, now or ever.

And it was exactly those occasions, known and studied by the exhausted observer, coupled with her knowledge of Rebecca Clark's physical and analytical capacities, that brought her nearer to sanity's edge than she had come for some time. Who was to say that Rebecca Clark had not, even within the last five minutes, received one of her supernatural visions? Who was to say that a new vision freshly received might not have revealed the very threat of which the blonde observer herself had knowledge? Who was to say that Rebecca Clark would not creep up from behind the observer as she sat there in her rental automobile and. . . .

Shaking her head violently, the observer pulled her eyes away from the couple, both of them still stretching their leg and back muscles on the grass of their tiny front lawn. Looking down and away from them, she tried to regain control of her thoughts. If somehow she were discovered by them, and if somehow she were forced to talk—and she shuddered at what "forced to talk" might entail—she knew exactly what she must say, how to say it, and when to stop talking.

She concentrated. She nodded her head emphatically to herself, her story clear in her mind. She had practiced for weeks.

Now suddenly hearing the soft, rhythmic, scraping sound of cushioned feet running on hard surface, she looked up quickly. The couple had begun to jog down the sidewalk toward, the observer knew, the hard-surface tennis courts a little more than a mile from the apartment. She saw that Matthew Clark cradled his left wrist in front of his body with his right hand. This expedient prevented the useless left arm from swinging inefficiently and distractingly as he ran.

Using her side-view mirror, the observer watched the two runners disappear into the distance behind her, then picked up her ledger, made another entry, and laid her head against the seatback. Taking a deep and relaxing breath, she closed her eyes gratefully in anticipation of ninety minutes or more of rest, and if she were truly fortunate, a few minutes of actual sleep. She found herself smiling faintly in embarrassment at her preposterous and terror-stricken reaction to the sight of Rebecca Clark. The woman was a *schoolteacher*, and seer of visions or not, an ordinary person whose stature could not, should not, possibly produce these ridiculous emotional responses. Her father was right, the observer said to herself, smiling again. She could handle this stakeout business perfectly well, if she would simply talk to herself in ways that were not so grossly hysterical.

Her eyes had been closed, she thought later, for no more than two or three minutes when she heard a woman's contralto, *sotto voce*, inches from her ear, just outside the open driver's side window of the car. The authoritative, feminine voice, somehow both soothing and menacing, seemed to be coming from above and behind her, the words arrowing through the open car window like disembodied shafts of steel. *"You will tell me why you have been observing my husband and me. You will tell me for whom you work. You will tell me the nature of your assignment."*

The observer jerked forward with such a start that she cracked her nose on the steering wheel and uttered a vile oath in Italian. When, after a moment, she did attempt to speak, she did so while vigorously massaging the bridge of her nose with the fingers of both hands. She spoke halting but presentable English in an accent that was heavily Italian. Despite repeated rehearsals of her story, her explanation was anything but fluent.

"I . . . I . . . I have been . . . I have been hired . . . hired by a person friendly to you. You . . . you and your husband . . . are in much danger. My assignment is to . . . ah . . . to . . . to do an observing . . . of your comings and your goings at your home. I am . . . I am no problem to you. I am . . . I am a friend to you. I am . . . I am to assist in being . . . in being a protection . . . a protection for the both of you."

She stopped and lowered her hands from her nose, the pain having died slowly away. Satisfied that she had spoken her story coherently, though clumsily, she forced herself to turn her head to look back over her shoulder and into Rebecca Clark's hard, gray eyes. The thought crossed her mind as she did that these were the eyes of a woman who could be many things, including, if required, an uncompromising and implacable foe. And the Hebrew meaning, told to her by her father, of the Old Testament name "Rebecca" formed itself instantly in her mind: *Ensnarer.*

She resolved to continue her defense.

"Here," the observer said uncertainly, attempting a smile and turning her head away from the steely gaze, "I will show to you my identification document." With that, she reached across her own chest and into the oversized blue jacket that she had donned early that morning against the chill, yet had continued to wear through the heat of the early summer day.

Suddenly her wrist was seized in an iron grip and pulled violently up and away from her body. The inexorable force continued to lift and extend the woman's wrist until, finally, not only was her arm all the way out the car window, but her shoulder and now her head were beginning to follow despite the vigor of her resistance.

"Eeiiiiii!" she cried involuntarily, looking up in pain and fear at the assailant towering over her. Then she saw another, still larger, hand reaching across to encircle her tortured wrist with a grip of equal or greater force.

Her hands freed to go elsewhere by her husband's grasp on the observer's wrist, Rebecca quickly stooped and thrust her arms, head, and much of her torso fully through the car window, pushing the woman's face roughly, if inadvertently, aside with her shoulder. With both hands, she tore open the blue jacket, searching for the weapon she suspected she would find. Discovering none, she settled for the passport for which the observer had apparently been reaching, and the ledger that lay on the seat beside her. Then she extracted the ignition key from the steering column and stood up, opening the passport so that she and her husband could together examine the name, date of birth, city, and country.

Matthew Clark then released the woman's wrist unceremoniously, leaving the slight, disheveled figure to collapse momentarily, draped halfway out of the car's open window. Seeming to forget the would-be observer entirely, he then joined his wife in peering at the passport. The woman in the photograph was certainly the woman who writhed, gasping, under their gaze, though the likeness on the document showed a younger, fresher face, together with neatly brushed, shoulder-length, dark brown or black hair. The couple examined the identifying text: *Camposanto, Andrea Theresa. 15 agosto 52. Roma. Italia.*

The Clarks exchanged glances, and at his wife's nod, Matthew opened the car door and gestured for the woman to step out. "Walk in front of us," he said tersely, then stepped aside as the captive moved into the street and toward the front door of the flat.

Once inside the apartment, Rebecca indicated a straight-backed wooden chair, and the woman took the seat without hesitation. The couple, still standing, looked down at her searchingly. The Englishwoman, still holding passport, ledger, and car keys, moved her eyes from the captive to the ledger, and began to leaf through the neat, handwritten, Italian entries, skimming the lines for the main ideas and reading from back to front.

While she turned the pages, her husband addressed the observer. "By which name do you call yourself?"

"Andrea," she replied, gracefully rolling the "r" and accenting the second syllable dramatically.

The husband nodded. "And you are—you will be on August fifteenth— twenty-seven years of age, consistent with your passport?"

The blonde observer replied simply, "*Si.*"

The wife looked up from the ledger and spoke again, her voice hard. "My Italian is weak, but your ledger seems to speak of your traveling from Rome to London for the explicit purpose of observing us. Explain."

Andrea Camposanto, massaging her superficially injured wrist, arm, and shoulder with her opposite hand, looked up at her questioner through eyes filled with a bedlam of pain, anger, and more than a little fear. But she squared her thin shoulders and spoke in a clear, deliberate voice: "My father . . . my father . . . he is . . . *Antonio Camposanto.*"

She paused and looked into, first, the wife's, and then the husband's face, clearly expecting some sign of recognition. She was not merely disappointed. She seemed dumbfounded by the absence of response.

"My father is . . . *Antonio Camposanto!* My father is . . . *famoso!*" She snorted in exasperation. "Antonio Camposanto is the world's *most famous* man of . . . man of . . . man of *detection!* No . . . *detective! . . . detective!* How can you not know his name? Do you not read your own newspapers? . . . Eh? . . . Do you not read of his solving the political murders in Roma . . . three years ago? . . . Eh? . . . Do you not read of his . . . of his . . . of his solving of the kidnapping crimes in Paris . . . and . . . and in Trieste . . . and . . . and in your own city . . . all in the last five years? . . . Eh? . . . He is . . . called upon . . . by police . . . everywhere . . . all over the world . . . to assist."

She searched their faces again, incredulous. "You *must* know his name! If you say you do not . . . if you say you do not . . . I do not even *believe* you!"

There was a brief silence. Then Rebecca spoke, the trace of a smile on her lips, a smile that, the captive noticed fleetingly, compressed the shallow V of scar tissue on her cheek ever so slightly. "We know your father's name, Andrea." She spoke the woman's name exactly as the woman herself had spoken it, rolling the "r" expertly and stressing the second syllable.

The woman's smile suddenly brightened the room.

"Ah!" she said triumphantly, tossing her head back. "*Ah!*"

The Englishwoman's face retained its faint smile. "What has your father's fame to do with your secret observation of my husband and me? What did you mean before . . . in your automobile . . . when you said we were in danger? What 'friend,' as you suggested then, has hired you to watch us?"

Here the suggestion of a smile disappeared, and she stepped nearer to her captive, moving her face within inches of the slight woman, who remained huddled, now shivering perceptibly in the blue jacket. "And what possible justification do you have for entering this apartment today in our absence? Can you give me even one defensible reason why we should not telephone Scotland Yard this instant?"

At Rebecca's allegation—delivered as an accusation—regarding her forced entry into the flat, the woman's face changed to an expression that the Clarks both interpreted as one of astonishment and grudging respect. "How did you know. . . . No. . . . Never mind."

Her brow furrowed briefly while she looked down at her hands, which twisted against each other in her lap.

"All right," she said icily, "I will tell you what you have asked to know, but you must promise . . . you must *promise* . . . that you will not . . . that you will not for any reason . . . notify the Scotland Yard, yes?" She arched her eyebrows in expectation of a quick affirmative.

"No," replied the couple in forceful unison.

The woman snorted again, turned her head disgustedly to one side, and glanced behind her at the front door. When she turned her head again toward the couple, she saw that the wife had lifted the telephone receiver from its cradle, at the same time inserting the index finger of her right hand into the rotary dial. Then she began to operate the phone, removing her finger after dialing each number to allow the dial to make its slow, clacking return to its initial position.

"Stop!" said the captive with some urgency in her voice, lifting the palm of her right hand. *"Per favore,"* she added. And again, "Please, *signora* . . . please."

Then she raised her hands to her face and covered her eyes, sighing as she did. Finally, she lowered her hands and looked up. "All right," she said, her eyes on the telephone. "All right. I will talk to you."

Rebecca Clark replaced the telephone receiver in its cradle and stood looking closely at Andrea Camposanto, who sat staring down at the floor, her hands working against each other in her lap. The shapeless blue jacket made her look even smaller than she was. All combativeness and indignation seemed to have vanished with the threat of police involvement. Yet Rebecca found an idea forming in her mind: *This person fears Scotland Yard, but she fears something more than that. Much, much more than that.*

And immediately the captor stepped forward and, with her right hand, extended the ledger, passport, and automobile keys, holding them until the prisoner raised both hands, took the items and, confused, looked up from her own hands and to Rebecca's face. But Rebecca had already turned away.

She lifted a straight-backed wooden chair matching the one in which Andrea Camposanto sat, and moved it to a position just in front and to one side of her. Then, still dressed for tennis and still perspiring lightly from her brief run, Rebecca sat down. Sitting erect in the chair and placing her hands in her lap, she looked up at her husband, who continued to stand and watch his wife intently. "Matt," she said softly, "would you be a dear and make tea for the three of us?"

Without a second's hesitation he nodded and left the room, and the prisoner realized that, inexplicably, all definitions had suddenly changed. She was now a guest. Her captor had become her hostess. And the changes had materialized in a barely perceptible flash of recognition: the captor had seen something, sensed something, *recognized* something in her prisoner.

And both women guessed, though dimly, that the Englishwoman had caught the scent of an unnatural fear . . . an unnatural fear somewhere deep within Andrea Camposanto. And that scent had triggered some long-buried recollection in Rebecca's memory, a reluctantly remembered terror of something both monstrous and unspeakable, something once defeated, but not conquered. Something scattered incoherently around the edges of her mind and soul.

Andrea Camposanto continued to stare uncomprehendingly at the woman who had been her quarry for all of twelve hours, and who with consummate ease had reversed their positions. Having suddenly become the Englishwoman's captive, the Italian wondered if this sudden transformation from captor to hostess was the first step in another lightning maneuver, this one designed to convert physical capture into psychological capture. A tactic that would, if successful, change the prisoner into, first, an admirer, and then, a follower. She had been warned that Rebecca Clark had the power to capture her enemies in many ways.

Now her hostess was speaking again, her voice still soft, her eyes searching for something in the face that looked back at her, a face still guarded and bewildered. "You are free to leave, Ms. Camposanto," the voice said with such courtesy that the guest found herself believing the words immediately. "But," the voice continued, "I prefer that you stay and talk. I want you to speak to me about your presence here in London, and here in this neighborhood. I want to begin to understand why you are here.

And . . ." and here the voice hesitated for a brief moment . . . "and I want to know why you are afraid . . . of Scotland Yard . . . and if I am not mistaken, of me . . . and perhaps, of something else as well. . . ."

Though she did not smile, the Englishwoman's tone and demeanor were no longer threatening. "Please. Take your time," she added mildly. She had closed her mouth definitively as the final syllable had been spoken. She raised her chin expectantly, but her gaze was noncommittal. Utterly relaxed, completely in charge, Rebecca awaited Andrea Camposanto's reply.

The visitor returned her hostess's gaze unsteadily, her mind a thicket of tangled assumptions, orders, directives, and fears. For this, an arm's length away, was Rebecca Manguson Clark, the mere thought of whom had sent shock waves of unbridled fear, time after humiliating time, surging into her soul. And yet this very tigress had abruptly and courteously returned her passport, ledger, and car keys, and had added that she was free to leave.

In this confusion of mind, no words came to Andrea Camposanto. She turned her head and searched desperately about her, realizing as she did that she had no idea why she looked about, nor for what. She did know that a sense of desperation should still be flowing through her, and yet both terror and desperation seemed to have vanished. She lowered her head, shuddered, and closed her eyes.

Suddenly she felt a hand on her shoulder. Her hostess had risen, moved to a position beside her chair, and now rested her right hand on the guest's left shoulder. The grip was ambiguous, neither painful nor soothing.

The melodic contralto came again. And this time the voice seemed to the guest to come as a consequence of temblors pulsing through her hostess's body, passing down the length of the sinewy right arm and hand, thence into and through her own spectral, skeletal shoulder and torso. Rebecca Clark's words no longer came to her guest as simple auditory phenomena. Andrea Camposanto found that the combined vocal and physical experience was hypnotic, overwhelming.

"Talk to me, Andrea. *Parli. Per favore.*"

Silence.

The captive-turned-guest could never thereafter recall at what point she decided to speak, but within perhaps a half minute she began to hear her own voice, at first timorous, then gradually surer of itself. Yet, as she spoke, she remained conscious, not solely of everything she said, but as well, of everything she did not. And what she did not say, she knew, would in the end make all the difference.

The instant she began, the hand left her shoulder. Her hostess returned, catlike, to her seat, crossed her legs at the ankles, and leaned forward, eyes fixed steadily on the trembling speaker's face.

The guest, pausing to turn her shoulders to one side in order to place her ledger, passport, and keys on the lampstand beside her chair, turned back to her hostess and asked, "Mrs. Clark, do you . . . I'm sorry . . . forgive me . . . do you . . . do you know *Congressus Evangelicus*?"

Rebecca paused. "If you mean, do I know of the international conferences by that title . . . yes."

The visitor looked up.

"And you know Dr. Eleanor Mason Chapel." This was spoken as a fact, not as a question.

Rebecca's eyebrows moved. "Of course."

"I wish to explain," the guest continued, "that . . . because your friend Dr. Chapel is in danger . . . so you, and your husband also, are in danger." She paused, now searching Rebecca's face. "Dr. Chapel's danger . . . is your danger. *Capite? Capisci?* You are understanding what I am saying to you?"

As she said this, the guest's hands made an interrogative gesture. Although her expression was hopeful, fear twisted the shape of her voice into something thin, shrill.

Rebecca looked closely at the woman who sat, tense and miserable, before her. She studied the eyes. There was truth in their weary earnestness, but there was also concealment. "I understand the words you just spoke," she finally replied. "That does not mean that I understand what you are talking about."

"No. No, of course not. I will say more." Here the guest looked down again. When she resumed, she continued to look at the floor. "The conference—the *Congressus Evangelicus*—it is being held . . . this time . . . in San Francisco . . . in the United States. There is . . ." and here she searched for words . . . "there is the . . . the *controversia* . . . regarding the . . . the. . . ."

Now she looked up helplessly, shrugging her shoulders. "Ah . . . maybe you would say . . . *ah* . . . I don't know. I don't know how to say this." Then, her eyes searching the ceiling, she murmured, *"Tema?* . . . eh? *Tema?"* She groaned and turned her eyes to her hostess again, shrugging once more, shaking her head in frustration. She raised her hands to her face, covering her eyes.

Rebecca leaned toward her guest and touched her knee lightly. "Is there controversy, Andrea, regarding the theme of the conference? Is there a dispute?"

The guest looked up quickly. "*Si. Si.*"

"Is the conference position statement. . . ."

At this phrase the guest's eyes widened and she straightened in her chair. Her excitement was obvious. "*Ah . . . ah.*" She nodded her head.

Rebecca continued. "The two earlier *Congressus* assemblies issued position statements that became well known, Andrea. Is there a dispute regarding a position statement, or some other official statement that the participants might—or might not—like very much?"

"*Si. Si,* there is dispute. Dr. Chapel—Dr. Eleanor Chapel, your friend—she is . . . she is a problem for the . . . the people of power . . . the people who were leading the other meetings . . . in the other cities. She is a . . . a . . . a threat to them, they think. The statement . . . statement of position . . . that they want to make, she does not want them to make. She has, they think, a differing statement of position, one that the people . . . the . . . the. . . ."

"Delegates?"

"*Si* . . . the delegates . . . may . . . may like her statement better. . . . She is a problem for them, and they are . . . they are maybe to do something to her . . . and also to you . . . and even also to your husband."

Rebecca leaned forward again. "Why, Andrea? If powerful individuals think that Dr. Chapel may prevent their reaching their goals, I can imagine why she might be endangered. And certainly, if she is endangered, and if my husband and I can do anything to prevent their. . . ."

She sat back in her chair. The gray eyes moved away from the guest and looked toward the window. Then she nodded. "I see. They know if Matt and I learn Dr. Chapel is endangered, we will take whatever action we can in order to. . . . That's it, isn't it? That's what you mean. That's why you said that her danger is our danger. Yes?"

The guest sat erect, excited, and clapped her hands like a little girl. "*Si, si.* They know what you have done before. . . . They know who you are. . . . They know what you do. . . . They think Dr. Eleanor Chapel might . . . ask for you to come to her. . . . And they think you might . . . might . . . " She stopped and shut her eyes tight, searching her English vocabulary. Then she opened her eyes suddenly and continued. "They think you might *receive* something. . . . They think you, Mrs. Clark, might somehow be . . . ah . . . *instructed* to do something. . . ."

Rebecca smiled. "They fear that I might receive another series of visions?"

"Ah," she said. "*Si.*"

Rebecca thought for a long moment. "And you, Andrea? What is your assignment? And who assigned you?"

Here the guest smiled again, the same radiant smile that Rebecca first saw when she acknowledged that she and her husband indeed knew the name of Antonio Camposanto. Now, when the great detective's daughter spoke again, she seemed to be bursting with pride. "My *father!*" she said, her chin rising. "My *father* . . . assigned me to you. *He* sent me here, to London."

"And to do what, exactly, Andrea?"

"To protect you, of course."

Rebecca's face did not change in response to this revelation, but she worked to suppress a smile. The idea that this frail creature, unable to observe their apartment without immediate detection and equally unable to prevent her own capture, would have been assigned by the Italian detective to protect Rebecca and Matthew Clark was an irony that appeared to escape his daughter completely. Rebecca nodded. "I see," she said simply.

At that moment Matt Clark appeared in the doorway, carrying a small tray with three teacups, a teapot, and ancillary items required for the late afternoon English courtesy. He placed the tray deftly on a small table just inside the doorway, shifted his good hand from the tray to the table's under-side, and lifted the entire thing, carrying it easily to Rebecca's side.

She glanced down at the tray and saw that the thoughtful arrangement of items included her small blue Church of England prayer book, given to her by Matt the previous summer to replace the one that had been lost in the boating accident—no, she corrected herself—in the murder. She looked up at her husband. Their eyes met and spoke with that silent clarity known best to those who have become one flesh, and as she knew he would, he excused himself and retreated down the hallway to the bedroom. The women were alone again.

They were silent for several moments while they "did" their tea, and then Rebecca asked her question directly: "Andrea, when your father envisioned our endangerment, tell me what he meant, and tell me how he imagined your intervention. You'll forgive me, please, if I say that you do not seem to be trained either as an observer or as a combatant. And you are not armed. How, precisely, would you protect us, and from what?"

This last, taken immediately as an insult, produced a flood of emotion in the guest, all of it readily visible on the surface of her thin, irregular countenance. "Ah," she sputtered angrily, " . . . ah . . . but you are wrong, *signora!* You are completely wrong! I am . . . I am . . ."

And suddenly the hot tears flew from her eyes, her shoulders slumped forward, and her chin fell toward her chest. She raised her hands to her face once more, and—immediately—she felt Rebecca's physical presence. She looked up, startled, and found the face close, gray eyes boring in, yet not unkindly. She felt long fingers on her thin shoulders.

"Andrea," her hostess said intently, "I do not doubt that you are here to report our movements to your father, and to inform him by telephone if something happens to us. I have no difficulty believing your assertion that, if Dr. Chapel is in danger, then we are in danger, as well. I have no difficulty believing that you are here to help us, and that your father wishes to protect Eleanor Chapel from someone. Those things I can believe.

"But there is one thing I cannot believe, and one additional thing that I do not understand. What I cannot believe is your selection by your father— an internationally preeminent law enforcement official—to fly to London to provide *protection* for my husband and me."

She paused, still studying the face before her.

"I think this. I think if protection were your father's goal, he would have assigned two or more law enforcement veterans from his staff in Rome, and he would have asked that Scotland Yard become directly involved in support of those efforts. That is what I think.

"And so," and here she enveloped the guest's small hands in her long, strong ones, "I think he sent you here . . . at least in part . . . so that *we* might become involved in protecting *you.*"

The guest stared, dumbfounded. The flow of her tears stopped as if closed off by the sudden turn of a valve.

She looked into the wide gray eyes, eyes that were set in a face as exquisitely beautiful as any she had seen, a face with elegance undiminished by the vicious scar that dominated its right cheek. This was the face that had repeatedly sent her heart racing in fear, the face of a seer of visions whose intellectual and physical exploits had been inflated to such proportions that her mind could only stagger under the weight of the legend. And here was the legend, her captor and her emancipator, holding her hands tenderly, staring into her eyes from inches away, and now reading her mind.

Now the seer was speaking to her again, softly, insistently.

"Do you need protecting, Andrea Camposanto?"

The guest lowered her eyes to her hands, each of them encircled by those of Rebecca Clark, cradled with enough force to communicate the paradox: immense strength coupled with intolerable tendresse.

"*Si*. I need the protecting," she replied quietly. And, from her right eye, a solitary tear escaped and ran haltingly down the still young, weathered skin.

"From?"

She sighed. Her reply was a whisper. "I cannot say to you the answer."

"Because you do not know?"

"Because I cannot say to you."

There was a pause. A second tear escaped and trailed its sibling along the same path.

"All right. You will not tell me what you need protecting from. That's all right. You have given me a great deal, Andrea. Now, give me an answer, if you can and if you will, to my remaining question." She paused again. "Tell me why your father and his Rome law enforcement colleagues would be involved in protecting an American scholar on United States soil from . . ."

Rebecca stopped and smiled again.

"Ah, I see," she replied to her own question. "Of course. Many of the original and current leaders of *Congressus Evangelicus* are Italian . . . and probably Roman. If any of them were thought to be conspiring. . . ."

Again she paused. Then she rose and slipped back gently into her chair. Beginning to nod her head thoughtfully, she said slowly, "Your father is providing protection for Eleanor Chapel because the threats to her originate in his own jurisdiction . . . originate in Rome. He wishes first to protect her. After that, he is trying to ascertain the nature of the international threat, if any, to *Congressus* itself. In this, he has begun to anticipate threats against my husband and me."

Rebecca paused again, then continued, speaking as much to herself as to her guest. "He wanted you to observe us and to report to him, yes, but he *expected* us—eventually—to discover your surveillance. And he expected you, in the end, to come under *our* protection . . . Matt's and mine. He believes we can protect you from something, and from someone, better than he can . . . better than Scotland Yard . . . better than anyone."

Rebecca stopped and looked into her guest's face inquiringly. Immediately she realized that her speech had become too rapid, her vocabulary too rich. She decided upon a simple summary question.

"Andrea?" she said carefully. "Your father will protect Dr. Chapel, and your father hopes we will protect you, his daughter?"

"*Si, signora.*"

Rebecca nodded. She looked away, then returned her eyes to her guest.

"But you will not tell me from whom we must protect you." She paused again. Then, leaning forward, she spoke with a finality that led the guest to understand that the interview was nearing its end. "If those from whom we must protect you were simply the official leaders of *Congressus Evangelicus,* we could retrieve those names with one telephone call to a London or San Francisco newspaper. The threat to you is, in the end, from something or someone who must be behind or below or above those official leaders. Someone whose identity you know, but are afraid to tell me. And you are more afraid to tell me this name than you are that, without the name, I will be unable to protect you."

Rebecca saw that Andrea had followed little of this last, but decided not to press further.

She stood abruptly, turned, stepped to the tea tray, and lifted from it the palm-sized prayer book. Then she turned again to face her guest. Looking down at Andrea Camposanto, she prepared to speak her benediction. "You and your father believe that, because I have been chosen in the past to receive . . ." and she hesitated for a heartbeat "chosen to receive God's messages . . . that I am the person most likely to be able to protect you from something more powerful than anything your father believes that he can face and defeat."

As a third tear followed its sisters down the guest's face, trickling steadily alongside her nose and then downward to her lips, it found, unlike the first two, an upturned corner of Andrea Camposanto's mouth. This was not, to be sure, the radiant smile that had brightened the room when her father's name had been invoked previously. This was instead a hesitant smile, the tentative smile of a soft, thin shadow of hope, silent and ephemeral.

The guest bowed her head and closed her eyes, knowing that her hostess, holding the prayer book near her face, awaited the gesture. Andrea heard the resonant syllables as they flowed from the throat and lips of Rebecca Clark, her voice steady and clear:

> O most powerful and glorious Lord God, the Lord of hosts, that rulest and commandest all things. . . . Stir up thy strength, O Lord, and come and help us; for thou givest not alway the battle to the strong, but canst save by many or by few. . . . [H]ear us thy poor servants begging mercy, and imploring thy help . . . that thou wouldest be a defence unto us against the face of the enemy . . . through Jesus Christ our Lord. *Amen.*

Seconds after "amen" had been spoken, the two women looked up, and again their eyes met. After another long moment, Andrea Camposanto looked down again, closed her eyes once more, and whispered, *"Grazie. Grazie."*

Both women knew to Whom the simple expression of thanksgiving had been addressed. And both women knew something of the nature of the Enemy that they would ultimately face, though perhaps only one could have provided a truly authentic description. And both women knew, though as before, one far better than the other, that without the God-sent strength of angels, they would have no more chance against such an Enemy than a sparrow in the teeth of a hurricane.

Chapter Three

MATT CLARK RETREATED SOFTLY DOWN THE APARTMENT'S short hallway to the bedroom as soon as he read in his wife's eyes and face her silent request that he leave her alone with Andrea Camposanto. He closed the door carefully, then stood still and listened.

He heard what he had expected to hear: indecipherable feminine murmurs. *Good*, he thought to himself.

For while he did not wish to eavesdrop, he wanted to attend to the volume and especially to the tone of the two voices. Rebecca was, he knew, as certain as was he that the mere suggestion of alarm in her voice would send him crashing down the hallway and back into their presence.

Matt did not sit down. He remained at the door, leaning against the wall, his right hand resting lightly on the doorknob itself. Taking a deep breath, he looked across his and Rebecca's bedroom to the window that faced the street.

To his mild surprise, a smile spread gradually across his thoughtful face. The smile got his attention and he thought casually about its origin. This seemed an odd time to be smiling. After all, the world had once more turned itself unceremoniously upside down in the space of a few hours. In one sense, the change was on cue. It was time. Two years ago, there was his parents' inexplicable kidnapping in Central Park. And one year ago there was Rebecca's arrival in New York City and the immediate and shocking dissolution of their relationship. And both times, of course, there were the visions, the dreams, and the nearly overwhelming force of an Evil that bid fair to consume them both.

And now this, almost precisely twelve months after the second intrusion, another vision . . . another dream . . . another . . . what? Whatever it might be, why on earth should that smile have crept across his face a moment before? And he knew.

Out of the violence of the twin maelstroms twelve and twenty-four months earlier had come new life for Matthew Clark. Each time, as he had been buffeted by the forces that swirled through and around him, he had been infused with wonders he had never known, wonders that had never before even approached his consciousness, wonders at which he would have scoffed had anyone been so crass as to introduce the thought of them to the thoroughgoing skeptic and materialist that he had shaped himself to be.

Thus, the smile. His wife's dream—and now the mysterious and inept Italian observer—might well presage maximum danger once again. But if experience thus far could be relied upon, there would be not just danger, but opportunity. And if that opportunity were seized . . . if duty were accepted . . . if obedience were once more attempted in the face of the unknowable . . . then more wonders would welcome Matt and Rebecca Clark.

The smile remained on his face while a postscript flitted across his mind. He nodded his head slightly in surprise. For he saw—and knew that he saw—that he no longer feared death. It would have been easy enough to form that thought yesterday: not yet thirty years of age, in fine health, doing nothing more dangerous each day than walking to school and back home. But suddenly and certainly mortal danger was just steps away. And under these new circumstances to become aware that death was not the bête noire it had once been . . . well . . . that was as significant a departure from the Matt of two years earlier as could be imagined. And certainly worth a smile, not of self-satisfaction or smugness, but of wonder and gratitude.

For he knew now, and knew in his bones, that death would be but a transition from this to something glorious beyond imagining. And so he shook his head in amazement at the new life toward which Rebecca and the others had pointed until he himself had finally both comprehended and experienced the saving grace of God. New dangers . . . new opportunities for obedience . . . and an Eternity though which to move forever after.

Within the ancient walls of a tree-canopied hilltop cemetery on the outskirts of Rome, Anna Angelini, satisfied with the look of the fresh flowers on and around her mother's gravestone, sighed deeply and closed her eyes. She allowed her head to fall against the seatback of her small sedan, her wrists resting on top of the steering wheel. Then she allowed her mind to play through the day of the funeral two years previous. Maria had been six then, Paulo but four, and they had both seemed more concerned for Anna herself in her grief than to grieve themselves. And she had let them care for her, deciding that allowing herself to be helped by her children was the best gift she could provide for them.

She yawned and stretched in the cramped driver's seat, now running her fingers through her short-cropped brown hair, eyes still closed. A small wrinkle appeared on her forehead as she thought about her tight fit behind the wheel of her car. It would be easy, she thought idly, to blame the automobile manufacturer for this tightness of fit, but she knew that the blame, if that word applied, lay with herself. She simply was not getting any exercise whatsoever, and had not since the birth of their second child. And that was six years ago! *Plenty of time to add weight*, she thought to herself. Four or five pounds a year. Six years. Making it all the more inevitable was her deep-rooted delight in cooking the family's traditional pasta dishes, the succulent aromas from their rich sauces filling the rooms of her home every afternoon.

Eyes still closed, she moved one hand to the lower rim of the steering wheel and felt for the distance between the wheel and her stomach. She found that there was none. Sighing again, she adjusted her position in the seat. She had some time ago begun to choose ample, loose-fitting blouses that hung down to her hips. Her prevailing theory was that such coverings allowed a generous imagination to view her as having the same small waist she had before and for some time even after Maria's birth eight years previous.

She shook her head in resignation. The truth was undeniable. The care of her family and the love of her church took such precedence over her physical appearance that the chances of a return to her pre-maternal figure were nonexistent. That led her somehow to picture, in comic contrast, her beloved aunt Eleanor Chapel, two inches under five feet in height and probably eighty pounds total. Just like Anna's mother.

At that thought she smiled and lifted her head from the seatback, opening her eyes and looking out over the unevenly manicured cemetery, remembering little Maria's solicitousness at the funeral, even at graveside. Thus absorbed in the remembered image of the child's concern for the adult, her eyes drifted across the rows of grave markers and came to reluctant focus on an image that presented itself in the rearview mirror. There, in the medium reflected distance, sat a black Mercedes. Her eyes narrowed and she stared at the image in a puzzled effort to retrieve something from her memory. This dark, muscular sedan at the main gate to the cemetery . . . Had she not seen that very automobile just the day before when she had met the children after school?

She frowned. Yes . . . yes . . . she was sure of it. The vehicle was unique not just in its glistening blackness, its size, and the extremely heavy tint of its windows, but also in the thickness and height of the antenna that rose from its rear deck, high over its roofline. That was the very automobile that had sat across the street while she and Paulo had chatted, waiting for Maria to emerge with her classmates.

The thought had actually crossed her mind that she would expect such a vehicle to belong to a diplomat, someone from one of the embassies in the city. Yet she was not aware that any diplomat's child was enrolled in this small Catholic elementary school, located, as it was, far from Rome's embassies and their enclaves.

Now she looked away from the mirror and shrugged. There was nothing about her or her family that could possibly inspire someone to shadow them. But the coincidence was unnerving. She looked once more at the image of the Mercedes. It appeared darkly ominous, stationed at the cemetery's only vehicular gate, its occupants entirely unobserved behind the near-black windows.

Were they looking at her? She smiled again. What a ridiculous notion. Why would she draw the conclusion that, since she could not see them, they perforce must be looking at her?

She leaned forward, switched on the ignition, shifted into gear, and moved her car forward. She steered through the narrow roadway's twists and turns, following the irregular circle that it traced around the cemetery perimeter and back toward the exit. Momentarily out of sight of the gate, she was nonplussed, yet relieved, to reach the exit and find that the mysterious sedan had disappeared. She shook her head reproachfully at her brief bout with "paranoid cognition," as she had learned to call any guarded or suspicious thought in her days at university, and turned her attention to the mental grocery list she had begun to form earlier in the day.

A half hour later, Anna Angelini, happy with her shopping, especially with the fish selection available that morning, emerged from the grocer's with produce sacks nestled in the crook of each elbow. She found herself actually breathing heavily under this modest burden, and again formed a remorseful thought about her failure to exercise. Really, she thought to herself, she simply must develop some way to maintain her family and church priorities and yet attend regularly to her health and her weight and her girth and. . . .

She had turned left along the sidewalk toward the parking lot adjacent, and suddenly found herself actually looking for the black Mercedes out of the corner of her eye, searching the slowly moving line of traffic and the vehicles parked along Via Juliette. And just as she began once more to scold herself for such foolishness, she saw, near the intersection just beyond the parking lot, the apparition itself.

Against every rational impulse within her, knowing the preposterous nature of the thing—the idea that anyone would actually shadow her—she found herself stopping in the middle of the sidewalk. Her heart was in her throat as she tried to speak to herself in the same way she would speak to Maria or Paulo if either child suddenly felt "followed by bad people."

But nothing availed. She simply stood, gaping openly at the dark-tinted windows of the Mercedes from a distance of perhaps one hundred feet. And then, heart pounding, she turned abruptly, walked back to the entrance to the grocer's, placed her burdens on the bench just inside the door, and sat down heavily.

Her mind fought against itself. What could this possibly mean? Why would anyone think to follow her? Then her mind flew to the children. The Mercedes had been at school the day before. Whoever was in that automobile . . . those people knew where Maria and Paulo were right now.

She felt as if she were beginning to suffocate. She found herself fighting the urge to telephone her husband.

Mario Angelini, managing editor of a major textbook publishing house and two years her senior at thirty-two, already tended to view his wife as an hysteric. What would he say if she phoned to report that a black Mercedes had been shadowing her for two days? He might laugh, she thought to herself, but more likely he would simply make that disgusted noise that he preferred, a throaty, inarticulate harrumphing sound that she had learned to dislike from the earliest moments of their relationship.

If not Mario, who then? Her priest? The police? One of her neighbors? They would all treat her as an overimaginative child. She ran her fingers through her hair in disgust at herself. Other women would contact their husbands in a flash. She took a deep breath, and resolved to make the call. Perhaps, if he did not simply laugh or harrumph, he would suggest that she phone the police. But more likely he would just tell her to walk to her auto, get in, and drive home. And she knew, if he insisted on that course of action, she would do exactly that.

She sought the grocer, and he, seeing her struggling with two sacks of his own stock, was gracious. He helped her to his tiny office at the rear of the store, dialed her husband's number as she spoke it to him, and left her in private.

"*Pronto! Eh?*" said Mario Angelini brusquely.

"Mario? Mario?" said Anna tentatively in her musical Italian, "I . . . I'm sorry to interrupt. Are you in a meeting, I suppose?"

His voice softened. His wife rarely phoned him at the publishing house. He appreciated her restraint in that regard and assumed that she would not interrupt his day without reason. His Italian was rapid-fire: "Are the children . . .?"

"*Si, si,* they're fine. It's just that. . . ." She began an embarrassed, yet reasonably organized account of her three separate encounters with the black Mercedes. At the end of her narrative, she emphasized afresh that she had first noticed it at school the day before, and that, whoever this was, they clearly knew where the children were right now, and obviously could go there at any time.

Finally she stopped, out of breath, and waited nervously for her husband's response. It was unexpected.

After a lengthy silence, he said quietly. "Anna . . . I've seen it, too."

"What? When?"

"Yesterday and today, when I left the house and drove toward Via Principesa. I noticed that huge antenna, and had the same thought you did. *Why would a diplomat's vehicle be stationed in our neighborhood?* I just thought it odd, that's all. It did not so much as cross my mind that the car had anything to do with us. But if the same vehicle was at school, and then at the cemetery, and now just outside the grocer's . . . I don't see how that could be coincidence, Anna."

Another silence ensued.

"What should I do?" she asked quietly.

"You stay there. Telephone the school now. Tell them I am coming for the children. I will get them and then we'll come for you.

"After you speak with Sister Bernadette, wait a half hour and then step into the alley behind the grocer's. Yes. That's right. Next to the loading dock.

"After that, we'll drive straight to the precinct station. I want to talk to the detectives about this. I want their advice about the children, right now . . . today."

San Francisco/Berkeley: 8:02 am/Friday
New York: 11:02 am/Friday
London: 4:02 pm/Friday
Rome: 5:02 pm/Friday

"Let the minutes show that the June — meeting of the faculty of the Pacific School of Religion, Berkeley, California, is in session at 8:02 am."

The dean's tinny voice droned from the front of the smallish assembly, and in the tradition of Pavlov's finest, sociology of religion professor Richard Mabry's mind instantly turned to other things. On this particular morning, his mind oriented itself eagerly in the direction of Lois Tanaka, seated conveniently two rows in front of him and just to the right of his line of sight to the dean's podium. He stared at her left earlobe, visible below the pulled-back raven pageboy that, in his mind, was her trademark. She sat motionless, erect and demure, somehow lending a certain distinction to the dull gray folding chair in which she sat, seemingly riveted by the dean's mind-numbing announcements. Swinging from the earlobe was a gold earring that formed a Japanese character, he supposed, or perhaps it was just some abstract design that he could not distinguish from a Japanese character. He didn't care which it might be. His fascination was with the earlobe and the ear itself: such an extraordinarily delicate anatomical design. A veritable flower made from flesh and blood. . . .

After several moments of uninterrupted concentration on his colleague's earlobe, skin texture, and partial profile, he felt a nudge in his rib cage and sat up with a start, jerking his head back and to the left in surprise and confusion. A pair of glistening blue-green eyes stared ambiguously into his, and the small smile in the elfin face of the gray-haired Old Testament professor at his side formed itself into a question. In rather a strong stage whisper, Dr. Eleanor Mason Chapel asked, "Do you suppose you are actually *present*, Dr. Mabry?"

He then realized that, twice a year, roll was actually called—and this was one of those times. "HERE!" he shouted hastily, to the uproarious laughter of his colleagues. Still facing Eleanor Chapel, he saw out of the corner of his eye that Lois Tanaka had turned her head nearly all the way around to look at him over her shoulder, along with nearly everyone else in the room.

"We thought you were probably 'here,' Richard," said the dean from the front of the room in his mildly sarcastic way. "Thank you for providing confirmation."

Then, turning to the secretary, he added in his formal manner, "Please continue with the roll call."

Richard Mabry gave Eleanor Chapel an embarrassed smile. "Thanks," he whispered, rolling his eyes and shaking his head miserably.

"In love again, are we, Dr. Mabry?" she whispered softly, leaning toward him and cutting her eyes teasingly toward Lois Tanaka.

He lifted his hands helplessly and blushed. The distinguished visitor had spoken to him only a few times during her semester in Berkeley. That one of those times would come in the context of this humiliating display of adolescent, study hall behavior was the sort of embarrassment he would rather have spared himself. Why did his mind still at times seem to be searching for the same distractions he sought in junior high school?

This question sent his thoughts off in another direction for several more minutes. He then realized belatedly that the roll call was over and that the dean had leaped immediately to the heart of the agenda. And now one of his more opinionated colleagues had risen to his feet and had begun fulminating, but *about what?* He tried to attend.

"And so," the professor of abstract philosophy continued with an obvious sense of his own importance, "I want to urge that we enact a resolution, I hope unanimously, and I hope this very morning, in support of a *Congressus Evangelicus III* position statement to the effect that Christianity must acknowledge the crippling Eurocentrism of its historic tenets, together with the compelling need to adopt a theological platform that is truly multicultural and broadly multiethical. The *Evangelicus* conference will afford the perfect opportunity, through a powerful and contemporaneous position statement formulated by its steering committee"—here he turned his eyes toward Eleanor Chapel and paused meaningfully—"and subsequently endorsed by the delegates, to bring the faith more fully into the modern global community and that community's proper concerns and issues. The current draft position statement fails utterly to address these issues, and I suggest, will place Christianity at very real risk of coming to be viewed as, simply put, without so much as a trace of relevance to today's world, its issues, and its peoples.

"I think we would all agree, at the very least, on that much? I propose we, as a faculty, draw up a resolution to that effect, and urge it upon the conference steering committee leadership here in their final days of debate"—he turned his head once more to glance purposefully in the direction of Eleanor Chapel—"in the full expectation that the committee will incorporate our resolution's language and spirit into its official position statement. By this means, we will have acted responsibly in what can only be considered a worldwide crisis for the faith and the church. By influencing the conference's position statement in this direction, we will have given great momentum to the vector the church must take in the remaining years of the twentieth century, and will have provided a powerful platform for its launch into the twenty-first. It is," he closed in tones heavy with dramatic emphasis, "our last, best chance to preserve the faith as a force in these perilous times."

Richard Mabry saw that one of the New Testament professors was already on his feet in reply, his beet-red face an alarming contrast to his snow-white beard. "Nonsense! Nonsense!" he shouted. "We've seen, right here in the San Francisco Bay area in the last fifteen years, the kind of chaos and carnage and confusion and calamity that results when the compass spins out of control instead of pointing north steadily. Authority is undermined; sexual deviance runs rampant; hallucinogens become *de rigueur.* If we are going to draft a resolution for the conference steering committee's consideration, I suggest that it endorse a return to the elegance and simplicity of the eternal verities. Yes. *Yes,* I say: the *eternal verities.*"

With that, he sat down abruptly and heavily, breathing hard.

The professor of pastoral counseling, completing her first year on the faculty, raised her hand tentatively, received the dean's nod, and said quietly, "Weren't we supposed to open the meeting with prayer, or am I confused?"

Before her question was fully out of her mouth, two of her colleagues, one on each side of the room, were already on their feet and speaking loudly. Richard Mabry decided to attend to the one on the far right, who was both senior to and louder than the other, on the assumption that the junior of the two would soon give up and sit down. She did, and the professor of Christian rhetoric continued.

"As one of the sponsors of the conference, our faculty has an obligation, I submit, *not* to take a stance on anything at all. We have implicitly endorsed the fact of the conference by assuming the role of sponsor, and the conference steering committee, co-led by our own esteemed colleague Dr. Chapel, bears the responsibility for advancing a *Congressus III* position statement at the proper time for action by all delegates. No doubt Dr. Chapel and her committee will fulfill their obligation in this regard with distinction.

"As for our own role, let me note that two-thirds of the Pacific School of Religion faculty, as individuals, will be making appearances at one point or another as speakers, panelists, or chairs of sessions. Our faculty's diversity of viewpoint will speak for itself. We probably have no more real consensus on the conference's main themes than we have on anything else. I suggest we simply offer our services, as individuals, in support of those who are on the program. In that way. . . ."

Richard Mabry felt himself slipping away again. He allowed his eyes to return to Lois Tanaka's earlobe, this time the right earlobe, since her head was now turned fully in that direction to attend to the rhetoric professor's developing minilecture. Interesting, he thought to himself, that this earlobe seemed distinctly different in several of its details from the other. Squinting at the elusive lobe that threatened at any moment to be covered by some new movement of the young woman's head or by the forward tuck of her pageboy cut, he began determinedly to enumerate the array of differences. . . .

And so the first part of the meeting passed, with Richard Mabry silent and lost in his own thoughts. Sooner than he could have imagined, he found himself again startled to realize that the room was stirring and that the first break in the morning session was beginning. He wondered briefly what had transpired. Then he wondered how long the break was to be. Usually, the dean announced a fifteen-minute break, faculty members dispersed to their offices to make phone calls or to review their correspondence, and the meeting reconvened a half hour later with about three-fourths of the members present.

But then he noticed that, of the people still in the room, only two were still seated: himself and the visiting professor of Old Testament, who remained at his side. Then he realized, with some discomfort, that she was looking directly at him with her dancing eyes and her bemused expression.

Disconcerted, he smiled at her uncertainly. "Well," he said hesitantly, "I guess I'll go catch up on some paperwork."

He leaned forward to rise to his feet and found her hand on his forearm. He sat back and looked at her inquiringly.

She smiled. "What are you doing, Dr. Mabry?"

"I beg your pardon, ma'am?" he replied. He did not usually employ the constructions "ma'am" or "sir," but her overwhelming professional stature, coupled with her age—probably twice his own, he guessed—led him to use the term of respect without thinking, and to be glad that he had.

"I said, 'What are you doing?'" She smiled again. "I've noticed at other meetings that you seem to take your mind elsewhere almost immediately, and that your technique seems to entail prolonged concentration on any one of our several young female faculty members. We've just had a revealing discussion during which almost half the faculty spoke at one point or another, and I think you probably heard none of it.

"So, I wonder what you're doing, not so much now, in this meeting, but more generally. Do you consider teaching and research and writing to be your vocation in the traditional sense?"

She paused, still staring at him in a way he could not interpret. Was this condescension? Was this arrogance? Was this some misguided maternal impulse? Or was it something he simply could not read? And now she was talking again, not waiting for a reply to her initial questions.

"Is this a Christian calling and commitment, in your mind? Do you even *want* to be doing this?

"And what, let me ask while I am in the process of making you angry, is your view of women, Richard Mabry? Is it, in fact, about them that you seem to daydream continually? Do you actually court these young colleagues of yours, or just indulge your imagination as a device for getting yourself through meetings without falling asleep?"

She stopped talking momentarily and smiled brilliantly at him, disarming him just as he was beginning, indeed, to feel angry. Then she spoke again, and, to his amazement, with real passion. "What are you *doing,* Dr. Mabry? Are you trying to do something with the gifts God has given you? If so, what?"

He smiled with embarrassment, looked down, and shook his head. He should just tell her, respectfully, to mind her own business, he thought to himself. But there was something in her tone, and in the weight of the questions, and in the unspoken assumptions under them, that stayed him.

He swallowed.

He turned his face back to her and tried to smile again. He failed, and then found himself saying simply, his expression somber, "I don't know what I'm doing, Dr. Chapel. I'm almost thirty years old, and I don't feel I've progressed, in some ways, from the way I was in junior high school. I'm smart enough to keep up with my academic work—then, as a student; now, as a teacher—without too much investment of time and energy. I like to . . . well . . . think about them . . . women, that is . . . but I usually can't get up enough nerve to ask them out."

Then he added, somehow wanting very much for her not to misunderstand him, "I'm not handsome, you know, or athletic. I'm just bookish. A bookworm."

Then, after a moment, he said, "I don't think a woman like . . . well . . . like Lois Tanaka . . . would be interested in going out with me."

He paused, his eyes now on the floor, and mentally acknowledged his complete confusion. Why was Eleanor Chapel talking to him at all? Why would she care one way or another about someone as shallow as he must seem to her? And why, equally mysterious to him, was he making any response to her?

Yet somehow he felt impelled to continue. "I don't know what I'm doing, ma'am. Sometimes I feel I should just go back and start over, if I knew how. I guess it must show?"

She thought for a moment. "When we break for lunch later, walk down the hill with me and I'll treat you to a sandwich."

Before he could so much as nod in assent or lodge an excuse, she bounced up from her chair and was gone. He realized after a moment that she had not issued an invitation; she had just given him an order.

San Francisco/Berkeley: 12:02 pm/Friday
New York: 3:02 pm/Friday
London: 8:02 pm/Friday
Rome: 9:02 pm/Friday

Eleanor Chapel placed the half-eaten tuna sandwich on her plate, took a sip of iced tea, and looked across the small, circular table at her luncheon guest as he sat contentedly over his meal of tomato soup and club sandwich. She moved her chair slightly to interpose their table's oversized red-and-white-striped umbrella between the noonday sun, not yet overtaken by the broad overcast pushing in from the Pacific, and her unshaded eyes. A week after the close of spring semester at the University of California, the delicatessen's patio was deserted except for the two of them. She smiled at him as she spoke.

"Richard, I have a surprise for you. On behalf of the *Congressus Evangelicus* steering committee, I want to ask you to become a member of the committee as it enters its final days. The conference is upon us, and as we have begun to hold meetings almost nightly, we have realized that our burdens are multiplied by an odd lack of foresight on our part. In staffing the committee, we simply ignored the field of sociology of religion. We don't even know how it happened, but it did. And as the committee members have wrestled with the remaining decisions, gradually it has become clear to them that we should ask you—and two other sociology of religion scholars whom we similarly respect—to help us in our closing deliberations.

"Tell me what you think."

She watched his face.

He stopped chewing and stared at her. Then, eyes wide in disbelief, he resumed for several seconds and swallowed. "Well . . . I . . . ah . . . I don't know what to say, Dr. Chapel. That steering committee of yours has some terribly high-powered people on it. And there are already, I think, three general sociologists from area universities on the committee . . . I realize they are not in the sociology of *religion* field . . . but still . . . they are preeminent scholars . . . and they have well-deserved international reputations. Why, I haven't done anything to distinguish myself professionally, compared with those people.

"I just don't see how I'd be able to contribute, especially this late in the process. The steering committee was formed a year ago, wasn't it?

And the other thirty or so members have been enrolled on the committee all that time? You want to add three new people to the thirty who've been working together for a year, and who have formed a shared vision. . . . And the conference starts just ten days from now? I'm flattered, Dr. Chapel, but. . . ."

Eleanor Chapel leaned forward and shook her head. "First, Richard . . . there is no 'shared vision,' as you put it. There is, rather, growing division and gnawing anger and burgeoning incivility. And there is a critical issue still under debate, and it will probably remain under debate until a few hours before the opening ceremonies, and maybe even after the conference has actually begun.

"That issue relates strongly to today's faculty discussion—the one you missed while your mind languished in Lois Tanaka's vicinity—and the issue has importance beyond anything I ever imagined at the start. The conference program has been printed in a way that leaves the final session's agenda flexible. Specifically, the printed program does not say whether or not there will be an effort to present, and to seek the delegates' endorsement of, an official position statement. You're aware, of course, that this is only the third time the conference has been held—twenty years ago in Rome; ten years ago in Rio—and, at the conclusion of each of the first two, a position statement was offered the delegates for their consideration."

Mabry nodded. He had stopped eating.

"Those two position statements were, in the eyes of newspaper-reading Christians—and non-Christians—around the world, the *only* publicized and well-understood outcomes of those first two international conferences. The position statements were short, well-crafted, and easily remembered by anyone with the slightest interest. Church leaders, politicians, and lay people all over the globe knew those position statements and could paraphrase them in two or three quick sentences. There were some who claimed that those statements were among the most widely quoted words that Christianity, as an interfaith body, has spoken in the whole of the twentieth century.

"And yet, the steering committee has become divided on the question this time. And it would seem to be mostly because of me, Richard."

He smiled. Her statement did not surprise him.

She raised her tea glass to her lips and took a small sip, then looked up at him again as she placed it on the table.

"The silly committee," she continued, "decided to feature me as a presenter and panelist and television interviewee more than a year ago, even before I had made arrangements for spending this semester on the West Coast. And I was to be featured, you'll understand, as representing a minority view on the subject of Christian seminary education and church leadership. A *minority* view.

"It was a gesture of good will on the committee's part, decided upon partly because I'm a woman, partly because I'm Southern Baptist, and partly because I'm just plain old, and it made the core of leaders, those who led also in Rome and in Rio de Janeiro, feel generous, even magnanimous, that they had agreed to give such a powerful and visible platform to someone holding views with which they themselves largely disagreed.

"And"—here she smiled—"in fact, it *was* generous and magnanimous of them. It truly was."

She looked away for a moment, then returned her eyes to his and continued. "Then, when they read the announcement of my upcoming sabbatical at PSR, and realized that I would be so readily accessible to them, the committee's old guard thought it would be equally generous and magnanimous to invite me to membership on the committee. So, I agreed to join them, and then, in an especially stunning lapse on their part, they asked me to serve as a co-chair of the thing!"

Richard Mabry, sipping his soft drink thoughtfully and smiling at her self-deprecating way of presenting the steering committee's pursuit of her, nodded his head. He was intrigued. He had already known most of what she had said, as indeed did nearly everyone with an interest in *Congressus*. But hearing her own account of the events transfixed him, made him almost giddy that she would honor him with a private, extended explanation. He forgot for the moment the context: her incomprehensible request that he, an academic nonentity in comparison to some of those already on the steering committee, serve with them in the committee's final days of deliberation.

The humility that he felt was not feigned. He tried to focus.

"The problem," she continued, animated as usual, "from the old guard's standpoint, is that I've managed, through simple and wonderfully civil debate—civil until quite recently, that is—to influence my colleagues on the committee and, through them, the overall *Congressus III* agenda to such an extent that my once-minority view is now given roughly as much play in the conference schedule as is the once-majority view. And equally staggering, the steering committee itself has come to be split into armed camps."

His eyebrows lifted. This was news.

"First," she explained, "there is the old guard, as they actually call themselves, comprising a dozen of the thirty members. These are the men who crafted the original position statements in Rome and Rio, and who drew up the draft statement that served as the committee's unofficial point of departure throughout last summer and fall. The group includes the other co-chair, Niccolo Giacomo, and by and large comprises men who are about my age or older.

"Second, there are the reactionaries, as they were at first contemptuously called by the old guard, and as they have now playfully begun to call themselves. They number another dozen or so and encompass a broad age range. They include some of the women who serve on the committee, and they talk at times as though their stance on the issues were perfectly consistent with mine. On some days, in some discussions, I think it may be so. On other days, in other discussions, I think not.

"And that leaves a half-dozen undecideds. They were the first members to push the rest of us to broaden the already unwieldy committee so as to include several sociology of religion scholars. Eventually the old guard agreed, and others followed suit. By now almost everyone on the committee—though not I, you understand—believes that sociological concepts should inform the discussions more than they have to date."

She paused and looked at him inquiringly. "Shall I continue?"

He looked away from her for a moment, frowned slightly, then turned back to her and said simply, "Almost everyone, but not you?"

She nodded matter-of-factly.

He started to pursue the obvious incongruity, then, after a moment, thought better of it. Deciding quickly on a different tack, he asked, "Dr. Chapel, do the other two newly invited sociologists work from a perspective similar to mine?"

She smiled. "No, they do not. In its strained condition, the committee was careful to issue what it considers a balanced set of invitations. One goes to a scholar whose published work conforms largely to the old guard's stance; another goes to one whose views fall in line with the so-called reactionaries' position; and a third goes to one whose perspectives seem to fall outside, or beyond, either of the other two.

"You are the first of the three. You are the old guard's choice."

Richard Mabry received this news with a profound sense of embarrassment. He knew that he was, there on the patio, in the company of academic greatness. And he knew Eleanor Chapel had no use for the position held by the self-described old guard, nor, in necessary consequence, for his own.

Having looked away from her as soon as she spoke her final words, he now forced himself to engage the eyes that he now perceived as accusing. He knew the eyes had not changed. But deep humiliation had altered his perception of Eleanor Chapel as dramatically as if she had just announced that she had proof of his having plagiarized material for a research article. Fleetingly, he tried to imagine how he would feel if he had actually done such a thing, and then been identified by a distinguished scholar as the clear choice of *the committee for the sponsorship of academic plagiarism.*

He shuddered.

He cleared his throat. "Well," he said rather loudly, trying to put a brave face on his statement, "I question whether or not I *should* have been the old guard's choice, Dr. Chapel. I'm not at all certain that their position and mine fit together very well. Can you summarize their position for me in your own words, so that I might evaluate this . . . ah . . . accusation . . . for myself?"

Here he forced a laugh from himself, hoping to elicit one in return. He was disappointed. His luncheon companion simply nodded and began. He wondered if she thought of her invitation as, in fact, an accusation.

"Let me just paraphrase the draft position statement, Richard, since it was the old guard that developed it in the first place. I doubt if this will depart much from the actual verbatim, since every discussion the committee has ever conducted both started and ended with the text."

She paused briefly, collected her thoughts, and began.

"The conferees of Congresssus Evangelicus III *hereby declare their unanimous support for the following overarching themes: first, revision of seminary education worldwide, in every root and branch of the Christian family, so to emphasize theological, organizational, and financial unity— that is, ecumenism—for seminarians at all levels of preparation; second, innovative seminary curricula that give highest priority to cutting-edge organizational and facilities growth principles and concepts, to include external and internal marketing, capital campaign planning and execution, and endowment growth and investment policy; and, third, immediate steps designed to promote the integration of undergraduate with seminary*

education so that strong preference is given in seminary admissions deci-sions to individuals whose college and university academic fields of concentration are those consistent with the second theme, noted above."

She stopped and looked at him in a way that he found unnerving, and yet, from an independent observer's standpoint, would perhaps have been described as expressionless. He looked away again, his mind searching for escape.

Suddenly he seized upon one of her earlier remarks. "Dr. Chapel," he asked quickly, "I understood you to say that the dozen or so . . . um . . . *reactionaries* on the steering committee believe their position to be opposed to that of the old guard, and, at least on some days, as you put it, consistent with your own. Is their position truly in opposition to the summary you just provided? And, if so or if not, how does your actual position read, in your own words?"

He sat back, satisfied that the mental agility he had summoned in offering this two-headed question would buy him considerable time to find some other avenue of retreat. The thought then crossed his mind that he could simply have said yes—perhaps even no—to her request that he serve on the steering committee. That might have ended the entire discussion and sent them back up the hill to the afternoon faculty session, the matter closed at once.

But he had been too desperate to move himself from under the weight of her implicit disapproval. He wanted to demonstrate to her that, in fact, he agreed with her. That he agreed with her on . . . well . . . everything about everything. He wanted her approval and admiration. Yet, she and the committee had read his published articles. They knew what he thought. It was all in print. How could he possibly extricate himself? And why was he, theoretically a grown man and a mature professional, still so terribly anxious to have the approval of those whom he highly respected?

No, that's not it, he reminded himself. He wanted the approval of every person in the world, whether highly respected or not. He could not truth-fully comfort himself with the thought that it was the respect of the *few* that he sought. It was, in fact, the respect of all.

Richard Mabry, quite simply, liked to be liked. At times, he very much disliked the person he was.

But just then Eleanor Chapel, having taken a last bite of sandwich and another sip of tea, began to reply. He shook himself from the depths of self-reproach.

"I haven't time to do justice to either question, Richard. We need to start back or we'll be late to the faculty meeting. Let me give you a fast overview."

She began.

Neither party to the small luncheon was aware that their entire tete-a-tete had been observed professionally and dispassionately by a pair of eyes hidden in the shadows of a storefront entryway across the street from the delicatessen. At times, the street was so quiet that the gargantuan figure could nearly hear the dialogue, especially when Eleanor Chapel's high voice was at its most animated.

But the shadowy man-mountain had no interest in the conversation itself. He simply awaited his opportunity. He had begun to sense that it was near at hand.

SAN FRANCISCO/BERKELEY: 12:22 PM/FRIDAY
NEW YORK: 3:22 PM/FRIDAY
LONDON: 8:22 PM/FRIDAY
ROME: 9:22 PM/FRIDAY

The ornate, curved handle of a heavy and highly polished walking cane clutched tightly in his gnarled left hand, Sidney Belton moved slowly and steadily northward along Broadway. Upon reaching Columbus Circle, he began to work his way counterclockwise around its irregular circumference.

Though the coolness of evening had descended earlier upon the cities of Rome and London, New York City's mid-afternoon heat was still near its midday peak. And so Sid Belton found himself sweating profusely as he struggled toward the Central Park South pedestrian crossing. He had for some time been making his way determinedly toward the Mayflower Hotel's street-front restaurant, the cozy dining room where he had held his first conversation, a year previous, with a certain Old Testament professor who, a half year later, had become his wife.

A distant observer might have mistaken him for an ailing octogenarian, but closer inspection would have revealed a much younger man. It was his stature, posture, and manner of walking that would have suggested the more advanced estimate. Sidney Belton was, in fact, not yet fifty years old, some fifteen years younger than his wife who, in a contrast that amazed and delighted him, appeared to most people to be the age that he himself actually was. If informed of a fifteen-year difference in the ages of the two, no stranger would have selected Dr. Eleanor Chapel as the elder.

For Sidney Belton was stooped, wizened, rumpled, and of one piece with his disheveled clothing. He might have been five feet eight inches tall, if somehow stretched to full height, but his rounded shoulders and perpetual head-forward position made him appear considerably shorter. His weight certainly was under 140 pounds, perhaps well under.

Had an observer been allowed to examine the odd little man at truly close range, such a privileged and trusted person would have quickly discerned the terrible and somewhat recent burn scars on his right hand, coupled with a deformity of some sort in the same arm, an arm which seemed to have no range of motion whatever at its right-angle-crooked elbow. The same observer would have seen on the craggy face as well, the rough traces of carefully stitched scar tissue, the gruesome result of a vicious and prolonged beating, an attack obviously carried out with one or more heavy, blunt instruments.

And if the same privileged and trusted observer had been permitted in private to examine the small figure's naked torso, such an observer would have been appalled to see mounds of jagged scar tissue, the visible dermatological response to more than two dozen pieces of shrapnel. It had been this damage from a homemade grenade that had led the New York City Police Department to place its finest detective in an early retirement program reserved for the permanently disabled. That had not, however, prevented Belton's NYPD superiors and former colleagues from bringing him regularly into their most troublesome and convoluted deliberations, nor had it prevented the distinguished detective from prospering as a private investigator.

His eyes were deep-set and oddly black, childlike in their dispassionate assessment of the world. These were eyes that never missed anything . . . ever. At this moment, the eyes were busily examining the ever-shifting maze of reflections in one storefront glass display after another, reflections that told him everything he needed to know about the slender, well-dressed, and carefully coiffed man who had been shadowing him for the last four blocks.

The detective had known immediately, ten minutes before, that he was being followed. Decades of heightened sensory alertness had told him within seconds that the slight young man who carefully studied each store-front's wares long enough so as to remain fifty feet behind him was not, in fact, studying anything offered by the stores themselves. No honest perusal of the merchandise at hand could result in equal time and attention being given to such disparate commodities as swimwear, furniture, cameras, women's handbags, and office supplies.

And so, thoughtfully, Sid Belton approached the intersection of Central Park South and Columbus Circle, taking his position among the dozen or so pedestrians awaiting the signal to cross. When the *Walk* sign appeared, he took four shuffling steps into the street, planted the heavy walking cane firmly, pivoted completely around, and strode back in the direction from which he had come, thereby passing within inches of his red-faced and nonplussed shadow.

He then walked twenty feet to the nearest storefront and waited, watching both from the corner of his eye and in the glass for his pursuer's return. As he expected, the confused young man soon came hurrying into the reflection, realizing too late that, with no obvious ruse readily at hand, he would now have to pass close behind the detective or give up the charade entirely.

As the erstwhile shadow passed behind Sid Belton on the momentarily quiet sidewalk, the detective, without turning around, thrust the metal end of the heavy wooden walking cane backwards so quickly and accurately that the tip caught the young man in mid-stride, tripping him at the ankles. His fall was hard and uncontrolled. Though he caught himself with his hands in time to prevent his face from smashing into the grime of the sidewalk, the young man's chest hit heavily and an involuntary *uhhh* escaped his lips.

He lay momentarily stunned, unmoving.

At the instant the tip of his cane found its target and the inevitable toppling movement began, Belton spun around with an agility altogether improbable for one so physically diminished, and almost faster than the eye could follow flipped open a recessed trigger mechanism inside the curved handle. Still using only his left hand and arm, he then drove the rounded metal tip of the cane into the back of his prostrate victim's left hand as it pressed against the concrete. With his right hand the detective simultane-ously, despite the complete immobility of his elbow joint, reached with long-practiced dexterity into his own inside coat pocket to withdraw his private investigator's badge.

All in less than three seconds of actual elapsed time, Sidney Belton had sent his adversary to the pavement, jabbed his weapon's blunt metal tip into the back of the young man's hand, and with his right, held aloft his credential for the visual inspection of anyone—citizen or law enforcement officer—who might be unsure as to which of the two to assist.

The detective spoke rapidly in his raspy, guttural Brooklynese: "Before y'think about tryin' to move, pal . . . I gotta tell ya there's a three-inch spring-loaded blade in the end of this cane and I got my finger on the trigger. The blade'll go through that hand of yours, and every muscle and tendon in it, like a butcher knife through a cream pie. Y'know what I mean, pal?"

The terrified young man muttered an affirmative.

Continuing to hold his credential aloft, Belton continued. "Okay. I got a few questions for ya, buddy. If I was you, I'd prob'ly answer 'em as fast as I could.

"Y'know what I mean, pal? Know what I mean?"

CHAPTER FOUR

"AND SO," ELEANOR CHAPEL WAS SAYING TO HER YOUNG companion, "when I arrived in Berkeley at the start of the spring semester and first met my steering committee colleagues, the so-called reactionaries did not so much oppose the whole position statement as they did its third part, the one about seminary admissions policies. Most of the people in that group teach in seminaries. They viewed the implications of the third part as threatening.

"And you see why, Richard?"

He thought for a moment, then nodded. "They didn't want their seminaries' admissions policies changed by the position statement. They might've been okay with the first two parts—unity in goals, and a new focus for the curriculum—but not the part about who gets in school, and how?"

"Yes, exactly. But then, I'm afraid, I began to ask questions in the meetings. A lot of questions, Richard. Annoying questions."

Richard Mabry leaned forward.

She continued. "I asked things like: How, precisely, would our churches, led decades from now by seminarians taught under these themes, differ from other types of organizations created in the public interest? What, exactly, would make them *churches*, distinct in some way from other kinds of institutions that act for the general betterment of society?

"Or how, specifically, would the implied theme of *accumulation of wealth and property* conform to the meaning and message of the New Testament . . . or is that issue unimportant?"

She thought for a moment, and then continued, her voice sure, her cadence rapid, her delivery honed through countless classroom presentations and faculty dialogues.

"And why, explicitly, Richard, would it be necessary for these new seminarians to be *Christians* . . . or would the presumption of seminarians' prior commitment to Christianity have become irrelevant?"

His eyes widened.

She paused again, looked down, rummaged briefly in her purse, and extracted two ten-dollar bills. She looked toward the deli for a staff person. Seeing none, she resumed.

"I discovered, Richard, that my questions found receptive ears. As the months have passed, about half of the thirty members of the steering committee have, at one time or another, begun to express reservations about the original draft statement. None of them—the questioners—is, to be sure, among the old guard, and so the draft statement still has a solid core of support. But now, with the conference agenda so evenly balanced, and with the committee in a condition of some confusion regarding the draft position statement, the only real consensus we have had recently was around the suggestion of adding three scholars from your field: sociology of religion."

At that moment she caught the eye of a staff person, who hurried onto the patio, accepted the two bills, and retreated back into the building. Richard Mabry, seeing the interview was ending and not wanting to abandon the conversation without hearing at least a summary of the revered scholar's own position, persisted, asking almost desperately, "But Dr. Chapel, what of your own perspective?"

"Oh," she replied, holding her notebook and purse in both hands and sitting on the very edge of her chair, obviously prepared to rise, "I'm sorry, Richard."

She turned her eyes away and spoke, looking toward the Berkeley hills that rose to their heights virtually from her elbow. "My position will disappoint you, because it has nothing to do with sociology. It does have *implications* for sociology, just as it has implications, I suppose, for everything in the world."

She turned her eyes toward him.

"My position—if I dare dignify my thoughts with so grandiose a term—is as simple and as unadorned as Christ's message itself. We—all of us: Catholic, Baptist, Anglican, Eastern Orthodox, Methodist, Pentecostal, Presbyterian, Nazarene, Lutheran, all of us everywhere—are here on earth for *evangelical* reasons.

"Matthew 28, Richard. The risen Christ's charge to us all: *Go ye therefore and make disciples. . . .*

"And," she added, nodding her head slightly in confirmation of the simplicity and truth of her own words and looking at him intently, "that's all . . . really . . . truly. . . . That's all.

"I know . . . I know . . . so many of our colleagues want to run from that word—*evangelical*—as if it were wrapped in something sticky."

She paused and smiled at the image, then added, "But it is the correct word, Richard, always and forever.

"And so my position is that we are here simply to spread the Good News. And that means that churches . . . in order to be *churches* . . . must do that first and foremost, whatever else they may do."

She leaned toward him, hands still clutching her purse and her notebook, and added in her high, clear voice, "That, in turn, means that seminaries must attract people who are 'called'—please note the word—'called' to a life of spreading the Good News, and who wish above all to study the scriptures and commit themselves to a life of sacrifice and persuasion on behalf of Him who has called them.

"Everything else . . . *everything* else . . . is secondary to that. And there is very little more to say, Richard, about my position, though I will proceed to say what little there is."

At this he smiled, and she returned his smile, mixing in a fleeting touch of her tinkling laughter.

She brought her summation hurriedly, speaking more quickly as the time for the faculty meeting's resumption approached. "I'm *not* opposed to ecumenical and other unifying efforts. I'm really not, despite what many think. I'm just focused on something else. I teach Old Testament using the lens of the New Testament, a controversial idea in itself to some. But it fits absolutely this simple focus on the Good News.

"And this simple focus is what must support *any* Christian tradition in order for it to be a *Christian* tradition.

"So, that's what I think, Richard. And that's what I do.

"Everything else is either beside the real point, or—and this is pertinent to that draft position statement—*incompatible* with the real point."

She stopped and looked closely at him. Richard Mabry seemed to be staring straight through the remains of his sandwich. When he looked up, his brow was once more creased in earnest puzzlement.

"Why, then," he said in soft confusion, finally confessing to her the obvious, "would *you* want me on the steering committee, Dr. Chapel? It's clear that I am expected to supply a sociological perspective, and beyond that, to argue the particular sociological perspective implied by the old guard's viewpoint . . . to support fully the draft position statement . . . even though, I admit, when *you* summarized it, well . . . I experienced some misgivings about it. . . .

"Still, on balance, I do believe that we must move seminary training in the direction of sound management concepts integrated with sophisticated economic theory, and I think a powerful endorsement of that approach from *Congressus III* will push seminaries in all parts of the world in that direction. And I admit that I don't see any of that as necessarily weakening the Christ-centered emphasis you just articulated."

He glanced down at his feet, astonished at his own forthrightness in this terrifying conversation, reduced to momentary silence at the effrontery of his words. How dare he stand in brazen disagreement with one of the world's most distinguished Old Testament scholars?

But the words had been spoken. There was no taking them back. Mabry raised his hands to his face, swallowed, and prepared to continue, knowing there was no retreat.

Like a child, he found himself peeking at her through his fingers, trying to gauge her response from the expression on her face. He sensed that she was trying to decide whether or not to allow his statement to stand unchallenged.

He dropped his hands and said timidly, a hopeful smile forming on his lips, "Do you want to demolish me now, Dr. Chapel, or later?"

To his immense discomfort, she did not smile in return, but said simply, "Now."

He sat back, mentally girding his loins.

"Richard," she began after another moment, "do you actually believe that the ultimate goal of those who are, quite literally, *invested* in this position statement . . . do you believe that their ultimate goal is to effect the changes outlined by the statement itself? Do you think that their long-term vision of the impact of all this has to do with *curriculum?*

"Think, sir, for just a moment, about what comes after that. You're a sociology of religion teacher and researcher and theorist. You understand and teach about the behaviors of large groups of people and their organizations. You understand what they call church marketing: shaping messages so as to influence groups of people in particular directions for particular ends. So, what comes next, Dr. Mabry? When 'power structures' are put into place in accordance with 'power-base organizational and marketing theory,' as those in your field like to say, what follows?"

She stopped and lifted her eyebrows. He saw that she would wait for a reply. He looked away, thought for a moment, and responded.

"Well, eventually the organizations begin to transform themselves."

"Yes," she said, "and, in this case, ultimately into what?"

A dark curtain seemed to drape itself over his mind for several moments. Then a small candle flickered there, weak and uncertain. As he examined the tiny flame more and more closely, he suddenly recoiled and actually gasped aloud. He looked up at her.

Then he shook his head. "Oh, no, ma'am, you can't possibly think that. . . ."

She nodded. "Oh, yes, I do, indeed, think that," she said.

He found he could hardly form the words, but he desperately needed to hear her say that she, in fact, foresaw something other than the astonishing image forming in his mind. And so he said, speaking slowly and hesitantly, "Do you mean . . . that you can imagine . . . something like . . . well . . . churches *without worship,* Dr. Chapel? Churches *without sacraments?* Churches that are just . . . well . . . I guess . . . service organizations . . . sort of like YMCAs or YWCAs . . . or . . . maybe . . . influencers of public policy? Lining up with or against political parties and political candidates and accumulating money to give or withhold for particular political purposes . . . and . . ."

His mind returned to his initial words. "And . . . churches *without worship,* Dr. Chapel? Really? You mean . . . you mean all of that? You mean all of *that?*"

"Of course," she said simply and without hesitation.

He stared at her again.

"Think, Richard," she said, "of what would follow from a generation— or two or three—of seminarians trained to regard their churches as financial entities, institutions to be managed and transformed into power-base economic platforms in support of activities in the public interest, or in support of particular causes, broadly speaking. Think of what shape these churches would begin inevitably to take. Not right away, but eventually. And just think of the financial opportunities that would accrue: real estate speculation, life and health insurance brokering, full-service funeral and burial services, food, clothing, books, movies. . . .

"How would it be otherwise, Richard? Once the accumulation of wealth and power has been officially institutionalized, how could the outcome possibly be different? Church leaders will be judged on their ability to manage their organizations, to be responsive to the marketplace, to be as nimble as small businesses . . . and for the same reasons: to anticipate society's material wishes and perceived needs, and to address those, whatever they may be."

She paused, looked away from him for a moment, and then returned her eyes to his.

"I ask again, Richard, how could it possibly be otherwise? Young church leaders, having been educated to think in this fashion, would in the normal course of events take a hard look at the sorts of things that scare some people away from Christianity.

"And what are those scary things?" she asked, not expecting a reply from him, and indeed, not waiting for one. "They are those things that have to do with *commitment* to Jesus Christ and the miracle-universe that attaches to Him: redemption, resurrection, eternity. . . .

"These frighten certain people away—these things require devotion to the final and supreme level of Truth, and to all that goes with it—these things force people to change their priorities profoundly.

"And so, if you are a shrewd and management-savvy young church leader thoroughly educated in the ways of the marketplace, and if you've placed those things highest in your priority lists, you'll begin to reduce your emphasis on things supernatural, Richard, because those things may frighten your people away, you see? You'll develop sermons that focus on anything . . . *anything* . . . other than sin and redemption, miracle and eternity. You'll place less and less emphasis on baptism and holy communion, and you'll place more and more stress on entertainment and self-help and personal financial planning and international political issues and . . . oh, Richard! . . . I could go on and on.

"And I suppose I have," she acknowledged, shaking her head. "But once I get going on this topic, it's hard for me to find the brake pedal. Anyway, I'll stop. I've said enough. You certainly by now know exactly what I foresee, and I would imagine that by now you are wondering why you ever asked my viewpoint in the first place."

His mouth had fallen open as she had gone on and on, and now he dropped his head once more to his hands and closed his eyes. He found himself wishing he could be anywhere else in the world at that moment, anywhere that would remove him from the pressure he now felt, pressure to agree with the academic giant sitting just in front of him, along with equal pressure—honest, heartfelt pressure—to reject her ravings for what they were: outrageous and insupportable depictions of a Christianity that would never be allowed to materialize . . . never allowed by any Christian . . . whether follower or leader.

And then he remembered what she had said about whether or not the *Congressus* vision of seminaries would even require the seminarians themselves to be Christians. He frowned and shrugged away this ridiculous idea.

He shook his head, collected himself as well as he could, allowed himself a deep breath and looked up at her. He shook his head again.

"No, Dr. Chapel . . . no. It's not going to happen. It can't happen . . . it just can't.

"There is a huge difference in the idea of church leaders being educated and prepared to build churches into financially stable institutions with great power to reach out and to position themselves in the marketplace, and in church leaders arriving at the point at which they want to turn their organizations into *de facto* community service and public policy operations . . . in fact, into actual wealth-generating machines to serve the public good as they define the public good.

"No, ma'am, you're just wrong about this. That line will never, never be crossed. You're drawing a picture that's just too far-fetched."

She looked at him for a long moment. Then she sat back and nodded. "Well, I will hope you are right, sir, but I am convinced that you are not. I don't know what your reading is, for example, on the European church as an institution in the days of Martin Luther, but what exactly was Luther protesting against if it was not the church as a materialistic power broker, in fact, a wealth-generating machine? What was he fighting if it was not the power-and-profit motive as the basis for the church's decisions and

practices? How do you account for the Reformation that followed? Or for
the Counter-Reformation that followed that?"

She sighed. Then she shook her head and added, "In any case, Richard,
there is nothing in the *Congressus* position statement as it now stands,
nothing whatever in that statement on the future of seminary education,
that is consistent with *anything* in the Gospels."

Her brilliant eyes rested on his face for a moment, eyes that were kind,
gentle, even motherly, but challenging him fully to contradict her statement.

He said nothing.

There was a lengthy pause. Richard Mabry dropped his eyes and looked
down at his feet.

But Mabry found, through the fog of confusion and inadvertent intimi-
dation that Eleanor Chapel induced in him, that he was actually, at last,
beginning to relax. This last exchange had finally decided him.

Eleanor Chapel, preeminent scholar or not, had simply gone too far to
be taken seriously. The further the conversation had gone, the clearer
everything had become in his own mind. He knew what he thought about
these absurd notions of hers. Her earlier persuasiveness faded from his
mind and he found himself already beginning to form an image of her as a
radical, an extremist, certainly, at the very least, an alarmist.

So, at length, he decided simply to move the conversation back to her
original invitation to him. Though she would have been disappointed to
know that she had driven him back to his own ground, the truth was that
she had. He suddenly felt that the *Congressus* committee did indeed need
him and his perspective.

"Well," he began again, "thank you, Dr. Chapel, for all of that. I know it
would have been easier. . . ." His voice trailed off.

After a moment, he resumed, "But let me ask once more why you would
want me to do this, ma'am. Even if you're just doing this because the
committee asked you to, why would the old-line members entrust you with
the task? Why would not the other co-chair, or another member from the
old leadership, speak to me about this?"

She nodded and replied immediately. "First," she said, "you were
mistaken just now to suggest that I do, in fact, want you to serve on the
committee. I do not. I am not in support of inviting three religion sociologists to join us. I stand in opposition to the idea as another waste of people's
time, including yours, Richard.

"I am issuing the invitation because you and I are colleagues at PSR. None of the others has an affiliation with our institution. And beyond that, the old-line members, although they *oppose* me, do not in the least, as far as I know, have an inclination to *mistrust* me.

"I think that's all."

She paused for a moment, smiled to herself, shook her head thoughtfully, and then continued. "No," she added, "no, I'm afraid that what I just said is wishful thinking.

"I've no doubt that some old guard members, and perhaps others, as well—but only *some* of them, Richard—suspect that I have written a competing position statement, and fear that I will offer it to the conferees as an alternative to the committee's official draft statement. And I think that the rules of procedure actually do permit a co-chair of the steering committee to do such a thing.

"So, they fear, not only might their statement fail to pass . . . it might actually be replaced by a statement with which they are in earnest disagreement. They—some of them, that is—have become very, very mistrustful of me.

"But insofar as the group's attitude toward you is concerned, the old guard members simply want what they regard as the 'new standard' sociology of religion position strengthened, Richard. It provides a powerful justification for portions of the position statement. You have nicely articulated its basic premise, that—in my words, not necessarily yours—*an organizational and financial power platform must first be built to achieve maximum impact in any charitable endeavor*. They tell me that you have, in fact, articulated it better than anyone. They do know your work, Richard, despite your modest assessment of it.

"Believe me, the old guard members very much hope you'll accept, and even the most mistrustful of them did not, apparently, wish to expend their political capital insisting, over Dr. Giacomo's objections, that he meet with you rather than I, as your faculty colleague."

"And have you?" he asked, smiling.

"Have I what?" she replied.

"Have you written a competing position statement, as some suspect?"

He was staggered to see her face flush angrily. She sat forward in her chair, even more erect than previously, and stared at him, tiny nostrils flaring, blue-green eyes now blazing with a fury that turned him to stone.

"If I had written such a statement," she hissed at him, "I would have announced my intention to do so, and would have immediately distributed the statement to all committee members, so that they could respond to me, face to face, in the privacy of a committee session."

Richard Mabry, his face now as pasty white as Eleanor Chapel's had suddenly become fiery red, began to stammer an apology, followed by a retraction. "Please, Dr. Chapel . . . I'm so sorry. I meant nothing. I was just making the kind of stupid conversation I've always thought was . . . funny . . . or something. . . . Please . . . I'm sorry. I didn't mean the question as a serious . . . ah . . . challenge to you of any kind. . . ."

She rose quickly, unsmiling, and said simply, "Excuse me, please," in a curt whisper, and walked swiftly into the building. He saw that she had left her notebook and purse on the edge of the table, an indication, he assumed both hopefully and fearfully, that she would return.

The sudden flare-up of scholarly temper was observed thoughtfully by the shadowy giant across the street. The mind behind the hooded eyes was not surprised at the apparent eruption; that mind had studied its subject well, and knew the subject to be both volatile and capable of behavior best described as overtly combative. Though it did not know her luncheon companion, it could guess the nature of this young man's indiscretion. The ponderous yet somehow gracefully athletic figure smiled to itself. Then it stepped from the curb and strode rapidly and forcefully across the street.

When Eleanor Chapel returned in five minutes, two men's faces turned toward her. Her eyes wide, she stared at the figure that stood before Richard Mabry. The immaculately dressed intruder dwarfed her luncheon guest, though Mabry was standing, too, and was himself of at least average height. If she had been asked to guess the man's weight and height, she might have suggested nearly three hundred pounds on a six-foot nine-inch frame. And she would have been correct within twenty pounds and one inch, for he was actually that much heavier and taller than such an estimate would have suggested. Everything about him was oversized: head, shoulders, colossal hands, and enormous girth.

Eleanor Chapel remained completely still, the exterior door of the deli closing slowly behind her. Her eyes fixed themselves on the huge man's face. He was dramatically handsome.

His forehead was high, a receding hairline accentuating both the massiveness of the forehead and the touch of gray that brushed his temples. His dark eyes were bright and penetrating—characteristics apparent even from the twenty-five-foot distance between them. His jaw was square, though his jowls evinced the sagging looseness brought on by age and decades of rich food. A heavy salt-and-pepper mustache covered his upper lip and gave his face a sternness, even a slight severity. He appeared to be approximately fifty years old.

Suddenly moving around the table, he advanced on her in six enormous strides, and to her astonishment, bowed deeply before her and with a grace that she would have thought impossible for one so extravagantly oversized in every dimension. Then, stationary in his exaggerated bow, he spoke to her from that position, his eyes at her feet, his voice a booming replica of intermediate-distance thunder. *"Signora,"* he said, accenting the second syllable dramatically and rolling the "r" with a flourish, "it is with the . . . the greatest pleasure . . . and with the . . . the most superior honor . . . that I introduce myself to you."

Then, pulling himself to his full height, now towering a full two feet above her head, he announced in tones that would have done justice to the public address amplification of a king's arrival: "I am . . . *Antonio Camposanto!*"

And with that, he bowed again, and with at least as much drama of movement as in the first instance. The thought flitted through her mind that he was perhaps about to fall to one knee before her and to raise her hand to his lips.

But no. He rose again to his full height, and looking down kindly at her, he broke into a dazzling smile showing bright, white teeth that stood out in brilliant contrast to the heavy mustache.

Eleanor Chapel saw that Richard Mabry, meanwhile, had moved tentatively to the man's side, and that he looked up at the giant with the wonder of a child in the presence of some storybook character toward whom he felt some combination of awe, fear, and uncontrollable curiosity. Seeming to tear his gaze from the countenance of Antonio Camposanto with the greatest difficulty, Mabry at length turned his eyes to her and waited breathlessly for her response, still shaken to his core by her outburst and vaguely relieved to be in the presence of this stunning and wholly unexpected diversion.

He waited a long time, for neither party stirred.

When the silence was finally broken, it was the woman who did so. Her words could not have been more surprising or confusing to Richard Mabry had she announced the end of the world. Turning her face fully upward to Camposanto's, and fixing her gaze on his gently downcast eyes, she asked, speaking softly and, thought Mabry, with the first trace of fear he had detected in her in the five months he had known her, "Detective, is my husband . . . ?"

Instantly both massive hands rose to his chest, palms opened to her in a gesture of reassurance. He shook his head quickly. "You are to have no fear as to the safety of your dear husband, *signora*. I have him under surveillance, as, if I may anticipate other areas of your most obvious concern, I have also under surveillance your friends in London and your family—most especially your angelic grandniece and your . . . ah . . . most energetic grandnephew—in Roma."

Mabry, thoroughly mystified by every word spoken, turned his eyes back to Eleanor Chapel, his relief palpable that her anger at him had been so totally—though he knew, perhaps temporarily—deflected. Again, he waited some time for a response. When it came, it only deepened the mystery.

For Eleanor Chapel had begun to laugh. At first, it was her tinkling, delicate laughter, the laughter in which he had delighted from the earliest faculty meetings that he had attended with her. Then it grew less familiar and took on a less controlled, almost hysterical quality. She doubled over, laughing still harder and holding her stomach with both hands, gasping for breath.

At this, Mabry realized quickly, Antonio Camposanto was as surprised and uncertain as was he himself. Camposanto even turned his head and glanced briefly down at him, his eyebrows arched quizzically. Mabry shook his head, smiling vaguely. Both men turned to face the diminutive woman and watched silently as she regained control of herself, wiped her moist eyes with the tips of her index fingers, and both her hands again holding her stomach, raised her face once more to Camposanto.

"I'm so sorry, Detective," she said to him apologetically. "That was rude. Please forgive me. It's just that . . . I understood you to say that you have my husband and my London friends *under surveillance.*"

Here she paused and raised her own eyebrows, looking for confirmation. He gave it with a nod of his head.

This time she did not laugh. "Detective Camposanto," she said, "I am disappointed in you."

Mabry, looking at her carefully, saw that she meant this.

"Exactly how," she continued immediately, "would you place Sidney Belton or Rebecca Clark *under surveillance?* Surely you are aware that neither he nor she can be . . . ah . . . 'watched' without their immediately becoming aware of the situation? Surely you know that, probably within minutes or even seconds, your . . . operatives . . . would find *themselves* under surveillance?

"Is it possible that you know my husband or Mrs. Clark so little that you do not know how quickly they will identify—and defeat—any such effort? And I might add that, depending upon the response from your operatives, it is even conceivable that those in your employ may find themselves momentarily in a position of some hazard.

"Please, Detective, explain your thinking."

Antonio Camposanto's eyes flickered in Richard Mabry's direction. There was no other perceptible response from him.

Eleanor Chapel turned abruptly to Mabry. "Thank you, Richard, for joining me for lunch. I must ask you to leave us. Now."

As Mabry turned in utter perplexity to go, he felt his upper arm suddenly enclosed in massive pincers that, in size and strength, put him in mind of some kind of monumental, hinged and forged steel machinery. It was Camposanto's right hand.

A deft movement of that hand spun Mabry around to face Eleanor Chapel once more. His mouth was agape, and he stared alternately from one face to the other. He could not speak.

Eleanor Chapel, her voice soft, looked first at Camposanto. "Thank you, Detective," she said. Then she added, turning to Mabry, "Richard, until *Signore* Camposanto or I release you from the promise you are about to make, you must speak of his presence here in California to no one. Do you understand?"

He swallowed, glanced down at the gigantic paw that continued to envelop his upper arm, and croaked, "Yes, ma'am."

"Say it," she insisted.

"I promise . . . not to speak of . . . Mr. Camposanto's presence here in California . . . until you or he releases me from the promise."

Instantly his arm was free. His upper arm felt as though it had been compressed into something no more than half the diameter it had been just seconds earlier. Stumbling in consternation and humiliation, he turned to go. As he retreated unsteadily across the patio toward the sidewalk, he heard over his shoulder Eleanor Chapel's strong, clear, high voice: "Richard, I'll need your answer this afternoon. We want you on the steering committee!"

He did not reply or so much as turn around. He staggered onto the sidewalk, and without consciously deciding to, began to run.

San Francisco/Berkeley: 12:52 pm/Friday
New York: 3:52 pm/Friday
London: 8:52 pm/Friday
Rome: 9:52 pm/Friday

Warm and moonless nightfall had enveloped the inner city of London by the time a dark-clad threesome emerged from the dilapidated flat and crossed the street, walking quickly and without speaking, to the small sedan. Each was encumbered by backpack and hand-held carrying case. Rebecca Clark slipped behind the wheel and started the rough-running motor of the rental car, while her husband took the seat to her left. Andrea Camposanto, apologizing softly for the filthy interior of the vehicle that she had littered with wrappings, newspapers, and magazines, moved into the left rear seat behind Matt Clark.

Following the murmured apologies, a tense silence began.

Rebecca deftly maneuvered the sluggish sedan ever further into and about the convolutions of city center. At length she directed the struggling auto into a dark cul-de-sac, pulled over to the side of a bedraggled residential street, turned off lights and engine, rolled her window down, and listened. After two full minutes, she nodded to her companions. They stepped from the car as one, then strode together to the end of the street and across the small grassy park that separated the cul-de-sac from the thoroughfare into which it had once emptied. Hailing the first taxi to appear, the three climbed into the rear seat. Rebecca bade the driver circle the next block not once but twice. She then asked him to pull to the curb. With the car's lights and motor off, she allowed two more minutes to pass, watching and listening, all windows down. Finally satisfied, Rebecca gave the driver an address, and appearing to relax for the first time, sat back, nestling between the shoulders of her two companions on the taxi's narrow rear seat.

In fewer than ten minutes, the taxi stopped, disgorged its passengers, and departed. With Rebecca leading the way, they walked quietly down an alleyway to the next parallel street, turned left onto the broken side-walk, and two doorways from the alley, passed through a small swinging gate in a four-foot-high chain-link fence. They passed around the left side of a small frame house, stepped up onto its four-by-four-foot back stoop, and paused. Again they waited, listening, before Rebecca reached into a pocket of her jet black, lightweight tennis warm-up jacket, removed a key, and extended her hand toward the keyhole.

The key never reached its mark.

Suddenly the door of the darkened room opened. Rebecca, unsur-prised, stepped instantly into the void, followed closely by Matt. Andrea Camposanto, momentarily assailed with doubt, hesitated. But only for one long second. She felt her wrist once more seized by a powerful hand, drawing her irresistibly forward. Before she could protest, she felt herself crossing the threshold. Then she sensed the door swinging shut softly behind her.

San Francisco/Berkeley: 1:15 pm/Friday
New York: 4:15 pm/Friday
London: 9:15 pm/Friday
Rome: 10:15 pm/Friday

At very nearly the same moment, in an affluent suburb of a far more ancient city than London, Mario Angelini took his wife's soft, smooth, increasingly plump hands in his own, fingering her several rings and looking earnestly and lovingly into her face. "They're asleep," he said simply in his rich Italian baritone, indicating their children's bedrooms with a quick movement of his eyes.

Anna Angelini spoke softly, the music in her high voice still noticeable despite the near-whisper she used to reply. "Mario, tell me again what the detectives said to you at the precinct today. With Paulo whining so, I couldn't attend to you earlier. It seemed to me they said nothing at all."

Her husband shrugged his shoulders. "Well, they certainly said nothing helpful," he replied. "They minimized the possibility of some threat to us or the children. They noted the prevalence of such vehicles as the black Mercedes we have seen—huge automobiles with heavily tinted windows and large antennas—in a city where embassies and the Vatican draw hundreds and even thousands of dignitaries in a continuous stream. They pointed to the obvious: neither you nor I saw the license plate on the car. We cannot know it was the same vehicle in each instance. We are not to worry, but are to get in touch with them if the . . . well . . . surveillance . . . seems to continue."

She shook her head, squeezing each of the hands that continued to caress hers gently. "*No,* Mario! People in that car were watching us. I know it. But why? What are we to anyone?

"Think, Mario . . . *per favore* . . . that limousine was parked at the main gate of Mother's little cemetery. It remained there until I moved my car . . . and it has appeared at our little school . . . and it has appeared at our little market. . . . Mario! There are no attractions for dignitaries at those places, no matter why some high-ranking personage might have come to Rome. They are studying *us* . . . they want *us!*"

Anna Angelini's hands withdrew from her husband's and flew to her face. She began to sob, her soft body immediately wracked with a pent-up fear that spilled forth into her husband's open arms. And Mario Angelini held his wife tenderly and without speaking.

He had no other comfort to offer.

San Francisco/Berkeley: 1:20 pm/Friday
New York: 4:20 pm/Friday
London: 9:20 pm/Friday
Rome: 10:20 pm/Friday

An ocean and two continents—more than six thousand miles of terrain and water—to the west of the sobbing Anna Angelini, her beloved aunt Eleanor Mason Chapel and the recently arrived visitor still shared a table on the deli's quiescent patio. Richard Mabry, propelled by the lingering sensations of Antonio Camposanto's bear-like grip on his arm, had fled up the hill toward the seminary nearly a half-hour previous, while Camposanto, holding the professor's heavy metal chair with one hand as if it were a plastic toy, had assisted her as she sat. As soon as the visitor had pulled his own chair to the table, or as near the table as a human of such dimensions might attempt, the professor had spoken.

"Forgive me, Detective, for my impetuous demand. I'd no right to insist that you 'explain your thinking,' especially in front of Dr. Mabry. I was rude. I'd no right to insist upon such a thing under any circumstances at all. I should, if I'd had my wits about me, have simply thanked you for providing protection for my husband and friends and family."

The detective smiled and shrugged his outsized shoulders. "I had done the . . . the surprise to you, *signora*," he said simply. "The rudeness was entirely mine, though I intended nothing of that sort. But I do wish to acknowledge that it would be of the greatest favor to me—if you would be so kind as to talk to me—before I do the talking to you . . . about the . . . ah . . . situation . . . in which we find ourselves. Would you object . . . please . . . so much as to do the talking to me? What has been happening here? What has happened to you, *signora*?"

She responded quickly. "The first thoughts that raced through my mind as soon as I saw you—there was no need for you to identify yourself; you are not easily mistaken for any other person in the world—were simply that your presence here and now could explain itself only in connection with this absurd business about the *Congressus Evangelicus* position statement.

"I've known, of course, from the start that the conference's position statement would be of far-reaching importance: to the steering committee's old-line leaders, many of them your countrymen; to the world's seminaries and universities; to the vocation—the calling—of Christian leaders everywhere, and . . . well . . . to the very definition of the Church Universal. And it seems increasingly obvious," she added, her words slowing, "that it's important to those with—or interested in—church-owned art objects, property, land and buildings, financial holdings of every imaginable sort, in every corner of the globe. And perhaps this last is of particular importance to law enforcement people like you, sir, and like my husband?"

She paused to consider her own statement. He waited, as unmoving as the looming hills to their east.

After another moment, she continued. "I've known from the first, Detective, that my presence on the steering committee might lead to my becoming a threat to . . . to vested interests . . . in *every* category."

She paused only long enough to raise her eyebrows. His response was a small smile that moved the heavy mustache slightly upward at its corners. His face and form were otherwise completely still.

"My husband," she then continued more rapidly, "has cautioned me repeatedly by telephone and by letter, insisting that I was placing myself in danger by . . . well . . . as he said several times . . . by just being myself in a . . . um . . . how did he put it? Oh, yes . . . in a 'high-stakes game' such as this one has become. And I have scolded him repeatedly about seeing danger lurking around every corner."

She smiled then, remembering.

"I have scolded him, yes," she continued. "But I have listened, too. Sidney Belton, as you know well, sir, is no coward and has a shrewd eye for danger."

She looked away from the hooded eyes for several seconds, now smiling both inwardly and outwardly at the image of her husband of six months.

"When I saw you standing here with Richard Mabry a few moments ago," she continued, "my very first thoughts were of Sidney, and then of my family in Rome, and then of my friends in London. My immediate feeling was that you must be here to protect me, and perhaps them, from . . . well . . . from somebody or something. . . ."

Hesitating then, Eleanor Chapel looked at her digital watch, noted that the time for the faculty meeting's resumption had passed, and sighed. Shaking her head, she added ruefully, "There is no point in my trying to get to the meeting on time now, Detective. I have already talked your ear off, and you, I'm certain, have things to say to me. I have not yet even allowed you to begin.

"I was just thirsty for a professional ear, *signore*. I miss Sidney so much. I never imagined this separation would be so hard. . . . But I was thrilled to see you, right from the first moment I realized you were actually here. Sidney has spoken of you often in the year that I have known him, sir. He has read your books, your articles, your reports—everything you have written, I think—with great care. I know of no one in the field whom he respects more than Antonio Camposanto."

She stopped, seeing him tense and move forward in his chair, an arresting series of movements in one so huge, movements accompanied by creakings of wood, groanings of metal, and an unintelligible, threatening sound from deep in the detective's throat. "Your voice is a bell, *signora*," he said softly in an impossibly low murmur. "It . . . how do you say it . . . it *carries* on the breeze."

Adjusting his position in his chair, much of his weight now on his forearms as he leaned across the table toward her, he continued. "Allow me to . . . to say the situation . . . as I understand it, *signora*. . . .

"My . . . ah . . . sources . . . my informants . . . in my own city, elsewhere in my own country, throughout the whole of Europe, and yes, *signora,* around the world . . . began recently to warn my office in Roma of a . . . of a corruption within the *Congressus Evangelicus* movement. I was not surprised by this.

"As you just suggested, Dr. Chapel, when an organization's decisions begin to take on sufficient . . . ah . . . financial consequences and . . . ah . . . could I say . . . ah . . . consequences for power . . . and . . . ah . . . consequences for the careers of powerful people, then . . . well . . . those in position to be . . . ah . . . threatening to those . . . to those consequences . . . those threatening ones . . . will become . . . ah . . . ah . . . what is the word . . . ah . . . targets . . . *si* . . . targets. . . . targets of those who wish to remain in the position . . . in the position of strength . . . in the position of power. *Si?*"

She nodded.

"You, *signora,* have become a . . . a target. You, *signora,* are now in much danger. And likewise, *signora,* your family in my city is now in danger, simply because those who wish to stop you . . . those ones . . . those ones understand . . . they understand that you will . . . you will . . . ah . . . ah . . . regard the threat . . . *si* . . . the threat . . . to your niece and to her children just as you would regard a threat to yourself. In fact, they know that you will regard a threat to them—to your niece and her children—as of *more* concern than a threat to yourself. *Si?*"

Again, she nodded, adding a quiet, "Yes."

"*Si.* And so I have come to California so as to protect you, *signora.* The San Francisco Bay area police forces . . . they know that I am here and they understand why. . . . And that is because some of the leaders of *Congressus* . . . some of those who stand to lose . . . who stand to lose the most in power and in money . . . should your views prevail . . . are from my own city. The local police here stand ready to assist . . . ready to assist me . . . whenever I request such an assisting from them."

"And my niece and her family in Rome?"

"Ah. . . . Anna Angelini and her husband and the little ones in Roma . . . my entire police force is alerted to protect them, and I have placed a special . . . as *Signore* Belton would say . . . a special *shadow* to observe them at all times.

"They will be cared for, *signora,* do not worry for them."

"And in New York and London?"

Here the great detective smiled, the thick mustache rising gracefully at its corners. "As you suggested before, *signora,* neither Detective Belton nor *Signora* Clark will likely need the protecting in the way that you and the little ones in Roma might need the protecting. But those who have studied your life well enough to make this . . . this . . . threatening . . . this threatening against you . . . will know not only that you have a . . . a . . . what is the word . . . ah . . . *vulnerable* . . . yes . . . a vulnerable family in Roma, but that you have a husband in New York . . . and . . . as you say . . . some . . . ah . . . some *friends* . . . in London . . . any of whom . . . all of whom . . . would fly to your side in a moment.

"So, although *they*—*Signora* Clark and Detective Belton—are certainly not . . . not . . . not *vulnerable* . . . in the way that you or the young Angelinis might be vulnerable, there may be an attempt upon them in advance . . . in advance of some sort of . . . of threatening . . . of threatening upon you . . . or upon your family in my city, in order to . . . to. . . . "

"To *preempt* their movements to assist me or my niece."

"*Si, si, signora.* To *preempt,* indeed."

Still leaning forward across the small table, Camposanto stopped, his dark eyes studying Eleanor Chapel's face. Her eyes were down as she concentrated on the implications of his words.

Then she looked up, the blue-green orbs clear and unafraid. "What do you want me to do, Detective?"

He smiled, his mustache again moving upward in response. "Since you will refuse to do what I would prefer—I will pass over the suggestion . . . the suggestion that you withdraw from this . . . this . . . this arena of danger and return immediately to your husband in New York City."

"Yes. Pass over that."

"So, I will suggest instead that you move ahead with your program, your agenda. Keep your schedule. Attend your meetings. Make your speeches.

"Know that I am with you, watching from somewhere difficult for you and others to see. Size is not . . . not . . . ah . . . not an obstacle . . . for one who knows how to be invisible under all circumstances. And know that I have immediate access . . . access to the police in this city . . . and in the neighboring ones . . . as well as command of the detective units in Roma . . . as well as friends and colleagues in Scotland Yard . . . and in the New York City Police Department.

"These bad ones—the ones who wish to stop you—they are not prepared . . . not prepared for what I and my associates can bring against them, *signora*." And here he smiled once more. "You should go forward with your life, Dr. Eleanor Chapel. Yes. Go forward with your life.

"Antonio Camposanto will be there to guard you. You will be safe, your loved ones will be safe, your agenda will be completed, and you will be victorious over these bad ones . . . yes. . . .

"Antonio Camposanto will be there to guard you, Signora Chapel."

SAN FRANCISCO/BERKELEY: 1:54 PM/FRIDAY
NEW YORK: 4:54 PM/FRIDAY
LONDON: 9:54 PM/FRIDAY
ROME: 10:54 PM/FRIDAY

As Eleanor Chapel opened the door to her upstairs office in the PSR administration building, she realized that the ringing telephone she had heard as she padded down the corridor was her own. Breathlessly, she reached her desk and snatched the handset from its cradle. She spoke her name, gasping, into the receiver. The voice she heard was precisely the one she expected: raspy, guttural, and unutterably welcome to her ear.

"Eleanor!" it said tensely. "You okay? Yeah? You really are? Yeah? You *sure* you're okay? Yeah? You're *completely* okay?"

It was her happy laughter that seemed finally to reassure Sidney Belton, when nothing she merely *said* could accomplish the task.

"Well," he continued after a pause, "I had a little run-in here in New York with a fella says he's workin' for Antonio Camposanto. Says Antonio isn't in Rome. Says he's right there in Berkeley with you. Have you seen him yet?"

"Yes! Yes, Sidney! Antonio Camposanto! Here! Think of it!"

"I *am* thinkin' of it, Eleanor. I've been thinkin' of nothin' else since my little tiff here with one of Antonio's boys. I figure you won't be surprised to know I'm at LaGuardia right now. I got a direct flight from New York to San Francisco. Leaves in half hour. Gets me there, with the time change, some time after 7:00 PM Pacific. A taxi oughta get me across the bridge and into Berkeley by . . . let's see . . . I'm thinkin' 9:00 PM your time, latest. Maybe a little before.

"You got one of your steering committee meetings tonight? Yeah? Can you tell Antonio I'll meet him at your apartment at 9:00 PM? You got some way to reach him? Yeah? Think that'll work?"

"Well," she replied thoughtfully and happily, "I don't know that he will want to come to the apartment, dearest."

"Yeah . . . that's right . . . good point . . . just tell him that I'll be there at the apartment by 9:00 PM and let him figure out how he wants to get in touch with me. Just be sure to let him know I'll be there, and that I wanna talk to him *tonight* . . . not tomorrow . . . *tonight.*"

San Francisco/Berkeley: 1:59 PM/Friday
New York: 4:59 PM/Friday
London: 9:59 PM/Friday
Rome: 10:59 PM/Friday

Andrea Camposanto, daughter of the great detective, her bone-deep fatigue momentarily forgotten, squinted as the lights came up in a subterranean, bare-walled cavity somewhere under the small house she had so unceremoniously entered forty-five minutes earlier. She and her companions had waited for that interminable length of time, crouched in absolute silence in, she presumed, a kitchen, while the home's apparent owner had moved softly from room to room and from window to window, searching for

. . . what? She had stopped trying to comprehend and had turned her efforts increasingly to fighting her own exhaustion. Whatever was to happen to her, she must remain alert and aware. Her father would accept no less.

Now, as her eyes found their sight, she found herself staring at the person who, she did not doubt, had been the one to seize her wrist on the back stoop. Though Rebecca was just at that moment introducing the young man to her, there was no need.

This was Luke Manguson, twin brother of Rebecca Manguson Clark. In Andrea Camposanto's mind, his legend was, on the natural level, at least on a plane with that of his sister. It was true that, unlike his sister, he was no seer of visions . . . at least, not yet . . . not insofar as she knew. But his physical prowess and mental acuity were indeed legendary to those who, like Andrea, had studied carefully the twins' exploits of the previous two years.

Physically the two were little alike, aside from the ramrod posture they shared. Luke was an inch shorter than his six-foot tall sibling, but his breadth was astonishing. The muscles of his chest and arms rippled through almost any clothing he chose, and the triangularity of his physique had turned as many young women's heads as Rebecca's willowy height and sinewy elegance had turned young men's.

Like Matt Clark, Luke Manguson had served his country for five years as a naval officer. In Luke's case, this had meant service in the Royal Navy, and his service, unlike Matt's, had included the sort of prolonged and specialized training that had proven indispensable during the danger-laden adventures of the past two summers. Royal Navy Lieutenant Manguson had been selected early in his career to serve as an officer-leader of ship-to-ship boarding parties. This entailed a small, elite team's forcing its way onto hostile decks, often at night, not infrequently in the face of determined resistance. Hand-to-hand fighting was the rule rather than the exception. Firearms, more often than not, played a minor role or no role whatever.

And so Luke's skill in the nonlethal use of force to penetrate defended positions of all kinds, and in the planning and reconnaissance necessary to bring an effective plan to its maturity, had proven to be crucial during the previous two summers' crises. Luke had been relied upon by Rebecca, Matt, and the others involved to spearhead both the planning and the implementation of each divine charge delivered to them via Rebecca's visions.

Andrea found herself staring at the chiseled features of her host. Then she realized with a start that he had been speaking to her.

She shook her head at him, smiling through her embarrassment. *"Per favore?"* she asked.

"I was just saying, Andrea, that I am honored to be in the company of the great detective's daughter. We are gratified that he has chosen to involve himself in efforts to protect our great friend, Dr. Chapel, and to ask you to conduct surveillance of Rebecca's and Matt's home. Thank you."

She beamed at him, her pride in her father and his reputation again bursting from her. *"Grazie, signore . . . grazie."* She looked down at her hands, still smiling delightedly at the effusive words of admiration from Luke Manguson.

Luke then turned his eyes to his sister and waited. He had known from the urgency in her voice on the telephone that once more they were to be called into action. He assumed that, again, Rebecca's great gift would be, at least in part, the vehicle for their summons. His face was alive with a mixture of eagerness and tension, but he did not speak further. He knew his sister.

He knew she would speak when she was ready.

CHAPTER FIVE

SAN FRANCISCO/BERKELEY: 2:05 PM/FRIDAY
NEW YORK: 5:05 PM/FRIDAY
LONDON: 10:05 PM/FRIDAY
ROME: 11:05 PM/FRIDAY

REBECCA OPENED THE SESSION BY "EXPLAINING ANDREA" more fully to her brother. In the telling, she placed her emphasis not upon the details of the famous detective's assignment of his daughter to surveillance, nor even upon the reported threats to Eleanor Chapel, facets of the situation she had outlined to him by telephone. She placed the weight of her explanation instead upon the daughter's unwillingness to speak the name of the person who, Rebecca was intuitively certain, stood behind and above the threat to Dr. Chapel.

The Italian woman appeared to listen to this monologue stoically, or perhaps not at all. Her eyes were not on the speaker, and it seemed that her mind might not be either.

Luke nodded repeatedly as Rebecca spoke. When his sister passionately concluded the first segment of her report with the phrase, " . . . the ancient Enemy's unceasing efforts to eviscerate the body of Christ," his eyes narrowed and his jaw hardened, but he shook his head in response to her raised eyebrows and murmured quietly, "No, dear . . . no questions yet . . . please go on."

Andrea Camposanto had, in fact, given up immediately on her tentative resolve, despite her limited mastery of English, to follow Rebecca's conceptually sophisticated explanation. As soon as she had surrendered in that effort, she rather happily began to drink in every feature of the look and manner of the fabled Luke Manguson, sitting just eight feet away from her, concentrating on his sister's every word and inflection. Andrea found herself staring openly at him despite her unexamined awareness that Luke could hardly be blind to her impropriety. At least, she hoped that her naked stare would be interpreted by him—by all three of them—as mere impropriety.

Why, she thought to herself as Rebecca developed her story to Luke, did everyone seem to speak of the sister as the physically astonishing one? Yes, certainly, Rebecca Clark was as exquisitely beautiful as any woman on earth, but her brother. . . . It was *he* who bespoke angelic presence to Andrea Camposanto: a rugged Old Testament goodness, purity, and physicality coupled somehow with the suggestion of "threat most formidable" to any evil unfortunate enough to trespass upon his spiritual or familial territory.

So she continued to gape, fascinated and captivated. And she found herself beginning to smile. So much had happened in this day. Could this still be the same day that began an eternity ago with her pulling her rental sedan into position across the street from the Clarks' flat? It seemed impossible. Yet here she was, seated in the presence not only of the supreme ensnarer, but also in the presence of the ensnarer's storied twin brother, in some ways even more awe-inspiring than his sister.

But now Rebecca had paused, listened to Luke's short response, and had begun speaking again. Now her subject was the early morning vision that had imposed itself on her sleeping mind an hour before Andrea Camposanto had arrived to establish her pre-dawn surveillance. Rebecca had begun to speak much more slowly and simply, wanting her captive-turned-guest to understand as much as she possibly could.

Looking alternately at her brother and at the woman, Rebecca took them both through the vision's taut sequence of images, her husband providing the several embellishments he had managed to elicit from her during their early morning dialogue. Even so, she took only minutes to provide this sketch for her rapt audience, eager as she remained to stress the *fact* of the vision over its details. Even at this stage of the incipient crisis, Rebecca, her husband, and her brother knew full well that it was the *occurrence* of the supernatural intervention that carried the importance.

For the vision, they knew, was but a harbinger. It had provided the opening scene in the first act of a drama that, no doubt as before, would prove itself to be at once holy and terrible. The vision had not given its recipient a specific command to specific action. The critical message, for the moment, was simply the fact of the vision. And that central, awful fact was certainly enough. It affected the four of them profoundly, each quite differently from the other three.

The young Roman had felt almost immediately a return of the near-paralyzing fear that had consumed her more than once that long day. She knew, of course, that she was in the presence of the seer. But to hear the supernatural images described by the voice of the seer herself was newly terrifying. Consequently Andrea Camposanto's mind was able to process nothing of what she heard. Her hands shook, her lips quivered, her breath came in short gasps.

Matt Clark found himself struggling, to his great disappointment, with a range of fears and hopes and thrills hardly different from those he had encountered two years before, when he had been a new Christian caught up in something far more alien and disorienting than anything he had faced in his five years with the U.S. military. Now, as then, he sought desperately to ground himself as he knew Rebecca and Luke always did with such apparent ease.

He found, however, that he could not. And he found that now that they were in Luke Manguson's company, his sense of inadequacy in the face of imminent threat was multiplied. Alone that morning with Rebecca, he had been the voice of calm and assured reason. Now, face-to-face with Luke, he felt only his sense of Christian cowardice, his persistent inclination to relapse into his pre-Christian reliance on his own resources, meager and fragile, rather than what he knew to be the Source of all courage. He looked at the floor and shook his head in abject self-recrimination. A *fair-weather Christian,* he thought to himself. Always unready for the storm. Pathetic . . . inexcusably pathetic. . . .

Luke Manguson was not an introspective man. Like his sister, he was oriented always toward action. Unlike her, he did not tend to work through the complexities and subtleties of a problem prior to shifting into his planning-for-action mentality. It was not that he had not the capacity for such. His intellectual acuity was indeed at Rebecca's level. But through natural inclination, and as well, through long-standing practice, he habitu-ally moved in a straight line to identify and isolate threats of any and all kinds, whether in the form of a flawed understanding of some calculation bedeviling one of the boys whom he taught daily in his neighborhood's Anglican junior school, or an unidentified radar contact seen on the screen of one of the Royal Navy ships on which he had served. Or this. His mind was already racing to establish connections between his sister's vision and the imminent threat to Professor Eleanor Chapel implied by the Italian detective's involvement with the Old Testament scholar. And implied as well, intriguingly and ominously, by the Camposantos' purposeful and calculated engagement of Rebecca, Matt, and Luke in the developing drama.

Alone among the four, Rebecca Manguson Clark was focused upon the possible linkages among the suggested threats to Dr. Chapel, her newly received vision, and the last two years' month-of-June crises. Yes, the central perpetrator in the first instance was dead. She—and she alone among them—had witnessed Meredith Lancaster's execution. But she and her colleagues had known all along that others had been involved in that first crisis, and that some of them were Americans, or at least had operated from American soil. And in the second instance, there had never at any time been real clarity regarding the mastermind behind the interconnected plots they had faced. Certain leaders had been jailed, true, including Cameron Stafford, Matt Clark's mentor and Eleanor Chapel's colleague. But there was at least one other who seemed at times to outrank Stafford. They had never been able to place him in an organizational universe, though he had at one time provided his name, Edward Jamieson, to Matt. Rather, he had provided *a* name to Matt. But the truth was this: Edward Jamieson's actual identity and role had never been determined to anyone's satisfaction.

Finally Rebecca looked up from her eyes-downcast study of the past and the present. No one had spoken for some time. The others, lost in their own thoughts, awaited her next question, instruction, or observation.

She looked at Matt to see if he had anything further to add for Luke's edification. He shook his head, and then she made the same silent inquiry of Andrea Camposanto. The Italian turned her palms upward and shrugged, a small smile on her face, a gesture both of acceptance and futility. She was aware that she had been privy to a firsthand account, albeit in a language which she understood imperfectly, of something that, had it been spoken in any other company or uttered by any other person, would have seemed so strange as to be laughable. In this setting it was not laughable. It was overwhelming.

Finally Rebecca turned back to Luke, leaned forward, smiled, and reached forward to squeeze her brother's hand. Then she sat back and nodded to him.

He spoke immediately, his intensity and clarity still further spellbinding the detective's daughter, whose eyes once more could move to no other face but his. "The old-line *Congressus Evangelicus* leaders," said Luke, "with their obvious vested interests—financial and other—in their draft position statement, comprise the most obvious of the potentially injured parties, should Dr. Chapel's views prevail. Yes?"

His twin nodded her assent.

"And yet, you believe, Rebecca, that Detective Camposanto and his daughter, although they may indeed be concerned about those mostly Italian . . . gentlemen, are in fact far more concerned about someone else . . . someone whom the daughter will not name? Yes?"

Rebecca looked at the Italian and replied in the affirmative, while Andrea Camposanto dropped her eyes in humiliation at the transparency of her cowardice. Playing the coward in front of Rebecca Clark had been difficult enough; this was very nearly unbearable. Her eyes on the floor, she shook her head and said nothing.

Luke paused, his head turned to one side, his distantly focused gaze an inverted reflection of the concentration he maintained on the central question.

When he turned back to his sister, he spoke to her through eyes that had become little more than slits. She knew this look from having witnessed his protective anger a thousand times over their years together. The look meant that he was already straining toward a hypothesis.

"So, aside from the old-line *Congressus* leaders, Rebecca, who stands to lose . . . whose interests stand to suffer . . . who will become the injured parties, should Dr. Chapel's views prevail? Do we know?"

"No," she replied immediately. "We do not know. And the truth is that right now, Luke, we don't even know the core issue. The draft position statement, I understand, has not been treated by the *Congressus* steering committee as secret, and has possibly been published, but I know nothing of it.

"I can only surmise this: since the *Congressus Evangelicus III* theme deals with leadership, power, and organizational structures, and since so many of the committee members are themselves seminary faculty and administration, seminary training in all corners of the world and across all traditions within the faith must be a primary focus of the statement. If so, the stakes must be high, as Detective Belton would say, beyond anything we here in this little room can possibly imagine. And Andrea has told us that Dr. Chapel has become endangered through her advocacy of some unpopular—or, if not unpopular, at least unfavored—perspective."

To Andrea Camposanto's surprise, Rebecca then smiled at her brother. The smile seemed actually mischievous, though nothing in the tone of the exchange had suggested anything but high drama to that point.

"Do we strike out for California in the morning, Luke?" said Rebecca, the enigmatic smile still lighting her face and compressing the long facial scar intriguingly. "Or are you going to explain to us that this is another trap—the bait for Evil's hook—a fresh attempt to bag the lot of us by luring us to a would-be rescue that will finally prove our undoing?"

Here she actually laughed aloud in her light contralto at the same moment that Luke scowled at her in mock indignation. He shook his head at her, then sat back in his chair and rolled his eyes toward the ceiling, breaking into a broad grin despite himself. "You have no more respect for your brother's high wisdom now than you did when we were ten, do you, dear?"

He turned to Matt. "Your wife is every bit as annoying as a grown-up as she was as a brat of a little sister, Matt. Can't you get her under control?"

At this all four burst into new laughter, even Andrea Camposanto, who, though she was unsure about the nature of the joke, could see that her companions were happy somehow. Accordingly, her own laughter was the genuine laughter of one who is able to appreciate joy and affection, whether finding it intellectually comprehensible or not.

The "little" sister then rose from her chair, took two swift steps forward, bent down, and enveloped her "big" twin brother in a ferociously exaggerated bear hug. In a stage whisper in his ear, she said loudly, "So, do *you* telephone the Royal Air Force now to persuade your colleagues there that they should make room for two Navy reserve officers and their companions on a military flight to the U.S. in the morning, or does Matt make the call?"

Luke chuckled. Then, after a pause during which Rebecca released him and stood before him, he looked up at her and said, "Rebecca, the first call needs to be to Dr. Chapel in California. We need information from her, and we have information to give her." Here he looked at Andrea and nodded.

"After that," he added, "I'll call the RAF."

As Rebecca laughingly threw her arms around her brother's neck late Friday evening in London, Eleanor Chapel sat at her desk in California and ruminated prayerfully about the situation. Her husband's phone call had thrilled her to her toes. Childlike, she had jumped and clapped her hands, her musical, high laughter filling her small office to overflowing. Then, glancing at her watch, she had scooped up her notepad and hastened toward the closed office door that opened onto the second floor hallway of the PSR administration building. The faculty meeting would by now be approaching its first afternoon break, and she wanted at least to get a sense of the debate.

She reached for the doorknob, still chortling in joyous anticipation of Sidney Belton's late evening arrival. But as her fingers neared the door, she froze, arm and hand outstretched.

An observer might have guessed that she had just remembered something important, or had just changed her mind about going to the faculty meeting, or had just realized that she had neglected to tell her husband something and was considering trying to reach him at the airport before he boarded his flight. But it was none of these that had stopped her so suddenly.

A thought had been, as she loved to say, "thrown at her brain." Nothing dramatic on the order, say, of Rebecca Manguson Clark's visions. No stupendous forecasts, no cryptic warnings, no thunderous commands. Not that, certainly.

But in their own way, messages that were just as clearly the Holy Spirit's workings within her as any cataclysmic vision ever delivered to Rebecca Clark. And, as Eleanor Chapel knew well, Rebecca herself—whether in actual prayer or not—routinely experienced the Holy Spirit's leading in this same ordinary fashion, countless times and in countless venues, throughout her life. Messages that were small, yet clear. Messages that, unlike the great visions, could, at least in a sense, be studiously ignored, provided one were determined to regard them as "whims" or "stray ideas" or "odd promptings" . . . and, if ignored often and consistently enough, perhaps then harder and harder to perceive under any circumstances at all . . . until at length, one might succeed in becoming hardened, calloused, armored . . . encased so thickly that only a colossal shattering, precipitated either by disastrous life events or by God's overwhelming shafts or both, could penetrate the fortification.

For perhaps twenty full seconds, Eleanor Chapel stood motionless, her right hand nearly touching the doorknob. Then, slowly, her hand fell away to her side and she turned back toward her desk. Crossing the room thoughtfully, she circled the desk and sat down. Then she leaned forward, placed her elbows on the desk surface, and bowed her head until her forehead rested lightly in her open hands. In that position she began to pray silently.

After several minutes she looked up. Deliberately, she then turned to a blank page in the folder that she kept with her, and after a moment, lifted her pen from the desk.

Less than five minutes later, as she wrote steadily in her fluid script, the telephone on her desk rang again. This time the voice on the other end of the line was that of Rebecca Manguson Clark in London.

The two women spoke for fifteen minutes, exchanging information and encouragement. At length they hung up, each of them thoughtful at the other's words, and one preparing immediately for action.

SAN FRANCISCO/BERKELEY: 3:10 PM/FRIDAY
NEW YORK: 6:10 PM/FRIDAY
LONDON: 11:10 PM/FRIDAY
ROME: 12:10 AM/SATURDAY

The faculty of Pacific School of Religion was startled some time later when, having reassembled at the conclusion of the first afternoon break, it found itself watching the distinguished visiting professor of Old

Testament purposefully scurry into the meeting room from the doorway at the front. Latecomers habitually entered faculty meetings from the rear, slinking to their seat or not, according to the sense of embarrassment or privilege they happened to feel. Observing Dr. Eleanor Chapel at this moment produced surprise among the faculty members for two reasons. First, her tardiness of more than two full hours was itself a novelty. Some had begun over the spring semester actually to check their watches for accuracy in concert with the moment of her arrival at any meeting.

Second, she had not only entered the room from the front, but having taken several steps toward the podium from which the dean held forth, she had there, in front of all, come to a dead stop. There she remained, facing him, still and quiet, requesting—perhaps demanding—the floor both with her stance and with her eyes.

The dean's voice gradually trailed off. He looked inquiringly in her direction. "Dr. Chapel?" he said tentatively. "Is there something . . .?"

She did not reply directly. She simply said, "Thank you," as though he had formally yielded the floor. Then, turning to face the faculty, she began to speak, her voice clear and high, confident and unwavering.

She made no apologies. She simply began.

"Because my home is in New York, because my seminary is in New York, because you have been so generous as to take me into your organizational family for a semester, I have spoken my mind in our meetings rather less often than my colleagues in Manhattan have come over the years to expect. Less often, in fact, than I myself would have thought possible from my decades-long track record as a dyed-in-gray-wool contrarian."

Here she paused while a good natured rumble of appreciative and respectful laughter rippled through the meeting room.

"I think that many of you believe," she continued momentarily, "because of my semester-long reticence, that you know at least the general shape of my thoughts vis-à-vis the *Congressus Evangelicus* position statement . . . and, if I am not mistaken, about many other things as well.

"I will be leaving you soon. But before I do—and even, as you see, before this faculty meeting moves to its conclusion and certainly before the *Congressus* steering committee convenes this evening—I wish to tell you what I think, fully and completely."

She paused again, glanced at the dean, and waited while he, without a word, stepped away from the podium and resumed his seat. He kept his eyes fastened on her, as did everyone else in the room. She did not move to the podium, but resumed her monologue from the spot at which she had stopped upon interrupting the session. Her hands were at her sides, a small folder of notes in her right, nothing in her left. The faded tennis shoes squeaked briefly while she pivoted to face the faculty squarely, the drab gray of her neatly tailored suit and the matching gray of her luxurious but tightly bound hair brightened by the trademark splash of red silk scarf.

"I think this," she said in her bell-clear voice. "The education of Christian seminarians around the world is a precious and holy charge. Precious and holy. In fact, it is, I have always contended, more closely akin to bearing and raising a child—something I confess I have never had the chance to do—than to anything else to which I can compare it.

"We seek now—we, the *Congressus* leaders—to formulate a statement that, whether we wish it or not, will be studied closely by seminary faculties around the world. Some will adopt its conclusions wholesale. Others will adopt its main ideas. Others will study the statement and reject it. And still others . . . I can't guess how many . . . will simply ignore the statement.

"Those seminaries that adopt the *Congressus* statement wholesale and those that more selectively adopt its main ideas can be expected to number in the several thousand. The individual seminarians who will thereby be influenced by the *Congressus* position statement will number in the many thousands, and conceivably, over the years and decades, in the hundreds of thousands. And the number of individual Christians—church members— eventually to be taught and influenced by these seminary graduates over those same decades and, via these new traditions, over the centuries. . . ."

She stopped and looked down. A sudden sadness seemed to emanate from her downturned face. One could not be certain she was not crying.

The room was silent. The faculty was riveted. No one moved. No chair squeaked. No foot shuffled. No pen scratched. It seemed that no one breathed.

Eleanor Chapel looked up and took a deep breath, a barely audible sigh escaping her lips. Her blue-green eyes were dry.

"The professional life of a seminary professor . . ." and here she looked lovingly around the room, seeming to affix every member individually with a visual caress, ". . . is extraordinary in its demands. We are expected by others to be scholars . . . and indeed we expect that of ourselves . . . at the same time that we are expected to maintain an energetic and exemplary commitment—spiritual, behavioral, even organizational—to our Lord and Savior . . . to Him whom we purport to serve every moment of our lives.

"Yet the two do not always mix easily."

Her eyes continued to survey the room thoughtfully.

"Some of us," she resumed after a moment, "begin every class meeting with prayer. Then, having just engaged the Lord of the Universe with our words and minds and hearts, we open our texts and our Scriptures and begin to perform scholarly analysis that is pertinent to the very Supernature—the divine Trinity—that we dared to address in our prayers just seconds before. The *hubris* implicit in that act of scholarship is staggering, and yet we believe that this is, indeed, our calling. It is our vocation to prepare spiritual *and* academic masters, church leaders who can serve their flocks and at the same time write and speak with informed authority about Holy Scripture and its implications for our lives.

"How do we reconcile these two shafts in the daily and hourly practice of our vocation? How do we dare to inspect and scrutinize that to which we bow the knee and toward which we prostrate ourselves in supplication and obedience? How do we muster the reverential arrogance needed to study that which we worship at the same time that we cloak ourselves in humility commensurate with the inadequacy of our scholarly tools—our necessarily limited brains and nervous systems—to address and, in some sense, to measure and to assess the activity, the messages, and the historic and current purposes of Almighty God?"

Again she paused, the bright eyes scanning the room, her face somber.

"My answer to my own question is that too many of us do this badly, and not just badly, but dangerously. By that I mean that too many of us err on the side of a secularized and unholy scholarship, unable to find the middle ground . . . the *only* ground."

She paused, glanced down at the notes held in her right hand, and resumed immediately. "Seduced by the success of our secular academic kindred—secular sociologists, psychologists, semanticists, philologists, historians, philosophers, biologists, chemists, physicists, astronomers, epidemiologists—whose research targets do not include Supernature, or perhaps better, whose research targets can be pursued *as though* Supernature were not layered into their data, we adopt their premises, employ their methods, and sometimes, draw their conclusions . . . for the former will result in the latter as often as not.

"As for us, members of the seminary professoriate—whether our chosen disciplines are in the Testaments themselves or in any of the derived studies: theology, ethics, history, Christian education, pastoral counseling— we, all of us, go to our sources seeking direction.

"My own field is Old Testament. If I lead my students into my field's original sources, as I do almost daily, we may together on any given day examine a passage traditionally suggesting a divine hand on the reins at a critical moment, a divine hand that led an individual or a group toward a life-changing decision or action."

She glanced down again at her notes, then looked up.

"For example, we may trace Ruth's dogged and touching allegiance to Naomi. We may analyze the details of Ruth's subsequent marriage to Boaz. We may study the marriage's recorded lineage. And in the process, we may immerse ourselves in the intricacies of Jewish law and custom and in the minutiae of transfers of Jewish property and obligation. If that is *all* we attempt, we may elevate ourselves, in our own minds, to the imagined level of our secular peers, thus proving to ourselves that we are *scholars*. And we may thereby duly impress our students, our colleagues, and our administrators—or so we think.

"But to what end?"

The blue-green eyes searched the room. "Have we deepened the *holiness* of the material for the future clergy who study at our feet? Has their Christianity been enriched by a renewed sense of awe at the Lord God's continuous sculpting of our common history?

"Do the seminarians in my Old Testament courses revel in the Holy Spirit's ancient activity? Are their hearts filled with a joyous confidence in God's historic and inevitable purposes, or with His holy persistence in the long preparation of a people and of a world for His incarnation in the person of Jesus Christ?

"Or have I simply emptied the Book of Ruth—in the example I have chosen—of every trace of the Living God, leaving little but the shattered fragments of a scholarship pursued without reverence, without humility, without faith, without prayer, and without the clarity furnished by Christ's eternally transforming lens? Have I, in fact, applied secular research premises, methods, and instruments to material so inherently and supernaturally powerful that the material simply breaks the instruments in my hands, leaving my students holding nothing more than brittle splinters and isolated shards of meaning?"

She glanced down again at her notes, paused, then raised them nearer her face and read aloud. "C. S. Lewis once wrote, 'The great spirit you so lightly invoked . . . is present: not a senile benevolence that drowsily wishes you to be happy . . . not the cold philanthropy of a conscientious magistrate, nor the care of a host who feels responsible for the comfort of his guests, but *the consuming fire Himself . . . persistent . . . despotic . . . jealous, inexorable, exacting. . . .*'"

Then came a surprise. As she tried to continue, her voice suddenly caught in her throat. She stammered briefly, attempted several times to go on, and fell silent. She looked down, gave her notes for the moment to a solicitous colleague who sat nearly at her feet, moved her index fingers up to and under her small spectacles, and wiped brimming pools of tears from each eye. She swallowed, looked up, and accepted the return of her folder with a small smile and a nod.

Only then did she realize that the dean was at her side, seeming to tower over her although he was of no more than average height. He patted her lightly on the shoulder in a movement at once so clumsy and so heartfelt that every faculty member present was moved by the administrator's incongruous coupling of adolescent ineptitude and brave compassion. Then, with equal unease and embarrassment, he turned and walked back to his chair, lowering himself awkwardly into his seat.

After another moment, the rapt audience heard Eleanor Chapel's voice rising again. It was the same strong voice with which she had begun: high and clear, floating above the heads of those present on angelic wings and descending to their ears as lightly as an early morning prelude to the sun's heraldic interruption of the darkness. The bright, blue-green eyes, peering with a fresh and youthful exuberance over the small eyeglasses, held the assembly helplessly captive.

"And now," she said, " . . . and now comes *Congressus Evangelicus III* and its eagerly awaited—or dreaded—position statement, a roughly one-hundred-word pronouncement, like its two predecessors, crafted to be both memorable and of long-lasting and worldwide impact. You have all seen and contemplated the draft statement, both unofficially and officially released by the steering committee.

"And so, having seen the freely circulated draft, and having just listened to my preamble, you can each, I've no doubt, readily summarize my viewpoint, can you not?" She paused, smiled, and continued. "Yes. You can. But I, inveterate explainer that I am, will provide my own words.

"My view is this: An emphasis in seminary curricula on financial and organizational power bases will tip the scales so far in the direction of the secular perspective that the most successful and influential church leaders will be those *who are not Christians at all,* and who can, therefore, move unencumbered—that is to say, without a Christian frame of reference constraining them theologically and ethically—through the mine fields represented by money, power, fame, property, and political and social influence. And they will lead the churches, one by one, in the direction of something that, at this moment, most of us cannot so much as begin to imagine: that is, the church-without-worship, the church-without-sacrament, the church that exists solely to provide community service and to influence public policy. The yardstick for a church pastor's success will be primarily financial, the measurement of accumulated assets and those assets' judicious use in support of communities and causes.

"That very yardstick is, in fact, already the essential measure of success for many churches, despite their disclaimers."

She stopped to survey the small sea of astonished faces before her, some literally with mouths agape, others shaking their heads in the first milliseconds of mounting outrage, and others simply staring in disbelief. For a moment she appeared ready to exit through the doorway from which she had emerged minutes earlier, her statement completed. But then she seemed to reconsider and, having tentatively moved toward the doorway, turned back and prepared to offer an impromptu addendum.

"Think, please," she said softly, her voice nonetheless carrying easily to the rear of the meeting room, "of any of the great figures in our tradition."

She paused. "Choose *any,*" she insisted.

"Moses . . . Isaiah . . . John the Baptist . . . Paul. . . . Choose *any.* Recall to your mind the names of your own favorites. The men and women of our deep history . . . our more recent history . . . our current greats. . . ."

She smiled.

"Did they not have in common, above all, a certain divine energy . . . an uncompromising commitment to their individual ministries . . . a clarity rooted in their individual summonses to obedience. . . . Yes. Yes. And if our seminaries succeed at anything that actually matters from the perspective of eternity, then they must first succeed in multiplying the commitment and the sense of commission that individual Christian seminarians bring with them to their studies, so that each one of them may live a life that is, above all, awash in the Holy Spirit's mountainous and purifying waters."

At the word "awash," she made a small gesture with her left hand. Coming from one so small and heretofore so still, the gesture seemed to flow over her audience like a wave of fresh baptismal water. And then it was gone.

"And if that is done, and done *well*," she concluded, "then we may dare to teach our seminarians anything we choose that may be pertinent to church leadership, yes . . . even including, I've no doubt, concepts related to such things as 'contemporary financial investment policies and principles.' But—you must hear me on this—if such concepts are put first . . . or even second or third or fourth . . . if accumulation of wealth and property and power lies at the center, then the only hope for our churches is that good Christian people will set their minds to ignore us . . . and to ignore our graduates."

Again it appeared to her audience that she was about to make for the door. But again she halted, faced her colleagues fully, squared her small shoulders, and added only this: "Each of you remembers that the Lord God called to the boy Samuel. And each of you remembers that Samuel replied in the words we all know. *'Speak, for Thy servant is listening.'* Let nothing we may say or do seek to replace God's call with anything smaller than the greatness of His own voice. For the Old and New Testament lessons are for us unmistakable on this point of holy discipleship: *If it is fundamentally power and authority and position that our seminarians seek, they must find the seminary door closed.*

"And it is we who must close the door, and hold it fast shut until they come seeking something else, and that something else only: holiness and service, and—yes, quite possibly—*something very like poverty*, all in the name of Jesus Christ our Lord and Savior."

Chapter Six

AN HOUR AFTER ELEANOR CHAPEL CONCLUDED HER remarks to the Pacific School of Religion faculty, more than six thousand miles to the east of her, on a darkened street in the ancient city of Rome, a jet black Rolls Royce Phantom V Park Ward touring limousine with right-hand drive pulled up noiselessly behind an equally black, left-hand drive Mercedes-Benz 600 sedan.

After a moment, three dark-clad figures emerged from the Rolls and two more from the Benz. The five moved together through the affluent neighborhood's only alleyway, arriving after a short walk at a high, vertical wood-plank fence. The fence, they knew, encircled a modest, grassy expanse that provided a tidy play area for children. It had been constructed two years earlier with painstaking attention to detail by the home's owner for his two children and their friends. The gate's simple latch-and-lock mechanism had been designed to be operated only from the inside, but proved the work of only a moment for the visitors.

Obviously familiar with the layout of the yard and of the house itself, the five proceeded confidently to the wall-mounted, ground-level, metal-encased box through which both power and telephone lines passed into the basement of the house. After two minutes' work to sever the home's only link to the outside world, the five moved to a nearby basement window. One of their number then swiftly manipulated a glass-cutting implement that included a small suction cup placed snugly against the pane, and having quickly cut and removed the single pane, reached inside to release the locking device. Two of his colleagues then raised the window sufficiently to admit each of the five singly.

Once inside, they proceeded with the same assured confidence to the basement stairwell. At the top of the stairs, they gathered tightly together in the large kitchen, and standing stock still, listened for two full minutes.

Upstairs, Mario Angelini, restive even at one-thirty on a Saturday morning, had heard the faintest suggestion of a metallic click through the open rear window of his and his wife's second-floor bedroom. Rising quickly and looking out the back, he had seen faintly the shadows of figures moving across his back yard. He had then crossed swiftly to Anna's side of the bed and, in the dim light provided by the small night light near the telephone, had begun to dial an emergency number.

Anna's eyes had then flown open in instantaneous terror and Mario had quickly placed an index finger to her lips, urging her to silence. Then he had waited in grim agony as the rotary dial clacked its slow way back into position after each number had been dialed.

Finally, blessedly, he heard the ringing sound in his ear. One ring . . . two rings . . . and the phone went dead.

Absolute silence blanketed the room, the house, and the neighborhood.

Anna threw the covers aside, rose, and together the two glided wordlessly into the hallway, and without prearrangement, moved singly to each child's bedroom. They returned in seconds, Mario cradling the sleepy daughter, Anna carrying the squirming son. They paused at the top of the stairs, listened and looked, heard and saw nothing, and descended rapidly to the small foyer.

Mario, holding Maria in the crook of one arm, reached for the deadbolt slide on the front door, moved it gently, and then heard behind him a muffled scream. Turning his head, he glimpsed dark figures swarming toward them. He tried to cry out.

It was too late.

San Francisco/Berkeley: 9:00 pm/Friday
New York: 12:00 am/Saturday
London: 5:00 am/Saturday
Rome: 6:00 am/Saturday

Sidney Belton paced impatiently back and forth through the small living room in his wife's compact apartment on Scenic Avenue, having arrived by taxi from the San Francisco Airport less than half an hour before. Nervously watching the former NYPD detective, seated in one corner of the room in a straight-backed wooden chair, his shadow-turned-captive-turned-colleague cowered in silence.

As with his daughter in London, Antonio Camposanto had placed this miserable young man, his soon-to-be son-in-law, in position to provide amateur surveillance on the eminent New York City private detective. He had done this in the certain knowledge that the shadow would quickly be converted into, first, a suspect, and then, after interrogation, into one whose protection could be most efficiently guaranteed by the original object of the surveillance. The ploy had worked to perfection twice now, once on each side of the Atlantic.

At five minutes after the hour, the telephone rang in Eleanor Chapel's apartment and Sid Belton moved immediately to lift the receiver with his good arm and hand. "Belton!" he barked into the phone with the same New York City brusqueness he had honed for two decades as the NYPD's premier detective.

Hearing nothing, he said again, even more sharply, "Belton!"

"Ah," came the rich, deep, rumbling response, "you have arrived safely, my friend."

"Detective Camposanto?" said Belton. "Where are ya?"

"Please, *signore*," came the reply. "Please exit the building at the rear. I will come to you by automobile in three minutes. And, *per favore*, please bring young Giuseppe along with you, *si?*"

"Okay," said Belton, "but are y'sure you wanna have the young man along on this? He might be better off just. . . ."

He heard a click on the other end of the line.

Fifteen minutes later, the three men—the two detectives and their anxious, bewildered young associate—waited in Antonio Camposanto's rental sedan fifty feet from a flight of steps marking the border of the opposite side of the PSR campus from Eleanor Chapel's apartment. The steering committee meeting was being held on this Friday evening in the PSR administration building, and Antonio Camposanto had asked the committee chairwoman to exit on the side away from her home, toward the Bay, explaining that he would be better able to remain unobserved from that position. Eleanor Chapel had made clear that she expected the meeting to end at 9:30. In her role as co-chair, she was usually able to start and end meetings at very close to their scheduled times.

The men were not disappointed. At 9:35, they observed Eleanor Chapel and a handful of other committee members walking down the steps toward the near sidewalk. They watched as she said good night to her colleagues, turned away from them, and hurried toward the car. As she neared the vehicle, she heard the impossibly deep voice from the driver's seat directing her away. "No, *signora*," said Antonio Camposanto quietly through the car window, "continue past us to the corner and wait. We will come to you."

SAN FRANCISCO/BERKELEY: 11:07 PM/FRIDAY
NEW YORK: 2:07 AM/SATURDAY
LONDON: 7:07 AM/SATURDAY
ROME: 8:07 AM/SATURDAY

Standing in his London kitchen completing cold breakfast preparations for his overnight house guests, Luke Manguson lifted the telephone receiver before the second ring. "Yes?" he said tersely.

"Luke? Sid Belton here, in California. Everything okay there? Good.

"Listen, Luke," Belton continued, "when Rebecca called Eleanor earlier, she said you were all gonna go to the air base this morning, headed for California. That right? Yeah? Don't do it, Luke. Don't come to the U.S. at all. We got a change in situation. We got a big change.

"Y'got a pencil, Luke?"

In his rough, clipped Brooklynese, Belton proceeded to outline the fresh developments. Detective Antonio Camposanto had just been notified by his staff in Rome that, overnight, Eleanor Chapel's niece Anna, her husband Mario, and their two children had been taken forcibly from their home. Mario had been executed in their back yard with a bullet to his head, fired at point-blank range.

A message later telephoned to the Rome police by the kidnappers had been explicit: the children were sequestered in Rome, their mother elsewhere. Their ransom demand was not for money. Their demand was that Eleanor Chapel remove herself entirely from the *Congressus* proceedings, that she return immediately to New York City, that she sever all ties with the steering committee, and that she place herself under a sort of house arrest, moving only between her New York home and office, until *Congressus III* was over.

There was more. The press—Italian or American or other—was not to be notified. Even the steering committee itself was not to be notified, except of the obvious fact of Dr. Chapel's having been called unexpectedly back to New York. Further, Dr. Chapel's husband, the formidable Sidney Belton, was to remain uninvolved in the case. And in a startling development, Rebecca Clark was to travel from London to Rome forthwith. Once on her way there, she would be given instructions regarding the children's location. They would be released into her custody, and into her custody only.

There was no mention of Anna Angelini's fate or future.

There was one further surprising piece of news. Antonio Camposanto's younger daughter, Sophia, a Roman in her early twenties, had also been kidnapped as part of the same operation. No further details would be supplied regarding the two kidnapped women, the police had been informed, until *Congressus III* had ended.

Luke, writing furiously, asked the detective to slow down several times, but otherwise said nothing until Belton finished his summary. He then scanned his notes, nodded to himself, and said simply. "Detective, what do you make of all this?"

"Well, Luke, the fact that Mario Angelini was murdered tells me that these tackling dummies aren't foolin' around, y'know what I mean?"

"Yes, sir, Detective," responded Luke Manguson with a smile at this sudden reacquaintance with the street-level vocabulary and unique speaking style of Sidney Belton.

"Beyond that," Belton continued, "I gotta tell ya that Antonio Camposanto is a mess . . . a complete mess . . . because this grade-school ploy of his—y'know, puttin' his family members on stakeouts when they don't know what in the world they're doin'—has finally backfired on him."

There was a brief pause.

Luke spoke again. "What do you mean, Detective? Andrea Camposanto is with us, as you know from Rebecca's call to your wife. Was his other daughter—Sophia, you said—on some sort of surveillance when this happened?"

"Yeah, Luke. Right. Forgot to explain that part.

"Antonio put the older daughter on Rebecca and Matt, and he put the younger daughter on Eleanor's family in Rome—the Angelinis—and he put Sophia's fiancé, Giuseppe something-or-other, on *me*, if you can believe it."

"What? Some amateur was watching *you*, Detective?"

"Yeah. For about five minutes. Nearly bloodied him good before I figured out what was goin' on. Anyway, Antonio's big plan, to get these young women and the fiancé under some kind of protection by us, worked okay, I guess, with the older daughter you've got with you, and with this doofus that was followin' me. But Antonio seemed to think that Sophia would be safe, because she was watchin' the Angelinis in company with two of his best men on the Rome police force. I really don't know what happened there, and I don't know if he lost the two men in all this. I just know the little that I said a minute ago."

Another pause ensued.

"Can you make sense out of this idea that Rebecca is to collect the children from the kidnappers, Detective?" said Luke, incredulity in his voice. "I'm trying to grasp the reasoning there. Is there any?"

"Any what, Luke?"

"Any reasoning."

"Yeah, Luke, there's reasoning. These low-life types we're dealin' with here obviously want Eleanor out of the way of the *Congressus* goings-on. But they wanna give her just enough hope, y'know, that they'll actually return her family members—the three that are still alive, that is—without any further damage, y'know what I mean? They want her to start thinkin' in terms of at least a *show* of cooperation on her part. See what I'm gettin' at? They kill Mr. Angelini, makin' sure we know they're tough. Then they take this humanitarian step of offerin' to get the children into safe arms. They want Eleanor to start *thinkin'*, y'know? To start weighin' one thing against another.

"I gotta admit, it's not a bad approach, Luke. So, sure . . . there's plenty of reasoning goin' on over there."

Belton paused for a moment, then resumed.

"Anyway," continued Belton, "it looks to me like they're hopin' to reassure Eleanor as much as they can, by sayin' they'll let the children go, so she'll begin, they hope, to consider at least backin' off the *Congressus* stuff long enough to get those kids in Rebecca's hands. And Luke, if they've studied Eleanor as much as they'd have to just to understand how much she cares about her niece and the children, then they're also gonna understand how much Eleanor trusts your sister.

"I'm thinkin' that these people understand there's nobody in the world that my wife would trust more to collect these two kids than Rebecca Manguson Clark, y'know what I mean, Luke?"

Luke turned the idea over in his mind, nodded to himself, and then asked, "And you think the kidnappers will actually give the children to Rebecca, Detective?"

Belton snorted disgustedly. "They'll hold *all* the cards. So, they might, but I think that if they do anything at all about returnin' the kids, they might *exchange* them for Rebecca, Luke. All they want is for Eleanor to believe that they *might* release the kids if she'll just let go of her *Congressus* activity and go back to New York. They wanna pry Eleanor outta here, and while they're at it, if they can get their hands on your sister, too . . . well . . . they know enough to understand that that'll hurt Eleanor plenty *and* will take away one of our weapons.

"These people know about the visions, Luke. They're bound to be somehow part of the same old network we've been fightin' every summer for three years now. They've got to be at least generally aware of the cathedral visions two years ago, and the arena visions last year. These guys'll just *assume* a new set of visions is underway, with your sister on the receivin' end, as always. Gettin' Rebecca held captive somewhere, they'll know for sure, will cripple any efforts we could possibly make to foul up their plans.

"And Luke? Don't forget that they'd like to get their hands on you, too. They know the two of you are a pair, and that your sister depends on you for a lot when she gets into these scrapes.

"Y'know what I mean, Luke? Know what I mean?"

Luke thought for a moment. "Yes, I know what you mean, Detective, but, I must say, if these people are so clever, how do they manage to misjudge Christians so consistently? If they understood anything really well, they'd understand that your wife is most unlikely to cave in to this sort of pressure, and as for my sister. . . ."

He paused and smiled to himself, deciding not to speculate further about Rebecca's decisions. After a moment, he spoke again.

"What's our next move, Detective?"

"Well, Luke, like I said, Antonio is a mess because his younger daughter got snatched, and because he feels like he has let Eleanor down—and me, too—by settin' somethin' up in Rome that didn't work out. So, he's not much use to us right now. He's not thinkin' straight."

Luke made a deep, disgusted noise. "I'm not sure he was thinking straight at any point in this, Detective."

"Yeah, Luke. You got that right," said Belton. "But he is thinkin' straight enough not to try to insist that Eleanor leave Berkeley just because Sophia Camposanto and the Angelinis are captives. The bad guys may not understand that, but Antonio, at least, sure does. He knows not to tell me to try to send Eleanor home to New York on the theory that we're supposed to *trust* these pork chops not to hurt his daughter and Mrs. Angelini and the kids.

"Anyway, what I think is this. The bad guys have got blood on their hands. Maybe they didn't plan to kill Mr. Angelini, but it looks like they did. What that means to me is that the Rome police are gonna go after those turkeys with everything they got. I can't see any point in any of us doin' anything at all right now.

"And, for sure, you and Rebecca and Matt and the Camposanto woman would be nuts to head for Rome just because they've made this statement about releasin' the children only to Rebecca. I say do nothin', Luke. Just sit tight. I'll stay in touch with ya. If y'need to phone us, call here, at Antonio's hotel suite. He's in the bedroom tryin' to sleep right now, but this is gonna be our headquarters . . . know what I mean? Here's the number. . . ."

Luke Manguson placed the telephone receiver in its cradle and remained facing the wall. He sensed someone was now in the small kitchen with him, and turned to see Rebecca, fully dressed and ready to head for the air base.

"Good morning, brother," she said, her expression serious. "Who called?"

SAN FRANCISCO/BERKELEY: 11:25 PM/FRIDAY
NEW YORK: 2:25 AM/SATURDAY
LONDON: 7:25 AM/SATURDAY
ROME: 8:25 AM/SATURDAY

Rebecca listened intently while Luke summarized the detective's phone call, referring often to his notes as he went. When he finished, he looked up at her and saw her shaking her head thoughtfully from side to side.

Then she said simply, "No."

"'No,' what, Rebecca?"

"No, we cannot 'sit tight,' as the detective understandably wishes us to, Luke."

"We can't?"

She sighed, turned her back to him, removed a drinking glass from a cupboard, and poured herself a measure of orange juice. She downed the drink quickly, and placing the glass on the counter between herself and her brother, looked him evenly in the eye.

"The dreams again, dear. The dreams again."

She leaned back against the sink, crossed her arms, and looked down, thinking. When she spoke, she was remembering, describing, recreating the newly received, early morning dream.

"The essentials were the same as in the first, just twenty-four hours before . . . is that possible?" She nodded to herself and continued. "I saw through the eyes of someone else, someone who, I now think, given what you've just told me about the detective's call, is being held captive somewhere.

"Just as before, she looks out from a third- or fourth-floor window, I think, over a courtyard filled with people looking up toward a church on the other side. It is the same church as before: the impossibly long flight of stone steps, an elaborate façade, a stained glass image above two enormous main doors. . . .

"And as the dream goes on, the captive grows increasingly frustrated, pounding her fists on the window sill, as before. I see her hands . . . her fists . . . in the vision as my own hands, but they are clearly not mine, since these dreamed hands are plumper, with short fingers. And the rings are all wrong . . . for my hands, I mean. And she pounds her fists and digs her fingernails into the window sill, just as in the first dream."

Rebecca paused and looked up at her brother just as her husband entered the room from behind her. She smiled quickly at the sight of her beloved, and spun around to embrace him in early morning joy.

Still holding Matt around the waist, she looked back at Luke, who was beaming with pleasure at this rare treat: seeing his twin and her husband just as they were starting their day. Rebecca explained quickly to Luke, "I awakened Matt as soon as the dream ended early this morning, and told him all I could remember, Luke."

Then she looked up at her husband and said, "Detective Belton phoned just before I came into the kitchen, Matt. It seems a great deal has happened in the last few hours, all of it bad."

Following this cue, Luke quickly reviewed his notes for Matt's benefit, then nodded for Rebecca to continue.

"Matt," she said, looking up at her husband and still holding him around the waist, "I feel that my two visions are almost certainly depicting a captive, given Mr. Belton's information. I don't know what Eleanor Chapel's niece looks like, nor have I heard a description of Antonio Camposanto's younger daughter but, if one of them is a rather plump woman . . . ."

Just then Andrea Camposanto entered the kitchen, which was now beginning to feel crowded, and spoke brightly to the group. *"Buon giorno, buon giorno, buon giorno!"* she said, looking at each of her colleagues in turn.

"Buon giorno, Andrea," said Rebecca in return, while the men smiled and nodded their silent good morning to the newcomer. Rebecca and Luke then exchanged glances, and Rebecca turned back to Andrea and asked, "Andrea, your younger sister . . . Sophia, I believe? Tell me what she looks like."

Andrea Camposanto's face fell immediately. "Why do you ask this question, *signora?* And how do you even to know my sister's name? Has something happened? What has happened? Please . . . tell me . . . you must explain to me now."

The twins then took turns, using the simplest possible vocabulary, outlining the newly received information, including the reported abduction of Sophia Camposanto. At this, Andrea's knees buckled and Matt quickly gripped her shoulders, encircling her with his good arm, and helped her gently to a sitting position on the kitchen floor. Nothing was said for several minutes, while the threesome ministered to their companion, finally helping her to move into the sitting room so as to be able to recline on the small sofa. She curled into the soft piece of furniture and held her face in her hands, sobbing softly.

Rebecca, kneeling beside the distraught young woman, said gently but firmly to her, "Andrea, we must act. We are being called upon to assist. You must rise out of your distress and speak to us. Do you hear? Do you understand?"

She nodded and whispered, *"Si."*

"Tell me what Sophia looks like, Andrea," said Rebecca. "Is she thin, like you, or is she plump? Are her hands large and her fingers long, like mine, or are her hands small and her fingers short?"

Andrea moaned softly and whispered, "Sophia is tall, like our father, but very thin, like me. And she is beautiful, also, with hair like yours and the face of a goddess. Sophia is amazing. She is amazing, *signora.*"

"But her hands, Andrea?" persisted Rebecca. "Speak to me about your sister's hands."

Andrea Camposanto reached slowly for Rebecca's hand, held the hand near her face, and whispered, "They are like yours, *signora*, but . . . but . . . not so strong . . . not so much . . . not so very much muscles. They are very long . . . and very thin."

San Francisco/Berkeley: 12:05 am/Saturday
New York: 3:05 am/Saturday
London: 8:05 am/Saturday
Rome: 9:05 am/Saturday

By 8:00 am on this London Saturday, Rebecca had nearly finished recounting for her colleagues the new ingredients in her early morning dream, her second such vision in two days. They had for some time been seated in the compact sitting room that served as a family room in Luke's minimalist bachelor flat, Andrea now sitting up on the small sofa, with Rebecca beside her and the men occupying straight-backed chairs they had brought in from the dining area.

Rebecca had explained how, before her dreaming eyes, the indistinct stained glass figure above the church's ornate double doors had been transformed into stark relief by the setting sun's direct rays, a near-miraculous illumination that appeared to project the figure forward, toward the crowd of witnesses, from a dramatically bright and golden background. And she had described how the people in the courtyard below had then alternately clapped their hands and bowed their heads prayerfully at the spectacle high above them.

She had gone on, speaking slowly and using her most basic English vocabulary so that Andrea Camposanto might follow, to explain how she felt as she observed the stained glass figure: suffused at first with a sense of comfort and reassurance, just as in the first dream, although she still could not identify the figure.

But here she had stopped, looking closely at Andrea. "What is it, Andrea?" she had asked.

"I know this church, *signora*," the Italian had replied tentatively. "Is it of importance for you to know this church . . . or no?"

She had become the object of rapt attention.

"Andrea, you are saying you can identify this church?" asked Luke. "Are you certain?"

"*Si*," she responded, nodding her head. "I think anyone in my country knows this church, *signore* . . . this *duomo* . . . this cathedral. Italian people know . . . they know the window that shines with the sunset. We all know the golden glass . . . the golden window. And of course we know the figure in the glass."

"This church . . . this cathedral, you say? . . . This cathedral is in Rome, Andrea?" asked Matt.

"This *duomo* is not in Roma, *signore*," she replied. "This is the *duomo* . . . *scusi* . . . the cathedral . . . that was dedicated in the long ago . . . dedicated in the very long ago . . . to Saint Andrew the Apostle . . . I think in the five hundred years after the Christ . . . or maybe in the six hundred years after the Christ . . . I don't know. . . .

"I think that you, *signora* . . . would surely feel the . . . sense of comfort . . . of . . . of . . . reassurance . . . that you spoke of just now," she added, looking at Rebecca, "when you would look, even in this dreaming of yours, at the figure of Saint Andrew. . . . Yes . . . you would feel the comfort of seeing him . . . and of him . . . of Saint Andrew . . . *seeing you,* as we say."

Rebecca made a small gesture with both hands that was equal parts wonder and impatience. "But Andrea," said Rebecca, an urgency creeping into her voice, *"where* is the cathedral located? If not Rome, then where?"

"The cathedral that you are dreaming, *signora,* is on the Amalfi coast, perhaps one hundreds of miles south of Roma, and not so far from the island called Capri. It is in the town of Amalfi. A famous town. We have been to Amalfi many times, my family and I. We have seen the sunset window . . . the golden window . . . many times."

Rebecca, Matt, and Luke—each equally riveted and stunned—finally looked away from the bewildered Italian. They exchanged glances with each other. At length, Luke broke the developing silence. He addressed his sister.

"Detective Belton said that, according to the kidnappers, the children are being held somewhere in Rome, but the two women elsewhere. And your dream, Rebecca, is of an adult . . . or, at least, of an adult woman's hands?"

He lifted his eyebrows in Rebecca's direction.

"Yes," she said, "in my dream I see the courtyard and the cathedral. . . . It would appear that this must be the cathedral in Amalfi—the Cathedral of St. Andrew, Andrea?—through an adult woman's eyes, and I see her hands . . . her plump, short-fingered hands . . . when I look down. . . . And I see her hands becoming fists . . . fists pounding on the window sill. I have not yet been shown anything else about her surroundings."

She paused, then continued.

"The detective didn't suggest that the two women—Anna Angelini and Sophia Camposanto—are being held together in the same place, correct, Luke?"

"Correct," he said.

"And so," said Rebecca by way of further verification, "Mr. Belton said only that the children are being held in Rome, that they will be released only into my custody, and that the two women are elsewhere, yes?"

"Yes," Luke replied. "And before you go any further, dear sister, and start laying your plans to go to Rome, let me remind you as sternly as I can as your *older* brother, that the detective was quite clear that we should not make a move in any direction whatsoever."

"Oh, please, Luke," she said, turning her face to her husband, and rolling her eyes for her brother's benefit, "you don't think seriously that I am. . . ."

She stopped and exclaimed. "Oh! I failed to mention another ingredient in this morning's vision. This was the part that worried Matt more than anything else when I woke him and told him.

"This time there was a face, Luke. This time there was a woman's face . . . or, no . . . not so much her face as just . . . well . . . just her eyes and, I suppose, the *suggestion* of her face. The eyes seemed to rise over the whole dreamed scene, just after the golden sunset illumined the figure of Saint Andrew, and just before the vision once more returned its focus to my . . . to the woman's . . . own hands. These eyes—they were huge in comparison to the rest of the dreamed objects—seemed to loom over the whole landscape, so that, just after my keen sense of comfort at seeing the apostle, and just before having my attention again drawn to my . . . to the woman's . . . hands, I saw these eyes. They were angry, vindictive, sinister, threatening eyes."

Rebecca shuddered. Then she shook her head, drew a deep breath, and continued.

"And these furious eyes," she said slowly, "came to dominate the whole scene, even at the same time that the apostolic figure was highlighted by the sun, and even while the people in the courtyard clapped and prayed.

"And you remember, Luke, that in the first dream the stained glass image brought first, comfort, and soon after, something fearsome that seemed to demand a response—but I could not tell what sort of response?"

Luke nodded, as did Matt.

"This time," she continued, "I sensed that the response demanded of me was to . . . well. . . ."

Her voice trailed off and she looked to her husband for assistance. He turned his face to Luke's, and said thoughtfully, "When Rebecca woke me last night—actually this morning—to tell me the new vision, she could not seem to find words that satisfied her, at first or even much later, for this final part of the vision. We talked a little, and then she used phrases like . . . 'I felt directed to *stop that face,*' and then, later . . . 'I felt ordered to *break the storm* represented by the face,' and then, still much, much later . . . 'I felt commanded to . . . to . . . *put out her eyes* . . .' and then, finally, and quite definitely, '*to put out THEIR eyes*. . . .'"

He glanced at his wife, then continued. "Rebecca never felt at any point that she had been able to explain to me exactly what she had felt, but she wasn't able to come any closer than those phrases."

He looked at his wife, and she nodded.

"Luke," she began again, "I think that, even though I can't find any exact words for this, the woman's face connects somehow to . . ." and here she turned her face to the side to look directly at Andrea Camposanto, seated on the sofa beside her. Fixing the Italian with her steady, gray-eyed gaze, she continued, " . . . connects somehow to Andrea's refusal to tell me yesterday who or what, exactly, has terrified both Andrea herself and her father. I think these eyes, and this face, represent something behind and above the immediate threats to Dr. Chapel in California, something high above all of this flesh-and-blood evil that we have encountered each year, first in this country, then in the U.S., and now. . . ."

She looked back at her brother. "When I was directly, physically assaulted by supernatural Evil two years ago, you remember that I never actually saw the face of the Enemy . . . but . . . Luke . . . if this dreamed face that I saw this morning had been masculine, I would begin to wonder. . . . I would begin to wonder if that Jamieson man we could never identify last year might not be, in fact, something more than . . . actually, something *less* than . . . a human being."

She paused, reflected for a moment, and continued. "If this were a man's face, Luke, I would be asking Matt to describe for us again the features of that Edward Jamieson person who seemed so central to the evil last summer in New York. The fact that it is a woman's face suggests to me that even Mr. Jamieson, if that is, in fact, his name, was not at the top of the pyramid. There is someone even higher . . . someone above even Mr. Jamieson in all of this. And it is a *she* . . . or if not, it is the feminine face of the Enemy himself."

Then Rebecca closed her eyes as if concentrating with all her might. After a moment, eyes still closed, she murmured, "But it was *their* eyes . . . not just *her* eyes . . . and so. . . ."

The room fell silent. After a pause so long that Andrea Camposanto had begun to wonder if she had missed so much of the meaning of what had been said that, for some reason, no one was *supposed* to speak after Rebecca's monologue, Luke broke the silence.

"And so," he said somberly, looking toward his sister, "all said and done, Rebecca . . . you intend to defy the detective's clear directive? You intend to go to Rome immediately? You think that, to '*put out their eyes*,' as you said, you must go and attempt to get the children?"

She smiled at her brother. "I did not understand you to be passing along a 'directive,' Luke, but, rather, Mr. Belton's 'suggestion.'

"But," she continued, "you're absolutely correct, and it would not matter whether the detective had given us a directive or a suggestion or . . . well . . . or anything at all. We know what these visions mean. The three of us have been living with the visions and their consequences for more than two years now.

"And," she continued, her voice rising in strength, anger just behind the words, "we know enough to understand that to '*put out their eyes*' may well be a reference to much, much more than receiving these two children from their kidnappers . . . from these murderers. Receiving the children is likely to be only one small part of what we . . . of what I . . . will be called upon to attempt, Luke."

Here she turned again to Andrea, leaning toward her as they sat together on the small sofa. Andrea shrank back from the force that continued to build before her eyes, inches from her face. "And you, Andrea, although you were not with us then, you, through your father and his networks, are nearly as familiar with the simple *fact* of these visions, and with much of what they have meant, as are we, yes?"

Andrea Camposanto, eyes wide, murmured, "*Si,*" hoping that her answer was true.

Rebecca leaned back, away from the Italian, turned her face and her eyes away from them all, and took a deep breath. After a moment, she turned back toward her brother and resumed. Her voice was soft now, her words measured.

"This, dear brother, is the Holy Spirit at work . . . at work through me . . . for reasons known only to Him. And when our Lord and Savior orders me into danger through His Holy Spirit's visits to my mind . . . well . . . it just can't matter what any of us think. We are not allowed to be prudent. We are required to be obedient."

She stopped, looked down at the floor, and then up again at her brother. "Luke, I need to ask you to begin planning a trip to Rome for me. None of you, apparently, is required to go with me. But *I* must act, and foolhardy or not, it would appear that I must place myself in position to receive these two children from their kidnappers.

"Luke, can you have us—or me—ready to start by this afternoon?"

Luke said only, "Of course."

But he found that his eyes had drifted from their tight focus on his sister's penetrating gaze to the ragged scar that dominated her right cheek.

And as Rebecca turned her head slightly to look more directly into her husband's face, Luke continued to look long at his sister's scar.

The words that flowed through his mind as he stared at the scar were those that emanated from the dream when the furious feminine image had risen above Rebecca's newest vision. And the words held their own sense of terror: *Put out their eyes.*

Like his sister moments before, Luke Manguson shuddered.

SAN FRANCISCO/BERKELEY: 8:00 AM/SATURDAY
NEW YORK: 11:00 AM/SATURDAY
LONDON: 4:00 PM/SATURDAY
ROME: 5:00 PM/SATURDAY

Richard Mabry stole a sleepy glance at Giuseppe Basso, who, noticing, looked back toward Mabry and smiled hopefully. Perhaps this American would actually befriend him, would actually explain the mysteries he seemed continually to encounter in his few short days in this new country. Mabry groggily sensed the pleading note playing across the Italian's face, nodded vaguely but unhelpfully in his direction, and turned his attention to the threesome that carried the conversation in Antonio Camposanto's spacious hotel suite.

The Italian detective had done his best to explain to Mabry, rousted early from his Saturday bed by Eleanor Chapel's phone call, as he had explained previously to his prospective son-in-law, the nature of the new circumstances. Camposanto had noted matter-of-factly that he and Sidney Belton, both veteran criminal investigators, had agreed immediately that both young men needed their protection: Mabry, because he had been alone in public view with Eleanor Chapel, and then had spent several moments, also in public view, face-to-face with Antonio Camposanto himself; Basso, because he was, in prospect, a member of the Camposanto family through his impending marriage to Sophia. Whatever the nature of the kidnappers' designs upon Eleanor Chapel herself and her deceased sister's daughter and grandchildren in Rome, the obvious fact was that the kidnappers' net had spread beyond the Mason-Chapel-Angelini family to the Camposanto family as well.

No one close to Eleanor Chapel, or it seemed, to Antonio Camposanto, was safe. Yet it had been obvious from the first moments after the detective's Rome office had contacted him regarding the kidnapping that Professor Chapel was, under no circumstances, going to comply with the ransom demands.

"What kind of nitwits are those people?" she had huffed to Camposanto as soon as she had worked though the shock of Mario Angelini's murder sufficiently to consider the demands themselves. "Do they think I am myself nitwit enough to *trust* them? . . . Cowards . . . blackguards . . . brigands each? I am to *trust* them not to murder or harm the rest of my family—and yours, Detective Camposanto—provided I do as they say? I'm supposed to *believe* them and act accordingly?

"They actually think that I am going to shrug my shoulders and forfeit my vocation, my ministry, and my most sacred Christian obligations and duties because these bullies feel like threatening me or my family? I must tell you . . . if they murder my niece and her children as they did her husband, I will be heartbroken . . . heartbroken almost beyond mending. . . . But I will not miss one single beat on my march to my duty, God willing.

"People like these think that life or death is the ultimate threat. That's what makes them nitwits, you know. *Heaven or hell* is the ultimate threat. And they'd better get that figured out.

"Or are they just plain *crazy?*"

Neither detective—her husband or the Italian—had dared raise the question again.

A moment later Richard Mabry was startled out of his halfhearted efforts to follow the technicalities of the hotel suite's three-cornered conversation when the telephone near his chair interrupted Eleanor in midsentence. She made to rise from her seat, but her husband put up his hand and moved to the phone.

"Belton!" he barked into the receiver.

"Oh," he said, suddenly deferential, "how y'doin', Mrs. Clark?" Then, covering the receiver by turning the handset into his chest, he said unnecessarily to those in the room with him, "It's Rebecca Clark . . . in London!"

"Of course it is, dear," said his wife from her chair. "You're grinning like the Cheshire Cat. Who else could it be but Rebecca?"

Sid barked his laugh of delight, the laugh that Eleanor could, above all people, draw from him on virtually any occasion. And then, a moment later, serious once more, he began to listen intently, offering only the occasional "hmm," as Rebecca talked him through the situation in London and their decisions regarding their next steps. As it became apparent to him that the London group was going to disregard his strong advice to wait for the police-initiated outcomes in Rome before making any moves of their own, and especially to disregard his advice that Rebecca not take the kidnappers' bait by going there to "receive the children," his face fell, but he continued to be noncommittal in his muttered responses.

Eleanor watched his expression and listened to his murmurs and grumblings, and without difficulty guessed the general text of Rebecca's message. She guessed without hearing a word from Rebecca herself that a second overnight vision had led the Londoners to prepare immediately to go to Rome—probably all four of them making the trip, not just Rebecca—the detective's advice notwithstanding.

"Yes, ma'am," he was just mumbling in the receiver, "I got it . . . you're gonna leave long before daybreak . . . tonight . . . I mean, tomorrow morning . . . and *drive* all the way to Italy? Yeah? How does that work?"

He listened again, then muttered in mild embarrassment, "Oh . . . a car ferry to France? Didn't know y'could do that. Okay, I see."

After another moment of intense listening, the detective spoke his first full sentences in more than five minutes. "That's right, ma'am, Antonio's staff doesn't have any instructions yet from the bad guys about how and where you oughta go in Rome to collect the two Angelini kids. But those lousy pencil heads will call Antonio's people in Rome any time now, I'd guess. They know that their info has gotta be relayed back here to California, to Antonio . . . then back to London, to you . . . before anything can happen.

"What's that, ma'am? Oh, right . . . you'll just need to phone us every few hours until we can give ya what y'need to know. How long does it take to drive all that way, London to Rome? Coupla days, y'say? Really? That's all?"

Eleanor had studied her husband's face throughout the conversation, and had seen the sadness building in his eyes, in his voice, and in his sagging shoulders as he began to imagine what awaited these treasured friends and comrades-in-Christ upon their arrival in Rome. Then he looked up suddenly at his wife, gestured in her direction with the telephone receiver, and said quietly, "Eleanor . . . Mrs. Clark wants ya."

Fairly jumping from her chair to scurry to her husband's side, Eleanor took the receiver, reached up to stroke his arm tenderly, and turned her attention reluctantly from her husband's sadness to Rebecca's voice. "Yes, Rebecca, dear," she said.

Slowly settling into the chair his wife had occupied, Sid now took his turn in scrutinizing his spouse's every word, gesture, and facial expression. And so it was that he, and his three companions as well, heard curious words from her mouth and saw puzzled frowns crossing her face, soon after she had begun listening to Rebecca's questions from across the ocean: "Well, Rebecca . . . let's see . . . such an odd question . . . um . . . well, I know Anna wears the usual rings on her left hand—an engagement ring and a wedding band—and . . . hmm . . . I just can't quite picture . . . oh! Yes, Rebecca . . . on her right hand there is the prettiest little cameo ring . . . a Madonna and Child image. . . . I think Mario gave it to her on a wedding anniversary."

As soon as Eleanor had said the deceased's name, her breath caught in her throat. "Oh," she said sadly, "poor, poor Mario. . . ."

In a flash, Sid Belton was at her side—as were, to their mutual surprise, Antonio Camposanto and Richard Mabry—arriving simultaneously from opposite sides of the two small figures as they stood hugging each other, the phone hanging uselessly from Eleanor's left hand. Giuseppe, seeing himself the only one in the hotel room still seated, rose slowly from his chair and stood uncertainly, shifting from one foot to the other.

After a moment, recovering, Eleanor raised the phone to her ear, and said, "Rebecca, I'm sorry. Please go on."

As soon as she began to speak into the phone once more, Antonio and Richard, embarrassed at the awkwardness of their common gesture—neither of them having spoken to, or reached out to touch, either Eleanor or her husband—turned and stepped back to their seats. As they did, Giuseppe, equally embarrassed, sat down quickly in his chair.

As soon as they could attend again, the men heard Eleanor saying, "Well . . . yes, Rebecca, dear . . . Anna has had a tendency to gain a little weight after each child's birth, and like a lot of mothers, never quite lost what had been added. And I suppose she *would* use some Italian word like our English for 'chubby' . . . or 'pudgy' . . . to describe herself, though I don't really think that is quite fair."

Throughout this portion of the conversation, Sid stood beside his wife, his arm now around her shoulders, as she talked. At some point, as his eyes moved around the room, he noticed the intensity of Antonio's focus on Eleanor and the telephone receiver itself—a seemingly ravenous hunger for the telephone—and it occurred to him for the first time that the Italian would surely be anxious to speak with his older daughter.

Getting his wife's attention and indicating with his hand and his eyes that he would like to speak to Rebecca for a moment, he waited patiently until she could bring about a pause in the conversation. Accepting the receiver, Sid said, somewhat apologetically, "Mrs. Clark, y'know Detective Camposanto is sittin' here with us in the hotel room, and I'm sure he'd appreciate a word with his daughter. Is Andrea there with you?"

The gargantuan Roman smiled broadly at his colleague's gesture, and began to gather himself to lift his enormous bulk once more from his chair. But the diminutive American looked up and stopped him with a look and a small shake of his head. "Sorry, Detective," he said, handing the receiver back to his wife, "seems your daughter and Rebecca's husband, Matt, have gone out to get something for the four of 'em for their dinner. Rebecca says her brother lives like a man who doesn't know what a grocer is."

Camposanto nodded, his disappointment undisguised.

On the London end of the transatlantic connection, Rebecca was drawing the conversation to an end, noting aloud that, although it was still late afternoon in England, she and Luke and the others still had a great deal to do before bedtime, and they planned to arise at 2:00 AM on Sunday in order to be on the road by 3:30 that morning. Luke wanted them to be first in line for the automobile ferry to Le Havre.

"Dr. Chapel," Rebecca was saying as Luke Manguson listened to his sister with much the same intensity that the four men displayed in California as they listened to Eleanor Chapel, "before I go, I want to ask you something about Detective Camposanto. I realize that he is sitting right there with you. Will you be able to respond with just an affirmative or negative to a question or two? Yes?

"Well, these . . . um . . . odd arrangements he made for Sophia's 'protection,' as he so quaintly put it, and Andrea's and Mr. Basso's, strike us as so . . . well . . . amateurish . . . that we find ourselves wondering whether or not Mr. Camposanto can actually be trusted to make good recommendations to you and your husband, or to give the most carefully considered instructions to his staff in Rome. Do you find that you have . . . well . . . absolute confidence in the detective at this juncture, Dr. Chapel?"

She waited for an answer. After a moment, it came.

"So, you're doubtful, Dr. Chapel? Well, I must say . . . I must say that we hope and pray that you and Mr. Belton will speak privately to each other about Mr. Camposanto and his reliability under the circumstances. And I know that you will."

There was another pause. Neither woman spoke, both lost in thought.

Then, glancing first at her brother and then at her watch, Rebecca said quietly, "Dr. Chapel, I must be going." She listened, smiled, nodded, and then added, "Yes . . . yes, I know. You will do what you must. I know your duty is clear.

"And so is mine, Dr. Chapel." Rebecca sighed audibly. "We will be on our way in just a few hours, and we will telephone you periodically, at least until you can give us the kidnappers' information regarding the location of the children and their instructions for me.

"We will, in the end, unite them with their mother. And Dr. Chapel, I must say that I think, too . . . I think, too, that God will bless our efforts and allow us to succeed, and to live and to return home."

Again Rebecca paused and sighed, more audibly still. Then she added, speaking slowly and deliberately, *"But . . . if not . . ."*

Here, with the word "not" still hanging in the air, Rebecca gently placed the telephone receiver in its cradle.

And Luke Manguson, facing his sister across the small kitchen, nodded his head grimly at the words.

Chapter Seven

ELEANOR CHAPEL, HEARING THE CLICK ON THE OTHER END of the line as Rebecca hung up the phone in London, lowered her telephone receiver to its cradle. After a moment, she glanced around the hotel suite at Antonio Camposanto, Giuseppe Basso, Richard Mabry, and her husband, then said thoughtfully, "Gentlemen, this will seem rude, I fear, but I'd very much like to speak privately with my husband about Rebecca and Luke . . . and Matt . . . and your daughters, Mr. Camposanto . . . and my niece and the children. . . ."

She smiled shyly. "I simply want my *husband* for a few minutes. Can you understand, gentlemen? Does it just seem altogether too rude?"

Seeing each of the three smile broadly and begin to rise, she said quickly, "Oh, no, no, I don't mean you three should leave Sidney and me alone here. No, that *would* be extraordinary. I just meant that Sidney and I are going to go for a fifteen-minute walk, so that we can be alone and talk alone. Can you manage to forgive us?"

Once outside the first-floor suite of rooms that opened directly onto the parking area for the hotel, the couple joined hands and walked slowly together to the near sidewalk. There they turned eastward, away from San Francisco Bay, and strolled toward the rising sun as it climbed above the Berkeley hills. They exchanged details regarding Rebecca's explanations, descriptions, and plans, each probing to make sure the picture was as complete as possible.

Finally, after fewer than ten minutes of slow walking, they turned and started back toward the hotel. After several moments of thoughtful silence, Eleanor Chapel added, "Near the end, dearest, Rebecca asked me if I had absolute confidence in Antonio, given his—she used the word 'amateurish'—arrangements, and I admitted that I did not . . . not fully. . . .

"She urged us . . . the two of us, Sidney . . . to think carefully about what Mr. Camposanto's temporary confusion might mean: for us, for the Londoners, for his own police staff in Rome, for the captive women and the children, for everyone involved.

"And then, just before she hung up, she said that she felt that, even if the kidnappers were, as we all fear, laying a trap for her, that God would allow her and Luke and Matt to prevail, to unite the children with their mother, and to live through the danger, and in the end, to return home. . . .

"And then she said, as she hung up, '*But . . . if not . . .*'

"And then she was gone, dear. Those were her final words."

Sid Belton looked at his wife quizzically. "But . . . if not . . .?"

The Old Testament professor looked up at her husband and smiled. "It's Old Testament, dear. The book of Daniel, third chapter.

"The passage sends chills down my spine every time I think of it," she said softly, "even after all these years."

She paused thoughtfully, then continued. "King Nebuchadnezzar had just been informed that the three Jews he had set over the affairs of the province of Babylon had not been worshipping the king's gods, as required of all. The king, as the passage says, 'in his rage and fury,' challenged the Almighty, whom alone these men would worship, to rescue them from the furnace into which the king would cast each of them should they continue this defiance.

"And this was their answer, Sidney, that: '. . . our God whom we serve is able to deliver us. . . .

"'*But if not* . . . be it known unto thee, O king, that *we will not serve thy gods. . . .*'"

SAN FRANCISCO/BERKELEY: 12:45 PM/SATURDAY
NEW YORK: 3:45 PM/SATURDAY
LONDON: 8:45 PM/SATURDAY
ROME: 9:45 PM/SATURDAY

Richard Mabry stared, possibly for the first time ever, directly into the face of a woman to whom he was attracted. He found the experience, at that instant approaching perhaps ten seconds in duration, thoroughly unnerving. This was not the back of Lois Tanaka's head. This was not her raven pageboy cut, studied from behind; or her delicate earlobes or the gold earrings that formed the mysterious Japanese character; or her profile as she turned her head in response to a faculty colleague's having risen to address the audience.

This was Lois Tanaka, full face and close range.

She was breathtaking to him, and not just because of her exquisitely classical Japanese features or the delicate courtesy with which she attended to him. There was something about the way she looked straight into his eyes, as though he were the only person on earth at that moment, something about the way she waited in muted expectation for him to say something to her. It was almost more than he could stand.

He was conscious of the fact that seconds were continuing to tick past as they sat facing each other across the small table. He knew he had started this, having risen quickly to greet her as she stepped out of the delicatessen and onto its ample patio. He had managed a quaking "Good afternoon, Lois," then had held her chair and taken his own in a silence that had now threatened to grow to monumental proportions.

He dropped his eyes from her politely curious gaze and said a desperate prayer: "Father, please . . . give me words." Even as he said the small prayer, he was aware of how extraordinary it was for him to pray in this fashion: spontaneously and conversationally. What, he wondered in a flash of disorienting insight and yes, of actual reverence, was happening to him now?

But no sooner had he completed his small petition than he heard her voice, a response to his prayer that he had not envisioned: *Her* words given to *him*. "Richard," she said softly, "you were so nice to phone me. I had just been looking at my cupboard and realizing that I would have to go to the store right away, unless I wanted to make peanut butter and jelly sandwiches for my lunch. You rescued me!"

And she laughed softly, an intriguing murmur of a laugh, just stronger than a sigh, and low for a woman. She continued to look at him expectantly, but without demands, her sweetly demure expression and posture an irresistible invitation to speak.

Finally words began to come to him. "Lois," he said, hesitantly at first, "I called you this morning because . . . well . . . um . . . yesterday at the faculty meeting . . . during the morning session . . . Dr. Chapel asked me what I was doing. . . ."

He stopped and dropped his eyes again. He was an articulate person. Why could he not put coherent sentences together now, when it meant so much? But he heard her voice again and looked up quickly.

"Was she talking about how you made everyone laugh during the roll call, Richard?" she asked, her smile, still shy and small, growing slightly at the memory of the hilarity his belated response to his name had induced throughout the room.

He smiled broadly at this and at the very fact that she was working so hard, and yet with such apparent ease, to make this less difficult for him. It occurred to him that, despite her youth—she could hardly be twenty-five—this could not be the first time in her life that she had been face-to-face with a young man who found himself struggling to talk to her. Nor could it be the first time she had sought to put such a young man at his ease.

He tried to move on. "Actually, I meant something Dr. Chapel said to me after my . . . uh . . . entrance," he said, still smiling at her. "She asked me what I was doing . . . well . . . with my life . . . with my vocation . . . and . . . well. . . ." He looked away again, fighting against his habitual embarrassment at the very mention of attraction. "With my . . . uh . . . well . . . flights of fancy . . . about . . . about . . . well . . . women. I mean . . . women in general, you know."

He shook his head at himself and at her, trying to indicate that he had not finished his little statement. She waited, unhurried in her listening pose, at peace with herself, with Richard Mabry, with the universe itself.

"She also meant . . . you . . . Lois . . . she meant that . . . well . . . I was just sort of . . . well . . . staring at the back of your head . . . and wondering what it might be like to ask you out . . . you know . . . for breakfast, or coffee, or something."

He looked away, and then back at her. "Dr. Chapel saw me and noticed what I seemed to be doing, and what I seemed to be *not* doing, and . . . well

. . . asked me that question: What I was *doing*? And she really meant *doing*.

"Do you know what I mean, Lois?"

She nodded. "Yes," she said. "Dr. Chapel does not mince words. It's one of the things about her that I love and admire. One doesn't have to guess what she's thinking. She says what she means. I'd like to learn that."

She shifted slightly in the wrought iron chair, then added, "She wanted to know who you *are*, Richard. It's what we should all want to know about each other, don't you think?"

"Yes," he said quickly, "and I would like to be more like her, too."

Then he shifted in his chair, unconsciously mimicking her movement, and continued, "I was surprised to hear myself actually answering the kinds of things she asked me, but I did. And one of the things I said to her was that I guessed I was . . . well . . . afraid . . . actually to call someone like you and ask you out."

"Afraid of me?" she asked doubtfully.

"Well . . . no, not exactly. Afraid to ask you out. Or maybe that's the same thing? I don't know. Just afraid.

"And then," he continued quickly, "in the afternoon, when she came back into the meeting and interrupted the dean, and made her little speech, I was just overcome by the whole thing . . . by what she said . . . by how she said it . . . by what she taught me . . . by Dr. Chapel herself . . . by everything she said . . . by everything she is. . . . And when I got home, I just couldn't get her out of my mind . . . not just her speech, but her question of me in the morning: What are you *doing*?

"And I decided several things last night," he continued. "I decided, first, that she's absolutely right. I do not treat my subject matter with . . . as she said . . . with reverence. I do not attempt every class period to deepen my students' commitment to Christ and to His world. I do not lead them in prayer at the start of every period. I do not treat my job as my calling.

"And . . . one more thing. I am afraid of women. I am afraid of you."

Here he paused just for a moment, forced himself to look full into her face, and said firmly, "And I am, with God's help, going to change. I'm going to change a lot of things. This, I decided, was something I could change in just minutes. I decided I could just call you up this morning, ask if you would meet me for lunch at the deli, and see what would happen.

"And look!" he added delightedly. "You're here . . . with me . . . right now!"

At this she laughed again. The same laugh, low and soft and unembarrassed. She continued to smile, but said nothing. She apparently saw no need for words at that moment.

He decided, emboldened, to go further. Since he did not know how, and had no practice, he plunged in.

"Lois," he said uncertainly, his stomach suddenly in a knot, "you're just . . . well . . . just beautiful!" Instantly he dropped his eyes to the table, blushing furiously.

But immediately he heard her reply, soft, still, calm, unflustered. "God has blessed me in many ways, Richard," she said, "but beauty is not one of those ways. I am plain.

"But I know . . . I really do know . . . that you mean what you've just said. And it's nice that you seem to think me pretty. But Richard, you must remind yourself that whatever my appearance may be to you on this day, and whatever my appearance may mean to you on this day—this day when I am still in my youth—my appearance is, first, fleeting. And second, my appearance is not of my own doing."

He nodded. "Yes," he said simply. Then, somehow aware that he had fulfilled his mission, had taken his first small step back toward something he had once aspired to be, he sat back and smiled at her.

"You know what?" he said rhetorically, and not pausing, answered his own question. "We're having a date, Lois. An actual date. And I'm talking to you and saying things that I actually mean, and you're actually answering me in the same vein.

"This is a date, and it's . . . well . . . it's good!"

SAN FRANCISCO/BERKELEY: 6:00 PM/SATURDAY
NEW YORK: 9:00 PM/SATURDAY
LONDON: 2:00 AM/SUNDAY
ROME: 3:00 AM/SUNDAY

Rebecca Clark opened her eyes and, after several moments of searching the room without raising her head, found the luminescent face of her brother's digital alarm clock. Its red-lighted numbers displayed 2:00. *My goodness*, she thought to herself. *It's actually time to get up. Can that be possible?*

She sat up carefully, quietly, and waited for her eyes to begin to adjust. Without putting out her hand, she could feel the presence of her husband in the small guest room bed they had shared in the basement of her brother's compact home. Near her left elbow, Matt's symmetrical in-and-out breath came to her softly, that most familiar, regular, and reassuring of nighttime sounds, his barely discernable sleeping noises stored happily and systematically in her bank of auditory expectations after nearly a year of marriage.

The two of them had willingly accepted use of the bare-walled guest room, allowing Andrea Camposanto the use of Luke's own narrow bed, also in a basement room. Luke himself used the upstairs sofa in the sitting room. All four had slept soundly, if briefly.

Rebecca had had no dreams on this third night of the new visions.

Her eyes having made as much of an adjustment to the darkness as they were likely to, Rebecca leaned forward and, using one hand as a prop, rose slowly from the bed. She tiptoed to the small table on which she had placed her toiletry kit, felt for it, and lifted it carefully from the bare surface. She then glided cautiously to the doorway, one hand outstretched, feeling for the doorframe. Finding it, she slipped into the narrow hallway and crept to the door of her brother's bedroom.

In the faint light falling through the single half-window in the room, Rebecca could just make out the sleeping form of Andrea Camposanto. She could not hear the young woman's breathing, but on some exhalations there was a small, soft sigh that brought a smile to Rebecca's lips. This was a sweet sound, and formed an arresting contradiction to the hardness of the young woman's personality as it had thus far revealed itself.

No, Rebecca corrected herself mentally. The hardness of the personality she has *wished to* project to us.

Rebecca then turned back into the stairwell and crept slowly up the steps to the kitchen where a weak, shaded bulb provided the only artificial light in the house. Passing through the kitchen, she found the lavatory without difficulty. Moments later she reemerged, with gray eyes wide and a tautness, undefined, spreading through her muscles. Feline in every motion, she padded through the kitchen and moved silently into the hallway.

She stood motionless in the short hallway and listened.

Suddenly she heard a small noise from the direction of the front door and froze. A shape materialized rapidly before her eyes, a man's form, muscular and powerful, moving quietly but purposefully. The two forms stood absolutely still, staring toward the other in the nearly complete darkness.

It was the male that broke the silence. "Sis, if you do that again, I'm going to call Mum and tattle. . . ."

Bursting into near-uncontrolled laughter while at the same time trying not to wake the two sleepers downstairs, the two staggered into each other's arms. Small squeaks of laughter escaped Rebecca's throat, uncharacteristic noises that surprised and delighted her brother.

Finally they stepped back from the familial embrace, still gasping for breath. "Well," she struggled to whisper, "I should have known it would be impossible to move through the house without your knowing it, Luke, but I really thought I had made it somehow."

Luke slapped his forehead in the semidarkness in mock indignation. "What? Surely you jest, my dear. I was off the sofa and tracking you through the house before you'd put both feet on the floor downstairs."

"Oh, Luke," she whispered playfully, "sometimes I think you're nine parts animal. A very *good* animal, you understand, but some combination of seeing-eye guide dog . . . and Saint Bernard rescue dog and . . . well . . . forgive me . . . and Scotland Yard–trained Doberman."

He snickered affectionately at his sister's attempt at canine metaphor. "I'll accept that combination, I suppose," he whispered, "but I'd suggest our old girl, Mildred, as a reasonable combining of the best of all three."

There was a pause while both called to mind their family's three-legged border collie, an intelligent, devoted, and utterly fearless herding dog that the twins had rescued years earlier from a dog pack that had chewed her left hind leg clear through. Each knew that the other was smiling, imagining Mildred's energetic form, barely hobbled by her missing appendage, racing back and forth, herding actual squirrels and imaginary sheep, responding with joyful obedience to every whistle and shout from the twins. In all Mildred did, she fulfilled with every step and bark the purposes for which the Almighty had created her.

Then, as suddenly as it had begun, the laughter and the reverie were over. Luke glanced down at his wristwatch and pressed the small button to illuminate the digital display. "It's 0215, Rebecca," he said brusquely. "It's time to get moving. You'll get the others up?" Without further pleasantries, he turned away to complete preparations for their drive to the Southampton-Portsmouth area.

The automobile ferry to Le Havre, departing at 7:00 AM, would bring them to the French port city by early afternoon. They would motor across the Pont de Normandie, over the wide mouth of the Seine, and proceed south through the old battlefields of Normandy, skirting Paris well to its west. They would then travel south and east toward Lyon, then due south through Avignon, and finally to Marseille, reaching the area soon after midnight.

Luke's plan of campaign included a short rest in one of the small towns near the coast. The next morning would begin a purposeful drive along spectacular Mediterranean vistas to and through Cannes, Nice, and once in Italy, the E80 highway all the way to Rome. Luke intended to be ready to "storm the gates," as he had said, unsmiling, to his sister, when first light arrived on Tuesday morning.

Turning away from her twin, Rebecca descended the steps and moved to wake her husband. Matt was a quick riser, and was himself climbing the steps, shaving kit in hand, within two minutes of her gentle hand on his shoulder. Waking Andrea took longer and was less certain, since she appeared capable of collapsing back into sound sleep even after achieving a sitting position on the side of the bed. But Rebecca was persistent, and once she had the Italian on her feet and moving, she returned to the guest room.

She took a seat on the simple wooden chair near the bed, turned on the reading lamp, and opened the Bible that rested on the guest room's bedside table. She had been reading Ephesians as part of her daily regimen, and on this morning, she moved several chapters ahead of her leaving-off place, to the sixth. And there she read, slowly, prayerfully, saying the words softly aloud as was her lifelong habit:

> . . . Stand therefore, having your loins girt about with truth, and having on the breastplate of righteousness; And your feet shod with the preparation of the gospel of peace; Above all, taking the shield of faith, wherewith ye shall be able to quench all the fiery darts of the wicked. And take the helmet of salvation, and the sword of the Spirit, which is the word of God. . . .

Chapter Eight

THE LITTLE CARAVAN MOTORED STEADILY THROUGH THE early morning darkness toward the south coast of England, the two women leading the way in the sports car, the two men close behind in the sedan. Rebecca had been immediately at home at the controls of the small Alfa Romeo. It was the same runabout that had been loaned to the twins two summers previous by one of Luke's former Royal Navy comrades, and in which she and her brother had at that time negotiated a harrowing night-time escape from London.

Securing the Alfa had been simple. The nimble right-hand drive two-seater had been for sale when the twins had borrowed it originally, but Luke's colleague had later decided to keep the car as his spare. One phone call from Luke and the vehicle had been made immediately available and ready for their use.

Luke, keeping the more sedate Jaguar at a respectable distance behind the diminutive sports car, had taken longer than his sister to adjust to that auto's idiosyncrasies, of which there were many, but by now was settled comfortably.

Arranging to use the Jaguar had also been more problematic. Luke, in his planning for this incursion onto the European continent, had decided early on that all four would be included—Rebecca, Matt, Andrea, and himself—for tactical reasons, four providing more flexibility than two or three. Two cars would be required for the same reason.

Luke did not want to generate the paper trail that renting even a single vehicle would have entailed. And their own autos were congenitally unreliable, reflecting the twins' habitual disinterest in "nice things." They purposely lived close enough to their schools and churches to walk back and forth daily, and viewed a personal automobile as one might any necessary encumbrance, much as their century-previous forebears might have grudgingly owned a serviceable one-horse shay for weekly jaunts to church or to town for supplies.

Though reluctant to involve any of their family members, even indirectly, Luke had finally asked Matt to contact his parents in Birmingham. Luke knew that Paul Clark had purchased a quarter-century-old Jaguar Mark VII 120M, an elegantly understated classic with right-hand drive, four-speed manual transmission, and even a sunroof. This black beauty, which the senior Clark had procured and then immediately loaned to his son and Rebecca for their short wedding trip the previous August, was more attention-drawing than Luke would have preferred, but it fit his needs in every other way: large enough to seat all four of them if necessary, ample trunk space for their belongings and for the equipment Luke wanted with him, mechanically reliable, and reasonably fast and powerful, though no match for the Alfa from a performance standpoint.

On receiving Matt's telephoned request, Paul Clark had driven to London immediately, followed closely by Martha Clark in their family car. They had quickly seized the chance to see their only child and his wife, if only briefly. Matt's parents realized without any real explanation that once again a summer crisis was upon Matt, his wife, and her brother, but knew equally well that nothing would be divulged to them about the nature of the new emergency.

The elder Clarks spent an emotional fifteen minutes with Matt and Rebecca, spoke briefly with Luke, were introduced to Andrea Camposanto, and departed forthwith for Birmingham. Matt, following Luke's request, had asked his father to park the Mark VII two blocks away from Luke's home, in a small parking lot that was partially filled on Saturdays by neighborhood residents. Luke had moved the Jaguar from the lot into loading position near the house only in the small dark hours of Sunday morning, when the four had reached the point of being completely prepared to load and depart.

Aware from the start that both vehicles were right-hand drive, Rebecca and Luke knew that the trip across France and Italy would be technically challenging, as they would of necessity switch from driving the left side of British roadways to, upon debarkation from the ferry at Le Havre, the right side of French and Italian roadways. Nonetheless, they were grateful that they could be so well equipped for this foray on such short notice. The twins also knew that the two of them would do all of the driving. They were not willing to entrust either car to Andrea, uncertain as they were both of her driving skills and of her emotional stability. And Matt, with his useless left arm and hand, could not safely operate any manual transmission vehicle.

Andrea had nodded off to sleep almost as soon as Rebecca had reached the outskirts of London, her head lolling to each side as the Alfa Romeo swept through its turns on the sometimes intricate roadways southward to the coast. Meanwhile, Matt used a hooded flashlight in the Jaguar's front passenger seat, as he was busy studying the "charts"—a term both he and Luke, their naval vocabularies intact, used habitually with each other in referring to the detailed road maps they had secured. Luke had laid out the general track, then turned the details over to his former brother-in-naval-arms.

Once off the ferry in France, the Mark VII would take the lead and the Alfa would follow. The opposite arrangement had been chosen for the first leg of the trip because Rebecca knew these English roadways well. The south coast had long been a favorite Saturday-picnic destination of hers, so she was as comfortable leading the way through the darkened countryside as she had been on many a bright fall Saturday with family or friends.

The drive was finished quickly, and as Luke had hoped, their two-car parade filled the first two positions in the ferry line. With half an hour still to pass before daybreak, all four soon closed their eyes and dozed comfortably.

When the ferry crew arrived in a small van precisely at sunrise on this warm June Sunday, the eight veteran sailors, walking slowly together toward their imposing vessel, commented loudly and approvingly to each other regarding the appearance of the first two cars in the rapidly lengthening line of vehicles.

"Hey, Ed," bawled one, "that an Alfa Romeo in front?"

"I'd say 'tis, mate," said he. "But look at that Jag just behind. A Mark VII, it is! *That's* a beauty, I'll say."

The little cluster of men paused to stare, stepping closer to the two autos.

After a moment a new voice spoke.

"Hey, Will," said this third, rather too loudly, "speakin' of 'beauty,' have a look at the lassie drivin' the Alfa. How about a go at *that*, eh?"

The cluster then moved several steps closer still, peering at Rebecca's eyes-closed profile, her right temple resting lightly against the closed window of the driver's side glass.

Exactly at that moment, the right-hand front door of the Mark VII swung open rather violently and a ramrod-straight, barrel-chested young man stepped out, muscles visibly rippling through his short-sleeved shirt. He closed the Jaguar's door roughly, sauntered to the driver's side door of the Alfa Romeo, turned to face the eight civilian sailors, and leaned back deliberately against the sports car, his massive forearms crossed over his outsized chest. He looked steadily into the eyes of the surprised ferry crew, then smiled broadly. "G'mornin', mates," said Luke Manguson cheerily. "Were y'thinkin' of havin' a little chat with my baby sister this fine Sunday mornin'? Or maybe with her husband back in the Jag there?"

As the crewmembers' eyes followed Luke's glance back at the Mark VII, Matt Clark, awakened by the forcible concussion of the Jaguar's door, unfolded his long-muscled, six-foot four-inch frame from the opposite side of the car. He leaned against the roof of the Jaguar and looked evenly toward the sailors, saying nothing.

Luke returned his gaze to the ferry crew. His broad smile disappeared. "Or maybe you were just admirin' the car, eh?" he said quietly. "Not *really* starin' at the driver. Not *really* startin' to discuss my sister . . . this gentleman's wife. Eh?"

Then he smiled again. But this smile was different from the other. This smile, if a smile it was, seemed to comprise notification that there would be no further warning. Pleasantries were over.

The eight men, almost as in choreograph, touched their hands to their caps, and except one, began to turn away and head toward their waiting vessel. The one called Ed lingered just long enough to make a reply. "Very nice automobiles, sir," he said seriously. "It'll be our pleasure to deliver 'em both to Normandy.

"And, sir," he added, seemingly as courteously as possible, now beginning to move away with his shipmates but still looking over his shoulder at Luke, "I hope you'll not mind my sayin' that your sister's face . . . well . . . seein' her like that, sleepin' so pretty . . . just the sight of 'er makes me a little happier. No disrespect to her or you or the gentleman. God's own truth to that, sir.

"On the Bible itself," he declared. "The sight of 'er just makes me happier."

Luke found himself moved by this brave effort to deliver a compliment at once so simple and yet so encompassing. After a moment, still holding the man's gaze as he moved slowly toward his ship, Luke nodded his head in fresh understanding.

"Yes," he called out to the man, "and she does that for us all, sir. She always has."

SAN FRANCISCO/BERKELEY: 11:30 PM/SATURDAY
NEW YORK: 2:30 AM/SUNDAY
LONDON: 7:30 AM/SUNDAY
ROME: 8:30 AM/SUNDAY

Eleanor Chapel nudged her sleeping husband with a sharp elbow. "Sidney . . . Sidney . . . SIDNEY!" she said.

"Hmm?"

"The telephone, dear. Reach over and answer the phone! You *insisted* on having the thing on your side of the bed."

He complied sluggishly. Rolling away from his wife and onto his right side, thereby freeing his undamaged left arm and hand, he reached for the jangling instrument. Clumsily, he brought the receiver to his ear. Years of NYPD habit then broke through his nine-parts sleeping brain and he said with long-practiced, big-city brusqueness, "Belton!"

The voice on the other end of the line rumbled toward him softly but insistently. "Detective? Antonio Camposanto here. Are you awake enough to do the listening, *per favore?* I need for you to do the listening."

And then Camposanto waited courteously, listening to the rustling sounds of his colleague as he struggled to rouse himself. Finally he heard the same voice, nearly as deep as his own and now fully alive, coming back to him over the line. "Yeah, Detective . . . okay . . . I'm ready . . . shoot!"

"I have just completed the speaking with my staff in Roma, *signore*," said Camposanto. "I have an instruction from the kidnappers . . . the murderers. Can you write this instruction, *signore*? You must have the instruction on paper and you must have the instruction correct, my friend, so as to be certain that your friends in London are given the correct detail, *si*?"

"Yeah, Detective," muttered Belton. "Hang on a minute."

Belton turned to his wife. Her bright eyes were wide in the semi-darkness of the bedroom. "Can you help me out here, Eleanor? We gotta write stuff down."

Before her husband's second sentence was begun, she was already on her feet and scurrying, note pad and pencil in hand, toward the living room where the other telephone sat. In seconds, she lifted the receiver and spoke softly, "Detective Camposanto? Eleanor here. I'm ready to write, sir. Please go slowly. I don't want to miss a word."

Camposanto then explained that the retrieval instructions were extremely specific. Rebecca Manguson Clark would be required to appear at All Saints' Anglican Church, situated on Via del Babuino, between the famed Piazza di Spagna—the Spanish Steps—and the Piazza del Popolo, on Tuesday at noon, just over fifty-one hours from that moment. Directions to the children's exact location would be inserted in a large manila envelope and placed on a long table amid the clutter of church newsletters, meeting announcements, bulletins, and other communiqués just inside the doors to the main sanctuary. Mrs. Clark's name would be written prominently on the face of this envelope as it was placed among the jumble of documents. The table and the envelope would then come under constant surveillance from a remote point inside the church.

Mrs. Clark was to arrive at noon precisely. She was to enter, walk directly to the table, and stand beside it with her right profile in full view of anyone seated in the church proper. Her facial scar, the kidnappers' message emphasized, must be clearly visible to the person or persons who just earlier would have placed the envelope on the table, and who would by then be seated somewhere in the two-hundred-seat church, observing closely. If anyone other than Mrs. Clark attempted to take the envelope, the children would immediately be moved from the city to a location outside of Rome that would not under any circumstances be disclosed.

Camposanto paused, then continued. He spoke deliberately, translating slowly from his notes. Eleanor Chapel wrote silently. Her husband listened without comment.

"You, *signora,* are to depart California and return to your home . . . to New York City . . . without delay," said Camposanto quietly. "The kidnappers—the murderers—say that you are to depart by Wednesday midday, California time. They add that if you are still in this area on Friday evening . . . Friday evening in Roma, they say . . . then. . . ."

Camposanto stopped.

After a moment, Eleanor Chapel spoke. "Continue, Detective. If I am still in California by Friday evening, Rome time, then what? Go ahead. I must know."

Camposanto cleared his throat, drew a breath, and continued. "The murderers say that, if you are still here in California by then, they will execute one of the captives every forty-eight hours until all four of them are dead: my daughter Sophia; your niece, Anna; and the two children. All dead."

Silence ensued.

At length, Camposanto spoke again. "My friends, there are two more parts to this . . . this devil message. They say that no word of this . . . this connecting . . . this connecting between the kidnapping in Roma and these instructions for your removal from California, Dr. Chapel . . . of the removal of yourself from the *Congressus* steering committee . . . may be revealed to the newspapers . . . or to the television. They . . . the newspapers and the television . . . they know already, of course, of the Angelini kidnapping and the murder, but they do not know that there is this demanding of you. They do not know *why* there has been the Angelini kidnapping . . . and the murder of Mario. They only know that there has been such a thing. They have . . . speculated . . . that the kidnapping has to do with Mario Angelini and his publishing business . . . but they do not know. . . .

"And, at the last," he concluded, "they say that you, *signora*, and I, as the . . . how do you say it? . . . . as the . . . 'relatives of blood?' . . . eh? . . . . as the 'blood relatives' of the kidnapped women and children . . . must understand that the release of the children to Mrs. Clark is simple . . . ah . . . simple . . . *good will* . . . on their part. They say that they do not wish to harm or even to frighten the children. And they know that Mrs. Clark's location in London—a two-day drive or a two-hour flight to Roma—and her close friendship with you, Dr. Chapel, make Mrs. Clark the correct person of their choosing to receive the children."

Silence again fell, both in the hotel suite where Giuseppe Basso listened morosely to his future father-in-law, and in the apartment where Eleanor Chapel and her husband heard and considered these demands. At length, Sidney Belton said slowly into the receiver, "Eleanor, you got everything

written down? Yeah? Okay . . . well . . . we got it, Detective. . . . We'll talk. . . .
We'll talk and then we'll get back to ya. You still at the hotel?"

SAN FRANCISCO/BERKELEY: 7:00 AM/SUNDAY
LONDON/PARIS: 3:00 PM/SUNDAY
ROME: 4:00 PM/SUNDAY

Luke placed his transatlantic and transcontinental collect phone call to
Eleanor Chapel's apartment in Berkeley from a public telephone located
just south of Chartres, to the south-southwest of metropolitan Paris, along
the main roadway to Orleans. Writing rapidly as the professor spoke, he
recorded the kidnappers' lengthy message.

Eleanor Chapel read the message at something just slower than her
lecturing pace. Rebecca held a clipboard steady for her brother as he
wrote, replacing each sheet of paper as he neared the end. When the
message was completely recorded, Eleanor Chapel said that she wished to
add something to the message, and made clear that she wanted Luke to
hear her plainly.

"I want you to know," she said emphatically, "that I have made the decision, Luke, to comply with these instructions. I know what I said earlier,
and I know the consequences of responding to terrorists' demands—and
these *are* terrorists, so far as I am concerned—and I know that people who
would kidnap two children and murder their father and threaten to kill
their mother. . . ."

There was a pause.

"I know," Eleanor Chapel resumed, struggling, "that when you do what
murderers and terrorists tell you to do . . . I know . . . but Luke . . . Luke,
I *have* to leave and go to New York. . . . I just can't . . ."

She was interrupted at that moment not by Luke, but by Rebecca,
whose ear had been pressed to the receiver alongside her brother's. "Dr.
Chapel . . . Dr. Chapel . . . listen to me, dear. Listen to me carefully.

"This will be finished before then. We will be finished with all of this
long before Friday night in Rome. I promise you.

"God Himself has joined this battle, Eleanor," she continued, urgency in her low, forceful contralto. "This is out of your hands and into His, and now, through Him, into mine . . . into ours . . . into mine and Luke's and Matt's and even Andrea's. By Friday night . . . or perhaps well before . . . this will be finished, one way or the other. *It will be finished!*"

And after a moment, Rebecca added, "Remember, dear Eleanor, always remember: '*It is a fearsome thing to fall into the hands of the living God.*' Our enemies are soon to know this and to understand this, in ways they have perhaps never understood before.

"Do not think one single minute more about these murderers' demands, my dear Eleanor," added Rebecca, speaking slowly, as before, so as to lay emphasis on each word separately. "This *will* be finished."

SAN FRANCISCO/BERKELEY: 12:00 NOON SUNDAY
ROME: 9:00 PM/SUNDAY

As Giuseppe Basso settled into the rear seat of Richard Mabry's humble Plymouth Valiant, Richard looked over his shoulder at the unhappy young man. "You must be overwhelmed by all that has happened in the last few days . . . I mean . . . assigned to shadow Sidney Belton in New York City, of all things . . . then, after you were . . . well . . . ah . . . *noticed* by him . . . flying all the way out here . . . then learning that your fiancée had been kidnapped. . . .

"What do you make of all this, Giuseppe?"

Giuseppe stared at Richard without expression, his face a troubled mask.

Lois Tanaka, who had also been looking over her shoulder at the newly embarked passenger, turned her head toward the driver, her expression filled with good-natured reproach.

"Richard," she said softly, shaking her head and expressing an exaggerated solemnity, "you *must* become aware of your idioms. You cannot say to a native speaker of some other language who is still in his first week in this country, 'What do you make of all this?' and expect him to know what on earth you're asking of him."

Richard looked over at his teasing companion and smiled. "Well, Ms. Tanaka, language expert extraordinaire, just what should I have said?"

She replied by turning away from him and, smiling now at Giuseppe Basso, asked simply, "Giuseppe . . . are you hungry? . . . ah. . . . Are you . . . *affamato*?"

The two men, simultaneously grasping both the wisdom and the humor in this abrupt change of subject, broke into appreciative laughter. Basso, suddenly confident that he knew what had been asked of him, nodded his head, "*Si, signora*," he said gratefully. "Detective Camposanto . . . he does not eat the food for such a . . . a. . . ." and here he spread his hands wide so as to suggest Camposanto's stunning girth.

Suddenly the threesome found themselves relaxed in each other's company. As Richard steered the dirty, dented gray Valiant toward a small Italian restaurant a mile south of the university campus, a conversation of sorts developed with Lois in the role of questioner and Giuseppe endeavoring to respond coherently in his broken English.

By the time they arrived at the tiny restaurant, the two Americans learned that Giuseppe Basso and Sophia Camposanto had been formally engaged for about three months, that their families had carefully arranged the union, and that Giuseppe was certain he was much more satisfied with the betrothal than was his intended.

Minutes later, now sitting together at a window table, the threesome shifted the conversation by unspoken mutual consent from the engagement and some of its more unsettling aspects to the developing events involving Eleanor Chapel, Sid Belton, and Antonio Camposanto.

In his turn, Giuseppe spoke slowly, trying to make clear his impressions. "I think," he was saying, looking alternately at his two hosts, "that the detective . . . 'Papa Camposanto,' I am to call him . . . I think that Papa Camposanto . . . he does not know . . . what he should do. . . .

"He had the . . . the thinking . . . that Sophia . . . she would be safe with . . . with the . . . the arranging . . . the arranging that he had made in Roma . . . for her protecting. . . . And I think . . . he does not think very . . . very clear . . . or very well, sometimes . . . *capisci*?"

Heads nodded.

After a moment of visible struggling, he spoke again. This time it was not in response to a direct question. "I think . . . I think I tell you both of something," he said slowly, ". . . something from the last night . . . that I am so . . . confused. . . ."

He paused, searching for words, then continued. "There was the phone call last night to Papa Camposanto . . . from his staff in Roma . . . and it was the . . . the . . . demands. . . . It was the demands. . . ."

Then Giuseppe Basso, uncertain about everything—uncertain that he had fully understood the kidnappers' message even though Antonio Camposanto had allowed him to read his transcribed notes, uncertain that he himself should be party to the ensuing intrigue, uncertain, above all, that he should be relaying to his new friends any of the information that he possessed—plunged in, desperate, and reported laboriously to his luncheon hosts everything that he remembered from the previous night's telephone exchanges, first with Camposanto's staff in Rome, and then with Eleanor Chapel and Sid Belton at their apartment in Berkeley. At length he fell silent.

Both listeners understood that by now, the Londoners traveling on the continent would have been in touch with Dr. Chapel, and thus, would assuredly be in receipt of the kidnappers' demands. Both Americans also understood the ominous report. An uneasy silence ensued, and then Lois spoke.

"Are you afraid . . . for Sophia, Giuseppe?" she asked, peering at his face intently, trying to read his thoughts before he could express them aloud.

"*Si, signora*," he replied quickly, "but . . . I must tell you again . . . that . . . that I do not know my fiancée . . . very much. . . ." He paused and looked at his questioner closely, mirroring her efforts to read his face.

"Do you . . . do you know my . . . my . . . the meaning of this, *signora*?" he asked, the words coming slowly to his lips as he wrestled with translation from Italian thoughts to English words and sentences.

She nodded. "Yes, Giuseppe, I do know what you mean. You mean that this marriage has been arranged by your families . . . and that you have not been together . . . alone . . . with Sophia . . . very much. Or at all. You have perhaps had no . . . private conversations . . . just the two of you . . . at all. Yes?"

"*Si*," he said simply, "but I want very much for her to be . . . okay . . . you know? I want her to be okay and I . . . and I want to . . . to be with her in my country . . . and . . . and I want to marry Sophia . . . whenever our . . . our families . . . should make the arranging. . . . Do you see?"

As Lois nodded, grateful to have been trusted with such personal disclosures from one whom she scarcely knew, Richard joined the exchange—changing the subject so abruptly and callously that, to his amused astonishment, he drew a reproving, exaggerated-yet-delicate, right-hand punch to the bicep from his female companion. "Do you . . . are you hoping, Giuseppe," he had said in the process of inviting the miniature assault, "that Dr. Chapel will do what the kidnappers have instructed her to do?"

It was here that the small fist made contact with his arm.

Laughing delightedly at the blow and at the scowling, affectionate face behind it, he continued, undeterred. "And do you hope that Dr. Chapel will return to New York right away . . . to abandon the *Congressus* steering committee and to leave it to do its work without her?"

The Italian, studiously ignoring what he correctly understood to be flirtatious byplay between his hosts, pondered the question, then replied slowly, "I don't know. I don't know how I should be thinking of this. And . . . and I think that Papa . . . he does not know how to be thinking of this, too. I think that Papa . . . he does not . . . does not know how to think . . . how to think like the detective . . . when it is his own daughter who is the . . . the. . . ."

"The victim," said Lois, quietly completing the sentence.

He nodded. "*Si.* The victim."

The intense silence that followed was interrupted by their waitress, who efficiently took their simple order—pizza slices and soft drinks— and departed. As the young woman with the pencil and notepad moved away from their table, Lois turned her eyes away from the window to face their guest.

"Giuseppe," she said carefully, "do you pray for your fiancée? Do you believe that God can intervene . . . that God can . . . ah . . . reach down to help her? Or to help Antonio Camposanto to know what he should do? Or to help Dr. Chapel know what she should do?"

She hesitated, then stopped and waited for his reply. In the new silence, Richard, surprised at her purposeful redirection of the conversation, looked first in wonder at his companion, then turned his own eyes to Giuseppe Basso, who stared at the table for a long moment, then raised his eyes to the delicately feminine, distinctively oriental features of his questioner. "*Si, signora,*" he began simply. "*Si.* I pray for them all. And I pray for the . . . the. . . ."

"The kidnappers?" Lois asked.

"*Si, signora* . . . for the kidnappers. I pray for them also. I think that I do not know what to do . . . except this one thing. The praying, I know how to do. The praying, I know . . . it can sometimes . . . make everything okay. God . . . He can make everything okay. And I say to myself He will. And I think . . . I think . . . that He will make everything okay. . . . But I know that He needs for us . . . for us . . . here . . . to have the courage. . . ."

"'Here'?" Lois interrupted. "'Here' . . . on this earth, Giuseppe?"

"*Si* . . . here on this earth, *signora* . . . God needs us to have . . . courage to do . . . things . . . to help. And . . . I do not have the courage. I do not know . . . what I can do. . . . And so I worry that Papa . . . he seems not to . . . know . . . he seems not to have the courage. . . . He seems not to be himself, I think. . . .

"I know only to do the praying, *signora* . . . for Papa . . . for Sophia . . . for Dr. Chapel . . . for her family in Roma . . . for the . . . the London people . . . for Andrea . . . for the bad men who are doing this. . . . I know only to do the praying. . . .

"And so that is what I do. It is what I do . . . all the time. . . . *All* the time."

San Francisco/Berkeley: 11:00 am/Monday of the second week
Rome: 8:00 pm/Monday of the second week

As the two-car motorcade approached the outskirts of the ancient metropolis, Luke pulled the Mark VII over and onto an exit ramp, followed at a safe distance by Rebecca behind the wheel of the nimble Alfa. The two autos soon took a sharp right onto a small farm road. Then, after another half-mile, they moved off the unmarked roadway and onto a grassy expanse fronting a generous copse. Although the June sun had set long before, a near-full moon and cloudless sky provided ample light for the four as they stretched their cramped legs and stood gratefully at rest in the quiet summer air, the lights of Rome brightening the night sky in the distance to the south.

Rebecca looked up at the broad expanse above her. She shivered visibly. Immediately she felt her husband's strong right arm around her shoulders. She looked up at him appreciatively.

"Thank you, dear," she murmured softly, "but I wasn't shivering from cold. I was just . . . well . . . *quivering*, I suppose . . . at the thought of where we are at this moment on God's earth."

She looked to the south, and the others turned their faces to follow her eyes. "Just think! Why just down there . . . just *there*, in the distance . . . the apostle Paul *himself* sat in his prison cell, in chains, writing words that we all would read *today*, reaching us . . . teaching us. . . ."

Suddenly she wheeled, trotted ten steps to the Alfa, reached through its open right-side window, and extracted something. As she walked back toward the little group, her husband smiled, reached to his belt loop, and unclipped his hooded flashlight. Rebecca, already turning the pages of her small traveling NIV Bible, looked up gratefully at Matt, stood close against him, and turned to Paul's letter to the Philippians.

After a moment, she began to read aloud in her strong, low voice, from the first chapter:

> for whether I am in chains or defending and confirming the gospel, all of you share in God's grace with me. . . . it has become clear throughout the whole palace guard and to everyone else that I am in chains for Christ. Because of my chains, most of the brothers in the Lord have been encouraged to speak the word of God more courageously and fearlessly. . . . now as always Christ will be exalted in my body, whether by life or by death. For to me, to live is Christ and to die is gain.

She finished the passage, looked up at her friends, and closed her Bible, pressing it against her chest with both hands. Then she repeated, slowly and prayerfully, the encompassing and immemorial words of the great missionary: *"For to me, to live is Christ and to die is gain."*

She turned her face upward, gazing at the expanse of sky above her, and smiled. Then she dropped her eyes to earth, and after another moment, turned them back to her brother. She knew it was his time now, and that the minutes were precious.

But Luke did not move immediately to a presentation of the next steps in the plan. He wanted a prayer. Disciplined in his own private prayers, but uncomfortable and unpracticed in leading spoken prayer even for three other Christians, he asked Rebecca to lead them in a prayer of thanksgiving for their safe passage to this point. And she did, clear and unhesitating and confident in extemporaneous public prayer, a gift that had been hers from adolescence, now honed through twice-daily prayers in front of the girls in her Anglican school classroom.

After her whispered "amen," Luke launched his review of the coming twenty-four hours. For the other three, this was confirmation of a plan that had developed in bits and pieces throughout the previous thirty-six hours, following the telephoned relay from California of the kidnappers' directives. At each petrol stop during the long second day's journey, the plan had been fleshed out in increasing detail. "This," Luke began, "is where we will divide forces.

"Andrea," he said, turning his face to the Italian, "you understand your role." He spoke carefully to her, knowing she was translating as he went. "You are to guide Matt to Amalfi, to the Cathedral of St. Andrew . . . to the *duomo* . . . via the A12 to the Rome orbital; then, on the A2, to the Naples area; and finally, when you can pick up the A3 just west of Vesuvius, eastward all the way to Salerno—but no further. There you will find the Amalfi coast roadway and follow it back, traveling west from Salerno, to Amalfi itself. Yes?"

She nodded.

"And you must translate all road signs into English for Matt.

"And . . . whenever he slows the Jaguar, stops, or accelerates, you must handle the shift lever for him. This will be especially crucial on the Amalfi roadway, as you know from personal experience. Matt will be turning, slowing, stopping, accelerating, and turning again, almost without ceasing, once you leave the A3 and start back toward Amalfi from Salerno. Do you understand, Andrea?"

Andrea Camposanto looked down at her feet, frowning. After a moment, she said simply, "*Si.*"

The other three glanced at each other unhappily.

Before Luke could continue, the Italian looked up, her face contorted in anger. "*Non! Non!*" she suddenly shouted at him, her hands moving in tandem near her face, framing her shout. "Why . . . *why* . . . do you believe me, that Rebecca's dream . . . that her dream is of the place that I know? . . . *Why* do you believe me that I say that her dream is of the city of Amalfi . . . that her dream is the dreaming of the Amalfi *duomo*? Why do you believe me that I say all of this . . . that I saw all of . . . of . . . everything?

"*Why* do you make this plan to go to . . . a place . . . to a place that the *signora*"—here she gestured with both hands, dramatically, toward

Rebecca, who stood nearly in front of her—". . . that the *signora* has only *dreamed* of seeing . . . has only seen in her . . . her *visions* . . . her visions of . . . of she does not know what?

"You let me tell to you of the place of where she is dreaming, and you make the plans to go to the place of where she is dreaming, and you make the plans to go there without even a question of the truth of my telling to you, without even a *question*! You make the plans to go there, you make the plans to go there . . . and you show me the . . . the *trust* in what I tell to you!

"And now . . . and now . . . I cannot have the trust to *drive this car*?"

Her voice broke. She put her hands to her face and began to weep.

Rebecca, astonished at this outpouring, but never stunned into inaction when action might be called for, immediately stepped toward Andrea and placed two strong arms around her bony shoulders. She pulled her to her chest, both arms tightly supporting the wiry young woman as she sobbed uncontrollably.

Two full minutes ticked by in the dark silence, Andrea's sobs turning eventually into short gasps, and finally, into a prolonged series of irregular sniffles and sighs. At length, silence fell afresh about them.

Matt was the first to speak. He addressed himself to his brother-in-law. "Luke, I know we must divide forces in this way. I know you and Rebecca must handle the rescue of the children, if it turns out to be that, or escape from the entrapment, if it does not. I understand that it must be Rebecca who enters the church, and I understand that two hands and two arms are essential in the support role that only you can play. Only she can go in the church; only you can be her support person.

"So, yes, it's obvious that Andrea and I must start for Amalfi now to begin conducting our reconnaissance, so the basic surveillance will have been done by the time you and Rebecca arrive tomorrow evening. And of course," he added, his eyes moving briefly from Luke to the two women, "it is Andrea who knows that area and who knows that town intimately.

"But if I may say it, Luke, it is, as Andrea has just said, she herself who has interpreted the physical aspects of Rebecca's visions, and she who has recognized the Cathedral of St. Andrew and placed the kidnappers in Amalfi, and she in whose word we are placing *all* of our confidence . . . and, as she has just said so compellingly . . . our trust."

He paused and turned his face to smile in the direction of his wife, whose arms continued to envelop the small, still obviously distressed woman. "I know, Luke," he continued, "that I have insisted on driving the Mark VII from the moment the division of our forces became the settled plan. 'Never mind that I can't shift,' I've said. 'Never mind that my driver's license is restricted to the UK,' I've said. 'We just don't know Andrea, or her capabilities,' I've said . . . and I've said so at times in front of her, and at times, not."

At this last, he peered more closely in the women's direction, and realized after a moment that the Italian was actually peeking out from under one of his wife's arms. He smiled broadly in her direction.

Then Rebecca stepped aside, one arm still around the great detective's daughter, so that her angular, anxious face was uncovered. Andrea Camposanto looked up at Matt, her expressive eyes uncertain.

"Well," Matt continued, looking first at Luke, and then at his wife, "I was wrong. I was just wrong, Luke. Having only one hand and arm available is not just a matter of being unable to shift the transmission lever. There will be times, probably hundreds and hundreds of times, when the driver of this Jaguar will need two hands and arms *just to handle the turns,* to say nothing of moving the shift lever at exactly the right moment, at the instant the driver chooses to depress the clutch pedal. It is most decidedly *not* a two-person job.

"Andrea is the driver, Luke. She has to be."

Luke Manguson nodded briefly and looked down. All three understood that this was not a nod of agreement, but merely of reception of Matt's message. Luke Manguson, when thinking hard, actually *looked* like a man thinking hard. It was as though an engine had been given an extraordinary load to lift, and it was beginning to test its ability to raise the weight to the necessary level.

More seconds passed. No one moved, although Rebecca and Matt found themselves smiling in the moonlight at each other. Both seemed to know in advance the conclusion that was being drawn in Luke Manguson's capacious mind, and each waited in comfortable expectation for a known outcome.

Their affectionate gazes each to the other were interrupted by a movement from Luke. He looked slowly up at Andrea Camposanto and nodded. "Andrea," he said carefully, deliberately, "we believe God is with us . . . that we are involved in this at His direction . . . that you are involved with us as part of His plan for us . . . that you were given to us precisely because you could immediately identify the kidnappers' location as depicted in Rebecca's visions. . . .

"And it would never have occurred to us to think otherwise.

"But," he continued after a pause, "when it has come to the point of designing a workable plan of action, I confess that I did not carry that same line of reasoning any further. I did not form the perfectly reasonable thought that you, Andrea, have been given to us—divinely appointed, you understand?—not only because you could provide the location of the site to which the kidnappers have apparently taken, at the very least, Dr. Chapel's niece, Anna, whom Rebecca has repeatedly envisioned, but equally as well, because you know the coastal roadways to and from Amalfi and . . . obviously . . . because you can drive a manual transmission automobile better with your two hands and arms than someone who has the use of but one.

"I thought only of my military comrade, despite my original assumption that he could not drive these vehicles, once my mind turned to our final plan of action. I'm so sorry, Andrea."

He looked at her and waited. After a moment, she tossed her head back triumphantly. "Ha!" she said, placing both hands on her hips. "You admit you are wrong! And you admit I am right!"

Both sentences were spoken as accusations delivered to the vanquished by a victor. She stared at him, her hands remaining on her hips, apparently demanding that he grovel at her feet in order to earn her forgiveness.

Rebecca and Matt watched quietly, bemused.

Luke returned the challenge with easy grace. "Yes, Andrea, I do indeed. And, having made this admission of error, I now need you to handle this automobile with care and skill, and to lead Matt in the reconnaissance of Amalfi and of the buildings near the cathedral in which Anna Angelini— and perhaps your sister and the children—are held.

"And if you accept both my apology and this invitation, then you must follow whatever orders I give you. Only one person can be in charge of a mission of this sort. I am that person. Do you understand?"

His tone of voice was light; his demeanor was military.

Andrea Camposanto dropped her hands from her hips, then raised them to her face. She smiled, her hands now framing her thin face. "*Si, signore*," she said brightly. "I do understand. And I will not disappoint you, *signore* Luke Manguson. I will not!"

CHAPTER NINE

AS NOON APPROACHED ON THIS MEDITERRANEAN JUNE DAY, a tall, erect young woman approached All Saints' Anglican Church from the rear, striding quickly along the length of the narrow side street—actually an alleyway—that connected Via del Corso to Via del Babuino on which the church faced. The woman wore a dark blue tennis warm-up suit with full-length sleeves and side-zippered trousers lengthy enough to brush the tops of her light blue Nike running shoes as she walked. Her long, thick, black hair was drawn into a tight ponytail that swished rhythmically in concert with her rapid strides. She carried nothing in her hands, and moved with the catlike anticipation of one prepared to draw upon her considerable athleticism at the instant it might be required.

As she drew near the church property, she glanced upward toward the top of the high, smooth masonry wall that separated the alley from the small courtyard that lay directly behind the church building. Her eye quickly picked up that which it sought: two barely visible black metal prongs extending over the alley-side top of the wall. She dropped her eyes and continued toward Babuino, satisfied that what she had glimpsed was, in fact, the only visible component of the grappling hook and rope ladder combination placed in the predawn hours by her brother.

She knew that her twin had arrived on foot at the deserted alley shortly before 3:00 AM, had quietly and skillfully cast the hook-and-rope device into a tight metallic seat on the wall's fourteen-inch-wide crest, and had swiftly clambered to the top. Luke Manguson, perched there for no more than five seconds, had then pulled the rope ladder up, cast it down the inside of the wall, and descended using the ropey rungs, even more quickly than he had climbed.

Once inside the courtyard, he had completed preparations for his sister's escape route from the church, returned to the ladder, ascended, pulled the rope to himself, and then coiled the ladder carefully along the top of the wall so that none of the rope, and only two dark metal prongs on each side of the crest, would be visible from either side to a person looking up from street or courtyard level. Finally, he had attached a light-colored quarter-inch line to the end of the coiled ladder and dropped the virtually invisible line to the courtyard's grassy surface, there to await a fleeing woman's tug, a gesture that would cause the entire ladder to fall to the grass, the grappling hook still in place atop the wall.

Fewer than three minutes after his arrival at the base of the wall, Luke dropped from the fifteen-foot crest to the sidewalk with the confidence and agility of the Royal Navy boarding party commander that he had been not so very long ago. In seconds he was out of the alley and jogging through the darkened streets of Rome back to the waiting Alfa Romeo.

Throughout her brother's clandestine penetration of the church perimeter, Rebecca Manguson Clark had slept soundly in a nondescript hotel room on the northern outskirts of the metropolitan area. Luke and she had checked into the room just before 10:00 PM on Monday. Both had efficiently prepared for bed, engaged in their separate evening devotions, and passed quickly into sleep, she on the small bed and he on the floor, rolled in one of the sleeping bags he had pulled from the Jaguar's trunk—along with select pieces of mostly arcane equipment—before they had separated from their Amalfi-bound companions.

Luke had then arisen at 1:30 without need of an alarm, and indeed, had managed not to awaken his sister at all as he left the hotel for his night foray into the city. Now, as Rebecca approached Babuino, she paused, breathed deeply one time, and mouthed her prayer slowly to herself: *Father, protect me; Jesus, be present; Holy Spirit, give me strength.*

She knew that as soon as she stepped from the alley, she would come under intense surveillance and perhaps had been observed, before now, throughout her approach. Concluding her brief but intense prayer, now just seconds before the noon church bells would begin to toll, Rebecca stepped from the alley, wheeled right, and strode briskly toward the doorway of All Saints'.

The entrance to the church, she knew, was via a doorway that brought a visitor not into the worship center itself, but into a small, nearly circular anteroom directly under the bell tower. Leading thence from the anteroom floor were five marble steps that brought the visitor into a short passageway opening immediately into the sanctuary itself. Rebecca passed swiftly through the anteroom, pausing only to examine two other doorways that led out of the small space. She then proceeded up the short flight of steps and through the passageway, where she suddenly found herself in the sanctuary proper.

Powerfully conflicting inner suggestions, simultaneously of peace and of extreme danger, flooded her senses. She stopped, scanned the graceful expanse of wood and marble, identified the literature table nestled against the wall to her left, and without further hesitation, moved to its side.

She had glimpsed at least a dozen people scattered around the church, some seated, others kneeling in private prayer, but now she deliberately looked only in the direction of the table surface. There her eyes sought and found a manila envelope, placed nearly in the center. Scrawled across the face of the envelope was a name: Rebecca Clark.

Standing completely still, with her right profile exposed fully toward the interior of the sanctuary, the V of her scar in full view of anyone attempting to confirm her identity, she lifted the envelope and slid her finger along the sealed flap. She inserted her hand and removed a single sheet of paper. Five words appeared there, printed carefully in English: *Ensnarer— prepare to meet God.*

Expressionless, she instantly opened her hands, allowing envelope and note to tumble haphazardly toward the polished hardwood floor. As they made their erratic course downward, she spun and walked swiftly toward the anteroom.

Turning her head quickly to the left, she saw in periphery at least three looming shapes rising from their seats along the near aisle of the sanctuary. Rebecca broke into a run, descended the five marble steps in one long bound, and bringing herself to a halt in the circular anteroom, immediately heard loud, rough, male voices shouting to each other in Italian on the sidewalk just outside the closed doors fronting Via del Babuino.

SAN FRANCISCO/BERKELEY: 3:03 AM/TUESDAY OF THE SECOND WEEK
ROME: 12:03 PM/TUESDAY OF THE SECOND WEEK

With weapons for the moment holstered or sheathed, six very large men burst through the main doorway of All Saints' Anglican Church and found themselves face-to-face with three of their equally formidable colleagues in the suddenly too-small anteroom. Their leader, having just entered from Babuino with the other five, smiled grimly. Nodding at the three who had just exited the sanctuary, he indicated with a movement of his eyes that they should take the small doorway that led, by spiral staircase, to the top of the bell tower.

These three immediately began the arduous climb.

The leader was in no hurry to move to the other small doorway. He knew that it led, also by spiral staircase, down to basement level. He also knew there were no unguarded exterior doors leading out of the church basement. Anyone descending by those steps would necessarily climb that same staircase in order to depart. And since the entire basement was well below street level, there could be no windows affording an alternative means of escape. The leader could be a patient man, and in this instance, he found himself enjoying every moment of what he knew was a young woman's utter desperation.

In just two minutes, he heard the bell tower steps being descended with slow, heavy tread, and knew from those sounds that no captive was in tow. This was no surprise to him. His quarry would have understood, if she and her accomplices had managed to research the building's layout at all, that a descent to basement level would provide more opportunities to attempt concealment from pursuers than an ascent to the top of a bell tower, where there could be none.

Five minutes later, still moving systematically through the basement's meeting rooms and storage cavities, the leader heard a shout from one of his men. He, along with two others in his immediate company, wheeled and raced down the corridor that led to the rear of the building.

Arriving at the doorway to a small utility room, he saw one of his men crouched halfway in and out of a partially raised window. The window opened not onto street or alley, but merely onto a concrete chute that directed itself upward, apparently to the level of the rear courtyard. The opening at the top of the chute was secured by a heavy metal grate. The leader, now peering upward alongside the man who had made the discovery, indicated with a nod that he wanted the weight and strength of the grate to be tested forcefully.

Struggling with great difficulty into the narrow, constricted chute, the bulky henchman stood awkwardly, raised his hands to the underside of the grate, and pressed upward. To his surprise, it moved. At the urging of his leader, and indeed, with considerable physical assistance both from him and two others who attempted to crowd through the window opening and into the chute to assist, the beleaguered man finally slid the grate to one side and fought his way, his colleagues pushing clumsily from below, up to courtyard level. He rolled away from the opening and onto the grass.

The leader and his two comrades waited, still crammed into the concrete chute, while perhaps a full minute passed. Then their colleague's face appeared just above them.

He spoke in rapid Italian: "She didn't come out here, sir. There's no way out of this courtyard except through its gate into the alley. The gate is padlocked. Looks like it hasn't been opened in years. And there's no possible way she could've climbed that wall. It must be fifteen feet, straight up, no handholds. She's still in the church, sir. She can't be anywhere else. No possible way."

SAN FRANCISCO/BERKELEY: 8:25 AM/ TUESDAY OF THE SECOND WEEK
ROME: 5:25 PM/ TUESDAY OF THE SECOND WEEK

The Italian co-chair of the *Congressus* steering committee lifted the telephone receiver from its position on the spacious mahogany desk of his ninth-floor San Francisco hotel room. As he prepared to speak, he glanced northwestward out his window overlooking San Francisco Bay, his eye drawn immediately to the distant image of Alcatraz Island, an image that for untold years had served as irresistible magnet for a million wandering gazes from city to water. He spoke slowly into the receiver in his impeccable English. "This is Niccolo Giacomo speaking."

He smiled as the rumbling voice greeted his ear. The voice filled his mind and heart with an Italian spoken as only ancestral natives can, those multi-generational heirs of a language whose genealogy reached back to the very political and military world that Jesus Himself engaged. The conversation proceeded entirely in that language.

"I think, my friend," said Detective Antonio Camposanto, "that you will find it necessary to go forward without the presence of Dr. Eleanor Chapel."

"What do you mean, Detective?" said Giacomo sharply.

"She is simply overwhelmed, I fear," the detective replied. "The situation in Roma is a terrible emotional distraction to her, and the sad fact is that my people are no closer to a solution now than before. These unspeakable animals have communicated a horrible threat to systematically kill the captives if Dr. Chapel does not return forthwith to New York.

"I have found it necessary to tell her that I believe they are capable of doing exactly what they say."

"I am so sorry, my friend," said Giacomo.

There was a pause. And then he continued, "And how are you bearing up, yourself, Detective, with your daughter among the kidnapped?"

"I am able to remain focused on the work most of the time, Dr. Giacomo. And I pray to God without ceasing, my friend. It is all that I can do."

"Yes, yes, I understand, I do understand."

There was another pause, and then Niccolo Giacomo went on thoughtfully, "And you believe that Dr. Chapel has changed her mind about ignoring the attackers, as you at first reported to me, and will leave us to return to her home in New York?"

"I have advised her to do so, and I think she will accept my advice. I have tried to ask myself whether or not I would give that advice were not my own daughter among the victims. I think the answer is yes. And on that basis I have so advised her."

"And does her husband—Detective Belton, I think it is?—does he agree with your advice?"

"Indeed he does. He and I are old friends. We trust each other completely."

"Well," said Giacomo after a moment, "I certainly do not like the idea that terrorists can succeed in disrupting work at this level of international, and indeed, as we believe, of eternal importance, simply by being what they are: murderers and blackmailers. But I cannot in good conscience say that I could give Dr. Chapel any advice other than that which you have already given, Detective."

"Thank you, thank you."

"Should I endeavor to speak with Eleanor before she goes, Detective Camposanto?"

"No," the policeman replied quickly. "I have sequestered her and Detective Belton outside of the Bay area, and hope to negotiate through our consulate a military flight back to the East Coast for the two of them. I would prefer that she not use a commercial airport for this flight. I am mindful of the criminals' instruction not to allow the media to connect their crimes with their demands on Dr. Chapel. And I simply cannot guarantee her security, nor can my colleagues here in the area."

"Well," replied Giacomo sincerely, a sadness in his voice, "I will truly miss her. She has, of course, generated great problems for me in her persistent opposition to our position statement, but she has done so with the most perfect Christian charity and integrity. It was not a mistake to invite her to join us."

"Will you tell her those things, Detective?"

"*Si. Si.*"

"*Grazie.*"

SAN FRANCISCO/BERKELEY: 11:05 AM/TUESDAY OF THE SECOND WEEK
ROME: 8:05 PM/TUESDAY OF THE SECOND WEEK

More than two hours after Antonio Camposanto telephoned Niccolo Giacomo, Lois Tanaka and Richard Mabry stood at his hotel door and knocked twice. After a moment, the door swung open, filled completely by Camposanto's immense figure. The detective smiled broadly at the sight of the two, but made no move to invite them inside.

"Ah, my young friends," he said in English, gesturing expansively, "you are perhaps hoping to find Giuseppe here?"

Both nodded.

"He has, I'm afraid, decided to go for the long walk this morning. He said to me that he would not probably be returning until late in the day. I shall inform him of your coming to see him, eh?"

"Thank you, Detective," said Richard. "Would you ask him if he might telephone me this evening?"

"*Si*," replied the detective, nodding agreeably and reaching back with one hand to begin to draw the door closed.

But Lois moved forward quickly as the detective stepped aside to allow the door to shut completely. "Detective," she asked, peering up at his face and tilting her head to one side as he continued to retreat into his hotel room, "have Dr. Chapel and Detective Belton been here to see you? This morning or last night?"

The detective did not interrupt either his or the door's movement. "*Non*," he said simply and emphatically. The door shut fast, inches from the young woman's face, locking automatically.

The two visitors turned away slowly. As they moved back toward Richard's old Plymouth, he looked closely at his companion. Her face was ashen.

He stepped nearer and placed his hand on her arm. "Lois? Lois! What is it?" He searched her tense face for an answer and saw her eyes close.

She shook her head and, opening her eyes after a moment, gestured toward the car. Richard quickly stepped around her, opened the passenger-side door, and assisted her carefully to a sitting position, much as he might a child or an elderly person. She did not resist his efforts to help her, and in fact clutched uncharacteristically at his hand throughout the maneuver. Richard had never seen anyone faint except in movies, but he thought to himself, this surely is how a person would look just before losing consciousness.

Closing her door carefully, he swiftly circled the front of the car, all the while looking at his companion's face with mounting fear. As he stooped to slide in behind the wheel, he saw her raise her hands to her face, covering her eyes.

Seeing that she was not ready to speak, and indeed, seemed to be sinking down into herself as he watched, he started the engine, backed quickly out of the parking space, and sped out of the parking lot and around the corner, proceeding just far enough to seize a parking space removed visually from the detective's hotel room window.

He pulled into the space haphazardly, stopped quickly, switched off the ignition, and turned back to Lois. He slid across the Valiant's bench seat, placed his right arm and hand around her shoulders, and reached tentatively toward her right cheek with his left hand, although both her hands still remained in place, covering her eyes.

Cradling her right hand in his left, he pulled her face carefully toward his and then gently tugged her hands down, away from her eyes. Then, his face now very close to hers, he peered into her dark eyes and whispered, "Lois . . . Lois . . . talk to me . . . please. . . . What is it?"

Her reply was given in a whisper, one much softer than his, and he leaned still closer, the side of his face almost against her lips. "On the floor . . ." she murmured, her lips trembling, ". . . on the floor, Richard . . . just under the skirt of the bed . . . I saw . . . I saw the pin."

He moved away from her just enough to look at her more fully. He shook his head. "The pin, Lois?" He was still whispering. "What pin? I don't understand what you mean."

"The pin," she said, no longer whispering. "The pin that Dr. Chapel always wears on her lapel . . . the silver replica of a fountain pen. . . .

"Her pin was on the rug, Richard. It was just behind Mr. Camposanto, just at the edge of the bed . . . almost under the bed. . . .

"Richard!" she cried, her voice breaking in terror. "Richard! He has done something to her!"

SAN FRANCISCO/BERKELEY: 4:00 PM/ TUESDAY OF THE SECOND WEEK
ROME: 1:00 AM/WEDNESDAY OF THE SECOND WEEK

Richard Mabry sat down at the exact moment, almost to the very second, at which the steering committee's afternoon session was to begin. He looked quickly around the room as he pulled his chair up to the enormous conference table. It seemed to him that everyone was present except the one that he had spent the day worrying about.

Immediately Dr. Niccolo Giacomo called the meeting to order and asked for the minutes to be read. As soon as the opening formalities were complete, including a perfunctory prayer offered by one of the old guard Italians, Giacomo continued in his careful, flawless, academic English. The translators waited, silent, knowing that their services would be unnecessary until the discussion began to include, as it inevitably would, more technical and esoteric English constructions that would tax the nonnative English speakers' understanding.

"You are all aware," Giacomo resumed, "of the tragic events in Rome, the kidnapping of members of my co-chair's family, the murder of her niece's husband, the kidnapping of Detective Antonio Camposanto's daughter. . . .

"These things you know.

"What you do not know, and what I must tell you now, is of the threats that have been communicated to Dr. Chapel, via Detective Camposanto."

A small, barely audible gasp escaped several throats at once. Every eye in the room now locked itself onto Giacomo's face.

"The kidnappers," he continued after a moment, ". . . the murderers, have said to Dr. Chapel, through Detective Camposanto's staff in Rome, that they will systematically execute the captives unless Dr. Chapel returns immediately to New York . . . unless she immediately breaks off her involvement with this committee, and indeed, with the entire *Congressus* proceedings."

He paused and looked around the room.

"She will, accordingly, not be with us henceforth. She may in fact be en route to the East Coast of the U.S. as we speak. We can, in truth, only pray for her safety and for that of her family members in Italy.

"I must make clear to you, as well, that the murderers instructed the detective not to reveal to the media the connection between their abduction of these women and children and their demands that Dr. Chapel remove herself from these proceedings. It will be clear to you, then, that you will repeat that connection outside this room at the peril of Dr. Chapel's family, Detective Camposanto's daughter, and indeed, Dr. Chapel herself. Do you understand?"

He paused, looking slowly and meaningfully around the room.

"I admit that I do not understand how it is possible that a Christian debate focused on the education of seminarians around the world can transform itself into something as demonic as this . . . as demonic as murder, kidnapping, and blackmail. Or perhaps I do. Perhaps we have only to consider the word itself—demonic—to identify the source."

He paused again. Several heads nodded miserably.

"In any case, we will not stop, you and I. We will complete our preparations. With God's help and with His guidance, we will do our part to prepare for and to lead this magnificent conference. We will continue."

The ensuing silence grew long and was broken eventually by Giacomo himself, who then, his voice quavering at several points, offered an elegant prayer of intercession for Eleanor Chapel, her husband, and the kidnapped women and children. He included in his prayer emotion-laden phrases on behalf of the murdered husband of Anna Angelini, and he ended the intercessory plea with a fervent appeal that the committee might truly enact the will of the Almighty in its final deliberations.

His prayer complete, Giacomo said simply that he would need fifteen minutes of solitude in order to compose himself for the business of the meeting. He added that he assumed everyone present would want to use those minutes in prayer and contemplation. He then rose and walked to the door.

As his footsteps receded down the hallway, all thirty members of the *Congressus* steering committee bowed their heads as one in the stark silence and entered into their souls' individual sanctuaries. When Niccolo Giacomo returned after a quarter-hour, he found that no person had moved other than to fold hands and bow heads.

He sat down quietly, murmured a quiet "amen" in the enduring silence, and resumed the meeting.

Richard Mabry had spent the fifteen minutes in a state of nearly unbearable tension, his mind careening back and forth between outright terror, as he considered what might have happened to the couple and to his new friend, Giuseppe, and the purposeful sense of determination he had felt at the time he had entered the meeting room.

The terror was grounded in his and Lois Tanaka's fruitless search for Eleanor Chapel and Sid Belton, and the helplessness they had felt during the five hours that had passed since their brief visit to Antonio Camposanto's hotel. The fact that they could find no trace of Giuseppe Basso either frightened them nearly as much as the other. He would not, they knew, do what Detective Camposanto had nonchalantly suggested. Their new friend would certainly not have gone for a walk that would consume the entire day. He had no interest in exercise for the sake of exercise, and a real fear of exploring even the hotel's immediate neighborhood on foot.

The determination that Richard felt alternately with the terror was rooted in his and Lois Tanaka's conclusion—born in an agony of indecision and settled less than an hour before the meeting—that, first, Richard would attempt to represent Eleanor Chapel in this meeting, speaking from her perspective as he understood it, and in any other sessions that might be held in the final days before *Congressus*; and second, that if no word had been received from or about Eleanor Chapel, Sid Belton, or Giuseppe Basso by 7:00 PM—roughly the scheduled conclusion of the meeting—then they would attempt to reach Rebecca Manguson Clark in Europe by telephone. Richard had little confidence that either thing could be done successfully.

Regarding the first, he had no genuine stature with the committee. He might parrot Eleanor Chapel's positions on the issues, but he was not Eleanor Chapel. And regarding the second—reaching the fabled Rebecca Clark—he and Lois did not even know where she was, to say nothing of having some method of gaining entrance to the professor's apartment or to her office in order to research whatever contact information for Mrs. Clark might be discoverable there.

It seemed to them both that, in seeking such contact information, they would be more likely to be arrested by the campus or the city police than to succeed in any fashion whatever. The most likely scenario would be that they would be thrown in jail for breaking and entering long before they had begun to find Rebecca Clark's contact numbers.

But they could think of nothing better. And doing nothing was simply out of the question. They both felt themselves immersed in something of incalculable importance. Though Richard would not have put it this way even a few days earlier, they both felt that the issues were cloaked in the high holiness of a supernatural conflict in which they played an incomprehensible, but meaningful, role.

And so they would do the best they could. They would act in obedience. As they saw it, there was no other responsible choice.

Richard looked up from his notebook and realized that one of the old guard was in mid-proclamation, and that the translators were already fully engaged. The English translation of the last statement came to his ears: "And so, my friends, there can be no further equivocation. The draft position statement is the only statement around which we can rally the delegates. It proclaims the position of greatest strength . . . the platform of greatest influence . . . the edifice of greatest height. . . . The church universal *must* match the financial, commercial, and advertising muscle and technique of the secular economic engine . . . the global economic engine . . . or the church of Jesus Christ will be shunted aside as an irrelevance, unable to compete, unable to gain the attention of the world's literate peoples, and thus, also unable to gain the attention of the as-yet-educated. There is no choice, my friends. We must lead from strength. We must prepare our future priests and ministers of the Gospel to deal with the competing gospels of money, of power, of influence, of advertising sophistication beyond anything we have faced in two thousand years of ministering to the world in Jesus' holy name."

No sooner had the aging Italian begun to resume his seat than Richard Mabry had risen, pushing his chair back noisily. Niccolo Giacomo turned his surprised face to Richard and acknowledged him with a nod, but Richard had not waited. He had already begun.

"I have been profoundly disturbed," he said rather too loudly, his voice tremulous, "by certain things that Dr. Eleanor Chapel said to me privately just two days ago, when she issued her invitation to me to join the committee. I will begin by admitting that, at the time she spoke to me, I found myself simply dismissing her position as . . . well . . . naïve and . . . ah . . . antiquated."

He stopped and looked down. Struggling and confused, he sought desperately to recapture a sense of the prayerful commitment that he and Lois Tanaka had made to God and to each other less than an hour earlier. As his eyes closed momentarily, he suddenly experienced a mysterious, calming strength that swiftly flooded his senses, instantly overwhelming and finally subduing his confusion. He felt a surge of confidence radiating through him, flowing inexplicably from body to mind.

Never had he encountered anything like this. He was so surprised that he found himself wanting to ask his audience's indulgence, to leave the room and search for solitude, to engage privately in sensory recollection and reflection on the experience . . . anything that would allow him uninterrupted time to focus upon these transforming sensations. But this was, he knew, the juvenile and self-absorbed wish of the Richard Mabry of last week, last month, last decade. This was now. And this was the time to do nothing other than follow in obedience. And this meant action. This meant converting the miraculous internal experience of a moment into effective speech and action.

And so, while more seconds passed in the silent room, Richard Mabry gathered himself to proceed, consistent both with the charge and with the miracle.

He looked up at his colleagues.

As he did, a relaxed, happy smile suddenly played across his face, surprising both him and his onlookers. In immediate response, his anxious colleagues turned their faces more fully toward him, beginning to breathe again, their embarrassment on his behalf at his nervous, confessional beginning dissipating in the instant of witnessing his newly smiling countenance.

"I called Dr. Chapel's position both 'naïve' and 'antiquated,'" he said slowly, still marveling, still distracted by what had just happened to him. But he continued to gather his concentration. He could feel it returning. He began to look around the room, now engaging each individual singly with his eyes.

"I called her position both 'naïve' and 'antiquated,'" he repeated, "but it is not. Her position is . . . is simply 'old.'"

He nodded at them, smiling afresh. "It is as old . . . as old . . . as old as the Gospel itself."

He paused momentarily as the translators began their murmuring, unobtrusive work, then resumed. "I find myself thinking suddenly of the familiar words in the letter to the Hebrews: *Jesus Christ the same yesterday, and today, and forever.*"

Richard looked around the room yet again, took a deep and conspicuous breath, and continued, his voice growing stronger as he spoke.

"I thought, as I sat down in our meeting room today, that I would stand up and attempt to represent Dr. Chapel's sentiments in her absence. But, now that I am finally standing here in front of you, I find that that's not really what I feel . . . well . . . commissioned to do.

"I find that I just want to make a simple proposal, one that I think Dr. Chapel would endorse."

He looked down, asked himself if he could actually bring himself to speak the words that pressed to be spoken, and laughed aloud. Looking up, unembarrassed at having laughed audibly in the midst of the most august assembly he had ever addressed, he said simply, "I propose that we issue no position statement at all."

He smiled at the mixture of raised eyebrows, head-shakings, eye-rollings and unambiguous scowls that flooded the room. "No . . . really . . .

think about it," he said. "*Congressus* does, of course, have a tradition . . . a very short one . . . of issuing position statements on the occasion of its international sessions, but why should that mean that we must do that . . . again . . . this time? Why not . . . instead . . . do something like this?

"Let's hold up for our conferees' consideration two things," he said confidently, "and two things only, and not as 'position statements,' but as . . . well . . . informal 'affirmations.'

"Let's hold up, first, one of the creeds—the Apostles' Creed, I suggest, in recognition of its history, its brevity, its clarity—as a faith statement that we encourage all seminaries, their faculties and their students, to reaffirm, exactly as that very creed has been affirmed and reaffirmed for one-and-a-half millennia—that marvelous, ancient summary of the central components of the Christian formula. I mean . . . really . . . really, my friends . . . why not do that?

"A simple, straightforward affirmation of the Apostles' Creed would say plainly that we view seminary training and the shaping of our future ministers as necessarily rooted in . . . well . . . as the creed says to us, in our belief in 'God, the Father Almighty, maker of heaven and earth, and in Jesus Christ his only Son, our Lord. . . .'

"*Why not do that?*"

He looked around the room. The faces had resumed their previous mixture of affect: some curious, some courteous, some intrigued, some disappointed, some beginning to call up a residual, lingering anger.

"And then," Richard resumed, "having done that, we will be able to introduce the several themes of the position statement, but now in the context of something infinitely older, larger, greater. . . .

"Don't you see? If we start with the creed, we could, with that foundation stone, bring in our financial and organizational proposals not as elements of a 'position statement' at all, but as 'new points of emphasis for a new decade' . . . guidelines that would be consistent, when you think about it, with the title for this *Congressus* event itself."

He glanced down at a page on the table in front of him: "*Christianity, Leadership, and Power,*" he read with emphasis, "*Organizational Structures for the New Decade and Beyond.*"

Richard glanced at the chairman, and saw that Niccolo Giacomo was smiling his most paternal, indulgent smile, the sort of smile you might give a small child just at the moment glancing up from the puddle you'd cautioned him about moments earlier.

Suddenly unnerved, stricken with fear that no one was taking him seriously, Richard spread his arms, palms up, toward his colleagues in a gesture calling for support.

"Please!" he said plaintively, his voice taking on the adolescent, whining quality that he hated, "please . . . just consider these simple changes. We'd get to keep the broad themes of the position statement that so many of you have labored for, but we'd subordinate those themes to the ancient creed and thereby remove much of what Dr. Chapel and others among you have found wanting. We'd place the ideas in the safe cradle of the creed, and we'd diminish the threat that many see in them by making them 'affirmations' or 'recommendations' or 'proposed guidelines.'

"Please!" he said again, just as plaintively, "Please consider these suggestions. For Dr. Chapel's sake and for the sake of unity within our steering committee . . . and among the conferees . . . and throughout the whole world of Christian people . . . and other people . . . please!"

Richard stopped speaking and sat down abruptly, his knees suddenly weakening. He leaned forward and put his face in his hands.

He knew his performance had deteriorated at the end, had become terribly clumsy, even pitiable. He had known, even while delivering his message, that his words did not so much as approximate the impact that Eleanor Chapel's presence, oratory style, and content would have had.

His face still buried in his hands, he heard a strange sound from one end of the room. Without looking up, he realized that someone had begun to clap, and that now another had followed, and now yet another.

He took his hands from his face and sat back in his chair. Astonished, he glanced quickly around the room. The applause grew . . . not quite everyone clapping, but nearly so . . . applause that was both unforced and genuine . . . and continuing . . . and continuing . . .

He blushed violently and acknowledged his colleagues' generosity, smiling and nodding his head at them. They were good and kind people.

He looked down again and closed his eyes. *"Thank you, Father,"* he whispered. *"Thank you."*

He did not know whether or not he had changed anyone's mind, and he knew for a certainty that at the end he had spoken amateurishly. But he knew something else, too. He knew that he had been obedient—that he had done all he could at that moment—at that one, small moment that he had been given.

And he knew that God had commissioned him, Richard Mabry—ordinary Christian human being—to do this . . . this one thing . . . and that he had done it . . . and that he was somehow to continue to do what more he possibly could. This he knew.

CHAPTER TEN

NICCOLO GIACOMO LOOKED CAREFULLY AROUND THE ROOM at the thirty contemplative members of his steering committee who were present for this crucial session. Five of the members had spoken thus far, perhaps none as passionately or—apart from his hurried, shrill conclusion—as eloquently and persuasively as had one of the group's newcomers, young Richard Mabry. Now Giacomo, seeing no other members seeking the floor, turned his face to the old guard member whose argument in favor of the draft position statement had launched the debate some forty-five minutes earlier, and invited him to offer the finance subcommittee's new proposal and to introduce the afternoon's guest.

This caused a mild stir, since nothing suggesting a guest appearance had been found on the simple printed agenda that the members had received at the session's onset. The finance subcommittee chairman rose, cleared his throat, and began his explanation of the new proposal.

He, speaking for his subcommittee, wished to propose that the *Congressus* steering committee first endorse and then commend to the full *Congressus* assembly what he termed "a formal organizational and financial linkage between a to-be-permanently staffed *Congressus* organization, on the one hand, and the multinational fund known as the Phoenix Trust, on the other." At this, the Italian paused to distribute a small but professionally prepared brochure that set forth the proposal in outline form.

The finance chairman, watching the brochures circulate through the room, noted to himself with satisfaction that the group seemed utterly stupefied. He assumed correctly that the members had been astonished

equally by the phrases, "to-be-permanently staffed *Congressus* organization" and "multinational fund known as the Phoenix Trust" and
"organizational and financial linkage."

Having paused only briefly to assess the response of the group, the
chairman then led his colleagues through the proposal booklet with some
care, underscoring as he went the four salient points, each of which he
painstakingly summarized:

(1) *Congressus* would no longer be the name for a multinational
assemblage of Christian leaders and representatives meeting once per
decade, but a real, permanently formed and professionally staffed organization in its own right—lobbying, negotiating, and advertising at the
highest and most visible levels on behalf of Christian unification efforts
wherever such could be identified or created.

(2) The *Congressus* organization would be sited in New York City, near
the United Nations complex, against which it would comprise, in a very real
sense, a Christian analogue.

(3) The primary, and perhaps only, funding source for the organization
would be the Phoenix Trust, until now a mostly behind-the-scenes global
fund with freshly developed interests in supporting the worldwide
Christian unification movement with which *Congressus III* would be
forever identified.

(4) The Phoenix Trust had the financial, organizational, and media
resources and connections to bring any and all *Congressus* efforts to
successful conclusion, having served to date as the usually unidentified
colossus supporting a staggering array of multinational enterprises: tech-
nology, media (books, film, television), transportation, food and clothing,
and many others. The Trust had, a footnote in the brochure indicated,
also developed what it called "cooperative" relationships with a number
of governments in order to "facilitate its disbursement of funds around
the world."

When the finance chair then mentioned the current operating budget
for the Phoenix Trust, a collective gasp went up from the steering
committee members. Some of them knew that the figure exceeded the
national budgets of all but perhaps a dozen countries around the globe, and
even among those who did not, all knew that resources of such magnitude
would make *Congressus* an immediate and dominating player in any international conversation that it would henceforth choose.

There would be very little, in fact, that they might not accomplish with the Trust as the organizationally and constitutionally bound underwriter of the *Congressus* agenda. Some in the room, even during the fifteen minutes during which the subcommittee chair was still discussing the details in the proposal booklet, had already begun to imagine themselves holding positions of authority within the newly formed and underwritten *Congressus* organization. As an immediate consequence of this novel idea, those same members had, in a seamless, perilous and nearly instantaneous mental transition, begun to consider precisely which of the other committee members they must necessarily begin to regard as rivals for positions of true power.

For this, quite simply, would change everything.

At this point in the meeting, the presenter raised his eyes from his proposal booklet and nodded to a colleague seated near the door. The colleague rose immediately, and a moment later, stood respectfully aside to allow entrance into the conference room of the previously mentioned but still unidentified person known only as "this afternoon's guest."

The escorting committee member gently took the arm of the guest as she moved through the doorway, escorting her to the far end of the rectangular room, where a podium stood waiting for her. As the guest moved into place behind the podium, a screen descended silently behind her, while a projector, also silent, raised itself smoothly from a cavity in the boardroom table into its ready position about fifteen feet in front of her. The room had in seconds become filled with a palpable sense of excitement.

The committee members, both the men and the women, had gaped transparently—perhaps even rudely—at the woman as she had crossed the floor. They assumed that she must rank high in the Phoenix Trust's management hierarchy, and thus, that she must be among a select few who held the key to all real *Congressus* power and influence going forward.

And, if truth were told, they found quickly that, as someone at whom to stare, she was physically an arresting object. She was very tall—easily six feet without the polished, medium-height heels—and very slender. She walked and stood erect.

She was dressed immaculately in a tailored charcoal suit with a subtle diagonal pattern interwoven throughout. She was coiffed dramatically, her thick, long, blonde hair pulled back severely from her elegant face and held tightly in place by two intricately carved ivory combs. Those close enough and attentive enough could see that the combs were actually small masks of an especially macabre design, perhaps miniature replicas of the death masks commonly employed in some ancient cultures. From the combs, lustrous strands of blonde hair fell freely to a point midway down her back. Beauty, wealth, power, and authority all communicated themselves in an overwhelming package to the onlookers.

The woman seemed at first too young for one wielding such apparent influence in the financial world and beyond, but further scrutiny revealed a face that could be fifty years old, although somehow so free of the normal age markers—lines, saggings, graying hair and eyebrows—that it could also be ten years younger than fifty. And, if forty years of age without visible markers, why not sixty?

The guest now stood silent behind the podium, unsmiling, looking out over the assembled committee members. The members, looking back, began to trace with their collective eye still more detail of the mysterious speaker's features. They found themselves beginning visually to absorb a face and figure at once both elegant and plain: a woman whose appearance was studiously enhanced by the dramatic coiffure, macabre combs, expensive suit, fine heels, and regal bearing; and yet was also understated in her obvious refusal to utilize cosmetics or jewelry. She was fascinating to watch, and watch her they did.

The guest's cheekbones were high and prominent. The mouth, untouched by lipstick, suggested a practiced disdain. The overall thinness and angularity of the face, coupled with the cosmetic-free paleness of the skin, placed more than one in the room in mind of a glamorous, expensively dressed cadaver. But, beyond all this, there was yet another feature that set this woman apart from any other woman the steering committee members had ever seen.

It was her eyes. At first it seemed to some in the audience that her eyes were of no color at all. But as the committee members continued to stare transfixed at the guest, they began to realize that this woman's eyes were of such light blue that they were easily mistaken for transparent or, more accurately, for translucent . . . disconcertingly translucent.

There was something else disturbing about those eyes, or in the way this woman *used* her eyes. She did not, her audience began to realize, appear to focus her eyes on anyone or on anything whatsoever.

One by one, the audience realized the woman was blind.

As the seconds passed in absolute silence while the guest and her audience continued locked in a visual knot that neither could untie—the guest because she could see no one, the committee members because they could not stop staring at her—the members gradually began to acknowledge to themselves their intense discomfort in the woman's presence. Their only visible response to this realization was, singly, to begin to avert their eyes, until at length the woman seemed to look unseeing over a sea of disengaged faces, none visually attending to her.

The extraordinary silence, dominated eventually by the stunning absence of eye-to-eye transactions, continued for perhaps a full minute. Then the old guard member whose finance subcommittee proposal lay before the committee began finally to speak his introduction, leaving his place at the conference table and walking to the woman's side to do so.

Their guest's name, he said, was Dr. Helene Jamieson. She was a physician by profession. No longer practicing medicine, she now held the joint title of chief financial officer and chief operating officer with the Phoenix Trust. She was present to invite a decision that very hour: a decision that could affect Christianity's financial and organizational strength, said the subcommittee chair without obvious overstatement, for a thousand years.

At this, the Italian returned to his seat and Dr. Helene Jamieson began to speak.

The audience found her voice consistent with her beauty: precise, carefully modulated, unspectacular, and yet at the same time, utterly arresting. Working entirely from an extraordinarily precise memory, she quickly covered the Phoenix Trust's history by referencing the ten anonymous benefactors who created the trust; its mission of supporting humanitarian efforts in the public interest regardless of organizational type (volunteer, not-for-profit, for-profit, governmental, or various combinations of these); and its interest in establishing formal organizational alliances, especially with initiatives like *Congressus Evangelicus* that had already attained worldwide visibility but were as yet "financially and organizationally too immature to have substantial impact even on the late-twentieth century world, to say nothing of the world in the centuries—and yes, in the millennia—to come."

At this last statement, a thrill ran through the members, including Richard Mabry and others whose view of the draft position statement had become largely oppositional. They could not stop themselves. Their minds ran wild with images of *Congressus* influence all over the globe, going forward for thousands of years.

Not only was the atmosphere in the room electric, but the members' initial discomfort with the speaker's physical presence and demeanor had begun rapidly to diminish while she spoke to them. She seemed suddenly a very attractive figure in every way, comforting and stimulating at the same time. Hearts pounded with anticipation, excitement, and appreciation.

Dr. Jamieson then signaled for a film to begin. The Phoenix Trust's eight-minute cinematic introduction was effective. The audience saw the actual outcomes of the trust's financial support around the world: children, teachers, priests, ministers, rabbis, the underprivileged, the undernourished, the underrepresented, the disenfranchised, all receiving assistance for their long-term financial betterment.

At the film's conclusion, the guest moved to a simple recitation of the advantages of a *Congressus Evangelicus* marriage to the Phoenix Trust: the establishment of a permanent organization with virtually unlimited funding; the creation of a permanent site near the United Nations Plaza in Manhattan; the institutionalizing of sufficient power to channel countless billions of dollars over the years, decades, and centuries to seminary education worldwide, and through those seminaries, to their graduates' church and community efforts throughout their professional lifetimes.

Then Dr. Jamieson noted, almost as an aside, the single condition. The draft *Congressus* position statement would need to be endorsed overwhelmingly, preferably unanimously, by the steering committee, then and there. Not later. Then and there . . . in that room . . . and within the next half-hour.

The Phoenix Trust had no interest in throwing its resources behind any organization that had reservations about the centrality of its mission: unified, humanitarian, and financial assistance to all worldwide, via any new or existing channels of any organizational type whatever. It was simple. Accept and endorse this, or reject this offer forever.

Helene Jamieson had spoken for fewer than twenty-five minutes, including the time taken by the short film. Now she was finished. She did not ask for questions, and the group's feeling was that she had no interest in discussion. It seemed apparent that she wanted only one thing: a decision— yes or no—and she wanted and expected that decision immediately.

Feeling with one hand for the chair she knew had been placed beside and behind her, she sat down near the podium and fell silent. She had yet to smile.

As Helene Jamieson took her seat, her stunningly translucent blue eyes staring blindly and yet unambiguously in the direction of the steering committee chair, a pair of equally stunning feminine eyes shone in half-moonlit darkness nearly a half globe away. These eyes, deepest gray in color, peered intently at a very different kind of leader.

Rebecca Manguson Clark, Luke Manguson, Andrea Camposanto, and Matthew Clark now prepared, under Luke's direction, to swing into action across Amalfi's *piazza duomo*, confident that they understood their situation as well as it could be understood in advance and confident that their flexible plan of action was, in its very flexibility, the best that could be devised. On the previous night, Andrea and Matt had completed the 140-mile drive from Rome to Amalfi, where they initiated a most successful moonlight reconnaissance. Then after a short sleep, they had followed this with a more relaxed surveillance during the day and had experienced a still more spectacular success. So it was that, by the time Rebecca and Luke had arrived in the Alfa Romeo late Tuesday afternoon, the advance scouts were able to report a level of success beyond anything they had any right to expect.

Matt and Andrea located the likely holding cell for the kidnap victims within thirty minutes of initiation of night surveillance. Standing in town center and holding each other in a loose embrace to mimic the numerous pairs of lovers basking in a summer Mediterranean midnight, the make-believe couple adopted a stance with Matt facing the open plaza, and with the side of Andrea's face pressed against his chest. In this position Matt held an unobstructed view, over his companion's head, of the Hotel Centrale on the opposite side of the plaza. Holding Andrea thus in an embrace that to the other couples in and around the plaza looked utterly unexceptional, Matt had been able to keep the facing building under continuous scrutiny for so long that his main challenge had been keeping his colleague awake as she leaned comfortably and sleepily into him in the warm darkness.

Shortly after they had begun their strategically contrived embrace, Matt had collected his inert left hand in his muscular right, bringing both hands around to the small of Andrea's back. In this fashion he was able to provide support for her as she at times actually dozed, while at the same time he avoided the odd and perhaps attention-getting appearance of a man holding his beloved with one arm while ignoring her with the other.

From his position beside and almost under the long, high stone stairway up to the *duomo's* ornate entrance doors, Matt had studied each window in the hotel, straining to develop any clue suggesting which of the rooms might hold the captives. At no point did he doubt that the captives were, in fact, imprisoned in that very building, despite—or more precisely, because of—the fact that the primary evidence had been provided by his wife's supernatural gifts, and that the secondary evidence had been delivered via Andrea's supernaturally directed placement in their midst, her very life experience permitting her colleagues immediately to understand the victims' precise location.

Matt had seen too much in the two years previous, had experienced too much in that time, to entertain the slightest doubt regarding the validity of the evidence. The facts were there, as clear as his beloved's enchanting gray eyes. The supernatural origin of these facts did not make them less factual; it made them more so.

Thus, from the first moment of surveillance, Matt had concentrated only on the upper floors of the four-story Centrale, and on none of the other structures ringing the plaza. Like all of Amalfi's buildings other than the Cathedral of St. Andrew the Apostle that loomed immediately behind and over him, the Centrale was a small structure with no more than, he esti-mated, eight or ten rooms on each of its three guest floors.

A particular window had attracted his attention immediately. It squarely faced the cathedral steps across the plaza and was illuminated faintly from within, as was its adjacent window to the right. The similarity of the indirect illumination in the two rooms, coupled with the separation between the two—roughly twice the separation distance between other windows on the same floor—led him to hypothesize two connecting rooms separated by a windowless bathroom, with a light purposefully left on in that bathroom. This was, after all, exactly what one would reason-ably do if one were a parent sleeping with children in the same or an adjoining room.

Shortly before 1:30 AM, just as Matt had reached the absolute limit of his physical endurance and was preparing to arouse his limp and exhausted companion, he had seen faint silhouettes moving across the face of the right-hand window. One silhouette was that of an adult; the other, of a child.

Further reconnaissance at the midday following had confirmed the hypothesis. For several minutes, the two scouts had assumed the same lovers' pose they had adopted during the night. But they quickly realized that in the bustle of the noon hour there was no need for any such contrivance. They simply joined numerous other couples, individuals, and families who sat contentedly at various points up and down the impossibly long flight of cathedral steps and stared at and across the plaza, chatting, writing postcards, snapping photos, eating, and simply enjoying a fine Mediterranean June day.

Matt's and Andrea's persistent daylight scrutiny of the two windows identified during the night had eventually been rewarded in a fashion that left no doubt that the two rooms were, in fact, those occupied by Anna Angelini, Sophia Camposanto, and the children. Sometime in early-midafternoon, just as the two scouts were once again preparing to return to their nearby hotel rooms, a woman had come to the right-hand window and looked out over the plaza. The window was fast shut, despite the June heat and despite the fact that most of the hotel's windows had been thrown wide open by their sweltering occupants.

The woman had short-cropped brown hair and the rather round appearance of one who had never returned to what may have been a svelte, prematernal figure. She seemed to the two observers to be facing the plaza in a kind of grim fury, or perhaps truer, with desperate determination. Her hands clawed into the window sill at her waist. Her gaze seemed fixed on the façade of the *duomo* and on its stained glass image of St. Andrew the Apostle, sited well above and behind Matt and Andrea.

Then, after just seconds, the woman had been joined at the window by a second woman, much taller, thinner, and seemingly younger. She had been visible but for a moment, long enough to touch the first woman on the arm. They had both turned immediately away and disappeared from the observers' view.

Matt looked down at his comrade's face. Andrea Camposanto's eyes were wide, her hands covering her mouth. Tears rose in her eyes and began to roll down her cheeks. From behind her clasped hands she had whispered

to him. "Sophia . . . my sister . . . my sister. . . ." And she had lowered her
face into her hands and wept quietly.

Now, hours later, the foursome, each dressed in dark clothing, moved
quickly across the plaza from the shelter of the *duomo*'s high steps. They
moved straight toward the hotel's front doorway, no grappling ladders or
other climbing devices in their hands. They were going to walk straight into
the building.

Luke had considered many approaches to this rescue operation. All but
one scheme had involved use of grappling hooks and ladders, and all but one
had depended for success upon a great deal of accurate guesswork regarding
the layout of the hotel, and especially, regarding the positioning of the
captors. So, in the end, all approaches had been rejected in favor of a direct
frontal assault. The four would enter the hotel's front lobby—actually little
more than a small desk in a hallway—secure the "cooperation" of the desk
clerk, and move on from there following any number of possible scenarios
depending upon the information extracted from that unfortunate person.

The men, naval officers until just two years earlier, were armed. During
the previous day in Rome, Luke had purchased a medium-caliber military
handgun in an out-of-the-way pawn shop. It was Matt who now carried this
weapon, firmly gripped in his good hand. The handgun's magazine was fully
loaded, its safety off. Matt was ready to fire—to shoot to disable—at any
provocation. He held the weapon tucked into the right-side pocket of his
loose-fitting, lightweight sweatshirt.

Luke carried no firearm. Instead, he carried his standard array of knives
of varying size and shape, the largest now fitted into the heavy universal
handle that in itself comprised a formidable blunt instrument. Both the
large, fitted blade and five smaller, unfitted ones were slotted, along with
numerous other small tools and weapons, into a multi-purpose shoulder
holster which was in turn covered by a zippered sweatshirt that allowed
easy access by his right hand.

The women's hands were empty, and each walked arm-in-arm with one
of the men—Andrea with Luke, and Rebecca with her husband—simulating
the late-midnight strolling gait of couples in love. They stepped lazily up to
the hotel door, and Luke prepared to pull the door open so that the Italian
could enter first, prepared to address a desk clerk in his own tongue.

Luke reached for the door handle with his left hand and pulled. The
door did not yield. He instantly reached with his right hand into his

zippered sweatshirt, extracted a small object from one of the holster's leather slots, inserted the object quickly but carefully into the door mechanism, and then pulled again. The door swung open and Andrea stepped immediately into the dimly lit entryway.

A puffy, sleep-confused face raised itself from the small registration desk in the short hallway. The balding, diminutive clerk, suspenders awry, shirt untucked, eyeglasses askew, tried vainly to focus on the woman who greeted him cheerily with the words, *"Buon giorno, signore! Buona sera!"*

He stared foggily at her as she crossed in front of him and reached down to touch his arm, thus securing his complete visual attention. A second later, the confused clerk felt on the side of his face the cold steel of the flat of an enormous blade, pressed into place from behind his shoulder. The point of the knife extended well into the clerk's direct line of vision. Luke Manguson leaned in close behind the blade, while Andrea leaned in equally close from the other side. As this transpired, Rebecca and Matt moved swiftly past the threesome and into the ground floor's transverse hallway, there to stand guard during the first phase of the rescue attempt.

Surrounded by her formidable and experienced colleagues, Andrea Camposanto proved an excellent interrogator. In moments she had learned and had translated for the English-speakers many facts: the entire third floor of the hotel was occupied by two women, two children, and a host of men who appeared to be their "shepherds," as the clerk euphemistically called them in his nervous, rapid-fire Italian. The women and children were in rooms 303 and 305, on the front of the building, their windows facing the cathedral. The two rooms were joined to each other by a shared bathroom.

The men occupied the other six rooms on the floor and, the clerk explained, the doors to 303 and 304, and 305 and 306—pairs of doors that faced each other across the hallway—were never closed. He had seen all of this in his daily and nightly trips to the third floor with messages, food, drink, fresh towels, and the like, and he had been repeatedly admonished not to block the line of sight from 304 and 306 into 303 and 305, respectively. Two of the shepherds were always positioned just inside the even-numbered rooms, maintaining unbroken surveillance of the women across the hall.

The desk clerk seemed anxious to explain that the women were entirely private when they were in their connecting bathroom, and that he was quite sure that the shepherds never crossed the hallway to try to see the women when they were not within direct view. It seemed clear to him, however, that the shepherds watched the women with great intensity if they neared their windows, and he supposed that any attempt by the women to signal anyone in the *piazza* below would result in the most severe repercussions.

Andrea paused in her interrogation to look behind her at the Clarks, her eyebrows raised to invite new questions. Rebecca spoke immediately. "Ask him who is paying for the rooms, and who seems to be in charge."

Rebecca's eyes grew wide when she heard the clerk's reply: "*Signore* Edward Jamieson."

Although of the four, only Matt had ever been face-to-face with Jamieson, his very name validated for them the comprehensiveness of the evil that they had now faced in three countries and on both sides of the Atlantic Ocean. For it had been Edward Jamieson who had seemed to Matt to be obviously in charge of those who sought his, Luke's, Rebecca's, Eleanor Chapel's, Sidney Belton's, and Ellis Dolby's destruction twelve months previous, but only as an opportunistic embellishment to a much more encompassing plan.

And, they had earlier hypothesized, this same Jamieson may well have been instrumental twelve months before that in the kidnapping of Matt's parents and in the intricately fabricated scheme to alter Christian history and theology in a manner certain to tear at the very fabric of the faith worldwide.

Now Rebecca studied Andrea Camposanto's face and its reaction to the mention of Edward Jamieson's name. But it was not the Italian woman's face that displayed the reaction. Rebecca watched, surprised and yet not, as her colleague's knees buckled and she began to sink to a kneeling position beside the desk clerk. Rebecca moved to her side and placed her arm around her friend's shoulders, supporting her gently.

This simple act, collapsing in transparent terror at the mention of a name, confirmed everything Rebecca had hypothesized since her first inter- rogation of Andrea Camposanto in London, when the then-stranger was viewed as an enemy. This name—Edward Jamieson—was the name that Andrea had been afraid to utter or acknowledge. This name was the name that Antonio Camposanto had feared so much that he had arranged one daughter's preposterous surveillance of Matt and Rebecca Clark, another daughter's failed protection of Anna Angelini and her family, and most laughable of all, Giuseppe Basso's shadowing of Detective Sidney Belton.

Yes, this name—Jamieson—lay behind every evil that Rebecca, her family, and her colleagues had faced from the first. And this man—Edward Jamieson—had, according to Matt's testimony, displayed characteristics in the Brooklyn warehouse that had led Matt to question whether Jamieson's evil was "natural" evil or something well beyond that.

Yet, thought Rebecca in the brief silence as she continued to comfort Andrea, her own visions had suggested an evil that lay behind, below, and above even this. And that evil had been feminine. The phrase . . . the phrase with its plural reference . . . ran again through Rebecca's mind: *Put out their eyes. . . . Put out their eyes. . . . Put out their eyes. . . .*

She shuddered, shook her head to clear the images, and returned to the present.

After several minutes, Andrea found herself able to complete her interrogation of the desk clerk, and she stood aside while Rebecca and Luke trussed the miserable man and placed tape across his mouth, finally lowering him to a prone position behind his desk. After a quick briefing from Luke, the foursome was ready.

They knelt in a small circle in the transverse hallway, joined hands, and Rebecca led them in the familiar prayer: *Stir up thy strength, O Lord, and come and help us; for thou givest not alway the battle to the strong, but canst save by many or by few . . . a defence unto us against the face of the enemy. . . .*

SAN FRANCISCO/BERKELEY: 6:15 PM/TUESDAY OF THE SECOND WEEK
ROME: 3:15 AM/WEDNESDAY OF THE SECOND WEEK

Knife in hand and with Rebecca close behind, Luke ascended the north stairwell to the third floor as Matt, handgun ready, and Andrea climbed the south. Luke pulled the heavy metal fire door open enough to create a slit, peered down the dimly lit hallway, and waited until he saw Matt do the same from the opposite end. They then moved silently, Rebecca just behind, into the space between the closed hallway doors marked by the numbers 307 and 308, each occupied, they had learned, by those guards who were not on duty watching the hostages.

Matt and Andrea mirrored this movement and stood between closed doors marked 301 and 302. Edward Jamieson, they had been told, occupied 301. A chill passed simultaneously down the spines of the two as they stood now in such proximity to this evil. Both, in fact, felt exactly the same: as though Jamieson stared at them from just inches away, wild-eyed and ghoulish, through the door. Of the two, it was Matt who could pull this image from actual memory. But the image was hardly less real to the Italian. She, too, had known evil from close range.

All four of the rescuers could see that the doors beyond the ones between which they stood were open—305, across from 306, and 303, across from 304—and knew that only the feline silence of their movements had prevented armed men from pouring out of two of those rooms. Luke and Matt, crouching, weapons extended, began to move forward slowly using a rolling, noiseless heel-to-toe foot placement.

The two men stopped just short of the even-numbered doorways, the women inches behind them. Without signal to each other, Luke and Matt breathed deeply and visibly one time, then moved, lightning-quick.

Luke's adversary in 306 was reading in the dim light cast by a small lamp on a nearby desk, his magazine held close to his face, a large-caliber handgun lying at the ready on the floor beside his chair. His partner was asleep, fully clothed and face down on one of the beds, a pillow closing off eyes and ears from the light and the noise of his partner's rustling magazine pages.

The flat of Luke's enormous knife was against the first guard's anterior carotid artery before the hapless captor knew anyone was in the room with him.

His eyes wide in belated recognition, he dropped the magazine to the floor, terrified equally by the face inches from his own and by the cold, heavy steel against his exposed neck. Before the guard could so much as form a thought, Rebecca had quickly but silently applied a previously cut strip of duct tape to his mouth. She then assisted Luke as he tipped the straight-backed wooden chair quietly, even delicately, onto its back, the guard still positioned in it, and as Luke continued to press the flat steel against his neck, had tied the man's ankles to the legs of the chair and his wrists to its sides in such fashion that he was helpless. The two moved without pause to the sleeping guard, his eyes and ears still covered effectively by the pillow, and repeated the process in seconds, binding him securely by ankle and wrist to the four bedposts.

Just as they completed this task and turned away from the second guard, they heard a male voice shout out in alarm.

The twins' movements had been closely mirrored in 304 by Matt and Andrea. Their on-duty guard was actually dozing, head lolling on chest, when his eyes opened to find the muzzle of a pistol trained between his eyes from a distance of twelve inches. Andrea had taped his mouth and bound his wrists and ankles less skillfully and swiftly than her counterpart, but well enough. They had seen from the first moment that the room contained no second guard.

As they stood up, having lowered their bound enemy to the floor, still positioned in his wooden chair, they heard the noise of a toilet and turned to see the bathroom door opening, a burly figure preparing to exit. The guard shouted in alarm and stepped back, slamming the door. He wheeled to the door opposite, yanked it open, shouting to his comrades in 306, and was silenced instantly by an iron fist that smashed into his face with the thunderous force of a sledge hammer. Unconscious at impact, the guard toppled backward as a felled tree, crashing with a thud onto the tile floor.

Uncertain as to the effects of the guard's shouts on the presumably sleeping occupants of the floor, Luke reopened the bathroom door into 304, saw the trussed guard and the still-surprised faces of his two associates, and gestured toward the hallway.

All four raced into the hall through 304's doorway. Luke pointed for Matt to cover 301 while he moved to the other end of the hall with the knife. With his eyes, he directed the women into the captives' rooms.

In thirty seconds, Rebecca emerged from 305, followed immediately by Anna Angelini, carrying Paulo; Sophia Camposanto, carrying Maria; and Andrea, an arm's length behind her sister. The women and children sped to Luke's end of the hallway. Matt, handgun still pointed toward the other end of the corridor, backpedaled rapidly behind them.

Luke pushed the fire door open and stood aside while rescuers and rescued passed through and down the north stairwell. Just as Matt slid past and began his running descent, Luke saw the opposite-end fire door fly open and a wildly frazzled woman, screaming at the top of her lungs, entered the hallway. Luke watched, impassive, while she pounded on the door to 301 and shouted, "*Signore Jamieson! Signore Jamieson! Signore Jamieson!*" until the door to 301 opened and the man known as Edward Jamieson tore into the hallway. In his right hand was an enormous automatic pistol.

He looked to his right, saw his enemy, and raised the weapon to fire.

Luke slid easily behind the door frame while the fire door slammed shut, reached into his shoulder holster to remove a steel-and-rubber object, and slammed the small wedge-like device into the three-eighths-inch space under the fast-shut steel door. Then he spun and flew down the stairs two at a time, raced back along the ground-floor hallway, darted past the helpless desk clerk, and sprang from the door into the *piazza duomo*.

Edward Jamieson and his men, realizing finally that the north fire door could under no circumstances be moved by force, turned and sprinted to the south stairwell. They descended to the ground floor, feet clattering in a booted cacophony on the concrete-and-metal stairs, ran back to the entryway, and burst onto the plaza. There they glimpsed, in the combination of soft moonlight and hard street light, a sleek, jet-black Mark VII Jaguar with British plates turning right out of the plaza to head west on the Amalfi coastal road.

CHAPTER ELEVEN

A FERRARI DINO 246 GTS TWO-SEATER, GLISTENING RED IN the indistinct mix of street light and moonlight, leapt from the *piazza duomo* and turned right onto the Amalfi coastal road like a fighter jet on rails. Edward Jamieson, thoroughly familiar with the intricacies of the Ferrari's five-speed manual transmission and absolute master of the pursuit capabilities inherent in its precision-tuned engine, spoke only once to his passenger as he accelerated through the first four gears, alternately stomping the clutch pedal and the gas pedal, his shift-hand flying from steering wheel to shift control and back.

"Shoot out the tires when we catch them. I want all of them alive. Disable the car, but leave me with eight healthy captives. Understand?"

"*Si*," came the raspy, nasal, one-syllable reply.

The Italian gunman sitting close beside the American driver in the tight, two-person cockpit was hand picked by Jamieson himself, and had, in fact, been in charge of the kidnappers' security detail. He was no cipher.

Even so, as he checked his weapon, he decided not to ask his employer—whom he loathed with that peculiar intensity reserved by honest criminals for those who acknowledge no code at all—how he imagined that a shotgun blast might magically restrict itself to something as small as a tire. Especially, he mused, a blast fired from what would no doubt be an oblique angle, and from a distance of fifty to seventy feet from the window of a swerving, accelerating-and-decelerating Ferrari sports car, in the general direction of a swerving, accelerating-and-decelerating Jaguar sedan.

He mused further about the likely outcome of any shotgun blasts that might actually contact the fleeing vehicle, especially if any of the scattering pellets were to pound their way through the car windows and into the driver, who doubtless would be "the Clark woman," as he had heard her called most often. For that outcome would surely precipitate a sequence that would send the sedan into a tumbling, spinning, uncontrolled fall ranging anywhere from seventy to two hundred feet from roadway to water, or more likely, onto the jagged boulders that laced the Mediterranean waterline.

The gunman glanced to his left at the intent driver, shook his head surreptitiously in disgust, and removed two spare shotgun shells from the portable ammunition case that rested on the floorboard between his feet. He dropped the shells gently into a pouch attached to his belt. Then he rolled down his window and moved the already loaded, double-barreled weapon into firing position. As he did, the Ferrari completed its steep climb out of the village and screamed into a hard right-hand turn.

Simultaneously, the gunman saw headlights in the distance to his left, just across the small inlet around which the Ferrari would now move in a swift, 180-degree power turn. This was the kind of turn that, he and Jamieson both knew, the stately Mark VII sedan could not begin to match, even if it were not fully loaded with the additional weight carried by six adults and two children.

The gunman again shook his head. The presence of the children disturbed him deeply, and he hated Jamieson all the more because the man was willing to sacrifice these innocents for some obscure agenda of his own.

But this was his job. And this gunman was very good at his job.

As the Italian moved the polished twin-barrel weapon into firing position out the Ferrari's right-side window, one of his intended adult victims edged warily out of a doorway in Amalfi's village center. Matt Clark kept himself deliberately in the shadows of the oceanfront façade of the breakwater under whose parapet he had crouched with the women and children while his wife and brother-in-law had, moments before, led the pursuers to the west, toward Positano. Now he turned and signaled to the others.

They padded quietly forward, concealed within the shadows. Anna Angelini carried little Paulo in her arms, while the Camposanto sisters alternated in transporting the older child, at times hoisting Maria in their arms, and at other times shifting her onto their backs. All six understood that they were still in great danger. Although the Ferrari pursuit car had roared after the aging Jaguar with, presumably, two men inside, there would be a half-dozen or more others still in or near the plaza.

So, wordlessly and nearly soundlessly, the small party of women and children crept along behind Matt Clark, moving steadily eastward toward the adjoining town of Atrani. There the two-bedroom hotel suite used by Matt and Andrea since their arrival in the Amalfi area awaited the tiny band of refugees. In fewer than ten minutes, at the efficient but manageable pace set by Matt, they approached their aging hotel.

The hotel's rear entrance was nestled so tightly into the hillside separating the twin towns from each other that the women found it necessary to place the children on their own feet in order to negotiate the narrow walkway between the back of the hotel and the nearly vertical hillside that seemed to push against the hotel itself. At last they opened a back door which led directly into their suite, and sanctuary was theirs.

Matt, closing the door behind Sophia Camposanto, looked at his watch. It read 3:51. The graying of the sky in anticipation of daybreak would still be more than an hour away.

He turned and watched in satisfaction as the women moved expertly to attend to the children and to prepare them, for the second time that night, for bed. But now that they had all reached safety, his mind began to move inexorably elsewhere, as it had fought to do every moment since he and Rebecca had separated in Amalfi's village center.

Matt knew that he was infinitely better than he had been two years earlier at doing this, handling such proximity to his own violent death. And yet, he mused briefly, even then, first near Cambridge and then along the Welsh coast, he had performed capably in his first real experience of focusing outside himself while embroiled in a truly lethal cauldron, concentrating on obedience to the God he had just then begun to know, placing duty, purpose, obligation, and sacrifice ahead of himself.

Indeed, before and during the rescue they had just carried off in Amalfi, he had entered the fray with a confidence borne equally of belief and of experience, certain that he knew what God demanded of him and that he could perform responsibly in the fight. And certain, too, that he by now understood as fully as one realistically might understand such things, the nature of eternity and of Christ's promises to humankind. He was sure now of what awaited him on the other side of the great transition, and though he was not so naïve as to formulate in his mind some sort of explicit construct of a heavenly landscape, he knew beyond doubt that what awaited him was simply better than anything he could profitably imagine. And that was more than enough.

Now, however, safe in the Atrani hotel suite with his small entourage, his mind turned immediately to his wife, and he found himself again fighting to retain both his concentration and his composure. For this was the first time since he had, two years earlier, unforgettably encountered Rebecca Manguson as she had opened a heavy door in an ancient wall, striking him mute with eyes that drove all the way through him . . . the first time since that encounter that he knowingly stood safe while she faced death without him.

True, not many hours before this, Rebecca had entered the church in Rome knowing, as did they all, that it was likely a trap, while he and Andrea had moved to conduct their surveillance in Amalfi. But that had been markedly different from this. For in Rome, Luke had prepared the way for Rebecca in such fashion that the risks were at least somewhat controlled. Here, now on the Amalfi coast, they were not.

Standing under the seawall in Amalfi not long before this, he had seen and heard the Ferrari screaming out of village center, turning west toward the escaping Jaguar, and it had shaken him to his soul and beyond. It had, in fact, taken more mental discipline, physical self-control, and Christ-centered prayer and faith than he had known he could summon—to do what obedience demanded of him in that moment.

And yet, despite this . . . or, better, because of this . . . he had fallen to his knees in the sand under the seawall's looming parapet, in full view of the women and children. His face in his hand, he had sunk lower and lower onto his haunches, struggling to breathe as his chest seemed to constrict impossibly and his prayer fought like a sleep-wounded animal to extricate itself from his mind and body, thence to reach beyond itself to the Mighty Deliverer that it sought.

In that attitude, gasping for breath, he had felt hands on his head, on his shoulders, on his arms. Embraces, murmurings, caresses . . . adult and child alike . . . and he had gradually sensed his prayer moving out, moving beyond, borne on wings, and received and responded to in less than a supernatural instant of earthly time.

He had known his prayer was imperfect. He had known that it contained none of the necessary characteristics modeled by the Perfect One long ago. But it had seemed to form itself without his choosing and beyond his will. It had been this, and only this, over and over. . . . "Father, please don't take her yet . . . not now . . . not tonight . . . please . . . Father . . . please . . . not now . . . not tonight. . . ."

At length he had slowly risen from his knees, emptied; had stood erect in the grainy sand; had wiped his eyes with his good hand; and had turned and nodded his thanks to the five who peered anxiously up at him through the darkness. And then he had done his duty. He had led them away, away from those who would capture and kidnap and perhaps murder them each, and finally delivered them to this tawdry but expedient haven.

Now, he stood just inside the door to the suite, leaning wearily against the door frame, praying for his wife—the same prayer that he seemed helpless to alter in any fashion—yet at the same time attempting to focus on the larger crisis that linked them all. One by one, as the children's bedtime preparations completed themselves, the women began to return to the sitting room and kitchen-dining area that served as the suite's only gathering place.

Matt, still leaning against the door, looked up from his prayers and saw Andrea Camposanto peering at him intently, inquiringly, as she took her chair. He saw resignedly that, although not having spoken a question, she meant to have a response from him.

After several moments, he nodded in her direction, smiling gently. "*Grazie*, Andrea," he said softly. "Rebecca's okay . . . Luke's okay. . . . *Grazie.*"

And, a moment later, still smiling gently at her: "You were wonderful at the hotel, Andrea . . . truly wonderful. Your father will be very proud."

SAN FRANCISCO/BERKELEY: 7:22 PM/TUESDAY OF THE SECOND WEEK
AMALFI/ATRANI: 4:22 AM/WEDNESDAY OF THE SECOND WEEK

Anna Angelini, entering the sitting room, nodded at Matt without smiling and moved directly to the wall-mounted telephone. Matt noted to himself that the exquisite grief of a newly widowed mother of young children filled her hollowing, tear-stained face utterly, leaving no room for facial expression of any other kind. He watched and listened as she dialed and negotiated with an international operator. After a moment, Sophia Camposanto rose and crossed the room to stand close behind the woman who was, not so long before, merely her "assignment." Now she placed a long, elegant hand tenderly on the young mother's shoulder and saw the hand immediately brushed by Anna's small, plump fingers, the gesture gratefully reciprocated.

Several minutes of Anna's lyrical, staccato Italian alternated with long silences and deep sighs, Matt understanding little that he heard. But he recognized the repeated name of Eleanor Chapel, and so he knew that this was an international person-to-person call in which Anna Angelini sought to reach her cherished and imperiled aunt in California. He tried to focus, to keep his mind there in the room and not on a certain roadway winding high above the Mediterranean breakers west of Amalfi. . . .

At length he saw Anna's face change suddenly, a look of acute disappointment and puzzlement flashing across her anxious, saddening countenance. He strained to understand. . . .

SAN FRANCISCO/BERKELEY: 7:22 PM/TUESDAY OF THE SECOND WEEK
AMALFI/ATRANI: 4:22 AM/WEDNESDAY OF THE SECOND WEEK

Richard Mabry struggled to open the locked back door to Eleanor Chapel's Berkeley apartment, trying not to look helpless under the watchful eye of Lois Tanaka. Neither of them could think of any course other than to try to break into the apartment, search for a phone number for Rebecca Manguson Clark, and then, if successful, attempt to contact her. They had practically no expectation of success, but they knew that this Englishwoman was viewed by Eleanor Chapel as a solution, or as *the* solution, to threats and dangers that they themselves only dimly understood.

They saw no point in engaging law enforcement, given Detective Antonio Camposanto's influence within police networks everywhere, and had in the end decided simply that they were less likely to be arrested attempting a break-in at Dr. Chapel's apartment than at her Pacific School of Religion office.

"Are you making any progress?" whispered Lois, keeping her voice low as they stood in full view and within easy hearing of anyone passing through this interior hallway or even traversing the front or rear stairwells in the twelve-unit apartment building.

"Well . . . I'm not sure," Richard whispered in reply, furiously working his laminated driver's license card up and down the small crack between door frame and door. Although he was vaguely aware that the obvious presence of a dead bolt made his efforts futile, his determination to keep trying remained high, driven to irrational heights by Lois Tanaka's disconcerting presence.

He had had few chances in his life to appear heroic in the eyes of someone whose opinion he cared about, and perhaps none to appear heroic in the eyes of someone toward whom he had romantic hopes and fears. So, when it became obvious that jiggling his driver's license in the vicinity of the door latch was pointless, he stood, stepped back from the door, and prepared to crash into it with his shoulder.

His companion's bright black eyes grew wide. "What are you going to do now, Richard?" she asked incredulously.

"I'm going to knock this door down with my shoulder," he said with obvious disbelief in his voice.

She stepped forward and placed both hands on his right shoulder and arm. "You know, Richard, that's just something they do in movies. It doesn't really work like that."

"It doesn't?" he asked happily, thrilling to her touch and instantly oblivious to everything else.

"No," she answered. "But maybe there's a fire escape outside, and maybe we could climb up to the windows and somehow get in that way. A lot of these old buildings have those ladders. We ought to take a look."

He nodded in relief, and they turned away. They had taken only two steps when the very door they had sought to open swung noisily open, pulled violently from the inside. And there before them stood the very man whom they wished least to see at that moment, looking to them larger and more foreboding than ever. Detective Antonio Camposanto looked down at the two intruders, his handsome face a mask for the hostility and aggression they were certain he felt toward them.

He stared down at them for several moments, and then spoke, his impossibly deep voice reverberating up and down the bare hallway. "You were perhaps . . . ah . . . seeking to do the . . . ah . . . the breaking into the professor's place of residence? *Si?*"

The young couple was quiet for a moment, and then Lois began to attempt a reply. "Well . . ." she stammered . . . "well . . . we . . . ah. . . ."

"Yes!" interrupted Richard with an aggressiveness in voice and demeanor that surprised and frightened him. "Yes! We were, Detective. We want to know what you've done with Dr. Chapel. Where is she? Where is she right this minute? Tell us!"

He paused momentarily as a new thought fluttered past him, and then added, his voice now heavy with accusation, "And you! What are *you* doing here? Why are *you* in her apartment and she is not?"

Emboldened by her partner's recovery, Lois added excitedly and unapologetically, "Yes . . . yes . . . I . . . I saw her pin on the floor in your hotel room, Detective." Her voice was rising in pitch and volume. "Why was it there? What did you do to her? Where is she?"

"And why," added Richard for good measure as she concluded, "why was she not at the meeting this afternoon? Dr. Giacomo said she and Detective Belton might be on their way to New York right now, but that doesn't sound like them. They wouldn't run away from this or from anything at all. Where are they? What have you done with them?"

"Yes!" said Lois again, her voice still rising, now turning and taking one step back toward the giant Italian as he stood unmoving, filling the entire doorway to Eleanor Chapel's apartment, "yes . . . and where is Giuseppe? You said he had gone for a long walk, but we know he does not go for long walks. That's not what he does. What have you done with *him*?"

And finally the couple fell silent, quietly defiant, looking up into the huge man's stony face with eyes that simultaneously accused him and shrank from him. They waited, filled with a courage that they each seemed to be able to draw from the other.

Camposanto appeared bemused. He seemed to be turning over in his mind the question of whether or not to reply to any of their charges, or whether instead simply to shoo them away as the inconsequential interruptions they were. Finally, without altering his leaden expression, he said softly, "I am in the professor's apartment because she demanded that I bring to her the briefcase and the Bible that she requires. I am following her orders."

This last was accompanied by the faintest trace of a smile under the formidable mustache.

After several more moments of silence, to the couple's surprise, the man-mountain's next response was to step to one side and to give them one of his long, sweeping gestures, motioning for them to enter the apartment. There was even the suggestion of a slight bow at the waist, as he completed the dramatic and unmistakable nonverbal invitation.

The couple hesitated, looked at each other, back at the detective, and then, once more at each other.

Finally Richard Mabry squared his shoulders, turned his face back to Camposanto's, and said to his companion, still looking at the detective, "Lois . . . I'm going in . . . I'm going to go right in . . . now. . . . You go downstairs and wait for me in the front yard. If I'm not out in five minutes, call the police."

He was fuzzily aware of how empty the "call the police" threat sounded at that moment, but it was all that came to his mind, derived as it was from some hackneyed television or movie dialogue. But without further hesitation, Richard stepped boldly forward, passed under the towering figure that stood motionless at the doorway, and once he was inextricably inside the apartment, heard the door shut firmly behind him.

He was trapped. His mind seemed to be closing down. Then he sensed someone at his elbow. He looked down.

Lois looked up at him, bright eyes beaming.

The two stood staring at each other, uncomprehending, and then sensed the gigantic presence moving gracefully around them both, now striding away from them through the hallway that linked the rear of the apartment to the front. They followed.

As the threesome passed in single file into the living room, a telephone suddenly rang out virtually at the woman's elbow, causing both young people to jump, startled, at the sound. Lois halted, looked at the men, first at one and then at the other, her eyebrows arching. In a movement that could have been choreographed, both men shrugged their shoulders and opened their hands in the characteristic gesture.

So it was that in California a young American woman lifted a telephone from its cradle. And, like a young Italian woman on the Amalfi coast of Italy, this woman's face was observed intently by her companions.

Thus, Richard Mabry, Antonio Camposanto, Andrea Camposanto, Sophia Camposanto and Matthew Clark watched as mirror-image looks of confusion played across the anxious countenances before them.

SAN FRANCISCO/BERKELEY: 7:29 PM/TUESDAY OF THE SECOND WEEK
AMALFI/ATRANI: 4:29 AM/WEDNESDAY OF THE SECOND WEEK

Matt Clark watched and listened as Anna Angelini began switching rapidly back and forth from Italian to English, assuring the long-distance operator in one language that she wanted to go ahead with her call despite the fact that the woman on the other end was not her aunt, while seeking desperately in the other language to determine the situation in California. At the direct query from the Italian, "Where is my aunt? Where is Dr. Eleanor Chapel?" Matt could tell from the taut, intensely expectant lines suddenly crossing Anna Angelini's face that no reply was forthcoming.

In Berkeley, Lois Tanaka had, upon hearing this question, simply stopped and stared into the face of Antonio Camposanto for a long moment, the telephone in her hand dropping slowly to her side. Finally she said, her voice flat with accusation, "She wants to know where Dr. Chapel is, Detective. As do we."

He stared back at her.

And then he replied simply, "Who . . . is . . . 'she'?"

"She says she is Dr. Chapel's niece."

And there, having listened first to the babel of confusion and then, within that one clarifying statement, having felt the weight of the universe lifted from his heart and soul, the Italian colossus rushed upon the diminutive American, snatched the phone from her small hand, and poured a stream of Italian into the transcontinental, transoceanic telephone line until he got what he had sought with all his strength: the voices of his daughters tumbling unencumbered into his desperate ears.

A comedic scene then duplicated itself on both sides of the world: Italians shouting ecstatically into telephones in their own language, stopping, turning to companions, changing to English, shouting to their companions in that language, listening to shouted questions in English, then turning back to the telephone to shout Italian questions and answers into that thoroughly overwhelmed device. They—all of them, in both settings—found themselves raising their voices ever louder in response to the self-feeding crescendo, now stopping to laugh and now stopping to cry.

Bedlam reigned.

But, ever so gradually, Matt Clark in Atrani, and Lois Tanaka and Richard Mabry in Berkeley, came to understand several things that had been grasped under the language-confused circumstances much more quickly by the four Italian speakers than by the English-only participants:

The kidnapping had ended.

All of those kidnapped, save Mario Angelini, were safe.

Eleanor Chapel, her husband, and Giuseppe Basso were also safe, according to Antonio Camposanto, having been sequestered so forcefully by him that, he explained in English, had anyone observed his security safeguards firsthand, they might have been uncertain whether the actions he undertook with the two small Americans and the young Italian had been friendly or hostile.

There had, in fact, been a physical struggle in Camposanto's California hotel room. The struggle had ended, according to his careful account, only when he had lifted the tiny professor bodily into his arms as though she were a child and carried her outside to a waiting van brought by local police at his request, with his American colleague, Detective Sidney Belton, limping behind and his prospective son-in-law trailing them all in anxious confusion.

Further, Camposanto had continued, an observer fortunate enough to witness that scene and its immediate aftermath, as he had been, could have borne witness to an improbable exchange between Eleanor Chapel and her husband, as they had settled reluctantly into the rear seat of the police vehicle, the professor grumpily straightening her skirt, blouse, suit jacket, red scarf, and upswept hair throughout the dialogue. Camposanto's detective-explicit account of the exchange, repeated with the extra-comedic touch provided by his effort to mimic the Brooklynese of the American detective and the Southernese of his professorial wife, then relayed with equal attention to dialectical detail by Sophia Camposanto for the benefit of her Atrani companions, moved listeners on both sides of the ocean to peals of delighted laughter.

"Y'know, Eleanor, Antonio's right," Belton reportedly had said to his wife once they had settled in the van. "We just need to get you outta sight for a little while. They're gonna take care of things over there in Europe—Rebecca and them, I mean—and they're gonna do it fast. She said so. Rebecca said so to us on the phone. We just gotta get you and Giuseppe here outta the way.

"Know what I mean, Eleanor? Know what I mean?"

The fortunate observer of the scene, continued Camposanto, would then have felt, rather than observed, a pair of blue-green eyes burning into Belton's black orbs in the shadowy confines of the police vehicle, its tiny dome light standing weakly between complete and semidarkness. "You let that man pick me right up off the floor, Sidney Belton," the professor had said accusingly to her husband. "You're supposed to protect me. What on earth were you thinking? Why didn't you just give him a good *whack*?"

The little man's lopsided grin had then emerged in the dim light, barely visible to Antonio Camposanto, who had turned almost completely around in the front passenger seat in order to absorb the rear-seat spectacle more fully.

"A good whack, Eleanor? I'm supposed to give this three-hundred-pound behemoth *a good whack*?"

Belton had then peered in Camposanto's direction as the front passenger seat groaned under the Italian's bulk. "Well," Belton had noted thoughtfully, "I guess I coulda *shot* him, Eleanor. But I was afraid he'd drop you, see. I just had your own interests at heart, that's all."

"Oh, for pity's sake, Sidney Belton," she had reportedly replied, "I don't know what I'm going to do with you. How in heaven's name did I ever allow you to talk me into marrying you?"

"Well . . . you really couldn't of helped yourself, Eleanor. Y'know, I just figured that if I asked you in front of the president of the United States and the First Lady you'd be too embarrassed to say no. So, I guess you might say I just outsmarted you, Eleanor. Know what I mean? You've never been able to keep up with me, y'know. I'm way too quick for ya. I just plain outsmarted ya, Eleanor . . . that's all. It wasn't your fault. Y'just weren't quick enough."

At that point Antonio Camposanto, according to his own account, had become unable to contain himself and had burst into a kind of roaring, bellowing laughter at this affectionate, mutually accusatory husband-wife exchange. And then, said Camposanto, the fortunate observer in the van would have heard this from the rear seat: a high, tinkling voice that was as soft as it was melodic.

"Yes, Sidney Belton, you did. You just plain outsmarted me. And I'm just so very, very glad you did.

"Now then," the soft voice had added, "do *you* know what I mean?"

SAN FRANCISCO/BERKELEY: 7:41 PM/TUESDAY OF THE SECOND WEEK
AMALFI/ATRANI: 4:41 AM/WEDNESDAY OF THE SECOND WEEK

Matt Clark's mind remained a confused jumble. He could concentrate for perhaps thirty consecutive seconds on the telephone exchange unfolding before him with its gradually clarifying images, before his whole being screamed at him that his wife was facing deadly force at that very moment . . . at *every* moment. Indeed, at one point he sank slowly to a sitting position on the floor, holding his forehead in his good hand. Immediately, as before, he felt feminine hands on his shoulders, comforting him, and feminine voices whispering prayers, just above his head.

He knew hazily that Sophia Camposanto was continuing to converse with her father in California. Through the agony he heard her repeat the name "*Signore Jamieson*" a half-dozen times as she spoke to the detective in their native tongue. Finally, in response to Anna Angelini's and Andrea Camposanto's insistent nudges, Matt looked up. Sophia, still speaking into the phone, was now looking directly at him. She began to speak again in English, loudly addressing both him and Antonio Camposanto, in California.

"Yes, Father, the walls of the hotel were as thin as . . . as . . . as paper. Our room shared a wall with the room of *Signore* Jamieson. In the nights . . . *every* night . . . he would speak in the . . . in the loud voice . . . in the loud voice, on the telephone, to someone named . . . Helene . . . he never said her last name . . . but they . . . he and the other person . . . seemed as close as family to me. . . .

"They would talk about everything . . . about Mario's death . . . about the children . . . about the . . . the bungled attempt . . . yes, that's it . . . the bungled attempt to capture Rebecca Clark and her brother in Roma . . .

about Eleanor Chapel and her husband in the U.S. and about their efforts to capture them or kill them . . . and Father, they would talk about you.

"They would talk about you . . . they would talk about how they knew you would do whatever they told you to do as long as Anna and I and the children were in their hands and you feared for our lives . . . and yet they were never *sure* of you . . . never *sure* that you were not . . . ah . . . *playing* them . . . that's what they said . . . *playing* them. . . .

"It made me very proud."

Sophia Camposanto paused, listened, and continued in English.

"*Si* . . . *Signore* Jamieson spoke to this woman about their control of so many things, Father, their control of newspapers, of television, of the cinema, of police forces, of *your* police force—even of some governments—or of some of the people in some of the governments. Of small armies, or of some of the leaders of some small armies, and of something called . . . ah . . . Phoenix Trust . . . and how they . . . this Phoenix Trust . . . how they were taking over the . . . the . . . ah . . . the educating . . . the educating . . . of ministers, of priests, of pastors, all over the world . . . I did not understand exactly how. . . .

"*Si* . . . *si* . . ." she continued after a slight pause. "This Phoenix Trust—and it seemed to me this woman—this Helene . . . was somehow above all of this . . . this Trust . . . and above all of the things that it could reach . . . above all of the powerful people that it could buy . . . above all of the things and people that this Trust could . . . could purchase, could acquire, for her or for him or for . . . well . . . I don't know exactly for who, for *whom*, for *who* . . . but it was all part of this Phoenix, Father.

"Oh, Father, it was terrible . . . terrible. . . ."

Sophia Camposanto listened again, but just for a brief moment, and then continued. "*Si* . . . *si* . . . the Jamieson man and the Helene woman on the telephone's other end, they wished to use the Phoenix money and influence and . . . and the Phoenix . . . ah . . . *squads of the gun* . . . how do I say? . . . the *gunners* . . . the *gunmen* . . . the *killers,* Father . . . to acquire everything they could and for the main purpose . . . for the main purpose of, well, of the corrupting . . . of the corrupting of everything, Father. First, of the church and of its seminaries. And then, through the seminaries, the ordained leaders of churches everywhere . . . to . . . to make the church leaders just like the leaders of everything that is a . . . a . . . *power thing* . . . like everything that seeks the *power* and . . . and seeks the *influence* . . . and

. . . and seeks the *wealth,* and seeks the *minds* . . . and seeks the *hearts* . . . and . . . and seeks the *souls* . . . the *souls* of everyone, Father . . . of . . . of *all of us* . . . *everywhere.*

"And . . . and, Father . . . for . . . for those who will not corrupt, for them . . . for those people . . . well . . . just *kill them all* . . . that's all . . . just *kill them* . . . just kill *us* . . . just *kill us all.*

"That's all."

Chapter Twelve

AS EDWARD JAMIESON'S GUNMAN CAREFULLY MOVED THE shotgun into firing position, its twin barrels now protruding from the right-side window of the Ferrari, Rebecca Clark worked to wrestle the Mark VII through yet another hairpin turn as she sped west along the Amalfi-Positano roadway. She knew that her sedan had no chance to outrun the high-performance vehicle that tracked her and that the chase would not last long.

Rebecca hoped, above all, that Jamieson believed that the Mark VII carried the kidnapped women and children, as indeed, he did. Her goal was simply to take her pursuer as far away from Amalfi as possible before being overtaken. She knew that every mile and every minute that she occupied him would provide her husband and his small band that much more margin for safety as they moved from the deadly environs of Amalfi to the comparative safety of Atrani.

She had no plan of campaign for the aftermath. She had only the certainty that her vehicle could not perform at a level even approaching that of the Ferrari. So she simply drove with all the verve and skill at her command, knowing without a trace of self-congratulation that few in the world could do this as well as she. If her automotive equipment had been the equal of Edward Jamieson's, she knew, she could drive all the way to Naples . . . to Rome . . . to Paris . . . to Le Havre . . . without his over-taking her.

This confidence of hers was not grounded in pride. It sprang from her conviction that the simple act of acknowledging the Source of one's gifts converted pride to humility before the essential vice could even form itself, and from her certainty that joy in one's own skill should be no different from, and just as pure as, joy in another's.

So Rebecca Clark drove not in panic, but in a fine and focused confidence rooted in obedience to the will of God. She moved the Jaguar's gear shift through its five speeds continually, using the three foot pedals with a consummate athleticism that was both familiar and yet freshly amazing in the eyes of her only passenger.

And she prayed. Rebecca knew that in the midst of fast-developing events, whether in her classroom in London or on this narrow, twisting Italian roadway, simple prayers, simply expressed, simply responded to, were best for her. So she repeated to herself, her lips moving silently, "Father, be present . . . Father, help us. . . .

"Father, be present."

As for the Jaguar's passenger, Luke Manguson was not observing his sister with vacant admiration for her driving skill. He was praying, also. His own prayer was as simple as hers, and yet it differed markedly from Rebecca's.

His prayer, in fact, echoed the prayer of his brother-in-law and naval comrade: "Father," he prayed, "don't take her now. Take me. Please, Father. My life for hers. My life for hers."

And while praying, Luke thought hard, unlike his preoccupied sister, about the soon-to-arrive denouement and its epilogue. The pursuers would have at least one firearm, he was certain, and it would be no mere handgun. The Ferrari would attempt to disable the Mark VII with gunfire, since Jamieson would know that he would not be able to run Rebecca Manguson Clark off the roadway with his smaller car against the skill and stubbornness she would bring to such vehicular combat.

No, as soon as the GTS overtook the Mark VII, Luke was certain a gunman would attempt to shoot out the sedan's tires, and if that shot could be well managed under these challenging circumstances, the crippled Jaguar would then, he knew, enter an adventurous and probably disastrous skid-and-spin. It seemed to him likely that even Rebecca Clark would be unable to correct for the physical forces that would throw their vehicle toward the mountainside that rose to their right or toward the precipice that loomed to their left.

If, however, they could manage to survive such an end, thought Luke, he planned to order his sister to crouch in the driver's seat after the car had ceased its skid, her head below the line of fire, while he leapt from the sedan and closed so quickly on Jamieson and his gunman that the gunman's firearm would become useless. Suddenly, it would be Luke who would be the better armed of the two. The largest of his knife blades was already inserted in its universal handle, ready to be clamped between his teeth as soon as, or possibly before, the Jaguar came to its inevitable stop.

Luke knew, however, that the question of whether or not his sister would comply with such an order as the one he contemplated—to crouch low in her seat—was another matter entirely.

"Sisters!" he muttered disgustedly under his breath, glancing sideways in the direction of his beloved twin. He knew that, had she heard him, she would have laughed aloud in delighted appreciation of his gruff display of brotherly love and anxiety.

Minutes passed, but only a few, before the twins became aware of the Ferrari's headlights, visible across the U of yet another impossibly tight turn as the roadway insinuated itself along the cliffs of the Amalfi coast. In another thirty seconds, the GTS had halved the distance. And in another, the two-seater, engine howling, flew around a right-hand bend at such speed that it nearly overran the sedan before Edward Jamieson realized how dramatically different the speed of the two vehicles had become.

He geared down and braked expertly. Then, seeing an opportunity, he whipped the wheel to the right and dodged to the right-hand shoulder. The Jaguar cut him off immediately, but too quickly for Rebecca to respond, Jamieson spun his steering wheel to the left, dropped the shift lever from third to second, slammed the accelerator to the floorboard, and threw the Ferrari into passing position. He was beside the Jaguar so quickly that the gunman nearly missed his chance.

But he did not miss his chance. He adjusted instantly and squeezed off both shotgun shells at once, the violent recoil sending the 240-pound Italian halfway out of his seat and nearly into the driver.

Jamieson braked again, the GTS dipping sharply in response, and jerked the wheel back to the right, slipping immediately into the lee of the Mark VII. Before he could attempt a studied assessment of the damage to his victim, both vehicles were already swinging into the left-hand curve that would take them back in the direction of the sea.

It was apparent to Jamieson that the shotgun blast had struck the sedan, and from its plowing, sluggish action in this turn, he surmised correctly that, in fact, the left front tire had been destroyed.

What Jamieson could not see or guess was that the wild, uncontrollable distribution of the double-barrel's pellet-spread had, given the oblique angle of fire, blasted not just the left front tire, but the left front and rear doors and windows, as well. Nor did Jamieson consider the fact, though he might have guessed, that the Jaguar, unlike the Ferrari, was a right-hand drive vehicle, and that the double-barrel shotgun blast that blew out one tire and both left-side windows had also pierced the neck and face of the front-seat passenger.

And so, as Jamieson slowed his two-seater, staying a prudent distance from the Jaguar's now-confused, erratic movements as it nosed left and right, fishtailing dangerously toward the approaching cliffs, he found himself muttering aloud, "Hold it on the road, Mrs. Clark . . . hold it on the road . . . I want all of you alive, every single one. . . ."

Then louder: "I have *uses* for you. . . . *Do you understand?*"

And then, screaming at the top of his voice: *"Hold that car on the road!"*

SAN FRANCISCO/BERKELEY: 6:44 PM/ TUESDAY OF THE SECOND WEEK
AMALFI/ATRANI: 3:44 AM/WEDNESDAY OF THE SECOND WEEK

Luke Manguson had reeled forward and across the seat toward his sister from the force of two dozen steel shotgun pellets and countless glass shards and splinters—shotgun projectiles and automotive detritus mixed together—splattering against and thrusting into the left side of his face and neck with the unmistakable sound of gunfire's products thudding into flesh, a sound that Rebecca had heard once before in her life and had hoped never to hear again. At the same time, she had felt the Jaguar's responsiveness deteriorate into a confused mush, and immediately had found herself wrestling the steering wheel with one hand and gearing down with the other in a near-hopeless attempt to bring the wounded sedan under control.

She sensed her brother struggling to right himself as she fought to manage the car's speed and direction. She doggedly avoided touching the brake pedal, slowing the sedan by use of its transmission gearbox only and seeking to bring the Mark VII to a controlled stop before it reached the next right-hand hairpin. She knew she had no chance to negotiate the sharp right turn with the left front tire obliterated, and she saw at the same time that a failure to stop the vehicle before reaching the turn would send them straight off the road and over the cliffs.

The last fifty feet of pavement disappeared steadily under the wheels, the Jaguar slowing noisily but in a nearly straight line, forced by its driver's expert gear reductions into dramatic, rear-wheel-driven deceleration. As the void materialized before her, Rebecca finally tapped the brake lightly, felt the Mark VII dive and lurch one final time to its left, and watched helpless as the front of the sedan crept over the edge of the cliff.

The nose of the vehicle then dropped hard onto its chassis. The automobile immediately high-centered, rear wheels beginning to lift from the roadway, front wheels hanging above the rocks over which the sea rose and fell some eighty feet below. After several moments of precarious, gravity-defying instability, the sedan was, Rebecca realized, actually still sliding perceptibly forward and now beginning to tip, its nose falling implacably, its rear lifting in unwilling concert.

Rebecca, her right hand on the door lever, turned to reach for her wounded brother to attempt to pull him across the bench seat and out the right-side door, with her, to the slender road shoulder onto which she hoped they might be able to fall together before the car slipped forward into its death plunge.

But she found that there was no brother for her to assist. The left-side door of the Jaguar was open wide.

Luke Manguson had vanished.

SAN FRANCISCO/BERKELEY: 6:45 PM/TUESDAY OF THE SECOND WEEK
AMALFI/ATRANI: 3:45 AM/WEDNESDAY OF THE SECOND WEEK

Edward Jamieson had skillfully brought the GTS to a careful and complete stop some fifty feet behind the erratically moving Jaguar. He had pulled all the way to the right-hand road shoulder, and this gave him a full,

albeit oblique, view of the right-side doors of the Mark VII, despite its
driver's last-second brake-tap that had swung the nose slightly to the left.
Jamieson caught his breath. He could see the Jaguar's rear wheels now
beginning to lift slowly from the road surface, its nose already dipping,
sliding toward the abyss.

Then suddenly he lost sight of the crippled sedan. Careening around
the turn from the other direction, a small produce-delivery truck traveling
west to east from Positano interposed itself, and its surprised driver seeing
the Jaguar's plight, screeched to a halt directly in front of Edward Jamieson
and his henchman. The truck, its tall and unwieldy cargo box completely
blocking the men's view of the Jaguar, was stationary for no more than five
seconds. Then its engine roared toward a fresh crescendo and it resumed
its precarious trek toward the grocers and restauranteurs of Amalfi.

Now the two men could see that during their brief visual hiatus the
worst had indeed happened: the Jaguar had vanished.

Jamieson's gunman had already opened the passenger-side door of the
Ferrari and now stood on the small shoulder of the road, reloading both
barrels expertly, keeping his eyes fixed on the spot where the sedan had
gone over the side of the Amalfi cliffs. So it was that both he and Edward
Jamieson could now see in the moonlight a dark-clad woman lying on the
ground at the very edge of the cliff, her hands gripping the soft clay of the
road edge, her legs hanging over eighty feet of empty Italian night.

Jamieson clambered quickly and athletically up and out of the low-slung
Ferrari. He and his henchman advanced rapidly along the roadway as the
woman, seemingly unruffled, pulled herself forward to transitory safety.
Within ten seconds of the Jaguar's plummet, Rebecca Clark stood fully
erect, her hands at her sides and her back to the sea. She looked through
soft moonlight into the faces of the two men, and not unimportantly, into
the enormous twin muzzles of the same shotgun that had just ended the life
of the Jaguar.

She turned her head and watched Edward Jamieson as he strode
quickly to the edge of the road shoulder and looked down. He swore. "No
survivors from that!" he said with disgust.

She turned her attention back to the shotgun.

The gunman held the weapon eye-high, actually sighting down the
center of the twin barrels at Rebecca's forehead, as though his weapon were
a small-caliber hunting rifle whose single round would need to be aimed

with precision. But he knew from long experience, as did his employer and his victim, that this weapon, fired at this range, would simply obliterate a human being whether aimed carefully or carelessly in her direction.

And there the three stood, unmoving, while the seconds ticked past.

Rebecca was relaxed. Her easy stance reflected the truth about her state of mind at that moment: a simple mixture of regret in the knowledge that her husband and her larger family would be stricken by her demise, and crowding against the regret, of anticipation at what momentarily awaited her at the great change.

For the final transition had presented itself to her numerous times in her nearly three decades of living. And here it was once more. For one who had not served in actual combat, Rebecca Clark was extraordinarily familiar with the immediate prospect of her own death.

The Scripture playing through her mind on this occasion comprised Jesus' words from the First Gospel: "And fear not them which kill the body, but are not able to kill the soul. . . ."

Her adversary on this occasion, Edward Jamieson, observing her now from the cliff's edge, was thinking hard about the situation he now faced, and in one sense, was thinking more broadly than Rebecca Clark. His first question had been answered. The others were obviously all dead. The Jaguar lay flat on its roof eighty feet below him, its wheels up, its back broken, water breaking insistently over its partially submerged trunk.

His second question concerned the woman who stood near him, serenely facing the shotgun's twin muzzles. Did he want her alive? Could she be used effectively as a hostage to extend the leverage he and Helene Jamieson had needed to control Dr. Eleanor Chapel? Or had that situation already resolved itself satisfactorily back in California? He thought it probably had.

In any case, he thought, the immediate prospect was something that he and his network had sought for a long time: the chance to end the life of Rebecca Manguson Clark under circumstances in which her death would be both verifiable to him and to Helene Jamieson, and yet untraceable by the authorities. He briefly considered the likely response of Helene and the others. Would the personally verified and untraceable murder of Rebecca Clark balance the scales against his loss of all the others as hostages? He thought it probably would.

He turned to his hireling. "Kill her," he said simply.

"Kill her."

The gunman heard the order and tightened his finger on the shotgun's trigger mechanism. The barrels were still aligned perfectly with Rebecca Clark's face, and so he found himself staring directly into her eyes.

She looked back, as she had been doing for perhaps a full minute, directly into his. He had not been able to read this look of hers. He had seen fear many times and recognized it with ease. He knew that sometimes the absence of fear in a victim's face was an illusion, a studied cover-up of terror that a soon-to-be-dead human refused to display for reasons of its own.

He saw none of that in this face. What was this he saw in the young woman's eyes and her facial expression? Where had he seen this before?

And he knew.

This was forgiveness. He had seen it on one other occasion, when he had been ordered to pull the trigger and end the life of a pastor who had refused a command to stay away from a scene of magnificent carnage that he and his men had produced in an obscure corner of a rural Sorrento cemetery. The pastor, arriving alone to attend to a newly prepared gravesite on behalf of the deceased's family, had heard the gunfire and had walked quietly into their midst.

When the order had come to execute the intruder, that young pastor had faced the shotgun in exactly the same relaxed posture and with precisely the same look on his face as the gunman saw now. Genuine forgiveness.

The gunman considered himself a Christian man. That is, he believed in God and he believed in Jesus Christ as Lord and Savior. He believed, and yet he had spent much of his life earning his living by threatening and in many cases, murdering human beings. He fully expected an eternity of punishment, but there were times when he dared hope for a different outcome, when he dared hope that his private, oft-repeated prayers for forgiveness might actually have the result that seemed to him to be prom-ised in the New Testament.

The gunman considered himself an honest murderer, threatening and killing people who, he repeatedly had convinced himself, deserved death. That young pastor in the long ago had been an exception. And here was another.

"Kill her, I said!"

The words went through him like a charged current and filled him with disgust. But this was his job, and he was very good at his job. And he had just sent two children and an uncertain number of adults, including the children's mother, to their deaths. What difference would one more adult make?

He resumed his concentration on the face of Rebecca Clark, and again tightened his trigger finger. He once more concentrated on the face before him, and this time, in addition to the forgiveness, he actually saw at the corners of her mouth the suggestion of a smile.

Not understanding or attempting to analyze the impetus he suddenly and overwhelmingly felt, the gunman slowly lowered the weapon, turned away from Edward Jamieson, walked deliberately to the other side of the victim , and one hand on the stock, lifted and tossed the shotgun over the precipice. He watched it fall in the pale moonlight for long seconds.

The other two, motionless, watched him in astonishment. They said nothing while he stood observing the shotgun's fall. They said nothing while he turned and walked back toward the Ferrari, its marvelous engine purring in eager readiness to roar away onto these roadways for which it had been created. They said nothing while he dropped into the bucket seat, wedged his bulk behind the wheel, moved the gear shift into first, and smiling to himself for the first time in his long memory, launched the GTS around the hairpin and into the night.

Edward Jamieson, stunned, watched the red taillights disappear around the curve and swore again. And then he fixed his eyes on those of Rebecca Clark, who had not moved except to watch with Jamieson as the gunman departed, and who now had simply turned her head back in his direction.

Alone at the cliff line, the man and the woman now stared into each other's eyes from a distance of no more than ten feet, he, facing her fully, and she, her back still to the sea, but with her face now turned fully toward him. Finally the man spoke.

"This will be better," he said simply.

Chapter Thirteen

LUKE MANGUSON HAD BEEN STUNNED INTO INACTION BY the shotgun blast for no more than the ten seconds it took him to realize fully that he was still alive. Immediately after this realization, he felt, rather than saw, his sister tap the brake pedal. Then he felt the Jaguar lurch slightly to its left. Finally, he felt his sister reach for her door handle.

He understood faster than thought that she would try to pull him across the seat and onto the slender road shoulder before the Mark VII plunged over the precipice. He knew in another millisecond that there would be no time for that maneuver, and that Rebecca's effort to save her brother would cost them both their lives.

Bleeding from dozens of shotgun, glass, and metal fragment wounds, but absolutely clear of mind, Luke grabbed his door handle, smashed his left shoulder into the door, and rolled out the left side of the sedan just as its front wheels nosed over the cliff and the chassis dropped hard to the edge of the roadway. Still visually hidden from the pursuers by the Ferrari's positioning behind and well to the right of the Jaguar, Luke lay momentarily almost under the Mark VII as it began to tip forward. Then he sprang up, groaning at the fiery pain that radiated through him from his fresh wounds, and prepared to rush the assailants before they could bring the shotgun into further play.

As he took his first step forward, clearing the side of the Jaguar and searching immediately for the Ferrari that he knew would be stopping, or had already stopped, just behind them, Luke was confused to see not the Ferrari but the side of a produce-delivery truck as it braked to a halt almost close enough for him to touch. Anger born of frustration flashed through him as he saw his chance for a surprise rush on his enemies vanish with the interloper's arrival at precisely the wrong instant.

Then, just as quickly, something else flashed through him and he leaped to the old truck's running board, thrust his head through the open right-side passenger window, and said in English, "Go!" As he spoke the word, he thrust his right hand and arm forward in the direction of the roadway. The message, delivered in any language, was not easily mistakable.

The young driver, thoroughly confused by the scene he had unexpectedly encountered upon rounding the hairpin, was immensely relieved to receive such an unambiguous order. He slammed his floor-mounted gearshift into low and roared away, leaving the now-plummeting Jaguar in his wake and passing the Ferrari at close quarters within seconds of collecting the apparition that now crouched on his right-side running board. As he passed the stationary Ferrari on his left, he glanced at the two men it carried, one of whom was standing and holding what appeared to be a shotgun, the other of whom was just beginning to rise from the driver's seat.

Both these men steadfastly ignored the produce truck as it made its way past them carrying its vegetable cargo and its hidden running-board passenger. Concentrating instead on their solitary prey, the obvious sole survivor, they moved swiftly in the direction of Rebecca Clark, who had been the only one to observe what had just transpired.

But in the darkness, even she was unable to see past her approaching assailants to the retreating delivery truck. Had she been able, she would have been dismayed to see her brother, weakened from loss of blood, fall hard to the pavement as he attempted to dismount the accelerating vehicle so as to rush to his sister's rescue from her enemy's rear.

San Francisco/Berkeley: 6:53 pm/Tuesday of the second week
Amalfi/Atrani: 3:53 am/Wednesday of the second week

"This will be better," Edward Jamieson said simply to Rebecca Clark as the two stood alone at cliff's edge, the Ferrari having just disappeared around the hairpin in one direction, the produce truck in the other, and Luke Manguson, bleeding and disoriented, lying two hundred feet away on the edge of the roadway.

With those words, Edward Jamieson immediately began to transform himself—or to be transformed—into the atavistic creature that had first made itself known to Matthew Clark in their isolated encounter in a Brooklyn warehouse twelve months previous. Jamieson began slowly to advance on his prey, his gait an odd, insect-like, mechanistic working of legs and feet toward a victim assumed to be paralyzed with terror at the mere sight of the apparition that he had so easily and so *naturally* become.

His lips curled back to reveal incisors of unusual prominence. His eyes widened to such an extent that white showed all around 360 degrees of each orb. His hands opened into claw-like appendages, each prepared to grasp and hold and incapacitate while, perhaps, mouth and teeth did their work.

As he neared the still unmoved and unmoving woman, he exhaled purposefully toward her nostrils and immediately she apprehended a moist, vile stench utterly unlike any she had ever encountered.

"This will be *so* much better," Jamieson murmured softly as he moved steadily closer, now almost to her side.

The woman he approached was, however, an altogether different woman from the one who moments before had faced a gunman with a double-barreled shotgun. That woman had exuded forgiveness, and equally, a full and complete acceptance of her own death at the hands of a henchman—a person embodying no great or original evil himself—who had been ordered to commit simple murder by an employer whom he despised.

This was not that.

This was purest Evil advancing upon her, Evil prepared to rend her with its own hands and teeth and toxic, incapacitating breath, and in part, for the simple and exquisite pleasure of doing so. Beyond that, this was an answer to the question of why her visions had portrayed a feminine face and eyes, and yet had communicated the suggestion of a plural antagonist: "Put out *their* eyes. . . . Put out *their* eyes. . . ."

This man, she was now given to understand with a suddenness and clarity that took her breath away, was himself the eyes of—and for—someone else. Someone feminine. Someone whose own eyes did not function at all. Someone literally blind, or figuratively blind, or perhaps both.

This, unlike the shotgun blast, was *not* something to be accepted.

From the moment Jamieson's gun-wielding lieutenant had tossed his weapon over the cliff and vanished into the night, Rebecca had no doubt that one of her options was simply to run away from Edward Jamieson. Regardless of the mechanics or efficiency of the gait he might find himself using during the commission of this particular predation, she would, on foot, be faster than he.

And yet flight did not so much as enter her mind. Instead, obedience . . . duty . . . purpose . . . obligation. . . .

These filled her mind and her soul and her body. These compelled her to face a monster who clearly relished this opportunity to kill her without weapons other than the ones he carried in his own person. A monster who wished literally to *taste* Rebecca Clark's death as an absolutely integral part of the pleasure that he expected to find in her murder.

And so she prepared herself for the fight without moving and without speaking. She simply awaited her adversary with a stillness that seemed absolute.

The fight was brief.

As Jamieson began to reach for the woman with his clawed hands, and as those hands moved to within inches of the woman's torso, she subtly shifted her weight to her left leg, and in a lightning strike as fluid as it was powerful, swung her right foot up, under, and through her opponent's jaw before he perceived that her foot had so much as left the ground. The force of Rebecca's sledgehammer stroke snapped Jamieson's head straight back, bent his spine double, buckled his knees fully, and sent him to the ground in one scant second of earthly time.

Edward Jamieson lay flat on his back, unmoving, mouth and eyes open in groggy stupefaction, dark fluid pulsing from the side of his lacerated mouth and fractured mandible.

Rebecca Clark stood quietly on the same spot she had occupied since rising to her feet minutes earlier, now looking down steadily at the enemy. After several moments, seeming to reach a decision, she walked carefully around to his side and paused on the edge of the pavement, the man-monster lying between her and cliff's edge. Staring down into the expressionless, bleeding face, she asked quietly, softly, "Who are you, Jamieson? Tell me. And then tell me *what* you are. I want to hear you say it."

Five seconds passed with no movement and no sound from either combatant, just the noiseless, steady flow of Edward Jamieson's lifeblood pouring down the side of his grotesquely distended face. Suddenly, hearing something indistinct behind her, Rebecca turned her head to the left, nearly all the way around, and looked down the roadway in the uneven moonlight. There she saw dimly a struggling human form advancing on hands and knees in her direction, its shoes and trouser fabric scraping audibly along the hard surface of the roadway.

Her brother was coming, but for once he was coming too late.

Edward Jamieson's talons had already inserted themselves like razor-sharp grappling hooks into each side of Rebecca's right thigh before she was even aware that her enemy was no longer prone and semiconscious. She spun her head and shoulders around to see the monster's jagged teeth, despite its bleeding, broken, misshapen jaw, advancing ravenously toward the flesh of her upper leg: this soft flesh and hard muscle that it had seized and now held, immobile, in diabolically powerful claws.

Rebecca had known for some time, at least since the time of her most recent vision, what would be required of her in an eventuality of this sort, and she hesitated not an instant. Bending her knees so as to drop closer to Jamieson's level—as he half-sat, half-crawled, half-rose to killing position, ready to release every toxin of his demon's chemistry directly into her bloodstream—Rebecca clasped her hands together, index fingers extended in parallel three inches from each other so as to form twin arrows of steely flesh-and-bone, and drove these two muscular shafts directly into the monster's unprotected eye sockets.

Her rigid fingertips drove into and through the creature's eyeballs, fully into its orbital cavities and then into the delicate neural tissues and sensors just beyond. Memory of the disgusting tactile sensations would sicken Rebecca for the rest of her life. But she did not shrink, nor at any point pull back from her two-handed thrust. She completed the full motion, extending her arms fully and then, as if in slow motion, feeling her fingers laboriously withdraw from the gaping, devastated sockets as the creature recoiled backward in agony, screaming through its disintegrating jaw and mouth and pulling itself at length away from Rebecca Clark's twin insertion points in its body and soul.

Edward Jamieson, reduced in less than a half-minute's combat with his long-sought enemy to a pathetic ruin, collapsed on the edge of the road shoulder, inches from the cliff line, moaning incoherently . . . but only for moments. Presently his agonized groans diminished and Jamieson's misshapen form rose quickly, almost athletically, to its feet. It then turned its head to one side, sightlessly gazing at Rebecca Manguson Clark and thereby providing her with a final perspective so disgusting that she spun around, fell to her knees, and retched uncontrollably onto the roadway.

In that position, her back to the cliff line, she did not see the creature turn its face away from her for the final time, nor move its feet laboriously so as to confront the precipice squarely, nor crouch slowly and awkwardly.

Nor launch itself into the void.

SAN FRANCISCO/BERKELEY: 6:59 PM/ TUESDAY OF THE SECOND WEEK
AMALFI/ATRANI: 3:59 AM/WEDNESDAY OF THE SECOND WEEK

Luke Manguson, semiconscious, felt his sister's touch and tried to look up. He could not focus his eyes for more than a moment at a time, but he had managed to see well enough at the instant Edward Jamieson leaped outward and into his own oblivion. And he had seen also Rebecca's crouching form, her back to the suicide, as she retched onto the road surface.

Now, still crawling doggedly on hands and knees, he feebly deflected her solicitous hands as she reached for him, murmuring in a voice just audible to her, "I've got to see the body, Rebecca. I've got to see it's dead. I've got to see the man's carcass. I've got to see it's dead *and* gone. Dead *and* gone."

Rebecca immediately gave up her efforts to get her brother to lie down quietly on the roadside in anticipation of the next produce truck's arrival, and fought gently past his protesting words and gestures to assist him to his feet. Then, together in mutual embrace, they half-walked, half-staggered to cliff's edge. Once there, Luke allowed his sister to lower him again, slowly and carefully, to his knees. Finally, her hands guiding and supporting him, he crawled forward until he could look down.

While Rebecca held him tightly, turning her face away, Luke forced himself to concentrate through the fog of abrasion, laceration, and concussion, and stared down toward the rocks eighty feet below him. At first he saw only the inverted wreckage of the Jaguar in which he and his twin had fled the Ferrari.

Then he saw in the inconstant moonlight, silhouetted against the whiteness of the rocks at water's edge, the remains of Edward Jamieson. Although the form was recognizably human, it bore no resemblance to the man who had skillfully commanded a Ferrari GTS just minutes earlier. This was a form broken into parts that lay in no reasonable geometric relationship to each other, and yet were still tenuously attached, one to another, by bone and sinew.

It was, indeed, "remains."

The Mediterranean tide was coming in rapidly. Luke watched, held tightly by his sister, her eyes still averted, while waves first lapped at the body and then began to swarm furiously around it, tugging and sucking as though determined to dispose of something terribly alien. Finally, the surging, roiling sea lifted the body from the rocks and ripped the thing that had been Edward Jamieson, torn and tumbling, into the depths.

Chapter Fourteen

REBECCA PEERED OUT THE CABIN WINDOW OF THE EIGHT-passenger jet chartered on her behalf just thirty-six hours earlier by the Rome Police Department in immediate response to an urgent request from Detective Antonio Camposanto. Dusk was beginning to fall over San Francisco Bay, but she could just make out in the fading light the irregular path traced across the water by the Oakland Bay Bridge. As the pilots lined up their rapidly descending craft with the Oakland International Airport runway, she could see as well, across the water, the uniquely elegant hills of San Francisco, and behind and to one side of the hills, the twin spires of the Golden Gate.

The trip had been grueling. The small jet's limited fuel capacity and the two-man crew's need for two prolonged respites forced stops in Dublin; in St. John's, Newfoundland; and finally, in Chicago, on the near globe-circling flight from Salerno, near Amalfi. Rebecca's thigh wounds, though already beginning to heal, throbbed intermittently.

Her companions on the long flight, her husband and Andrea Camposanto, though both uninjured, struggled with their own discom-forts. His was a function of the fit, or lack thereof, of his six-foot four-inch frame within the constricted space available inside the small-diameter fuselage of their charter. Hers was emotional: the result of an agonizing decision regarding whether to stay in Salerno with her sister and Rebecca's recuperating brother, or to join the Clarks on their mission to California. In the end, she had opted to go to her father's side. She acknowledged readily enough to herself that the decision had been reached in part because of the glances that Sophia Camposanto and

Luke Manguson had shyly exchanged between themselves when they thought she might not notice.

Andrea had noticed.

It was not, she had reminded herself, as though she ever imagined herself in romantic company with Luke. She had actually thought of him as unattainable by any woman. But given her glamorous sister's betrothal to Giuseppe Basso, Andrea had assumed she would be free at least to serve as an undefined companion to the injured man—perhaps a nurse of sorts—as he moved through his recovery from gunshot, concussion, laceration, and abrasion.

Antonio Camposanto's decision to request Rebecca's immediate presence on the scene in San Francisco and to arrange for her flight via his police department's transportation bureau had been prompted by his continued fear, despite his daughter's rescue from Edward Jamieson's kidnappers, that he had not the means to cope with Helene Jamieson. It was not that he thought his law enforcement networks unable to contend with the Phoenix Trust and its financial, governmental, media, and other operations. He had, in fact, taken the lead some months earlier in positioning Italian, French, West German, UK and U.S. agencies to attempt exactly that.

Instead, his fears were humiliatingly personal. His novel tactic of placing daughter Andrea and prospective son-in-law, Giuseppe, in stake-out positions against people—the Clarks and Sidney Belton—who would quickly detect, confront, and finally protect such amateurs had worked perfectly. His miscalculation had been to place daughter Sophia in a shadowing operation against the Angelinis, a couple who unlike the Clarks had no experience whatever in taking aggressive action against presumed threats to themselves and their families, and no capacity therefore to rescue and protect her. Sophia had been quickly snatched away from Camposanto's police colleagues by Edward Jamieson's veteran British and Italian operatives.

And now, even with both daughters safe for the moment and his presumptive son-in-law sequestered along with Eleanor Chapel and Sidney Belton, Camposanto continued to fear almost irrationally for them all. Yet it was not that he feared the Phoenix Trust as an organization.

Camposanto viewed the Trust as a monolith that had, as a complex criminal system like many others, insinuated itself into hundreds of other mostly legitimate agencies and organizations, eventually becoming formidable in many of the same ways that Mafias of various national origins had at various times and places become formidable. The Phoenix Trust was unique, speaking strictly in the organizational sense, in two ways: first, the leverage it chose to employ was almost entirely financial, with physical violence very much a last rather than a first resort; and second, the caliber, power, and multinational integration of the agencies and organizations it controlled or influenced together comprised a step substantially beyond anything that had ever been seen before.

Even so, none of that daunted Camposanto. In fact, he anticipated with eagerness the moment when he would unleash the combined law enforcement capacities of five nations against this massive, thousand-armed octopus, first slicing off its tentacles by the hundreds and then driving into and through the nerve centers at its core.

Yet he simply could not find the courage—if courage it could be called—to ignore Helene Jamieson's threats, both clandestine and overt, against his own family members.

Almost as soon as those threats had been lodged, issued as they were in an obvious preemptive maneuver against his newly formed multinational law enforcement group, Camposanto had concluded that the people he thought of privately as "the Belton group" would comprise his best and perhaps his only hope to save his daughters and Giuseppe Basso. If Sidney Belton's unique, specialized force could be induced to protect the Camposanto family members, Antonio Camposanto knew he would then be free from the familial fear that had so quickly crippled him professionally, a fear that continued even now to prevent his pulling the trigger that would propel his five-nation task group into action against the Phoenix Trust.

Camposanto's decades-long respect and affection for Detective Sid Belton, coupled with the Italian detective's detailed analysis of Belton's two-year involvement with Rebecca Manguson Clark, her family, and others, had finally decided him. He had concluded that only the Belton group carried the combination of expertise, skill, and as Camposanto thought of it, *divine weaponry* to go up against the two Jamiesons and win.

Now, one of the Jamiesons was reportedly dead by a kind of suicide, one induced by exactly the kind of confrontation Antonio Camposanto had prayed for: that is, one resulting from a face-to-face, close quarters encounter with Rebecca Manguson Clark. Camposanto found himself genuinely surprised, however, that the fact of Edward Jamieson's death had made him not less, but more anxious than before.

He found that he expected Helene Jamieson to retaliate immediately in response to her brother's death, and to do so in a white-hot fury. And that fury at its worst was, when directed at individual human beings rather than at organizations or systems, something that could not be stopped by any means that were at his personal or professional disposal. He was certain of this.

Theologically, Antonio Camposanto was not a sophisticated man. He was a believer who knew the Apostles' Creed by heart and believed every word and phrase of that ancient prayer. He read in his New Testament every morning as part of his devotional discipline, and he particularly loved to read and re-read the third Gospel. And that was so, he freely admitted to anyone who asked, for no reason other than the presence of "the Christmas story" with which it began.

He believed, too, in evil as an active force, a force operative every hour of every day, here on earth. He believed in an active, personal evil because first, that was what he understood the Lord Christ to have indicated at many points in His teaching and preaching ministry. And second, because he thought that the concept of an immediate, active, personal, supernatural evil could alone account for the kinds of things he had spent his life fighting against, first as policeman and then as detective. He was certain that evil was not the mere passive absence of good. It was much, much more than that. And at its worst and highest, it went far beyond anything that he could realistically combat, except within the perimeter within which his own soul lived and moved and had its being. That he could protect always. Evil could not breach his own Christian defenses without his consent.

But Helene Jamieson seemed to embody something beyond his reach: consummate, active evil at its worst and highest. It was not, certainly, that Camposanto thought of her as a feminine devil. His theological framework, if it could be called that, was not in the least systematic. He did not even care, if truth be told, what she was or what she was called. He simply knew high-order, active evil when he encountered it. And she was exactly that . . . supremely that . . . far beyond that of any individual he had ever personally known.

He had been face-to-face with her twice in his life. Both times the cold, viciously serrated, steely edge-and-point that seemed to emanate from her very core unnerved him in ways that he identified as clearly supernatural. In his life he had been in the presence of holiness, and he had been in the presence of its opposite. She was its opposite. Never mind that she was in person a slender older woman, and he was a mountain of a man. Never mind that her voice was low and soft, and his, octaves lower and resoundingly louder. And never mind, too, that she was so far as he knew always unarmed, and he, never without at least one sidearm and one edge. Her sightless presence *itself* weakened his knees and led him each time he had been in her presence to search for immediate escape.

In his analyses of the Belton group's forays over the preceding two summers, Camposanto had found evidence that this phenomenon that he called divine weaponry was present in strength and operating within the Belton group. He liked the term, which he had coined himself to describe something he was certain he detected in the action reports developed for him by Sidney Belton. The two of them had cooperated in this way for years, along with a dozen other extraordinary detectives in the five countries now in readiness to lead the movement against the Phoenix. The fourteen-member group had developed techniques for ferreting out evidence of supernatural involvement—Good or Evil—in the activities of the individuals and organizations they studied. In the Belton group's activities in the UK and U.S., they were certain that they had seen exactly that: supernatural involvement both within the Belton group and opposing it. And Sidney Belton himself, when eventually brought into Camposanto's network, had confirmed the hypothesis explicitly.

Camposanto and the others knew, too, that use of the term "the Belton group" was a diversion in itself, since Detective Belton was not the central character in the group's successes. He was the critical natural piece, a highly skilled investigator and a brilliant and creative hypothesis-formulator, but the group's supernatural receptivity and capacity were lodged elsewhere. Rebecca Manguson Clark had become Supernature's chief receptor, and when called upon, its chief vehicle for the implementation of supernaturally directed actions.

In the immediate crisis, Antonio Camposanto had begged Rebecca to allow him to arrange her immediate transport to California as soon as she and her husband had summarized for him by telephone the week's events in and around Amalfi. And he had told them exactly why.

"*Signora*," he had said to Rebecca in his uncannily deep voice, "I cannot do this without you. The dead man's older sister, Helene Jamieson, is the . . . the . . . ah . . . the *executive* of this organization that now holds half the world in its . . . its . . . its most *corrupting* hands. But she is more than that, *signora*. She is the . . . the . . . the *Evil* that is . . . ah . . . behind all of the terrible, terrible things that you and your husband and your brother and the detective have seen in the last two years, the one who decides what to destroy, and how to destroy. . . .

"And *signora*, she will . . . she will destroy my daughters and young Basso and Dr. Chapel and her niece and her children and Detective Belton, and if she can, you and your husband and your brother just as soon as she can, in the . . . in the *retaliation* for her own brother's death, *signora*. And please understand, I am without the ability to stop her from this, because I do not have the . . . the . . . the *powers* that you have, *signora*. I know that I, and those that I have assembled to help me, can stop her organization, the Phoenix . . . *si* . . . *si* . . . we can stop the Phoenix. . . .

"But neither I nor we, working together, can stop her, the woman herself, the Devil's . . . the Devil's . . . ah . . . how is it you say this . . . the Devil's *hand-maiden*. . . . I cannot stop her. I cannot stop the Devil's handmaiden, *signora*.

"You must come, Rebecca. You must come, *per favore*. You must face her yourself. You have what I say is . . . *the divine weaponry* . . . and there is not hope to stop Helene Jamieson by any . . . ah . . . by any merely natural method. *Signora* . . . *signora* . . . come to us, come to us now."

Rebecca had not given her assent immediately. She had asked him for three hours, and then she had first prayed and then slept, briefly and yet soundly, under her husband's watchful eye, at their Atrani hotel suite. In both conditions—in prayer and in sleep—Rebecca had come to know that her assent was not merely divinely authorized, but divinely commanded. For again, both while awake and while asleep, she had seen the furious feminine eyes looming over the Amalfi *duomo* and the courtyard and the golden window of Saint Andrew the Apostle. And yet again, she perceived in her waking and sleeping mind's eye the horrible command: *Put out their eyes . . . Put out their eyes. . . .*

Now she closed her own eyes in prayer as the lightweight jet aircraft's wheels brushed the tarmac of Oakland International Airport: *Father . . .*

please . . . no more death . . . no more violence. But Thy will be done . . .
please, Father. . . . Thy will be done in this and in all things. . . .

"Ms. Jamieson?" inquired the musical contralto with its precise Oxford diction, "This is Rebecca Manguson Clark, just in from Amalfi. I'm phoning to ask if I might come by your hotel rooms to see you this evening."

Rebecca stood in Eleanor Chapel's empty apartment in Berkeley. Helene Jamieson stood in her lavish San Francisco hotel suite, surrounded by the most magnificent art objects owned by the entire hotel chain, a chain heavily in debt to the Phoenix Trust.

The two women, separated physically by the chill waters of San Francisco Bay, now stood silent, one waiting for a response, the other deciding if and how to respond. Finally the older woman spoke.

"I'd like that, Mrs. Clark. Come now. Alone."

Helene Jamieson hung up without waiting for a reply.

Antonio Camposanto, in near-continuous telephone consultation with Eleanor Chapel and Sid Belton, had used Rebecca's thirty-six hours of air travel to set the stage for what he hoped would be the final act in Helene Jamieson's decades-long theater of malevolence. With assistance from female members of the San Francisco police force, he had procured clothing and footwear for Rebecca in correct sizes, according to Eleanor's estimates. He had arranged transportation: first, from Oakland airport to Eleanor's Berkeley apartment; and second, from there to Helene Jamieson's San Francisco hotel. He had prepared a briefing folder for Rebecca concerning the history of the Phoenix Trust and the two Jamiesons' ever more prominent roles in the organization as years had passed, a briefing Rebecca and Matt had together studied during the limousine ride from the airport.

Detective Camposanto had been persuaded by Eleanor and Sid that Matthew Clark, even though included in the briefing, must not accompany his wife to the presumed confrontation in San Francisco. The face-off should, they all finally agreed, comprise the purest Goodness versus the purest Evil in the plainest sense imaginable. No secondary or tertiary support should be present on either side.

Matt Clark, they knew, would not agree readily to the arrangement. His wife, they also knew, would quickly agree to it. And his wife, they knew still further, was the only one who could secure some sort of concession on the matter from her husband. They would leave that part entirely to Rebecca.

As for the likelihood of Helene Jamieson's receiving Rebecca Clark alone, they agreed among themselves that this woman's fierce pride would require the clearest, most solitary triumph possible under these circumstances. They remained confident that even if others were present upon Rebecca's arrival at the Jamieson hotel suite, such would be dismissed as soon as all had verified the absence of an entourage with the visitor.

Now, fewer than sixty minutes after the brief phone exchange during which she had received permission to visit Helene Jamieson—or more precisely, during which she had been issued a curt summons to appear— Rebecca stood in the hotel hallway facing the entrance to the Phoenix Trust executive's private lair. Rebecca did not hesitate. She stepped to the door, knocked twice, then waited several seconds until she heard the handle turn, saw the door open a few inches, and heard a voice from within say softly, "Mrs. Clark? Come in, please."

Rebecca stepped through the door and stood to one side while Helene Jamieson allowed the door to close. It shut itself noisily, emphatically communicating their complete isolation from the outside world.

A moment afterward, Rebecca spoke. "Thank you, Ms. Jamieson, for seeing me on short notice."

There was no change in the expression on Helene Jamieson's face. She stepped nearer the door, felt for the locking mechanism with one hand and turned the device to its locked position with the other. Pivoting gracefully toward her guest, she remained motionless, her back to the door. Her face was turned toward Rebecca; her unseeing eyes were unfocused. She gestured toward the seating area of the suite. "Please," she said, almost in a whisper.

Rebecca took several steps toward the center of the spacious, exquisitely appointed sitting room, stopped, and turned back to face her host. "I'll stand, Ms. Jamieson," she said evenly. "This will not take long."

"This may or may not take long, Mrs. Clark," replied her host.

The two women stood facing each other from a distance of no more than ten feet. An observer, had one been present, would have been struck by the physical similarities between them. Both were six feet tall. Both were dressed professionally, wearing low-heeled, cream-colored shoes and classic linen business suits. Neither was adorned by jewelry of any kind, nor by cosmetic enhancements to skin, eyes, or hair. Both were absolutely erect in their posture. The visitor's hair was jet-black, and fell in a straight, thick cascade over her shoulders and down her back. The host's hair was golden blonde, and though shorter than the guest's, on this day lay similarly unencumbered on her shoulders and back.

And the eyes. The eyes comprised the most striking feature in each woman's appearance, and yet one was seeing, and the other blind. Rebecca's gray eyes gazed steadily at those of Helene Jamieson, while the Phoenix executive's sightless, translucent orbs seemed to perceive the guest's presence by some mechanism other than lens and retina and optic nerve.

Finally, Rebecca spoke again. "Ms. Jamieson, I've come to bring terrible news, and to confess my personal role in the event."

The host did not move, nor did she in any way indicate having heard the statement. Seconds passed.

Rebecca resumed. "Your brother leaped to his death two nights ago on the Amalfi coast, just in front of me. I did not kill him, but I was complicit."

This brought the first visible reaction from the older woman: a slight movement of her fine nostrils. Nothing else.

Rebecca began to feel an unpleasant, tingling sensation in her extremities. She sensed her pulse increasing. A throbbing commenced somewhere within her head and was instantly echoed in her right thigh, under and around the wounds she had incurred at the hands of this woman's brother.

Rebecca closed her eyes for a moment, opened them, and then remembered that her adversary was sightless. At that recollection, Rebecca closed her eyes again and prayed, *"Father . . . help me . . . help me. . . ."*

Her eyes still closed, she spoke again. "Ms. Jamieson, I am certain that you have personally ordered every vile thing that has been attempted against me, my family, my Christian colleagues, and hundreds of thousands of other innocent people, just within the last two years. What you've done before that time, I've no idea, but I've little doubt it was more of the same.

"I don't know what you are, exactly, but I don't need to know that."

She paused again, now opening her eyes and seeing that her enemy remained exactly as before, unmoving and unmoved. The tingling in Rebecca's hands and feet had turned to pain, innumerable tiny needles pressing into and through her flesh. Her pulse continued to accelerate. The throbbing in head and thigh grew more pronounced and became somehow audible inside her brain. She gasped for air.

Rebecca reached behind her for the nearest piece of furniture, seeking physical support for her weakening body. There was none.

Steeling herself anew, she continued, her voice now oddly strained, yet still strong and animated. "I want to ask your forgiveness for my role in your brother's death, Ms. Jamieson. I did not force him to leap from that cliff. But I had hurt him terribly. He chose the action he took, but I had damaged him almost beyond recognition. I am so sorry. Please forgive me."

As she had said this, Rebecca's gaze had wandered away from the unseeing eyes of her host. Now, as her eyes returned to Helene Jamieson's face, Rebecca suddenly cried out in confusion and disbelief, her gray eyes widening in astonishment. Her adversary was clearly looking at her, *seeing* her.

Reflexively, Rebecca stepped slightly to her right, testing the impossibility that was presented to her senses. She saw the translucent orbs move confidently to follow her. "You can *see?*" she asked incredulously.

With a small nod of her head and the barest trace of a smile, Helene Jamieson replied softly, "I can see *you,* Mrs. Clark."

With this announcement seemed to come within Rebecca a sudden intensifying of the tiny daggers in hands, arms, feet, and legs, of the pounding in head and thigh, and quickly accelerating, acute muscular weakness throughout her body. Rebecca found herself beginning to sink to the floor slowly, almost carefully. In just seconds she lay on her left side, her eyes still fixed on her enemy's now-penetrating gaze as Helene Jamieson followed her guest's gentle collapse with her eyes.

Without a word, as Rebecca watched helpless from the floor, the older woman turned away, took two steps to a small table near the door, slid open its single drawer, and carefully removed a hardwood-handled stiletto, its steel shaft nearly five inches in length. She looked from the weapon to the prone Rebecca, and satisfied that Rebecca understood what she held in her hand, moved the point of the stiletto back down into the drawer, apparently to dip its already deadly tip into something liquid.

Then she turned slowly away from the table, holding the doubly lethal implement away from her body. Both women could see that the point now glistened with a liquid substance. Though Rebecca could not know the name of the toxin, she had no doubt that it would kill quickly.

"It's succinylcholine, Mrs. Clark. The synthetic form of curare. Supertoxic, you know. Intravenous administration causes immediate paralysis, including the diaphragm's musculature. Then lungs. Death by respiratory failure. You will turn blue as you die. You'll be fully alert cognitively. You'll *know* that you are dying, Mrs. Clark. You'll *know* death in a way that few ever have."

Now fully on the floor, still lying on her left side, completely prostrate and utterly helpless, Rebecca watched her host's slow approach. She closed her eyes again and prayed, as she had on another occasion when facing an Evil both incomprehensible and seemingly irresistible: "Father . . . help me . . . please . . . help me. . . ."

Eyes closed, awaiting the inevitable, Rebecca groaned in pain and frustration as Helene Jamieson's approach seemed to exacerbate both the thousand points of pain and the thundering throb in head and thigh. Rebecca opened her eyes and saw that her enemy had dropped gracefully to her knees in front of her, and had already begun to extend the poison-tipped stiletto toward Rebecca's exposed jugular.

"Father . . . help me live to stop this Evil . . . help me live to *stop this Evil* . . . help me now . . . please . . . help me *now*. . . ."

And the symptoms vanished.

They vanished so quickly and so completely that Rebecca could hardly fathom the change or even understand how to act on it. But act she did.

At the moment Rebecca's symptoms cleared, her adversary, confused, drew the dripping stiletto point back several inches from its position almost under Rebecca's chin. For the physical changes in her victim had been clearly visible to Helene Jamieson: the look of surprise on Rebecca's face, the sudden muscular tension around her eyes where before there had been flaccidity, the instantaneous return of color to Rebecca's pallid face, this last accentuated by the steady, irrevocable colorlessness of the V-shaped scar that so dramatically crossed her right cheek.

The moment of hesitation was fatal to the attacker. For before she could recover, she found that Rebecca's right hand had seized her left hand from above, thereby encompassing both the hand and the stiletto's smooth, rounded handle. In one fluid motion, Rebecca slid from under the weapon and slammed her enemy's wrist, hand, and poison-tipped stiletto into the hardwood floor on which she had lain a scant second before.

Then, gripping the same wrist with such force that Helene Jamieson cried out sharply and released the stiletto entirely, Rebecca athletically rose to her knees, reached for her adversary's right wrist with her left hand, and now held both wrists in an iron grip from which there could be no escape.

The combat was now literally hand-to-hand. Both women, dressed impeccably, were on their knees, their faces and chests inches apart. But only for seconds, for inexorably Rebecca forced her enemy's wrists to the vertical, pushing Helene Jamieson back helplessly onto her haunches. While both remained on their knees, Rebecca loomed over her opponent, now in complete physical control.

The two stared at each other for long seconds, breathing deeply from the effort, the one still fighting to escape, the other fighting to prevent the slightest movement. And gradually . . . ever so gradually . . . the struggle diminished until there were periods of apparent cessation of resistance by the older woman, followed each time by brief fits of struggle. And then finally, nothing.

Seconds ticked past, and Rebecca found herself beginning to smile gently down at her enemy. At this, Helene Jamieson averted her eyes, at first looking away, to the side, and then straight down into her own lap.

The silence grew long. And then Rebecca spoke, her voice soft.

"I forgive you, Helene. I forgive you for what you have attempted to do to my family and to others whom I have personally known," she said, speaking deliberately. "God may Himself forgive you also, for that and for the carnage that you have left behind you wherever you have gone. Carnage that, I'm quite certain, goes far beyond anything I might imagine. But you will need to ask Him for that forgiveness, you know."

The older woman, although physically submissive, jerked her head up and stared with hate-filled eyes into the scarred, beautiful face of her conqueror. And then she snarled, her voice no longer soft. "Why should I?" she said sharply, spitting the words at the younger woman.

"You know why, Helene," came the unhesitating reply. "You have the eternal facts. You know the eternal equation. You understand the blueprint of the universe as well as anyone alive on the earth today.

"You've just chosen to ignore the eternal facts. Or to hate them. Actually, to hate *Him.*"

A new silence ensued, one that was finally interrupted by Helene Jamieson, her gaze again falling toward her own lap.

"He won't," she said, her voice soft once more.

"He won't what?"

"He won't forgive me. Not after all that I've done. Not after all that I've built. You have no real idea how much I have changed the conditions under which humans live on this planet.

"Of course He won't forgive me, Mrs. Clark. That's just another of your Christian absurdities. He absolutely will *not* forgive me. Not ever."

"Well . . . He *may*, Helene. And He certainly *can*. And I came to you this evening to say exactly that to your face . . . to ask your forgiveness for being complicit in your brother's suicide, and to tell you . . . no, to *remind* you . . . that the Father of us all *can* forgive . . . even you, Helene. Perhaps *especially* you, Helene.

"You are not, after all, the most evil human who has ever lived. You are simply the most evil human I have personally known. But, Helene . . . for *His* forgiveness . . . you must *ask.*"

Another pause ensued. The older woman now rested passively on her haunches, her wrists still held tightly in Rebecca's hands, though now the Englishwoman chose to exert just enough force to maintain control should the physical struggle begin again.

Finally, Helene Jamieson looked away once more, her face thoughtful. Then she returned her eyes to Rebecca's. "What will He demand that I give up?"

"Everything, Helene . . . and nothing."

"Everything . . . I can't do that."

"You can, because He will come to you. He will not leave you comfortless. He has promised. No matter what you have been, no matter what you have done, you are one of His creatures. And—I know you know this—you must say this now to yourself, and then you must say it aloud so that I can hear it, because it is true and because you know that it is true.

"Think these words, Helene, and then say these words aloud to me. Do it now: *He . . . died . . . for . . . me.*"

The vanquished woman dropped her head fully, her chin now resting lightly on her chest, her eyes cast down. She was silent for many seconds, silent for so long that Rebecca grew uncertain whether or not there would be any response at all. But then Helene Jamieson slowly raised her face to the eyes of the victor, her own pale orbs glistening, and breathed softly each of the four words, as if testing each to see if it could possibly fit . . . could possibly have meaning for her . . . for Helene Jamieson: *"He . . . died . . . for . . . me. . . ."*

Then, continuing, struggling with each word: *"In His name . . . I . . . ask . . . forgiveness. . . ."*

More seconds passed. And then a powerful, prolonged, whole-body shudder passed through Helene Jamieson. After the shudder, in a transformation too rapid to follow, a twitching, jerking spasm. And after the spasm, an escalation of involuntary muscular contraction, growing rapidly until spasm became true convulsion. The woman, now beginning to moan quietly, remained upright only because Rebecca continued to hold her carefully yet firmly by her wrists. Eventually the convulsion peaked, accompanied by the wrenching cry of a long-corrupt soul.

And it was over.

Helene Jamieson, emptied, seemed now to grow gradually smaller and smaller, as though curling into herself. She slumped forward, her wrists still held, though very lightly now, by her longtime enemy and would-be prey.

The new silence grew very long, each woman's breathing now measured. Rebecca gradually lowered herself to her haunches, mirroring Helene Jamieson's position exactly. And then Rebecca allowed her hands, still gripping the other woman's wrists, to descend still further, and finally to rest lightly on her own knees.

After several more moments of complete silence, Helene Jamieson spoke again, whispering. "I surrender."

"You surrender what, Helene? To whom?" asked Rebecca gently.

More silence. And then, still whispering, "I give myself up to Him."

"To Him who died for me," said Rebecca.

"Yes . . . yes . . . to Him . . . to Him . . . who . . . died . . . for . . . me," repeated the other. Her words were barely audible to Rebecca. Yet the voice was clear, firm.

Rebecca released her former enemy's wrists. Helene Jamieson's hands, now free, went immediately to her face. Still sitting on her haunches, she shrank still further, now into a very small ball, face in hands. She began to sob, her shoulders shaking, a keening now issuing from her lips.

Rebecca reached forward and placed both hands in the soft, golden hair. "I'm so sorry about Edward, Helene," she murmured.

Now the older woman, her body seeming slowly to fill itself with the Good, with something altogether different from that which had just departed, her sobs and cries abating, at length looked up from her own hands. Rebecca's eyes grew wide once more in stunned amazement. The translucent eyes stared sightlessly, unseeing once more.

"Rebecca," she whispered, "I'm blind."

Rebecca paused, and then said, "I know."

"But . . . I could see *you*, Rebecca. . . . I could see *you*."

"Yes. I know."

Silence once again.

Then, from Helene Jamieson, "Has He accepted me?"

"Yes."

"But I am blind again?"

"Yes . . . but only in your eyes, Helene. . . . This time, only in your eyes."

CHAPTER FIFTEEN

AS NOON APPROACHED ON A MIDSUMMER BAY AREA SATURDAY, two cheerful couples took their seats at the small restaurant's only window table. Their view through the smeared plate glass was of Richard Mabry's dirty, dented gray Valiant, parked a few feet away from the front of the by-now familiar Italian diner a mile south of the UC Berkeley campus.

Lois Tanaka, seated beside Richard Mabry and next to the window, gazed at the car and shook her head. "Richard," she said, "would it be too hard just to spray a little water at the poor thing? Just look at her. She's clearly embarrassed to be seen sitting on the street in full view of everybody."

He glanced at the faces of the Italians seated across the table and replied, "You know, Lois, for such a language authority as yourself, you've committed an interesting false step with your relentless personification of my automobile. Our guests cannot possibly know what you're talking about."

At this, Andrea Camposanto turned her head to look at her companion. "Well . . . are *you* confused, Giuseppe?"

He smiled at her. "*Non*, Andrea . . . *non* . . . I know this Lois person is a lady crazy in the head . . . and that she . . . ah . . . that she talks to that car . . . just like it was a person . . . or . . . or maybe a pet. . . ."

He was interrupted by appreciative laughter from the other three.

"*Bravo! Bravo!* Giuseppe," said Lois. "You are so very correct! This car of Richard's is indeed a pet, a *girl* pet, and as you've noted so forthrightly, I am most certainly a lady crazy in the head."

In just seconds the pizza and drink orders had been taken by the young waiter, and Lois, her face now serious, looked across the table at Andrea's rested and relaxed countenance. "Andrea," she said, "we've been waiting so long to ask, because we've not seen you or Giuseppe for a while now, but would you bring Richard and me up to date on your father's work? Have all the arrests been completed, all around the world?"

"*Non*, Lois," she replied, "but Papa . . . and we . . ."—here she paused and glanced at Giuseppe Basso—". . . we will, all three, be able to go home soon. Papa has said just this morning that he can finish . . . ah . . . the . . . ah . . . what was his word, Giuseppe?"

"Ah . . . the 'coordinating,' I think," he answered, sounding out the syllables laboriously.

"*Si* . . . he can finish the *coordinating* of all of the arrests . . . from his office in Roma. He has been gone too long, he said to me, too long. . . ."

A thoughtful pause ensued, interrupted at length by Richard.

"And what about the Phoenix Trust's leader, the Jamieson woman . . . what about her, Andrea? Can you tell us what has happened with her?"

She nodded. "*Si*. Papa says she has been so . . . um . . . cooperative . . . and of a very great assistance to him and his . . . his team of detectives, Richard," she answered. "She has even made . . . with her own money . . . ah. . . ."

She looked again to her companion and he furrowed his brow for a moment and then supplied the word. "I think . . . I think it is the 'restitution,' Andrea," he said, again enunciating with great care.

She smiled. "Giuseppe is so very *quick* with his English, *non*?"

All three smiled in response, Giuseppe with his eyes downcast in genuine embarrassment at the compliment.

"But," she continued, "*Signora* Jamieson will face the long time in prison, no matter how much she assists Papa with all of this . . . and . . . and if she is held to be . . . guilty . . . in a *personal* way guilty . . . of murders, well, I don't know what will someday happen to her. This will take a long time to decide. This is . . . there are . . . many nations . . . many nations that have the involvement, you know?"

The Americans nodded.

"I understand," Richard said after a moment, "that the Phoenix Trust has been dissolved and its funds are now held by the U.S. government?"

"*Si*," replied Andrea. "I know little about this, but I know that there is no more Phoenix."

There was another pause as each member of the foursome considered what they knew—and did not know—about the conclusion of the *Congressus* crisis. Giuseppe Basso spoke next, looking alternately at the two Americans as he asked his question.

"And the *Congressus* meeting . . . and the statement of . . . of position . . . that was such a . . . a danger . . . such a danger for Dr. Chapel. How did the ending . . . ah . . . what was the ending . . . for her . . . for all of the people who came here . . . and for everyone . . . and for everything?"

The Americans glanced at each other. Lois immediately sensed a shyness in her companion, a companion with whom she had spent some portion of nearly every day or evening in the weeks since his first fumbling telephone call to her. She turned her face back to the Italians.

"You remember that Richard made a statement to the committee on the day that Dr. Chapel had been . . . hidden . . . by your father, Andrea?"

Both listeners nodded.

"His statement seems to have had importance to the group—though Richard thought he did it badly—we think because it brought Dr. Chapel and her viewpoint so clearly back into everyone's mind."

She was going to continue but stopped, seeing a movement from Richard's hand. After a moment, he spoke, addressing himself more to his companion than to the other couple. "Well . . . yes . . . maybe . . . the Eleanor Chapel viewpoint, restored to the committee members' minds, no matter how badly, by my little speech . . . did have some importance. But the more I think about it, Lois, the more I think what might have made the difference was not so much Dr. Chapel's viewpoint, as I tried to represent with my little proposal, but . . . well . . . the contrast between Eleanor Chapel's . . . ah . . . *self* . . . her remembered *presence* . . . and the presence in that room of Helene Jamieson.

"She was such a powerful presence, sitting there, absolutely unseeing and yet somehow absolutely seeing, and she was somehow so . . . well . . . *unsettling* . . . so . . . uhmm . . . so *unnerving* . . . so . . . well . . . I have to say it . . . so very *frightening* . . . that I've come to think that people on the steering committee felt there was a—this is hard to explain—a good-against-evil choice to be made between Dr. Chapel and her point of view and my proposal, and Helene Jamieson and her . . . ah . . . proposal . . . which, you know, was just as much threat or ultimatum as it was proposal."

Richard stopped and looked carefully at the Italians, wondering if they were following his explanation. He saw a small nod from each and, reassured by this and by the fact that Lois had not seen fit to interrupt with a clarification, he continued.

"I think some of the committee members were actually driven away, not only from the Phoenix Trust and all that accompanied it, but from the very position statement that they had lived with for so long. I think they saw, in the person of Helene Jamieson and in her ultimatum, how raw power actually looked and felt and tasted and behaved. How raw power, unleashed fully, in this case, on the steering committee itself, would play itself out in the world, first, of graduate students in our seminaries, and then, after that, on the people and churches and charities and businesses and governments and . . . well . . . on just *everything* . . . on everything *everywhere*. . . .

"I think the committee members finally saw the contradiction. They felt the absurdity. They understood the danger. They knew in their bones what was in the room with them.

"In any case," Richard continued after a moment, "the committee rather quickly declined Helene Jamieson's proposal. They excused her from the meeting and created a new subcommittee that in no time at all had put together an effective little package leading with the Apostles' Creed, some verses from the tenth and eleventh chapters of the Acts of the Apostles—the building of the early church, you know—and some suggestions about the importance of basic economics in seminary education. All of that *provided*, of course, that those economic principles were cradled in the Gospels and in Acts and in the summary of the whole New Testament message provided by the little Creed.

"It was quite astonishing, really."

His statement finished, Richard again looked across the table, asking with lifted eyebrows whether or not the overall content of his explanation had registered with the Italians. Again, he saw them both nodding thoughtfully and still looking at him intently.

"*Si* . . ." murmured Giuseppe, almost to himself. "*Si*. . . ."

Lois waited to see if Richard wished to continue or if the others were going to ask for more information. But all three seemed content.

So at length, she added, "The committee—with Dr. Chapel returning to her leadership role after your father, Andrea, gave the okay—finally decided to do almost exactly what Richard had begged them to do. And naturally, so did the conferees, once the actual sessions got underway. Almost *exactly* what Richard had suggested! Don't you think that's just *wonderful?*"

She turned, smiling, to look at him, and he looked down, still discomfited by the twin memories of his whiny, childish speech to the steering committee and by the enormous momentum his simple, crisp suggestion to feature the Apostles' Creed and the book of Acts and to subordinate the rest had gained with the entire conference. Suddenly he felt Lois put her hand over his, both their hands now resting on the checked, plastic tablecloth and beside the cheap, white paper napkins. He blushed deeply and glanced across the table at the Italians.

His eyes widened at what he saw. Giuseppe had mirrored the action exactly, and had covered Andrea's hand in nearly identical fashion.

Giuseppe, whose eyes had met Andrea's as their hands touched, now turned to face the two Americans. The confused looks on their faces did not surprise him.

"I know," he began, "that it was with the . . . the *other* sister that our families did the . . . ah . . . the arranging, but . . . well. . . ."

"When Papa understood," interrupted Andrea, "that . . . well . . . the *families* were nicely matched, but the *couples* were . . . ah. . . ."

"The couples were the *wrong* couples!" inserted Giuseppe.

"*Si! Si!*" laughed his companion. "It was the right families, but it was the wrong couples! And . . . when Papa understood . . . and when Giuseppe's family understood, we all made . . . ah . . . the *amending* of the arrangements. . . ."

"Which meant, you see," said Giuseppe, "that Andrea's sister and Rebecca's brother were . . . you know . . . free to . . . ah. . . ."

"To do the courtship!" blurted Andrea, beaming at the precision in her English word choice.

"*Si, si,*" he echoed. "Sophia and Luke! Free to do the courtship! *Perfezione! Eh? Perfezione!*"

London: 6:15 am
ONE WEEK LATER

Rebecca Manguson Clark knelt beside the small desk in her diminutive London bedroom. Her husband, she knew, was doing the same in the still smaller room adjacent that served as their study.

She opened her prayer book and, having composed herself for worship, softly murmured the words aloud:

> O Almighty God, who art a strong tower of defence unto thy servants against the face of their enemies: We yield thee praise and thanksgiving for our deliverance from those great and apparent dangers wherewith we were compassed: We acknowledge it thy goodness that we were not delivered over as a prey unto them; beseeching thee still to continue such thy mercies towards us . . . through Jesus Christ our Lord. . . .

Allowing the little book to close itself, Rebecca shut her eyes and continued, letting her mind and her prayer roam through the detailed mental list of thanksgiving, of adoration, of personal shortcomings and failures and sins, of requests for forgiveness for each, and of specific petition for the Holy Spirit's intervention and guidance and assistance and protection throughout the day upcoming. And, nearing her closing, she asked for His help in knowing how to approach her husband with that newly conceived fact with which she was now burdened.

She rose from her knees, and walking softly in acknowledgement of the likelihood that Matt was still engaged in his devotions, left their bedroom and padded down the hallway. She busied herself with preparations for a cold breakfast, interrupted several times by brief and ambiguous waves of light nausea. When Matt entered the room, he found her seated at their two-person dining table, her head down.

With his right hand, he reached to touch her hair and she looked up at him. Taken aback at the sight of her wan face, he dropped to one knee beside her, and his open hand now touching her pale white cheek, he spoke softly but with an intensity that surprised them both. "Rebecca? What is it? Do you not feel well?"

Covering his right hand with her left so that both rested against her cheek, she replied softly, "No . . . and yes."

Taking his good hand now in both hers, she moved his hand to her abdomen, and opening it against the flatness of her taut stomach, pressed it into herself. She leaned forward and kissed him tenderly.

"Dearest husband," she said, whispering, tears beginning to rise in the gray eyes, "this is the fourth morning in a row on which I have felt ill. Just the four mornings, you understand. Just for a short while each morning. And yet I am not ill in the least."

Matt's eyes grew wide. His jaw sagged. He began to smile, as yet still hesitant, wanting to hear explicit confirmation of the hope and joy that now surged from within him.

"My darling husband," she continued, still whispering, "right here . . . right *here*, under your hand. Right *here* . . . new life . . . new life . . . our child. . . ."

A sob of joy broke from her throat.

At the words, he straightened himself, still on one knee, pulled his hand carefully away from her hands and her abdomen, and encircled her neck with his strong right hand and arm, pulling the sweet-smelling blackness of her hair into his face. The long fingers of his right hand, encircling her head and hair, played across the V-shaped scar, caressing the irregular track that marked the right side of her face.

She leaned fully into him, her left hand still resting on her stomach, her right reaching up to hold and massage lightly the atrophied left shoulder and arm of her husband. She sighed contentedly, smiling to herself through her physical weakness. Tears rolled unseen down both cheeks, and she knew without looking up that her husband's own tears were flowing silently down his face and into her hair.

After a moment, she murmured to him softly, her face in his chest, "You know, dearest, everything will be different now, don't you? Everything will change now. It will change forever."

Seconds passed with no response, and then it came. "No, Rebecca," he whispered, his mouth near her ear. "No, my darling, not *everything*.

"For I will love you every day," he continued slowly, "and I will love you as no other man could ever love you. And we, together, will love the Lord with all our hearts and souls and minds . . . and we will raise our child to do the same."

He felt her nod against his chest.

He smiled to himself. "Many, many things will be different, Rebecca," he continued, "but not that, my darling, not that.

"Never, never that."

About the Author

WALKER BUCKALEW RECEIVED A BACHELOR'S DEGREE IN English and religion from Duke University before serving as an officer on the aircraft carrier USS *Constellation*. Following his navy service, Buckalew worked as a public school teacher and coach while earning his MEd and PhD degrees from the University of Wyoming.

Buckalew then embarked on a career in higher education, teaching at St. Lawrence University in Canton, New York, and the University of North Carolina at Asheville. He was later appointed president and chief academic officer at Cumberland University in Lebanon, Tennessee. Since 1989 he has served as a consultant to private schools throughout North America. He lives with his wife, Dr. Linda Mason Hall, in Richmond, Virginia.